99 Nightingale Lane

Nightingale Lane Publishing

Dedicated to my grandmother,

Caroline Violet Elizabeth Dobbs

CHAPTERS

Chapter 1
DECEMBER 1914

Carrie Dobbs shivered as she stepped out of the basement lobby. She inhaled a deep breath then sighed, releasing clouds of vapour into the night air before gently shutting the door behind her. Pulling her woollen shawl firmly around her shoulders she wrapped her arms around herself to keep out the sharp cold. Climbing the five worn stone steps that led up to the pavement, the ones she ascended once a week, she opened the black wrought iron gate which gave a familiar squeal, and stepped up onto the pavement. The gate swung back into position behind her and closed with a comforting click against the railings. She looked down at her feet and marvelled at the grey flagstones, so ordinary in the daylight but now overlaid in an intricate lace of frost and glistening with reflected light from the yellow orbs of the streetlamps edging the path. She walked to the centre of the pavement, the pale grey skirt of her maid's uniform skimming the path, and looked up at the imposing house on the tree-lined street. Heavy curtains were pulled across every window, a warm blush glow from the lamps inside penetrating the lavish ruby-red velvet. She looked away, a wave of loneliness and despair sweeping over her taking her breath away. Lifting her gaze back to the house where she had served as a maid for two years tears pooled in her eyes. She brushed them away with the back of her knitted fingerless glove, then reluctantly turned away from the house and began the two and a half mile walk home.

A swirling mist had settled around the tops of the streetlamps and she pulled the brown chenille tasselled shawl even tighter around her slim shoulders. As she reached the corner of Nightingale Lane, white-hot sparks from the chestnut seller's brazier pierced the darkness. The embers fell from the brazier in a shower and sizzled as they landed on the frozen flagstones. Carrie smiled, her spirits lifting as the delicious smell of roasted chestnuts floated down the street towards her.

The seller glanced up as she walked towards him, recognition crossing his face. He shovelled a scoop of chestnuts into a brown paper bag and held them out to her. 'Here you are, Carrie. They'll warm you right through.'

She smiled at him and shook her head. 'Not tonight, Joe. They smell so good they're making my mouth water but I can't afford it. The rent man comes tonight and we've got just about enough with this week's wages from Dad and me.'

He pulled a comical face which made her laugh. 'Have them anyway. My good deed for the day. Oh, go on,' he said, pushing them on to her. 'I might not get the chance to do it again.'

She stared at him. 'Have you been called up?'

He nodded. 'You'll have to get your chestnuts from someone else from now on. This is my last week. I leave on Sunday.'

'Oh, Joe. You must be so scared. And what about your family? Christmas is just around the corner.'

'Not scared exactly. I have to do my bit, don't I, for King and country. Look how many lads have already gone. I can't turn my back on them no matter how much I'll miss the kids.'

She leant forward and kissed his cheek. 'Good luck, Joe. I'll be thinking of you and all the other boys who've had to leave their loved ones. Stay safe. I'll try and pop in to see your Molly and the nippers over Christmas. Just to say hello, and maybe take them a few bits from the 'ouse if I can get them.'

'That would be so good of you, Carrie. My Molly's so worried. She says she don't know how she's going to make ends meet with the bit we'll get. I'll be sending her what I can but Lord knows if it'll be enough. We're living on scraps as it is.'

'I know. Everyone's having to tighten their belts what with the war an' all. I'll do what I can, Joe. I promise.'

He smiled warmly at her. 'I know you will, Carrie. You're a good'un you are.'

She continued her journey, her hands clasped around the bag of hot chestnuts. It gave her comfort, the heat from the chestnuts penetrating her woollen gloves but it didn't lift her heavy heart. She thought about Joe's wife and three children. The youngest was only a few months old and she knew there was a chance he might not see them again. It's so sad, she thought. So very sad.

As she neared her home the scenery gradually changed. The well-maintained lanes with their grand houses and imposing entrances were gradually replaced by grim tenement filled streets patrolled by small gatherings of unkempt children, unfed and uncared for, their noses running with snot and their faces unwashed of the grime of the dirty streets. Their thin cheeks were bright red and nipped with the cold. None of them wore a coat and a few didn't have shoes. Shoes were a luxury most parents could ill-afford. She heard some of the children coughing, the rasping hoop of tuberculosis or bronchitis infected lungs punctuating the screams of laughter as they fought to get their breath in the cold damp air. A few of the girls pushed battered prams made from orange boxes, the latest additions to their parents constantly increasing broods hidden amongst the dirty blankets. The babies cried for their mothers, wondering when their next meal would be, their tiny bellies craving milk. Their cries were ignored by the other children whose attentions were directed towards having as much fun as possible away from the reprimands of their parents who neither worried nor cared as long as their offspring were out of sight. Women stood on the corners of the streets; some were as "rough as 'ouses" as Carrie's mother would often say when she was on a rant, but some were ordinary women who didn't know where the next meal would come from and had to get money to feed their kids somehow. Their bodies were all they had left to trade with, and Carrie blessed herself as she walked by them, praying she would never be in the same position.

She shook her head, the contrast of the two worlds she occupied not lost on her. She realised that the disparity between the two was a secret given up more readily when night closed in. Nightingale Lane was unashamedly opulent, the brightly lit glass Tilly lamps decorated with crystals shone through sparkling windows and the pristine facades with gleaming black front doors fronting the lavish homes which were occupied by luxuriously dressed residents whose lives were relatively untouched by the war. They never went without a meal; the pantry at number ninety-nine was testament to that. It was always well-stocked with everything anyone could wish for and more besides, things Carrie hadn't even heard of and definitely didn't want to eat no matter how hungry she got. She stopped when she got to the corner and watched as a mother dragged her child into a slum, clipping his ear as he went. Here was her street. The gut-wrenching smell of boiled tripe and cabbage mixed with the throat burning odour from the tanning factory where her brothers worked was constantly on the air surrounding the dirty streets infected with neglect. The overwhelming and seemingly ingrained poverty and apathy of its residents lowered her spirits even further.

She thought of her home, picturing the scene in her mind's eye. Her mother, Florrie would be in the scullery with its unadorned painted brick walls and faded curtain suspended from a piece of fraying string fastened across the doorway into their tiny living room. Then she'd lean over the old range, putting together a meal with whatever she could afford to spare from the scant income Arthur, Carrie's father brought in from his job unloading the boats anchored at St. Katherine Dock. Her older sister, Elsie would be sewing by candlelight, squinting in the gloom, making clothes for her baby expected in January; her husband, Len already called up to fight in France. Her brothers, Tom and Alfie would likely still be at work in the tanning factory. Too young to join up, she knew if the war went on much more it wouldn't be long before it was their turn. She hoped and prayed that the war would be over long before then. After nearly five months of war the government would have them all believe the war would be over by Christmas. The front pages of the newspapers continued to tell their readers that 'Our Boys Will Be Home for Christmas'. They need to get a move on, she thought. Christmas is only three weeks away.

Her thoughts went back to the houses in Nightingale Lane. Some of them were already decorated with Christmas trees shimmering in the windows, and many heralded the arrival of the festive season with ornate wreaths of holly and dried citrus fruits displayed on the front doors.

As she stepped off the pavement an army truck turned into the street, passing her before she got to the other side. In the back, behind a divided tarpaulin sheet that flapped open as the truck rumbled over the cobbles, were five young men. A couple of them looked like they should have been at home with their mothers, not dressed in the now familiar soldier's uniform on their way to the fighting fields of France. Carrie shivered as she glimpsed their pale faces. She knew their brave expressions belied their quivering hearts as they travelled into the unknown.

She continued walking down Hanbury Street until she got to a shabby front door, painted brown as all the doors in the street were. Carrie took a deep breath and pushed against the door which dropped slightly as she opened it, scraping against the floor as she went into the gloomy hallway.

'Is that you?' a voice called out.

'Yes, Mum.'

'Are you late?'

Carrie hung up her coat and briefly closed her eyes, swallowing hard. 'I don't know. Am I?'

Florrie was in the living room, clearing the table of Elsie's fabric and threads.

'Mum,' Elsie cried. 'I'll do it. Look, I've lost me place now.'

'Well, Dad will be home in a minute. He'll want his dinner on the table after the hours he'll have put in. Come on, Elsie, you've been at it all day. I don't know what's taking you so long, my girl. You'll have to be a bit quicker at things than that when that baby comes. It won't wait for anything as and when it suits you, particularly if it's a boy.'

'You only had to say.' Elsie glanced across to Carrie and rolled her eyes. 'What is it, anyway? For dinner I mean.'

'Can you not smell it? Tripe and onions, and suet pudding and golden sugar for afters. And make the most of it. The food shortages aren't getting any better. I don't know what we'll do for Christmas, what with there not being much about. What little there is, is so expensive. Someone's making money out of us. It's always the working people what suffer the most.' She glanced at Carrie. 'I expect the Sterns are all right. If you could eat there more often it would be a great help, Carrie. It's a good job you're in work, my girl, although only God knows how long that'll carry on for. And when Alfie and Tom go off to war we'll have even less coming in.' Tears at the thought of her sons going to war filled her eyes, and she wiped them away with her pinafore then blew her not inconsiderable nose loudly on the floral fabric.

Carrie held the still warm chestnuts out to her mother. 'We could have these with our suet, Mum.'

Florrie snatched the bag from her. 'Chestnuts? What're you wasting money on bloody chestnuts for, our Carrie? For goodness sake, girl, we don't need chestnuts.'

'I didn't spend anything. Joe gave them to me. He's been called up. I think he just wanted to do something nice.'

Florrie's expression of annoyance fell from her face. 'Oh, well, in that case. That's different, that is.'

Elsie pushed herself off of the chair by the fireside and placed her precious baby garments into a wicker sewing box. 'Dunno what you're worrying about. If there's no food around to be bought it don't matter how much money we've got.'

'We still have to pay the rent. And buy coal,' said Florrie. 'You won't want to bring your little mite home to a cold house, will you? Tut, I dunno. Makes you wonder what the point is of bringing more babies into this world. I hope it's a girl you have, our Elsie. I couldn't bear to think of another of our boys going off to war.'

Elsie turned her head and looked at her mother crossly. 'For goodness sake, Mum. It won't go on that long. They said it'll be all over by Christmas. For God's sake, stop worrying. Len will be home by the time this one comes along, and he'll help us,' she said smiling to herself. 'He's clever is my Len. We won't go short then. He knows how to get money.' She rubbed her bump protectively.

'That's as maybe,' said Florrie. 'And I don't want to know where Len West gets his money from. It's bound to be dodgy, knowing him. He's got his fingers in too many pies, that one. He wants to be careful he don't get 'em burnt. And anyway. Who said? Who said it'll be over by Christmas. It'll be one of the shortest wars in history if it is. I don't trust 'em. They'll say anything to keep our mouths shut.' Florrie glanced at Carrie. 'You're quiet tonight.' She frowned. 'Not coming down with anything, are you? We can't afford to have you off of work, Carrie. We need every ha'penny.'

Carrie shook her head. 'No, I'm just a bit tired. Mrs Stern had us spring cleaning again this week.'

'Spring cleaning? In the winter? What's wrong with the woman?'

'They've got guests staying at Christmas. She said she wanted the house to look like a new pin.'

Elsie lifted her chin. 'Bloody 'ell, it's all right for some. I'd feel lucky if I had an old pin. Guests indeed. I suppose Her Ladyship's got a Christmas tree up already.'

Carrie nodded. 'And you should see what they've got in the pantry. I don't know where they get it all from. Some of it I've never even heard of.'

'Connections,' said Florrie, pulling a, "don't argue with me" face. 'That's how they do it. They're a family with connections. They know all the right people. It's because Conrad Stern's something big somewhere, you mark my words. He's not a man to be argued with. And his wife's not much better I'll be bound.' She glanced at Carrie. 'Couldn't you hide some of what's in their pantry under your coat, Carrie, before you come 'ome? They wouldn't miss any of it would they? They probably haven't got a clue what's in there. People like that...they never do know what they've got. I shouldn't think they've ever looked in the sodding pantry. Probably don't even know what one is. It won't mean anything to them but it'd mean everything to us. Maybe we could have a Christmas after all.'

Before Carrie could answer Arthur pushed the front door open, rubbing his hands together. He went across to the fire and stood in front of it, then turned and warmed his backside.

'Brr, it's bloody cold out there. What a day we've had down at the docks. That Frederick Day from Bucks Row had a pallet fall on his leg.

He'll never work at the docks again, poor sod. Reckon that leg of his is finished. Crushed like eggshell it was. 'Orrible. Blood everywhere. He'll probably have to have it off. I've never heard anyone scream like that before.'

'He's got kids, hasn't he?' said Florrie quietly, all of her previous vehemence fading in the knowledge of Arthur's workmate's accident.

Arthur nodded. 'Four and one on the way. God knows what they'll do. The only compensation I can think of is that he won't be called up, but they could very well starve. It's a bad business.'

Florrie beckoned him to the table. 'Well, you make sure it don't happen to you, Arthur Dobbs. You need both your legs and your arms, an' all. Now, you come and have your tea. You look like death warmed up.'

'Charming! What is it?'

'Tripe and onions.'

He sat at the table and looked at her aghast. 'Again?'

Florrie went into the scullery to get the pot of tripe. 'Oh, now, don't start complaining, Arthur Dobbs. It's all I could get and at least it's hot. Look, I've made some bread to dip in the liquor.'

Arthur sighed. 'I'm not complaining, Florrie. It's not your fault, love. Blame the Bosch, although they're probably eating worse than we are.'

'Serves 'em right,' said Florrie. 'It's what they get for being difficult.'

Arthur threw back his head and laughed, and Carrie and Elsie giggled. 'Difficult?' he cried. 'Bloody 'ell, Florrie. I think they're being a bit more than difficult, sweet'eart. You say some funny things, you really do. Better 'ope it don't get really bad. Don't know what you'd say then. Difficult indeed.' Elsie and Carrie joined him at the table, and Florrie put steaming plates in front of them. Elsie tucked into hers with relish, and Florrie was pleased with herself that she'd managed to feed her family on very little.

Carrie looked down at her plate. The folds of grey, rubbery tripe began to nauseate her and she pushed her plate away.

'I'm sorry, Mum. I'm not hungry.'

Arthur glanced across at her, frowning. 'You been eating at the Stern's again? You get decent food there, don't you? I'm glad at least one member of this family is doing all right.'

'I had something before I came home. You can share this between Tom and Alfie. They're always starving no matter how much you give them. They can have my share of bread too.'

Arthur patted her hand. 'You're a good girl. Always thinking about other people.'

Carrie smiled. 'I might take a bowl of hot water upstairs and have a wash before the boys come in. Is that all right, Mum?'

'Course it is, love. You go on up. You're looking a bit peaky tonight. That Stern woman works you and those other girls far too hard. An early night will do you good. What time you startin' tomorrow?'

'Er, usual time.'

Carrie took the knitted cloth that hung inside the inglenook and wrapped it around the handle of the huge kettle hanging in the fireplace which was black from age and use. She carried it into the scullery and poured boiling water into a chipped enamel bowl, then filled the kettle again and returned it to the hanger. Holding the edge of the bowl in both hands she negotiated the narrow wooden stairs, careful not to spill any of the boiling hot liquid. Upstairs there were two rooms, one for her and Elsie, the other for Florrie and Arthur. The boys slept downstairs, one on the sofa made up into a bed, the other on a mattress they kept under the stairs which they took in turns to use, the mattress being the more comfortable of the two. Carrie went into the small, sparsely furnished room and put the bowl down on a wooden dresser, then opened the one drawer allocated to her and retrieved a flannel, a small bar of lavender scented soap and a hairbrush.

She undressed in the freezing cold room where ice had gathered on the inside of the window and began to wash, enjoying the warmth of the hot water that steamed up the foxed mirror sitting on the old-fashioned chest of drawers, and breathed in the calming scent of lavender. When she was finished she pulled a clean flannelette nighty over her head and wrapped a pink knitted shawl around her shoulders. Then she got into the bed she shared with Elsie and pulled the covers up to her chin. The embroidered cotton pillowcase was cool against her cheek and she closed her eyes and sighed. When she was downstairs with the others she could forget the thing that had played on her mind for weeks, but every time she tried to sleep it came hurtling back to her. Even when she was asleep she would dream of it. She opened her eyes and stared at the wall, following the large split in the chipped plaster that went from the ceiling to the floor, thinking there was nothing like it at the Stern house where everything was perfect and beautiful. She couldn't imagine Mrs. Stern ever deigning to enter a room like the bedroom Carrie shared with Elsie, let alone their house in Hanbury Street which might as well be a million miles away from Nightingale Lane. Probably doesn't even realise places like this exist, she thought.

There was a soft rap on the bedroom door and she sat up.

'Who is it?'

'It's Tom.'

She relaxed back against the pillows. 'Come in then.'

A tall, fair-haired lad entered the room and Carrie gestured for him to shut the door. He closed it quietly and sat on the end of the bed. He stared at her as if waiting for her to say something, but she just looked down and played with the tassels on her shawl.

He tutted. 'Well?'

She glanced up at him, her eyes dark. 'Well, what?'

He stared at her and his jaw hardened. 'Come on, Carrie. Has anything happened?' She shook her head and he bit his lip. 'What're you going to do?'

'I don't know. I don't want to think about it.'

'But Carrie...'

She held her hand up to stop him. 'I know, Tom. I know.'

'Maybe you're ill.'

'It's making me feel bloody ill, I can tell you, worrying about it all the time. I wish I could forget about it. I wish it would just go away, but it doesn't matter what I'm doing it's still there. Anyway, you shouldn't be worrying about me. You should be thinking about yourself. You're nearly sixteen. You might be called up soon and you'll forget all about me, I can assure you. You'll have far more important things to think about.' They both went quiet.

'Is it a baby?' he whispered.

She nodded, the corners of her mouth turned down. 'I think so?'

'How far is it?'

'Three months.'

His mouth dropped open. 'You'll have to tell Mum and Dad, Carrie. And you'll have to tell him.'

'They'll find out soon enough. And I'm hoping he'll stand by me. It takes two, doesn't it, to make a baby. I didn't do it on me own.'

He blushed to his roots, and looked away, embarrassed. 'Well, when you put it like that.'

'I do put it like that. We made this baby between us and we're both equally responsible for it.'

'D'you think he'll see it like that? Why are you so sure about him? And what about his family. They're not like us, are they? They wouldn't understand how we live. They're different. They've got money and…and things. They live in a great big house. They're even a different religion.'

'And what religion are we exactly?'

'C of E, aren't we? We used to go to the church near Hanbury Street when we were kids. Mum used to take us.'

'And when was the last time you went there and listened to the sermon, and prayed, and sang hymns out of a hymn book?'

He shook his head. 'Can't remember.'

'Exactly. So what difference is it going to make?'

'It might make a difference to them.' She shrugged and looked away and he wondered if she'd fly at him when he said what he was going to say. 'I want you to tell Mum and Dad…before you tell him.'

She glanced back at him. 'I'm not telling them yet, and it's got nothing to do with you,' she said, pointing her finger at him. 'It's none of your business. Don't make me wish I hadn't told you.'

He got up and stood by the door. 'If you don't tell them, I will. I'll tell them you've got a bun in the oven. You need them, Carrie. You need your family, and you need Mum and Dad. He's not family. You work for his parents and he should have known better. I know I'm only fifteen, but even I know that. He's used you.'

'Tom! Please don't. I'll tell them when I'm ready.'

'No, Carrie. Tell them now, or I will.'

Chapter 2

The flames in the grate suddenly flared, and a hissing sound came from the blocks of wood Arthur had thrown on the fire, scavenged from a derelict building site near the docks. Carrie swallowed hard and glanced at Tom. He didn't move. They stood in front of their parents like two naughty schoolchildren waiting to be punished for some minor misdemeanour or other. Florrie and Arthur stared at Carrie in disbelief then Florrie's eyes narrowed.

'So, you're telling us you're in the family way?'

Carrie nodded. 'Yes.'

'And Johan Stern is the father.'

'Yes.'

'And you're three months gone.'

Carrie took a deep breath. 'Yes,' she answered, her voice almost a whisper. Arthur looked at Florrie and shook his head. He got up from his fireside chair and took the kettle into the scullery where he put two cups and saucers on the dresser. He spooned two small scoops of tealeaves into a teapot and poured boiling water onto them, replacing the chipped lid. He stared vacantly at the teapot as if waiting for it to provide a solution to all the ills that seemed to befall his family. After a minute he lifted the lid and stirred the infusion, replacing the lid again. He poured the tea into the cups and stirred two generous spoons of condensed milk from a tin into each.

Carrie leant back slightly and peered through the curtain dividing the sitting room from the scullery. She watched her father's methodical making of the tea, observed him moving about the compact scullery as though automated. Her heart clenched with sorrow. I've let him down, she thought. I've really let him down.

Arthur came through the curtain holding the cups and saucers and passed one to Florrie before sitting next to the fire.

'Drink that, Florrie. I think you need it. I know I do.'

Florrie sipped the hot tea, then looked up at Carrie. 'So, what are you going to do?'

Carrie stared at her. Was this all her mother had to say? 'I don't…I don't know. I hadn't got that far.' Her eyes went to her father who said nothing. 'I s'pose I'll have to find somewhere to live, won't I, until Johan and I decide what to do.'

'That's quite a name, isn't it?' said Arthur at last. 'Johan.' His eyes met hers for the first time. 'Does he know?'

She clutched her hands behind her back and looked down at her feet. 'No.'

Arthur sighed. 'Y'know Carrie, I thought you of all people had more sense. You're seventeen and unmarried. And now you've got a bun in the oven. Do you think he'll want to marry you, a scullery maid who works for his parents? You're the lowest of the low as far as he's concerned. He's used you, Carrie, and you've brought that trouble 'ome.'

'Johan loves me.'

'Does he?' Arthur laid his cup and saucer in the hearth and leaned back in his chair, folding his arms across his chest. 'And what about his parents. Do they love you? Do you honestly think they'll allow him to marry someone like you? They're Jewish, Carrie. They mix with people like them. They'll want him to marry one of his own kind.'

'But I'm carrying his child.'

'Says you,' said Florrie.

Carrie bristled at her mother's inference. 'What d'you mean by that?'

'It's your word against theirs. That child you're carrying could be anyone's…some little snot-nose wharf-rat working on the docks.' Arthur looked at her and frowned. 'Sorry, Arthur. You know I didn't mean it like that but you know full well what I'm saying.' Florrie's voice got louder. 'Wake up, Carrie, for goodness sake. You can't tell him you're pregnant. If you do you'll bring shame down on this family. You'll lose your job for definite because they'll have you out on your ear and that'll be that. No job, no money, and a heap of shame brought down on all of us, including Elsie and your brothers. We might be the people who do the jobs no one else wants to do, and we might not have a penny to bless ourselves with, but what we have got is our dignity, and you're not taking that away from us let me tell you that, my girl.'

'I have to tell him,' cried Carrie. 'He has a right to know he's to become a father.'

'He won't want to know, yer stupid girl. If you want to stay under our roof for the foreseeable you'll do as we say. You will not tell him. You will not. I will not have this family's good name dragged through the mud because you didn't have the good sense to keep yourself clean. I mean it, Carrie. Don't come up against me on this. I know what I'm talking about.'

Carrie looked up at Tom, hoping for support, but his head was bent and he'd closed his eyes. She nudged his arm to get his attention, then frowned at him wondering why he didn't speak up in her defence. He shook his head and looked sad but said nothing.

'I won't be able to stay at Nightingale Lane forever, will I?' she said to her parents. 'I'll start to show and then the game will be up. Surely if Johan knows about the baby we can make a home. Him and me. And the baby. And we can get married and…the family…you won't lose any dignity because no one will be any the wiser.'

Florrie left her chair and took her cup and saucer into the scullery. Carrie heard her drop them into the water in the washing-up bowl, then open the scullery door and go out to the yard where the outhouse was. Her eyes went to Arthur. She knew he'd always had a soft spot for her. She hoped he would see it from her point of view, but he simply lit his pipe, leaned forward in the chair and stared morosely into the fire.

Carrie knew she'd lost. She hadn't known what to expect from her family when she told them; she knew they wouldn't be as happy for her as they'd been for Elsie, Elsie was married, but she thought they'd take her under their wing, find a solution and support her plan to be with Johan. She stood quietly next to Tom as the fire continued to flicker orange light into the room like Morse code. The silence was unbearable and she felt the nausea that had woken her in the early hours for the past few weeks swirling around in her stomach and threatening to put in an appearance. She hesitated, then walked towards the stairs leading off the sitting room. She put a foot on the bottom step, and before going upstairs turned and looked back at Tom. He was rooted to the spot, his head down, his hands pushed deep into his pockets.

'Tom.' He looked up at her and she was shocked to see that his eyes were full of tears. She smiled at him and put her head to one side. 'Come and talk to me.'

He nodded and followed her up the stairs. 'I'm sorry, Carrie,' he whispered. 'I didn't know it would be like that. I thought they'd help you, y'know, tell you what to do.'

'They did tell me what to do.'

They went into the bedroom and Carrie scrambled under the covers, shivering with the cold. Tom sat on the bed and wrapped the eiderdown around his shoulders, pulling his knees up to his chest. 'What will you do? Will you tell Johan?'

'I don't think I have a choice, do I, Tom. You heard what they said. If I tell him I'm out of here. Where the hell would I go?'

'D'you love him?'

She nodded, and then a thought occurred to her. 'You haven't told Alfie, have you? Tell me you haven't told him.'

He shook his head, then looked pointedly at her stomach. 'But he'll notice, won't he, when you start to get bigger? He might be young but he's not stupid. Everyone will notice eventually.'

She nodded and stared off into the distance. 'Yeah. Everyone will notice eventually.'

Chapter 3

Carrie rose from her kneeling position in front of the grate and rubbed her hand across her forehead leaving a smear of gritty black charcoal on her skin. It was the fifth grate she had cleared, prepared, and lit that morning. She looked at the gilt clock on the mantelpiece. It was not yet six and still dark outside. She put both hands on the small of her back and stretched. At five months pregnant her body had begun to change and she wondered how long she would be able to disguise her swelling stomach. At home she could relax about her developing body; the whole family knew about her pregnancy and who the father was. All had been sworn to secrecy.

Every female member of staff at Nightingale Lane was expected to wear a plain grey long-sleeved dress, a white apron, white sleeve protectors; black for messy jobs, and a white bonnet that must cover the hair completely, the uniform that marked them out from their employers. The grey dress was changed every three days, the white cotton pinafore, bonnet and protectors, every day. The apron covered a multitude of sins, successfully concealing the roundness of her belly. Florrie had let out the seams of her grey dress until there was no more fabric left.

Being a maid for the Sterns meant Carrie must sleep-in at Nightingale Lane six days out of seven. The sixth day she could go home in the evening. The following day was her day off but she had to back at Nightingale Lane in time to help with the hot, milky toddies the family had before they went to bed. She rose at five every morning, poured water from a jug into a bowl in the bedroom, dressed hastily in the icy room, and went downstairs to the huge kitchen. There, she would light the hob on the cooking range ready for Mrs. Coyle the cook so she could begin the breakfast preparations at six and prepare breakfast trays for Mrs Stern and her eldest daughter, Olivia, who ate their first meal of the day in their bedrooms.

In the drawing room, sitting room, and study she would draw the curtains and check the rooms were in good order; in the dining room she would set the table for Mr Stern, Johan, and the two younger girls, Liliana and Rachel. After all this was completed, she would clean the grates and build and light the fires in each room, the job she hated most of all.

The four overnight maids shared two rooms in the upper floor of the house. The rooms were plain with dark green utility iron beds covered in a white sheet, grey blanket and pale green eiderdown. The girls shared a dresser and a washstand, jug and bowl. There was also a tiny table between the beds to give them a semblance of separation, a kind of boundary between them indicating their own small allocated space. The maid's shifts were on rotation, but every other week Carrie would share her room with her best friend, Pearl. This was the shift she loved the most because it meant she could spend time with her closest friend. Their shifts usually finished at about eleven-thirty by which time all the Sterns had retired, then Carrie and Pearl would run up four flights of back stairs to the top of the house where they would swiftly undress, giggling and shivering with the cold, and jump into bed. When they had snuffed out the candle on the dresser, the only source of light for their room, they would snuggle under the covers and talk into the early hours, whispering their innermost secrets to each other, telling each other of their dreams and aspirations.

'I'll probably marry William,' Pearl said one night. 'And have loads of babies.'

'Is it what you want, Pearl?' Carrie had asked her.

Pearl nodded. 'Why would I want anything else? He's already asked me. We're sort of engaged.'

Carrie had grinned at her through the darkness, and they'd each reached out into the cold and held hands across the divide between the beds. 'I'm so happy for you, Pearl. Will you have a party?'

Pearl laughed. 'No…no party, but I don't care. Me mum and dad can't afford anything like that, but as long as William and I are together, it's all that counts.'

Carrie wanted to ask her a question but didn't want to spoil her happiness. She looked at her friend and wondered if she envied her. She and Johan were so close, yet they couldn't announce their relationship like Pearl and William. Johan had said it wasn't the right time; that they should wait until he could speak to his parents about her. Well she had waited and they didn't seem to be any nearer to the "right time". Perhaps Johan will ask me to get engaged, she thought. We could have a double wedding with Pearl and William.

'I know what you're thinking, Carrie' said Pearl. 'William's been called up to fight, but if the war ends when they say it will we'll get married when he comes home. We've got it all planned. We'll marry at St. Mary's Church in Whitechapel. We're having pink roses and cream peonies because they're my favourite. I want an ivory dress made of silk, and a veil with a rose headdress.'

She lowered her eyes, then looked back at Carrie. 'Will you be my bridesmaid, Carrie? I would love it if you would say yes.'

Carrie squeezed her hand. 'Oh, Pearl, of course I'll be your bridesmaid. You're my best friend. I'd be honoured.'

That night, when Carrie and Pearl went up to their attic room, Carrie didn't take the stairs two at a time as she usually did, but ascended the stairs gradually, her breath coming in short bursts. Pearl glanced back at her and frowned.

'You okay, Carrie? You're not ill, are you?'

Carrie shook her head. 'No, I'm alright. I just feel tired. It's been really busy in the house today. Mrs Coyle's been on my back all day. Don't know what's wrong with her. Reckon she's going through the change.'

Pearl shrugged. 'Christ, I reckon she went through that years ago. She must be sixty if she's a day. And if she ain't she bloody-well looks it.'

Once inside the room Carrie sat on the bed and wondered how she would find the strength to get up again at five the next morning. She'd started to struggle with the early mornings. Pearl placed the candle on the dresser and got undressed.

'Jesus Save Us, it's like an igloo in here. I'll be glad when the better weather comes,' she gasped. 'I've never known it so cold. I wish the Sterns would put one of those little paraffin heaters up here. They can't know how cold it is.'

Carrie laughed. 'You say that every week. They don't know how cold it is up here, how could they? They've never set foot in this room, and they don't care neither. They're all nice and warm down there because we make sure they are. As snug as bugs in a rug. Not like us, shaking like jellies.' She waited for Pearl to get into bed then blew out the candle before taking off her dress. She wanted to tell Pearl about the baby but hadn't yet found the courage and she wondered what Florrie would say if she found out. Getting undressed for bed after her shift had become a nightmare.

Pearl had noticed Carrie had changed her routine and she leaned up on her elbow. 'Why do you do that?'

Carrie frowned at her in the darkness pretending not to know what she meant. Her breath caught in her throat. 'Do what?'

'Blow the candle out before you get undressed. You never used to.'

Carrie frowned. 'Didn't I?'

Pearl sat up in bed. 'You know you didn't. What's going on, Carrie. You've been different the last couple of weeks…y'know, a bit distant. Is it because I said William and me was getting married? I'll always be your friend y'know. We'll always be best friends, won't we?'

Tears welled in Carrie's eyes. She wanted nothing more than to tell Pearl how worried and upset she was, and how the thought of giving birth frightened the life out of her. Her family had forbidden her to speak about it to anyone else but she was fit to bursting with it and she needed someone to confide in other than Tom. Pearl was her closest friend. Telling her would be alright, Carrie knew she could trust her. She relit the candle, placing it on the little table separating their beds and sat down, warming her hands between her knees. 'I'm pregnant, Pearl,' she whispered.

Pearl's mouth dropped open. She stared at Carrie in shock. 'Pregnant? Wha…what do you mean? How did that happen?' Carrie looked at her and raised her eyebrows. 'Well, alright I know how. But, Carrie you don't even have a boyfriend. You spend all your own time at home with your mum and dad.'

Pearl got out of bed ignoring the cold and sat next to Carrie. She put an arm around her shoulders.

'Let me see.'

'No, Pearl. I'm embarrassed.'

'But are you sure, Carrie. Maybe you've made a mistake. You're so young, you could have got it wrong, you know. Let me see.'

'I'm only a year younger than you. I'm not an idiot.'

'No, course you're not. I wasn't saying that.' Pearl lifted Carrie's dress to her waist, then gently lowered it again. 'How far are you?'

'About five months gone.'

Pearl went quiet. 'You poor little girl. Who was it? Did he force himself on you? It happens you know, in these big houses. Who is it, Carrie? Who's the father?'

'Johan.'

Pearls hands flew to her mouth to stop her from crying out. After a few moments she lowered them to her lap. 'Johan,' she whispered. 'You mean Johan Stern.' Carrie nodded. 'But when? When could it have happened?'

'It wasn't just once. We're having a relationship, Pearl. We love each other. We didn't mean this to happen, it just did.'

'Does he know?'

'No. My mum and dad do, though. They said I'm not to say anything to Johan, but I want to tell him, Pearl. I think he should know he's got a baby coming.'

Pearl got up and sat over on her own bed opposite Carrie. She leant forward and reached for Carrie's cold hands, squeezing them tightly in her own.

'Carrie, listen to me. You mustn't tell him. Never. Your name will be mud and you'll never get your reputation back again. They'll deny the baby is Johan's. They'll say that a girl like you would go with anyone, and everyone in Whitechapel will know what you've done. Listen to your mum and dad. You'll have to leave here soon anyway because it won't be long before everyone will know. You're as skinny as a hairpin so you've got a bit of time. That's the one good thing about never having enough to eat. We never put on weight do we?'

'Surely he should know. We said we were going to be together…make a life. We agreed, Pearl.'

Pearl closed her eyes and when she opened them again, Carrie's deeply troubled ones were staring at her. She obviously hadn't heard the news. Pearl took a deep breath wishing she didn't have to be the bearer of bad news.

'Johan Stern *is* getting married, Carrie, but not to you, sweetheart. His parents have arranged a marriage for him with a Jewish girl who has just arrived in England from America with her parents for the wedding. Did he not tell you?'

Carrie shook her head miserably. Tears ran down her cheeks, all her hopes and dreams evaporating into thin air.

'I do love him, Pearl. Really, I do.'

Pearl nodded, her mouth a straight line. 'Yeah, well I could knock his bloody block off right now. Stupid idiot. He's used you, Carrie. I'm so sorry. I know you think he loves you and I wish there could be a happy ending for you, but I don't think it's going to happen. Where will you and the baby go? Will you live at your mum and dad's? Maybe, in time, you'll be able to pass the baby off as Elsie's.'

'She's already pregnant.'

'I know, but people have short memories. You could go away somewhere for a little while, p'raps to some relatives. You could get another job after the baby's born, but not here, Carrie. You need to get away from this family.' Carrie nodded and Pearl squeezed her hand again. 'It'll be alright,' she said. 'I'll do your heavy jobs until you leave. You've got to take care of yourself now, do you understand?'

Carrie nodded again, silent, unable to put words to the way she was feeling. Then a thought occurred to her. 'When? When is Johan getting married?'

'Next week, at the synagogue in Sandys Row.'

Carrie breathed a sigh of relief. 'So I won't have to serve. I'll be off shift, thank goodness. I won't have to see them.'

'No, you won't have to see him. Thank goodness.'

Chapter 4

The week went by too quickly for Carrie and the day of Johan's wedding seemed to speed towards her. Over the previous few days there had been much coming and going in the house; tailors, seamstresses, florists, and hairdressers, all dancing attendance on Mrs Stern and her three daughters.

'Anyone would think it was them getting married,' Pearl whispered to Carrie, grinning, as they cleaned the house from top to bottom yet again. Pearl rubbed the windows vigorously, taking out her frustration on the already gleaming glass. 'Honestly, how bloody clean does she want the place to be? We did all this a couple of weeks ago.' Carrie was polishing the best silver and was well aware that if Mrs Stern couldn't see her reflection in the cutlery when she inspected it she would come down on her like a ton of bricks. She didn't answer Pearl. She had a queasy feeling in the pit of her stomach and she knew it was nothing to do with her pregnancy. The thought that Johan would be married to another girl without even knowing he was father to Carrie's child filled her with sorrow. She tried to concentrate on the chores Mrs Coyle had given her, but all she could see in her mind's eye was Johan. Pearl glanced at Carrie and looked worried. 'You will be alright, won't you, Carrie? This is like pushing your nose in it. Try to be strong, sweetheart.'

Carrie took a deep breath as she buffed the silver with a cloth. Rubbing away my unhappiness, she thought. If only I could. 'I'm alright. At least I won't be here on the day they get married. It's worked out quite well, taking everything into consideration. At least I won't have to see him. I don't think I could manage that. It would be so hard watching him say all the lovely things to her that he said to me. And even if I had been due in to work I'd have had to come in. I can't take time off, can I? I need the money and I'm going to need it even more soon.'

'We've to black the range this afternoon,' said Pearl. 'I can't imagine why. We only did it recently. I don't think any of the guests will be inspecting the bloody range. They've probably never even seen one. I shouldn't think they could care less as long as their dinner arrives on time.' She smiled gently at Carrie. 'Don't worry, Carrie. You can do the top bits, I'll do underneath.'

'Mrs Coyle won't like that,' said Carrie. 'It's my job to do the rough stuff. I'm the youngest maid apart from the tweeny, aren't I? It's the rules.'

'Yeah, well, we're going to break the sodding rules. I won't tell her if you won't.'

Carrie looked at her friend, her eyes soft. 'I love you, Pearl. You're the best friend anyone could ever have. I'm so glad I've got you to confide in. I don't know how I'd have managed without you.'

Pearl's face broke into a smile. 'Get away with you, yer silly mare,' she said, her face flushing, but a smile danced around her lips and she looked pleased.

In the kitchen Mrs Coyle was loudly instructing the tweeny to wash the pots from lunch. The little girl pulled a face behind Mrs Coyle's back but got on with it anyway. The last thing she wanted was to have the cook's wrath come down on her. The last time she'd fallen foul of her it had lasted for days. The big woman was huffing and puffing and complaining about the amount of work she was expected to do with such a small staff. Her face was bright red and her wispy hair kept escaping from under her bonnet. She pushed it back under the headband, but the same grey strands kept falling in front of her eyes.

'It's no good, Carrie. You'll have to come in on your day off this week. I'm sorry girl, but them upstairs have just increased the number of guests they've invited to the wedding and we'll need more staff. Honestly, I don't know where it's going to end. It's bloody ridiculous.' Carrie froze, staring first at Mrs Coyle, then at Pearl.

'Carrie doesn't need to come in on her day off, Mrs Coyle,' said Pearl. 'We can manage alright. We've got the other girls, and the tweeny can come in, can't you,' she said to the girl. 'You won't want to miss all the excitement of a posh wedding, will you?' She looked hard at the girl, daring her to disagree. The girl shook her head. 'There you go. We're fine.'

'No, we are not fine,' said Mrs Coyle, her hands on her ample hips. 'We won't be fine because them upstairs have invited twenty more guests. Everyone will have to come in. I don't know where they're getting 'em from, I really don't. And don't forget, their rules for what they like to eat and what they can't eat need to be observed and respected. We need all hands-on board and that means Carrie as well.' She turned to Carrie. 'I don't know what the fuss is about. You'll get a day off in lieu, Carrie. And at the end, if there's food left over from the evening buffet you can take some home for your mum. I should think she'd like that. You young girls should think yourself lucky. It weren't like this in my day. Now, we really had to work for our living, and we didn't get no free food to take 'ome at the end of the day, neither. You young girls don't know when you're well off. There are great benefits to working in a house like this. Mr and Mrs Stern are very generous and you should be grateful, you really should.'

They rubbed blacking all over the range in silence. Carrie did the huge hob and hot plate while Pearl did the ovens. They both had a tin of polish in one hand, an old cloth in the other. They'd scoop fingers of polish onto the cloth then rub it onto the metal. When they'd finished, the range was matt with the black polish. Now they had to wait until it dried then polish it all off, which took an age.

'Shall we have a cup of tea?' said Pearl. 'I'm worn out after that.'

'Alright,' said Carrie. 'I could do with a cuppa.'

'That's right,' said Pearl, pulling off her sleeve protectors. 'Take the weight off your feet. You look done in, Carrie, you really do. You should be putting your feet up a bit in the afternoons.'

'What am I going to do, Pearl? It looks like I'll be here to see Johan get married after all. I don't know how I'll cope. I won't know where to look.'

Pearl poured hot water into the teapot and slammed the kettle back on the hob. 'I wouldn't give him the time of day if I were you. Has he sought you out? Has he tried to talk to you over the past few months? Has he hell. He couldn't care less. That's men with money for you. And you're probably not the first. You definitely won't be the last, that's for sure. I'd stake my wages on it. And that girl he's marrying better get used to it. She won't be the only one. I've no doubt he'll have plenty of other girls hidden away somewhere. Men like that always do.' Carrie hated it when Pearl talked about Johan like this. She was sure he did care, and that if he'd known she was expecting his child would refuse to marry the other girl. 'We're below stairs, Carrie. We're the ones who do all the fetching and carrying. We're here to make the lives of those who live above stairs comfortable. It's what they pay us for. And believe me, if they find out about you and Johan and they kick you out there'll be a queue of girls waiting at the door to jump into your shoes and your job. Everything is scarce right now, and Mrs. Coyle is right, although I wish she wouldn't keep going on about it. We are lucky to work here.' Carrie nodded, then opened her mouth to defend Johan but Pearl jumped in. 'And don't go thinking he gives a damn, Carrie Dobbs. He doesn't, you mark my words. All he thinks about is himself. If he did care about you his bags would be packed and standing in the hall and so would yours, and you'd be running off into the sunset together, instead of him primping himself up for his posh wedding day and you on your hands and knees rubbing stinking black gloop over a rusty old cooking range.'

Carrie went into the dining room where a huge dining table large enough to seat forty people was laden with food. A few months before, this sight would have made Carrie's mouth water. Instead, it just made her feel sick.

'We'll eat well over the next few nights,' whispered Pearl as they passed each other carrying trays of canapes. 'That's the good thing about posh people. They think it's rude to eat loads…unlike us. Look at 'em, picking at their food like sparrows. Can't see the point of Mrs Coyle cooking all hours for this ungrateful lot.' Pearl grinned at Carrie, who managed a watery smile. Pearl looked at her sadly. 'It's nearly over, Carrie,' she said quietly. 'They'll all be gone soon, and you can forget all about them. And him.'

Carrie nodded. As she wove her way between the Stern's guests offering tasty bites here, filling a champagne glass there, her eyes were trained on Johan. He looked so handsome in his grey wedding suit, a cream silk cravat tied elegantly at his neck and fastened with a ruby pin. Her heart lurched with need of him. I just want to talk to him, she thought. Just to hear him say my name. She glanced across at his new wife, Lisabet. Carrie swallowed the lump in her throat that threatened to choke her. Johan's new wife was beautiful, with expertly coiled conker-brown hair, creamy skin, and full lips. Her eyes sparkled with happiness as she enjoyed the attention of everyone in the room. All eyes were on her and Carrie knew Lisabet was well aware of it. Her laughter was like a tinkling bell, her posture elegant, almost regal, and Carrie could see she relished being the centre of attention.

Carrie's eyes went to Johan again as he watched Lisabet with pride, a smile of quiet entitlement playing on his lips. Carrie tried to catch his eye but he turned away to speak to a guest. I'm carrying your child, she thought, and you won't even look at me.

'Carrie.' Pearl called to her from the other side of the room. Carrie took a step back then turned and walked towards her. 'What are you doing?' Pearl asked her. 'For God's sake, Carrie, you'll give the game away.'

'I was just looking.'

Pearl sighed and put a comforting hand on her arm. 'I know, but you're playing with fire. Mrs Coyle said she'd noticed you'd put on weight and she can't understand how you've done it, what with rations an' all. If she puts two and two together you'll be out on your ear. Plus, there'll be questions about the father.' She dragged Carrie out of the dining room and into the vestibule. 'You have to wise up about this,' she whispered. 'I know this is hard for you but you've got to get your head together and think about you and the baby. Never mind 'im.' She glanced into the dining room where Johan and Lisabet stood closely together, laughing and smiling with the guests, and seemingly in love. 'He's married now, lost to you forever. Forget about him and move on, Carrie. He has a new wife and a new life. And you have a little 'un on the way. Move on.'

The sun had not yet broken through the early morning mist, but when Carrie looked up she could just see it as it lightly touched the slow-moving cloud with silver. Every cloud has a silver lining, she thought. She dawdled home, not relishing the thought of returning there, yet accepted there was nowhere else for her to go. Since her family had known about her pregnancy there had been a terrible atmosphere in the house. She felt awkward around her parents, and their indifference towards her, she knew, was brought about by their unease and disappointment at her condition. Her pregnancy was an admission of what had happened between her and Johan, and she felt embarrassed in their company.

Elsie had barely spoken to her since the night Carrie had told her parents about the baby. Pearl suggested it was probably because Carrie had stolen her thunder. Elsie was the eldest daughter and had been receiving all the care and attention from her parents since she'd been married, and when she got pregnant there was great excitement. Carrie knew Elsie liked to be at the centre of everything. 'Maybe she thinks you've ruined it for her,' Pearl said. 'She's probably jealous.' Carrie wasn't sure. Florrie and Arthur had shown only their dismay at the condition she was in and she'd certainly received no special treatment. Since the day she had told them they'd barely mentioned it, and Florrie had been particularly dismissive. Elsie had nothing to be jealous of. She was the one with the husband and comfy lifestyle, at least more comfortable than hers. Carrie had hoped their pregnancies might bring them closer, although she and Elsie had never been close. At nineteen Elsie was two years older than Carrie, but it might as well have been twenty-two they had so little in common. Even though they now shared a life-changing experience Elsie still had no time for her.

Florrie and Arthur always looked worried no matter what was going on. In the past it was because of the scant money they had to live on and it had never been easy. When there's little money and the rent's due it keeps you awake at night. And Arthur wasn't getting any younger. He had a terrible cough, and Carrie often heard him wheezing and spluttering in the small hours where he couldn't get his breath. He was getting on, his forties had brought with them some bad health; aches and pains, coughs and colds that lasted longer than they should. Doctors were out of the question. They couldn't afford the medicines so there was no point in consulting a physician. She worried about him most of all, but she knew why their worries were worse than usual, and she understood. The war had brought food shortages into the homes of families all over the country, and theirs was no different. Soon she would have to leave her position at Nightingale Lane, there was no way out of it, which meant a significant wage less and another mouth to feed. The bag of food Mrs Coyle had given her before she'd left Nightingale Lane; a peace offering from her for her parents held so tightly in her hand her fingernails cut into her palm, gave her confidence. She was sure her family would be pleased when they saw what she'd brought home. Everything made such a difference to them, no matter how small or insignificant it would have been to the Sterns.

She pushed the front door open and stepped into the hall. As she went into the living room she could hear voices coming from the scullery. She frowned and glanced at Elsie who sat in her usual place in front of the fire. She looked up from her knitting, and without a smile or saying a word in greeting raised her eyebrows at Carrie and then inhaled a breath she released as slowly as she could. Carrie could hear her mother and father's voice but there was another, a male voice she didn't recognise. The thick curtain between the scullery and the living room had been drawn across, so the voices sounded muffled and she couldn't quite make out what they were saying. She walked towards the scullery and pulled the curtain aside.

'Carrie!' Florrie jumped and her reaction at seeing Carrie standing in the scullery entrance made Carrie wary. 'I didn't think you'd be home today. You said you'd have to stay at Nightingale Lane tonight. Why aren't you at work?'

'Mrs Coyle said I wasn't needed. The guests have all gone home and the Sterns are resting after the wedding. I think they're glad to see the back of everyone to be honest. Even Mrs Stern was happy to see us go and she hates it if we don't work out our time to the last minute.' Her eyes went to the man standing behind her parents. He was tall with a slim build. His fine fair hair was parted in the middle and so thin his scalp showed through the greasy strands. His pencil-thin moustache was wispy and fair and wouldn't have been noticeable if it hadn't been for the streak of nicotine at the edges staining it orangey-brown. Smartly dressed in a grey suit and a white shirt with a highly starched collar, he observed Carrie with a scorn that shook her.

'This is Mr Bateman,' said Florrie.' Carrie stood still and said nothing and Florrie looked uncomfortable, an uneasy smile on her lips that didn't reach her eyes.

Arthur spoke up, his voice trembling. He could barely meet Carrie's gaze. 'Mr Bateman, that is, Sergeant-Major Bateman is with the Royal Horse Artillery, y'know in the army. He's been chosen to be posted to India. He's leaving in a few weeks.'

Carrie stared at her father. 'That's nice for him I'm sure, but what's that got to do with us?'

Arthur was about to say something but Florrie interrupted him. 'Mr Bateman has a proposition for us…for you.'

Carrie's heart began to beat wildly. She took a deep breath that wobbled in her chest, then breathed it out, a wave of dread prickling her skin. She knew how her parents felt about her baby. She also knew that if the father had been someone from their own kind, from a family who lived in the blackened streets they all knew like the backs of their hands they would have accepted her predicament far more readily. They would have pulled together like families do in times of hardship or crisis and forcefully encouraged her to marry the father of her baby. He would have been named and shamed and marched down the aisle with Carrie, and her shame as a pregnant girl without a husband would have been brief and forgotten by the next day. As it was she had fallen in love with a man who lived a life utterly different from her own, who lived in luxury they could only dream of and whose prominent position in his social class was certain. Florrie and Arthur had not mentioned Johan Stern's name from the day she had told them about the baby. It was as though he didn't exist.

'What on earth could Mr. Bateman want with me?'

'I know Mrs Bateman, Mr Bateman's mother. She's a fine lady,' said Florrie, turning to him. Sergeant-Major Bateman bowed his head with a small smile to Florrie in thanks her for her compliment.

'But that doesn't answer my question,' said Carrie. She took off her hat and put it on the table in the living room, then hung her shawl on the hook by the door. She knew they were watching her and she ignored them as they followed her into the living room. Picking up the string bag of food she held it out to Florrie. 'Mrs Coyle gave me these things for you. She said she hoped they would help. There's stuff in there I can't even pronounce. Look.'

Florrie tut tutted and waved her hand towards Carrie. 'Never mind about that. Mr Bateman's going to India and he wants you to go with him.'

Elsie snorted with laughter at Florrie's frankness, and Carrie's mouth dropped open.

'What? What are you talking about?' She put her hands on her hips and shook her head, astonished at what her mother was telling her. Then she stared at her father, her eyes imploring him to put a stop to whatever was happening. He averted his eyes, embarrassment and regret etched across his face. His shoulders slumped and he went back into the scullery as if he couldn't bear to hear anymore. Carrie fixed her eyes on her mother. 'I'm not going to India, or anywhere else with a...a...stranger. How can you even think such a thing? My home is here with you, and Elsie, and Tom and Alfie. And the babbies.' She put her hands on her stomach. 'This baby is your grandchild. Don't you care about that? I don't even know this...person.' She flung her hand in the direction of Bateman. 'And yet you're suggesting I go to India with a man I don't know... you don't know. And I don't give a rat's arse if you know his mother. You know a lot of people but I'm not going to live with them. How shameful would that be, Mum, to live with a man I don't know? You wouldn't do it. You wouldn't expect Elsie to do it, so why the hell should I?'

'That's not the point,' said Florrie. 'The point is you're in the family way and you're unmarried. You've brought shame on this family, Carrie Dobbs, and you owe it to me and your dad to do as you're told. We can't afford to feed you and another baby on less money. It was going to be hard enough with Elsie and her little 'un, and soon you won't be bringing home any money because you won't have a job. Jobs are scarce and you've thrown yours away. No, my girl, what you've brought home is a load of trouble and even more worries for me an' your dad to contend with.' She barely took a breath during her tirade and didn't stop long enough for Carrie to interject. 'And it won't be shameful. Nothing about any of it is shameful except you and what you've done.' She folded her arms across her ample bosom and stared at Carrie with sharp eyes as if daring her to argue. 'Anyway, it's been decided. You and Mr Bateman will be married in two weeks' time.'

Carrie's eyes widened. She turned to look at Elsie who was busy concentrating on her sewing, pretending to take no notice, and then back at Florrie. 'What? Why? Why does he want to marry me, someone he's never met in his life before and take on another man's child? No one else would want to do it. Why is he so different?'

'Because Mr Bateman has a good position in the army, and…as befits that position he should be married but he hasn't met the right person as yet. You'll live in his house in India and run his home, and you will do as you are told. You lost the right to say what you want and what you don't want when you laid down with the son of the people who were employing you, the ones who paid your wages and put food on our table. And you got more than you bargained for with Johan Stern didn't you, a man who doesn't want you and is now married to someone else? So much for him loving you and wanting to make a home with you, Carrie Dobbs!'

She lay on her bed, the curtains drawn across the window. Carrie could hear them talking, turning her life upside down, planning her future; planning her baby's future. How dare they, she thought. How dare they take my life and turn any way they want without bothering to ask me what I want. Even Elsie had looked upset which had surprised her. She wished Tom had been there. He would have stood up for her she was sure of it. Maybe he'll try and change their minds, persuade them that what they were planning was a really bad idea. Tom was on her side. He always was. He wouldn't want her to be sent to a country so far away they probably wouldn't see each other again and couldn't even imagine what it was like.

That evening, Florrie called Carrie down from her room to explain some of the strange food she'd brought home from the Sterns.

'It's a good job you brought this home, our Carrie. We had nothing in the cupboard for tomorrow. Trouble is I don't know what half of it is. Couldn't you have brought something we're used to?'

'I didn't get to choose, Mum. Mrs Coyle gave me the bag and that was that. I could hardly say, 'we don't like this or that so give me something else'. It would've been like looking a gift horse in the mouth.' She swallowed hard and shuffled her feet. 'Anyway, I would have thought you'd be alright now,' she said in a low voice. 'What's Mr Bateman giving you to buy me? Surely you're not giving me to him for nothing. Even I must be worth something.'

Florrie lifted her hand and slapped Carrie across the face. As Carrie held her smarting cheek, her mouth open with shock. Florrie looked directly into her eyes. 'You should think yourself lucky someone was willing to take you on, my girl,' she said in a low voice. 'Now, I don't want to hear any more about it, do you understand?' Carrie reached for the damp dishrag and held it against her cheek, still burning from her mother's slap. It was the first time Florrie had hit her with such force. 'You're getting married at the big church in Whitechapel. Mr Bateman has provided for a wedding dress and for some food afterwards at The Royal Oak. You'll sail for India the week after. You'll need to get your things together, the things you want to take with you, not that you've got much…a small case, that's all. Go back to Nightingale Lane tomorrow and tell them you're leaving, and for God's sake don't tell them why. And don't forget to pick up your wages. Your dad and me are going to need every penny seeing as we won't be getting any more money from you from then on.'

During their evening meal no one spoke. Carrie tried to catch Arthur's eye but his focus was on his plate. He'd allowed himself to be railroaded by Florrie, who, even though he had always said was a down to earth good women, the salt of the earth, was the driving force behind any decision made when it concerned their family and their home. He was rarely allowed an opinion on anything unless it coincided with Florrie's, and if he disagreed with anything she said, she would send him to Coventry for weeks during which time he would become so miserable and downhearted he would decide it wasn't worth the aggravation and agree with her anyway.

He didn't like Sergeant-Major Bateman. Arthur knew a bad 'un when he saw one, and even after the briefest of meetings he was sure Bateman was a man not to be trusted. His heart was breaking, and he had such a lump in his throat because of the pain he felt at deceiving his beloved youngest daughter he couldn't speak. He knew he should have taken Carrie aside and given her a way out, but he couldn't.

Florrie would have made his life hell. She had been so quick to take Bateman's offer of marriage to Carrie they hadn't even asked him his Christian name. All they knew was that he had achieved a reasonable position in the army and his reward was a posting to India, a foreign country they knew nothing about. If he'd been posted to the moon Florrie couldn't have been less interested. As long as it was away from Whitechapel, the place where they had lived all their lives and made their home when they'd married, and all the people they knew which was most of the community, she wasn't bothered where it was.

Part of him felt ashamed. He was ashamed because he knew he should have stood up to Florrie; told her she was wrong to send their youngest daughter away to God knows where. He knew it was possible they might never see Carrie again. The thought of it devastated him. Carrie had always been his favourite child. He admired her gumption and her quick wit, so unlike himself. And he knew deep down that his daughter was a good person. She'd made a mistake, allowed herself to be led on, believed Johan Stern when he'd told Carrie he loved her. He knew in his heart she wasn't the first girl to have been treated so shabbily and she wouldn't be the last. Yes, he was disappointed; if it had been Elsie he might have accepted it better, but he didn't feel Carrie's lack of judgment which was probably down to her naivety warranted her being sent away. He and Carrie had always been close, and now, at a time when she needed him most, when she needed support and guidance from her parents, he had turned his back on her. He got up from the table and went into the scullery, carefully placing his plate and cutlery in the soapy water, then opened the door to the yard.

'Arthur?' Florrie called out.

'I'm going out,' he answered gruffly. As he went to close the door he heard her complaining about him behind his back.

'S'pose he's off down the pub. He shouldn't be squandering what little we have on beer. It's all right for some.'

He sighed, then continued into the yard and out onto the back path with a heavy heart.

Chapter 5

Florrie Dobbs carefully ran her hand down the bodice of the ivory and mint green silk and lace dress hanging against the door. She reached for the scalloped hem and held out the full skirt, admiring the way the early morning light streaming through the window fell on the diaphanous fabric making it shimmer like spun gold. She let it fall and watched it billow like a cloud against the door as though in slow-motion. A surge of regret went through her. She shook her head to rid herself of the feelings she knew she mustn't have, the destructive thoughts that would ruin all of her plans and make her look weak in front of the family. And that couldn't happen because she was the only one who would make sure things were as they should be.

She sighed and folded her arms. Her thoughts went to her own wedding day to Arthur, and how little they'd had to be satisfied with, then and since. Everything had been such an uphill struggle for them; they'd never had enough money to live on, and it had got even harder when the kids had arrived. Of course, only she had known she was pregnant with Elsie when she and Arthur had walked down the aisle of the same church where Carrie and Mr. Bateman would marry. She remembered they had been teased mercilessly by their family and friends when she'd announced she was pregnant a short time after the wedding. There had been lots of ribbing about Arthur's prowess in the bedroom. Elsie smiled to herself, remembering how embarrassed Arthur had been. It was true enough though. She'd never had any complaints on that score. Elsie had been called a honeymoon baby and had come early. That's what they'd told everyone and it's what everyone had believed. Elsie had been small and rather pale when she came into the world, and it had helped Florrie keep her ruse going. And Arthur had never guessed why she'd been so keen for them to marry when they did. He'd just gone along with things, like he always did.

Florrie sat on the end of her bed and looked up at the dress that Carrie would wear at her own wedding. Carrie's such an ungrateful little wretch, she thought. It was only thanks to Florrie that she had the chance of a future and yet she was behaving as though it was a punishment. Carrie didn't know how lucky she was. Her daughter had made a mistake that affected the whole family, and she, Florrie, had simply taken the only steps she could to ensure no shame would be heaped on them. She'd heard about girls in Carrie's position, known women whose daughters had fallen prey to the sons of families for whom they worked. It never ended well. Many were ostracised by their families, often sinking into destitution after having been kicked out of the family home. Numerous young women were driven to walk the streets looking for punters, handing their babies over to unsuitable carers so they could earn a few shillings lying on their backs. She didn't want that for Carrie. People had long memories in Whitechapel, and there was no way she would allow her to bring a disgrace on the family that would stain its reputation for generations to come.

She knew Carrie was angry with her, and she acknowledged that if her mother had tried to marry her off to a stranger and sent her away she would have felt the same, but she'd married the boy next door, the one she'd sat next to in class until she left school at the age of twelve. Arthur was always the one for her, and even though it was clear to her he was devastated at losing his favourite daughter, she knew he would forgive Florrie in time. They would get through it like they'd got through everything else; the scrimping and scraping, the going hungry, the outbreak of war, Elsie's husband being called up after only a few months of marriage, and the certainty that if the war didn't end soon her own two boys would go the same way.

She took the dress from the door and holding it against her body stood in front of the mirror. She smiled at her reflection. She'll be alright, she thought. She'll be alright.

Chapter 6

Carrie and Sergeant-Major Bateman stood under the stone archway of the church door. The ceremony had been short and to the point, each saying their vows by rote, neither infusing the declarations with any meaning. There was very little congregation; just Carrie's family and her new husband's mother. There were also a few men from Bateman's regiment, but he didn't bother to introduce her to them. Arthur had given her away as was expected of him, but his miserable expression indicated how he felt. This wasn't the wedding he had imagined for his youngest daughter; instead he knew he was leading her to a life of uncertainty and very likely misery. Pearl followed them sedately up the aisle, Carrie's only bridesmaid. When Carrie had joined her intended at the altar she turned to give Pearl her flower posy. Their eyes met across the pretty mix of lily of the valley, freesia and gypsophila, Carrie's full of apprehension, Pearl's full of tears.

While they waited for the vicar to begin the ceremony, Carrie turned to Sergeant-Major Bateman. 'I don't even know your name,' she said quietly.

He lifted his chin and linked his fingers together in front of his stomach. 'Arnold,' he said staring straight ahead. 'My name's Arnold, after my grandfather.'

Carrie turned to face the altar and swallowed hard. 'Thank you.'

He nodded once. 'You're welcome.'

Afterwards, they gathered at The Royal Oak, a spit-and-sawdust pub that catered mostly for men from the docks and soldiers home on leave from the front. It was a place that Carrie had never entered in her life before, and probably never would have if it hadn't been for Arnold Bateman. Inside it was gloomy and smelt predominantly of cigarette smoke and spilt beer. Everything was stained ochre yellow, even the worn tapestry seats and the curtains which were thick with dirt and held back with red tassels stiff with dust. Carrie's heart sank. This wasn't the kind of place she had dreamed about or ever imagined she would have her wedding breakfast. She glanced at Arnold. And he certainly wasn't the man who had occupied her thoughts and dreams night after night.

Arnold went straight to the bar with his mates and ordered whisky for each of them. Florrie opened the door to the snug and poked her head into the room. Carrie glimpsed a table covered in a deep red chenille tablecloth, a few plates of sandwiches and tiny cakes dotted on the top. She looked up at Pearl who reached for Carrie's hand and held it tight.

'What have I done, Pearl?' she whispered, leaning her head against Pearl's shoulder.

Pearl shook her head. 'I don't know, Carrie but it's not looking good. Isn't there anywhere you can go, somewhere to get you away from all this? I don't know what the hell Florrie was thinking when she agreed to it.' She rubbed Carrie's back affectionately. 'At least you're a married woman now,' she whispered. 'That means you'll get some respect wherever you go. It's not like before when you were a girl with a bun in the oven and no man to stand beside you. And you could make up a story…say your husband's been killed in the war. People would believe that. There's plenty of them perishing at the front, isn't there?'

Carrie looked up into her friend's face. 'But I've no money. How will I look after the baby with no money?'

'What about your wages? There must've been a couple of weeks-worth with leaving pay.' Carrie looked over to Florrie. Pearl lifted her chin and tutted. 'Right. Got those too, has she?'

The landlady, a black-haired woman as wide as she was tall wearing a brown dress and cheap paste earrings came out from behind the bar and approached Florrie.

'You can go in now, Mrs. It's all ready. Mr. Bateman's paid so it's been taken care of.' Florrie nodded and beckoned the others into the snug. Carrie let go of Pearl's hand and walked towards Florrie with a heart as heavy as lead. A fluttering inside her made her gasp and she placed a hand on her stomach to let her baby know she had felt it. Suddenly a surge of love went through her. She had felt the baby's movements before of course, but for the first time since discovering she carried Johan's child she experienced a bond between her and her baby; an invisible unbreakable cord of steel that seeped into every cell of her body, from the top of her head to the soles of her feet. She wasn't just one person anymore. The baby she nurtured within her own body was the most important person in that drab little room in the Royal Oak, a place devoid of any real sense of occasion and so lacking in warmth. Carrie knew from that moment that whatever happened she wasn't alone. Her eyes went to Arnold again and her heart sank. He wasn't an attractive man. His age was difficult to place but Carrie guessed at around thirty. He was quite tall, almost six feet, and his body slender with no obvious muscle. His fair hair was very thin; she could see his pink scalp shining through the greasy strands where he'd combed it carefully into place. The skin on his neck was mottled with tiny bloodspots where the shaving blade had nicked him. She thought of Johan's thick dark hair and the way it curled over his collar, and his hard, well-toned body when he'd held her to him. Her chest tightened. I mustn't think of him like that, she thought. He can't help me now. Even if he wanted to.

The other guests squeezed into the snug and Florrie encouraged them to take a plate and help themselves to the sandwiches now stiff and curling at the corners. Arnold Bateman and his mates joined them briefly but were eager to get back to the bar. Carrie watched him from the door then looked back into the snug where her mother was holding court. Florrie held her china teacup between finger and thumb, her little finger raised the way she imagined all well-to-do ladies drank their tea. Her father sat in the corner of the snug nursing a beer. He looked like he was at a wake mourning the passing of someone dear to him, not celebrating his daughter's wedding. Elsie sat next to him. She looked ready to drop and kept shifting her swollen body from one buttock to the other on the hard, straight-backed chair. Tom and Alfie stood by her, leaning against the wood panelling, their eyes darting first to Florrie then to Mrs Bateman as the two women chewed the fat over their good fortune. The boys wore the same miserable expression as Arthur, their faces gaunt and pale, mirroring their wish of being somewhere else, anywhere but there. They held jugs of watered-down cider; a previously unbroken rule written by Florrie that her boys would never drink alcohol in public, relaxed that day because of the special occasion. They sipped at the jugs without enthusiasm.

Pearl sat next to Carrie and smiled at her. Her eyes locked on to Carrie's and the two girls knew this was their final moment together.

'I have to leave now, Carrie. I've to go Nightingale Lane tonight to cover your shift now that you've left. I think Mrs Coyle is planning to take someone on in your place. They've been seeing girls.' She screwed up her face. 'Funny looking lot.' She tutted. 'No one I'd want to share our room with, that's for sure.' Her eyes filled with tears and she grasped Carrie's hand. 'I wish you weren't leaving, Carrie,' she whispered. 'I don't know what I'm going to do without you.'

'Do you think they know why I've left? Mrs Coyle looked a bit suspicious when I told her I was leaving.'

Pearl shook her head. 'Now don't go fretting about that,' she said, patting Carrie's hand. 'Whatever they're thinking it'll last as long as yesterday's newspaper, and then they'll find someone else to talk about. Anyway, no one's said anything to me and if they do I'll shoot them down in flames.' She grinned at Carrie, trying to lighten the moment, then tightly grasped Carrie's hand again. 'You will write to me, won't you, Carrie? I know you'll be a long way away, but we'll still be best friends, won't we? And I want you to be my bridesmaid, don't forget. I couldn't have anyone else but you, and William agrees with me.'

Carrie smiled, wondering how she could be Pearl's bridesmaid once she was over the other side of the world. 'Of course I'll still be your bridesmaid. I wouldn't miss it for the world. I'll never forget you, Pearl, no matter what happens. You're closer to me than my own sister.' She glanced around the snug. 'Than anyone really. I'm going to miss you so much.'

Pearls eyes glistened. 'Me too.' She leant forward to whisper in Carrie's ear. 'If he's horrible to you or makes you do things you don't want to do, you just come and live with me and William after we're married. He wouldn't mind, he's a good man, and we'd both rather that then be worried about you in another country. Promise me, Carrie. Promise me.' She gripped Carrie's hands.

'I promise you, Pearl.' Pearl kissed her on the cheek then turned away and left the public house with Carrie staring after her, wishing she could follow her, wanting everything the way it had been before, and that she too was going with Pearl to Nightingale Lane where life had been so simple. Her thoughts went to Johan and her stomach lurched. And if she hadn't been so silly...thinking that someone like Johan would actually love her. Everyone had said he'd used her. It just hadn't felt like that at the time. She closed her eyes and wished she were somewhere else, anywhere but in a grimy pub that stank of cigarettes and stale beer. As she opened her eyes again Arnold Bateman filled her vision. This man was her husband, the man she'd just married, not for love like she'd always dreamed of, but for convenience, and not her own but her mothers.

'Carrie!' Florrie called her from across the snug. She'd had a sherry or two and her cheeks were flushed bright red. 'Mrs Bateman says you're to go home with her tonight. She's made up a room for you and Mr Bateman...Arnold.' She looked at Mrs Bateman and smiled ingratiatingly, 'And you'll stay there until you go to India.'

Carrie shook her head. 'No, I want to come home, Mum. I haven't packed my things or anything. And I'd like to spend another night at home…with you, Dad and the family.'

Florrie pushed a small worn leather case forward with her foot. 'I packed your case for you. Everything you'll need is in there. You're a married woman now, Carrie. You have to live in your husband's house, and that's with Arnold and Mrs Bateman.'

'But…I don't know them.' Her face was contorted with distress as she begged her mother. 'They're strangers, Mum. Please let me stay with you tonight.'

'No buts. It's how it is so it's best if you get used to it early on. You'll be leaving for India soon, and you can visit us at Hanbury Street to say goodbye. Then you can write as often as you want, if you get the time.' She smiled at Arnold Bateman again, and nodded to his mother.

Carrie looked down. Nausea swept through her when she realised her life with her family was over. She sighed heavily and glanced up again. Arthur, Tom and Alfie were staring at her. She looked at them, hoping her eyes would tell them how she felt. She glanced into the bar. Arnold Bateman was playing a drinking game with his friends, oblivious to her misery. He'd barely looked at her since they'd left the church. I'm just a thing, she thought. Someone to make him look good in front of his superiors. And someone to warm his bed. She shuddered at the thought. She looked back at her father and brothers who were still staring at her. She loved them so much, wanted to run to them and cling on to them hoping they could save her, but she knew by the expression on their faces even they had acknowledged she was lost to them, and there was nothing they could do for her now.

Carrie stood on the pavement behind Arnold and Dolores Bateman as they wrestled with the old front door of their house in Pratt Street in Camden. Arnold put his knee against it and when it still didn't budge, shoved it with his shoulder. A sound like a lightning strike ripped through the door as it split down the middle.

'For Christ's sake,' cried Arnold as the door fell in two. 'What a homecoming. I thought you'd spoken to the landlord about this, Mother.'

'I did mention it, Arnold, when he came for the rent last, but he didn't want to know. He said if we were that worried we'd do something about it ourselves.' She gathered herself up and took a deep breath before speaking. 'You did know about it, son. It's been needing a mend for months.'

'Yeah, well, I'm going to have to now, aren't I?' He gathered up the bits of wood and threw them bad-temperedly into the front sitting room. He looked crossly at Carrie. 'P'raps you could make yourself useful and brew some tea. You can see how we're placed here and there are no free rides. Me and Mother expect you to pull your weight until we go to India. And don't be using that baby you're carrying as an excuse to be idle. We're a bit sharper than that, aren't we, Mother?'

Dolores nodded and patted her son's shoulder. 'We certainly are, son. That's right, Carrie, listen to your husband. You'll know the scullery when you see it. Off you go.' Arnold threw back his head and laughed, then grinned at Dolores. 'And when you've done that you can help me make up the bed in Arnold's room. The sheets are still on the line in the yard. You can get them off and run an iron over them to dry them.'

Carrie put her case on the floor, took off her coat and laid it across an old moquette chair with wooden arms. 'Is there anything else you'd like me to do while I'm at it?'

Arnold straightened his back and narrowed his eyes. 'Don't use your smart tongue with us, Carrie Dobbs…and yes, in my eyes you are still a Dobbs. We've heard all about your independent nature and flippant remarks. And we also know what kind of a girl you are. Don't we, Mother?' Dolores nodded and Arnold continued his diatribe. 'We run a traditional and respectable house here, unlike your own it would seem.' He sniggered and Carrie threw him a look of utter loathing. 'You'll earn your keep while you're here. This is no meal ticket for you, Carrie Dobbs. You're expecting to eat, I take it?'

Carrie didn't answer him. She stoked the fire in the front sitting room, then unhooked the kettle off the hanger and went into the scullery to fill it with water. While the water heated she set out three cups and saucers on the wooden drainer, then spooned tea into the teapot. When the water had boiled she brought the teapot to the kettle and filled it, covering it with a cosy. She went back into the scullery and put the cups and saucers on a wooden tray, along with a tiny jug of milk and a bowl of sugar. She set the tray down on a table at the side of the fire, then went into the yard and pulled the sheets off the line. They were still damp. She gathered them up and took them into the house, laying them across the wooden chairs in the front sitting room to dry.

Arnold removed his suit jacket and fixed the two pieces of the front door together with a hammer and nails while Dolores went into the backyard to use the privy. Carrie poured tea into the three china cups and sat on one of the wooden chairs to drink hers, leaving the two comfortable chairs by the fire free for Arnold and his mother. When Arnold was happy with his handiwork he threw the hammer onto the table making a loud clunk, then flopped down in one of the chairs. He took his tea from the tray without thanking her. A silence between them followed punctuated only by the sound of the fire crackling in the grate. The snapping and hissing of the damp wood gave Carrie comfort, reminding her of home, and for the first time that day she felt she could relax a little.

When Dolores returned from the yard she took her tea from the tray and sat in the chair opposite Arnold, turning to Carrie.

'Thank you for the tea, Carrie. Perhaps when the bedding is aired you could help me with the bed.'

Carrie nodded. 'Yes, of course I'll help you, Mrs Bateman.'

Arnold glanced at his mother and frowned. 'Getting soft in your old age, Mother?' He threw back the dregs of his tea, then looked at her through narrowed eyes.

'Manners cost nothing, Arnold. Carrie has come here as your wife. She isn't a servant.'

He got up and shrugged on his coat. 'She bloody well ought to be after what I paid. And to think…it was me doing them a favour.' He threw a look of scorn in Carrie's direction, then went to the buckled front door and tried to open it, getting cross because it wouldn't budge. 'I'm going back to the pub. My mates are returning to the front tomorrow. I want to wish them well.' He went out of the thrown-together door and pulled it closed behind him without waiting for a response.

It was growing dark in the sitting room. Dolores got up and lit three candles, placing them around the room. She beckoned Carrie to sit in the chair Arnold had vacated.

'Come and sit with me in front of the fire, Carrie. It's very cold tonight. I thought once March and the beginning of April were out of the way we'd get some decent weather, at least good enough not to have to keep feeding the fire. Getting the wood is becoming more difficult. I don't know what we'll do if the war goes on too long.'

Carrie settled herself in the soft cushioned chair. Her swollen stomach felt unwieldy and uncomfortable and she was grateful for the offer. 'Thank you, Mrs Bateman. I don't want to be any trouble.'

Dolores leant forward. 'You can call me Ma if you like. I expect you wish you were with your own family, sitting with your own mother next to your own fire, but it is the way of us. If you marry a man in these parts you must live in his house. Do you understand?' Carrie nodded. 'I love my son, Carrie, he's the only son I have, but he doesn't know how to treat a woman. Arnold learnt everything at his father's knee and I'm afraid my husband didn't know how to treat a woman either. He was a bully like many men, and I'm afraid my son has grown to be just the same.'

Carrie's eyes grew wide with horror and her heart sank even lower. 'Could I not stay here with you when Arnold goes to India? I'm afraid Mrs Bate…Ma. I don't know this new country we're going to, and I don't know what it will be like there. I could stay with you, couldn't I, and help you in the house until the baby comes. I promise you I won't be any trouble. You won't even know I'm here. Please say I can.'

'I'm afraid not, Carrie. I know you're frightened, any young girl would be, but Arnold married you so you could accompany him to India as his wife. He has done well has Arnold for all his faults, and his position requires him to have a stable home life with children. It means you'll have a better house at the garrison. Your job will be to support Arnold in every way, and to entertain his guests. Arnold wants to be in a position of power and he needs you to help him get there by being a good wife. A very good wife.' She lowered her eyes to her cup, then glanced up at Carrie lowering her voice to an embarrassed whisper. 'You'll be expected to be his wife in every way, you know.'

Carrie leant back against the chair and closed her eyes. Arnold's thin, mottled face and lank fair hair loomed in front of her. The thought of sharing a bed with a man she'd met only twice, of having his hands on the most intimate parts of her body filled her with revulsion. She opened her eyes again to find Dolores Bateman staring at her.

'You must be strong, Carrie. You'll have to be very strong.'

Chapter 7

The candle flickered in the sparsely furnished bedroom, throwing large misshapen shadows onto the walls. Carrie undressed quickly and pulled on a flannelette nightdress and a knitted night coat. It was very cold; any warmth thrown out by the fire in the front sitting room seemed to get no further than the middle stair. Above it was bitter, even colder than Hanbury Street and nowhere near as comfortable. Carrie had always been aware of her humble beginnings because of the luxurious surroundings of Nightingale Lane, but she had to acknowledge her parent's house may have been shabby, but it was clean, homely and welcoming. Dolores had kindly given her an old pottery hot water bottle to warm the bed, and as Carrie slipped between the freshly laundered sheets she relished how wonderful it felt on her legs and body, a small comfort for which she was grateful.

Arnold hadn't returned from the pub and Carrie was glad. She'd purposely not blown out the candle because she didn't want him fumbling about in the dark and losing his temper when he came into the bedroom. She lay with the sheet and blankets pulled up to her chin and wondered how convincing an act she could pull off pretending to be asleep. What Dolores had said had frightened her. She had told her plainly that Arnold would expect her to fulfil her wifely duties, and she knew exactly what that meant. She turned on her side and snuggled down into the bed. Dolores had surprised her. It seemed that when Arnold was around she turned into a harridan and treated her the way Arnold did...like a servant, or at the very least an unwelcome guest. When they were by themselves Dolores was motherly and kind.

Carrie thought of Florrie and compared the two women. Florrie hadn't even talked to her about the baby or asked her how she was coping during her pregnancy, a show of concern she had hoped for regardless of the situation. Carrie was her daughter after all. She wished Florrie had put her arms around her to comfort her or spoken to her about what would happen during her confinement and birth, anything to show that she cared about her youngest daughter. Arthur seemed anxious not to go near her, particularly in front of Florrie. He was usually so affectionate towards her, they'd always had a close bond, but he had become a quiet, pale shadow of the man he was, and had barely spoken to her since she had told them about the baby. Carrie knew Florrie was angry with her. Not just disappointed...but angry. And she knew why. It was money. It was always about money. And Carrie understood. Florrie had endlessly had to make a little go a long way, and since the outbreak of war the expectation had been even greater. At present there was Arthur, Tommy and Alfie bringing in a wage to add to the pot, albeit a very small one. With the continuation of the war she would not only have lost Carrie's contribution but also theirs when the time came, which meant she would be down to one meagre wage of a few shillings to pay the rent and to feed three adults and a new baby. Carrie couldn't help wondering how much money Arnold Bateman had given Florrie. Regardless of much it was Carrie hoped it was worth losing her daughter for. She shook her head with sadness and promised her unborn child that if the baby was a girl and found herself in a similar situation Carrie would stand by her, no matter what the gossips said. She wondered at Florrie's love for her and how easily she had found it to let Carrie go.

Although unsaid Carrie felt Dolores seemed to understand Carrie's struggle with what had happened to her. She wondered why she was being so kind. In one week she and Arnold would board a ship and sail across the ocean to a country she had only seen in her atlas, and only then because she had searched for it out of curiosity about her future home. It was so far away. She had traced her finger from the little black spot on the paper that had "London" written next to it and followed a route across the world to India. She looked at the expanse of blue and the huge spread of continent between the two countries and thought she may as well have been travelling to another planet, realising at that moment it was possible, probable, she would never see her loved ones again. Then it dawned on her. Dolores knows her son, she thought, and she can't wait to see the back of him. She doesn't like him. What did she say before…Arnold learnt everything at his father's knee, and her husband was a bully? Dolores knows I'm going to have a horrible life with Arnold. She feels pity for me. It's why she's trying to soften things while I'm here.

Carrie buried her face into the pillow and sobbed until there were no more tears. As she cried she thought of her mother and father, and of Tom, the brother she had been so close to but who already felt a million miles away. She thought of Johan, of all the promises they had made to each other when he had held her close and told her he loved her. And she thought of Pearl, the most wonderful friend anyone could ever have. These were her people, her loved ones. She would soon leave them behind to begin a journey she didn't want, a voyage into the unknown to a country with strange customs, and with people she had never met and would likely be nothing like her. It was like a nightmare she would never wake from.

Chapter 8

Carrie stood at the dockside amongst the throng of passengers waiting to board The City of London clutching a small carpet bag. The noise of the chattering travellers was deafening, and the men loading supplies and luggage onto the ship shouted to each other above the hubbub making a huge din. Hoists rising high above the crowd deposited trunks and containers onto the decks for the crew to decant into the hold. Shrieking children ran around their mother's skirts, nannies pushed prams up and down the walkways attempting to comfort their charges, and young women stood detached from the maelstrom, just like Carrie, looking lost and alone, their faces pale, their eyes wide with anticipation…and fear.

Arnold was in the port office with their paperwork, waiting for it to be verified before they sailed. She watched him through the small square window in the door. He was laughing, sharing a joke with the officer who stamped their papers. Over the last few days she had tried to find something about Arnold she could like, a kind word of encouragement, a gentle gesture of concern for her and the baby, but he had shown her no warmth or concern whatsoever. He hadn't smiled at her once since their wedding. She was sure that he hated what was happening to them as much as she did, but because being married would give him a certain status he had decided it was worth any problems she may bring with her. She wondered why he hadn't met someone who could be a real wife to him, someone who could love him and play the part more convincingly than she was sure she could. She glanced through the glass again and she understood. She thought about Pearl and how much she loved William. She didn't care that he'd worked on the docks or been a bookie's runner. She just loved him with all her heart. Out of all the girls Carrie knew, Pearl understood how to pick a good bloke, and she probably wasn't the only one. These girls didn't look at what men did for a living because in Whitechapel and beyond in the neighbouring districts they all did the same things. They went for someone who took their eye and could return the love they gave, a man who was easy-going and kind and who wouldn't raise his hand to them or their children. Like Arthur. Like her dad. She finally worked out why Arnold hadn't been chosen by someone else. She had to acknowledge her husband was the most unappealing, unlikeable man she had ever met.

Dolores had continued to treat Carrie with kindness, but only when Arnold wasn't in the house. Clearly, she was wary of him, and if she had any cause to be severe with Carrie because Arnold expected it, she would always glance at her afterwards with a look of regret. Carrie had accepted it all with stoicism. In her heart, she wanted to find the courage to rail against the circumstances that had been forced on her, but after a good deal of introspection she had come to realise that there was nothing she could do. Arnold was her husband and she would have to do whatever he wanted. He owned her, had paid for her, and now she must do his bidding. He reminded her daily of her vows, to love, honour and obey, particularly the obey word which he emphasised. Fortunately he had not yet claimed his rights over her body. Every evening he would leave the house at seven and not return until after closing time, usually worse for wear. She made sure she was asleep before he returned, and if she wasn't she would pretend to be. Dolores also went to bed early to avoid him. Carrie found herself envying her. Dolores slept in her own bedroom with the door shut, and at least when Carrie and Arnold went to India there would be an end to her misery.

Arnold joined her on the dockside. He folded the papers precisely with his pale thin fingers and placed them into a battered brown leather attaché case, which made him feel important. Carrie had been amused when she saw the case and had wanted to giggle but knew she mustn't for fear of Arnold losing his temper with her. One of Mrs. Coyle's sayings was, 'Keep 'em sweet, girls. It's how to get the best out of a man. Let him think he's the boss and keep him sweet.'

'Our papers are in order,' he said. 'We have an interior cabin, not as well-appointed as a captain's billet, but it'll be adequate for our needs.' He glanced down at her. 'For God's sake, Carrie, buck up. At least make an effort to look like the wife you're meant to be even if you don't feel it. It's important that you try to be cordial with the wives of the men in my unit. They'll be doing their best to fit in socially with the others bearing in mind their husband's position and will be expected to behave respectfully and dutifully. You must do the same.' She stared at him and said nothing. He bent towards her, his face level with hers. 'I suggest you make the best of this, Miss. The alternative will not be pleasant, let me assure you,' he said through gritted teeth.

He straightened up then took her arm firmly, leading her towards the roped gangway which would take them onto the ship. On deck Carrie's heart dropped at the sight of so many people she didn't know. Many were in groups, obviously enjoying the opportunity to mix with their friends, relishing the thought of an exciting new adventure in a foreign country.

Arnold steered her towards a gathering of soldiers and young women. One of the men spotted them as they approached.

'Arnold. There you are. We wondered where you'd got to. Thought you chickened out, man.'

Arnold laughed. 'What me? Never.'

'Aren't you going to introduce us, Arnold?' said one of the girls, eyeing Carrie.

'Oh, yes. Er, everyone. This is my…wife, Caroline Violet.' Carrie smiled and nodded to them, wondering why Arnold had used her full name and not just the one she had always been known by.

'How long have you been married, Arnold?' asked one of the other girls. 'Can't have been very long. You weren't married the last time we saw you. That can only be what…four, five months ago, you know, at the Christmas get-together. You never mentioned a fiancée.'

Arnold nodded. 'Carrie…Caroline Violet and I got married last week. We're newly-weds.'

'Really,' the girl said, looking pointedly at Carrie's stomach. 'Congratulations, I'm sure.' She turned her back to Carrie and said something out of the side of her mouth that Carrie couldn't hear and which made the others in the group laugh. Carrie glanced up at Arnold who looked cross. He grabbed her arm and pulled her away.

'I think we should find our cabin,' he said coldly. 'And in future perhaps you could try to conceal your pregnancy. We don't want everyone making assumptions, do we?'

She frowned, the hairs on the back of her neck prickling with anger. 'What assumptions could they make? I'm eight months pregnant. How can I hide it, Arnold? All you seem to be worried about is what your precious friends think. Well, it might come as a huge surprise to you but I couldn't care less what they think. If you were that concerned you shouldn't have married me, but you did, so you're stuck with me, aren't you?'

She turned away from him, hating him more with every second that passed. He let go of her arm and strode ahead, searching the numbers on the doors for the cabins.

'We're on the wrong deck. We need to go down one. I s'pose you'll be alright to get there by yourself while I look for it? I can move faster on my own and I have to check in with my commanding officer before we sail.'

She sighed. 'What number is it?'

'Thirty-two.'

She shrugged and stared at him glassily. 'I might be pregnant but I can still count.'

He nodded without looking at her and left her in the corridor to find the cabin herself. She stared after his retreating back; watched him as he arrogantly walked towards the end of the corridor, then turn left to descend the staircase which would take him to the lower deck. The part of the corridor Arnold had left her in was beginning to fill with passengers looking for their own cabins. They smiled at her when they saw her, and she inclined her head to each in a gesture of politeness.

She followed Arnold's steps, taking her time to get to the lower deck which she quickly realised wasn't nearly as pleasant as the one she'd just left. The space was infused with a strange, cloying odour that she didn't quite recognise, a mix of the smell of meat cooking and something metallic, and the décor wasn't as well maintained. The paintwork on the pipes running the length of the corridor was flaking off the metal which was discoloured underneath with rust. The carpet underfoot, although meant to be a rich red was stained and threadbare and coming away from the sides of the floor. When she found the cabin she opened the door gently and looked inside. Their things had been left just by the door and there was no sign of Arnold. She stepped inside and after closing the door sank wearily onto the low bed, glad to be alone at last. Her head was pounding and she released a breath that she felt she'd been holding since she left the Bateman house. Leaning back against the pillows she closed her eyes.

She had visited Florrie and Arthur once more before she and Arnold had left for Southampton. Florrie had been awkward with her, talking about everything except Carrie's impending departure. Arthur had kissed her on the cheek before she left but had been unable to look her in the eye. Her eyes had filled with tears but she'd brushed them away. It was like everything she thought she knew, all that was familiar to her, had never existed. Her parents with whom she had lived all of her seventeen years had become strangers and a stranger had become her husband. She was totally alone. Except for her baby.

She put both hands on her stomach feeling the swelling bump through the fabric of her skirt. Johan's face emerged from her thoughts and her lips twitched into a small smile. He made me happy, she thought. Just for a little while. With a jolt she realised that whatever happened, wherever she landed, a part of Johan would always be with her. Their son or daughter was the unique blend of them both, and nothing could ever change it.

The ship was so vast Carrie was frightened of getting lost on the huge vessel. Being in a third-class berth wasn't unpleasant; they had a porthole in their cabin which gave her a view of the outside even if it was just the line between sea and sky, but as she explored the ship she became acutely aware of the differences between the level where her and Arnold's cabin was situated, and the first-class cabins that were on the higher decks. She realised that even on a ship the distinctions between Carrie and the beautifully dressed ladies on the upper deck were the same as when they passed each other on a London street. She admired them and they ignored her. It didn't greatly concern her. It was something she was used to. One of the lessons she had learned by being a maid to a wealthy household was that to the wealthy she had to be out of sight. The only way her employers should know she existed was because of all the things she did to make their life comfortable and not because of anything she hadn't done or because they could see her. She knew how to be invisible.

After a couple of days, she began to get used to life aboard ship, the noises, the smells, the movement as it continued its passage towards their destination; the port of Bombay. As she walked around the ship she said the word over and over. Bombay. Bombay. She loved the way it sounded, of how mysterious it was to her, and gradually she began to wonder with fascination about the place she would soon call home. She knew they would not stay in Bombay but travel overland from the port by train to the garrison town of Secunderabad, Arnold had told her that much, a canton where military personnel were stationed. This is where Arnold had been posted, and this is where her child would be born and raised.

With Arnold officially on duty with his regiment she often found herself spending her days alone. When the weather was good she would wander up on to the top deck where she could sit and watch as people continued their lives aboard the floating village. Many of the women had already formed friendships and were trying to replicate the life they had had back in England. When the weather was bright, little tables were brought out and covered with fancy tablecloths. The ship's most delicate china would be used to take afternoon tea, and they would order cakes and tiny sandwiches from the kitchens. The wives of Arnold's friends sat at the table and they would compose themselves as though posing for a photograph. They gossiped and giggled, and tried to outdo one another with their huge feathered hats and lavishly embroidered parasols. Carrie marvelled at their clothes. She had none of these things in her possession and felt like a visitor to a zoo peering into an exotic bird sanctuary.

That afternoon the sea was calm as the ship made its way into the Bay of Biscay between France and Spain. It was the beginning of June and although the sun was beating down on the deck the sea breezes were very welcome. Loosening her buttons at the neck of her dress, she sat on a deckchair and watched as flocks of seagulls flew down to the glassy stillness of the water, breaking the surface like arrows in flight as they hunted for their next meal. The exotic ladies were in their usual place, sipping tea with a tiny gloved finger raised, and flirting with the steward who attended them. They giggled mercilessly when his face turned bright red and whispered little comments to one another when he turned away. Carrie smiled to herself when he closed his eyes for a moment, obviously wishing he were somewhere else.

Suddenly, one of the girls left the group and walked towards where Carrie was sitting. She was petite and very slim. Her blonde hair was piled on top of her head in a tumble of curls and she wore a blush pink hat decorated with a veil of net that reached the bridge of her nose, trimmed with a posy of roses on the brim, the petals fluttering in the sea breeze. Her round-toed shoes were dove-grey with a strap around the ankle, and she carried a dove-grey fabric dolly-bag tied with cord fastened to her wrist. She sat in the deckchair next to Carrie and smiled.

'Hello. I'm Dorothy. What's your name?' She held out a hand encased in cream leather gloves buttoned to the middle of her forearm.

Carrie shook her hand. 'I'm Carrie Dobbs...I...I mean, Bateman.'

Dorothy nodded. 'I saw you here yesterday afternoon. Why don't you come and join us? We're all in the same boat...so to speak.' She laughed. 'It's nice to have someone to talk to, especially when our husbands are working.'

Carrie looked down. 'Er, thank you for the invitation but...I'm not sure I'd be welcome.'

Dorothy frowned. 'Why ever not? You'd be as welcome as anyone else.' Carrie didn't answer, and Dorothy looked over to the women who had suddenly realised she had left their exclusive group. They turned around on their chairs to see who she was talking to and when they saw it was Carrie their lips curled with scorn. 'Oh, I see. Look don't worry about them. They're very silly women who think they're a notch above everyone else. Please don't let it distress you. Who is your husband?'

'Sergeant-Major Bateman.'

Dorothy raised her eyebrows. 'Really. Gosh, I must say I didn't have him down as the marrying kind. In fact I'm not sure any of us did.'

Carrie looked at her. 'Oh? Why?'

'Oh, I don't know. He's what we would call an army man. You know, married to the army. You must be a very special girl to have caught him. And I see you're expecting a baby. Arnold must be delighted.'

'Er, yes…yes, I think he is.'

Dorothy looked at her hard, then took Carrie's hand. 'You know, Carrie, life in India is going to be very different from what you've been used to in London. We've all left our beloved families and friends behind. We've been told we must live there, somewhere most of the girls have never seen before, some of us against our true feelings because our husbands have attained a certain position within their regiments. You should expect a certain level of respect from him and from the other women. They're in the same position that you find yourself in. Your experiences may have been different when you were in England but when we get to India we will all be the same. We are all going to be lonely, we will all cry for our parents, and we will all wish we could go home. Don't isolate yourself. You will need the friendship of other women, particularly when your baby comes.'

Carrie looked down, then glanced up to see Dorothy watching her with sad eyes. 'I might be in the same position as you and your friends,' Carrie answered. 'But I'm not the same as you, Dorothy, or the other girls. Look at my clothes. It marks me out straight away. I have no tea-dresses or beautiful hats, or embroidered parasols. I can't sit with you because I'm not the same. Surely, you can see that. We're a different class. This is how it was in London and this is how it is here. Nothing has changed. Why should they accept me here just because we're on board a ship?' She lifted her chin to the giggling girls who sat together gossiping. 'They wouldn't have spoken to me before, would hardly have known I existed. Why should they now?'

Dorothy sighed. 'Why hasn't Arnold bought you the clothes you will need for the trip? The clothes you had in London will not be sufficient for a life in India, believe me. The climate is brutal. You're his wife. Why is he not showing you the respect you deserve?'

Carrie pulled her hand away from Dorothy's and placing her hand against the small of her back levered herself out of the chair. 'Thank you for talking to me. Yours is the first kind word I've had since we've been aboard the ship. It's cheered me up no end. I hope you enjoy the rest of the voyage and your time in Secunderabad. I think I should go back to our cabin. I need to rest.'

She smiled at Dorothy, and as she walked away tears pooled in her eyes. She brushed them from her cheeks before she got to the gaggle of women who were still teasing the steward. As she walked past them they went quiet. She felt their eyes on her back as she got to the steps leading down to the lower decks.

'That's right,' she heard one of the girls say. 'Back to where you belong.'

Dorothy returned to the table of women and sat down. 'That's enough of that,' she said in a cross voice. 'You should know better.'

Carrie made her way down the corridor to her cabin. Once inside she sat on the bed and threw her brown straw hat into the corner. She covered her face with her hands and sobbed. All she could think about was home. She wished with all her heart that she was back there, listening to Florrie complaining about everything under the sun and the rustle of Arthur's newspaper as he buried himself into it, trying to escape her nagging. She thought of Tom and Alfie and how she and they would laugh together, sharing a joke or playing a card game at the table in their front sitting room. It had been such a poor life, a simple life but she had always felt safe there. At least until they'd know she was pregnant. Since marrying Arnold she hadn't felt as safe as she did then, not for a second. All that she was and all that she knew were gone, and in their place was an acute awareness of not really belonging anywhere.

She rubbed the tears from her face. Dorothy had meant to be kind to her but it had made her feel worse because it had simply highlighted the void between her and the other girls. Now she would be frightened to go up on deck again in case she was ridiculed by them. She would have to stay in her cabin until they reached Bombay, no matter how long it took to get there.

Chapter 9

She woke with a start and leant up on her elbow. For a moment she couldn't quite work out where she was until she heard the creaking of the ship and the noise of seabirds outside the porthole. She licked her dry lips overlaid with a fine mist of salty powder. It covered everything, even their faces as they slept. Arnold lay on his back snoring loudly, his arms flung carelessly above his head.

Moonlight streamed in through the porthole and she looked down at him in the golden ray that highlighted the cabin. Strands of his limp hair hung down by his cheek. An image of him shoving her back on the bed and pushing his fleshy lips against hers played out in her mind's eye and she shuddered. It was a fear she had anticipated since their wedding night, yet he hadn't made any attempt to put his hand on her. This had surprised her because Dolores had made it very clear this was something she should accept with stoicism, no matter how unpalatable it might be to her. The nearest he had come to touching her was when he held her arm in front of the other soldiers and their wives, or when he rolled over in bed and flung an arm against her accidently. When this happened she moved as far away from him as she could, clutching onto the edge of the bed to stop herself from rolling onto the floor.

She lay back on the bed and stared at the moon. It shone like a huge gilded orb in the cloudless sky and she thought how beautiful it was. This would be so perfect she thought, if Johan were here instead of Arnold. She inhaled in shock as a pain flashed through her and gradually took hold, searing from the middle of her back across her stomach. It got sharper and more intense, taking her breath away. She sat up again, her breath coming in short gasps, her hands on her belly. Gradually the pain faded away and she lay back against the pillows with relief, burying herself under the covers and breathing deeply. The baby wasn't due for another three weeks and she had been confident they would have been settled in their new home in Secunderabad before then. She closed her eyes and took a deep breath, thinking about her life aboard ship which had become so solitary, she knew of her own making, without events to break up the time stretching out before her like a long, unbending road. More like a prison sentence, she thought. She wondered about the people she'd seen on deck, the never-ending socialising, sometimes bickering she heard from the other passengers, particularly the women. She had been assured by Arnold that when they got into the Mediterranean Sea there would be parties in the evening, high jinks the like of which she'd never seen before. She'd wanted to say she wouldn't see them now either because she felt so separated from the other passengers, thanks to him making her feel worthless, and thanks to the spitefulness of his colleagues wives. The previous evening she had heard singing from the deck. They sang songs she knew and would have liked to sing with them but she couldn't find the courage to leave the safety of the cabin and join in. I'd just as well be in the hold with the horses, she thought, for all the company I've had.

The day she'd met Dorothy she had lost the confidence to go up on deck where the air was purer and life was far more interesting despite Dorothy's friendly approach. No matter how pleasant she'd been towards Carrie anyone could see how different they were. Dorothy had been very kind to her, but she was still part of the group of women who looked down their noses at Carrie and their prejudice was difficult to stand up against. They knew what she was. They probably had girls like Carrie working in their houses or in their parents businesses. Dorothy was the kind of elegant woman who would have visited the Stern's home in Nightingale Lane, and she, Carrie, would have been the maid to serve them if the upstairs maid hadn't been available. She imagined Dorothy with Lizabet and Johan, sitting in front of the fire that Carrie would have cleaned and laid in the early hours of the morning while they were still fast asleep in their luxurious beds with the pale green and pink satin eiderdowns, or eating the breakfast she'd prepared. Dorothy was about the same age as Lizabet and the thought made her squirm with humiliation. I wonder if she meant it, Carrie thought, being nice to me in front of the others. Was it just for show or maybe she did it for a dare. How would I know how honest she is? I don't know her.

Another sharp pain flashed down her sides and across her belly. She gasped in shock then drew in a deep breath and waited for it to subside. This time the pain was far more intense and took longer to diminish. She got out of bed and wrapped her knitted housecoat around her, sitting in the hard, upright chair opposite the bed. The garment gave her comfort because it felt and smelt familiar, the washing soda Florrie used for the laundry, the scent of lavender from the bar of soap Pearl had given her for Christmas the year before. She didn't need its warmth, the temperature had risen to a muggy stillness the closer they'd got to the Mediterranean, but it was a remnant of her past reminding her of the time she'd spent at home in the bedroom she shared with Elsie. She hugged it to her. Please don't let this be it, she pleaded. Not now, not on this rusty old ship. She thought of her baby arriving into a world that was totally alien and felt a stab of pity then of guilt. I'll be the only one who loves my baby, she thought. No one else will. From now on no one I meet will have a connection to the new life I'm carrying. Not even my husband. And Mum and Dad won't even know they have another grandchild. She pulled her knees up as far as she could towards her belly and curled up on the chair. He or she will be my baby, my flesh and blood, she thought. Not Arnold's, thank God. Who'd want a father such as him? There was no love inside of him; no compassion, no nurturing. No nothing. It was like he was dead inside. Part of her felt sorry for someone who could feel so little and she wondered what had happened to him to make him so uncaring.

The next flash of pain made her cry out. Arnold snorted and stirred, then sat up, sleepily rubbing his eyes, surprised to see her out of bed.

'Why are you out of bed? What's the matter with you?' he said in a monotone voice laced with annoyance at being woken.

Carrie slipped from the chair to the floor and got onto her knees. She hung her head, resting her forehead on the floor, trying to speak through the pain. 'I think…' Her breath came in staccato gasps. 'I think it's the baby.'

'But it's not due yet. How can it be the baby? It must be something else.'

She shook her head, her hair brushing the floor. 'I don't know, Arnold,' she cried. 'Get someone…just get someone.'

Arnold sighed with irritation. 'Are you sure it's the baby? I don't want to bother anyone if it's not necessary. It'll look bad for me if I make a fuss and it's not necessary. Everyone will know about it. Maybe it's seasickness.'

'It's not seasickness. And it'll look a lot worse for you if my baby dies.'

Arnold threw on his jacket and left the cabin, returning a few minutes later with the nurse on duty. The woman smiled at Carrie and helped her to her feet.

'Can you get onto the bed?' Carrie nodded. 'Have your waters broken?'

'No.'

'When was the last contraction?'

Carrie lifted her face and looked at her questioningly, her brows knotted together. 'The last what?'

'The last pain? When did you have the last pain?'

'Just now.' She screamed as another pain took over her body. A few moments later her waters broke, gushing across the floor of the small cabin and the nurse ordered Arnold out of the room.

Your wife's in labour, Sergeant-Major Bateman. You must find somewhere else to stay for tonight.'

Arnold nodded and left the room without saying anything to Carrie. The nurse frowned. 'Your husband seems very nervous, Mrs. Bateman.' Carrie didn't answer her. She wanted to say that if she'd noticed his lack of concern for her it was because he couldn't care less and was more than likely cross because he'd been woken out of his sleep but she knew she mustn't. Arnold would get to hear about it and there would be hell to pay, and at that moment she had more to think about than Arnold and what his friends thought. She was terrified at the loss of control of her own body. She thought of Florrie, and no matter how angry Carrie was with her for forcing her into a situation to which she hadn't agreed, wanted her more than anyone. Her mother should have been with her. It was the way of things. When a baby was being delivered the maternal grandmother would be there. There was no one here on her side, no one to hold her hand and tell her everything was going to be alright. The contractions came one on top of the other leaving her little time to do the breathing the nurse instructed. 'You must try, Mrs Bateman. You'll cope much better if you get some rhythm into your breathing.'

'I am trying,' Carrie panted. 'I am.'

The nurse patted her hand and looked at her sympathetically. 'I know, dear. Just do the best you can.'

At a quarter to eight the following morning Carrie gave birth to a son. It was a moment of utter relief for Carrie…and when she saw her baby boy for the first time, complete and utter love.

'He's so tiny,' she said to the nurse, 'Will he be alright.'

The nurse laid the swaddled baby into her arms and smiled broadly. 'He's premature, my dear. He's smaller than we'd like, but he's a reasonable weight and seems strong. When you get to Bombay you must take him to a hospital and get him checked. And yourself, of course. We're rather limited on board as to the kind of care we can give you. If the authorities had known you were about to give birth it's quite likely you would have had to make the journey to India without your husband and at a later date.'

Carrie smiled. 'You were with me all the way,' she said. 'I felt safe with you and I don't even know your name.'

'Nurse Porter,' she answered. 'Nancy. You did well, Mrs Bateman, with virtually no pain relief. Your little boy is our first birth and very likely the only one. We have no other impending births recorded. Your son is special.'

'Thank you. And it's Carrie. My name's Carrie. Has my husband been told?'

'Yes. We got a message to him. He said he'll drop by as soon as he can.' Carrie nodded. She wondered what his thoughts were now that he had a stepson. She made a bet with herself that the news she had given birth to a boy had barely caused a ripple in his heart. She was in no hurry to see him.

The rest of the voyage went by in a blur. For the first few days she remained in the cabin as she had before the birth, but as the temperature rose she realised it wasn't healthy for either her or the baby to be cooped up, so she swaddled him lightly and took him up on deck. She kept a look out for the women who had taunted her and found a deckchair out of the breeze and out of their way. Some of the other passengers stopped to congratulate her, saying they had heard about the birth because it had been the only one on board. Someone asked the baby's name and she looked at them blankly, then felt embarrassed because she hadn't thought of a name. She'd had no one to tell so it hadn't occurred to her. Arnold had shown no interest in the boy and hadn't asked her what she would call him.

'Er, John. Yes, that's his name. John.' They had nodded, and someone had said, 'That's a fine name'. She had been pleased, wondering why she had so suddenly decided on the name, John, then realised that the one person in her mind since the birth had been Johan. She looked down at the slumbering baby and smiled. 'Your name's John,' she said. 'What else would it be? It's perfect for you.'

She looked up and saw Dorothy walking briskly towards her. Carrie's smile slipped from her face and her stomach rolled with anxiety as Dorothy sat on the deckchair next to her.

'I heard you'd had the baby. Can I look?' She gently pulled the blanket back from the baby's head. 'Oh, how sweet. Boy or girl?'

'A boy. John.'

'Oh, that's a nice name.' She glanced at the baby again. 'Gosh, his hair his dark. And Arnold's so fair.'

'Yes, but I'm dark, and so are my family. He must take after my side.'

'Yes, I expect that's what it is. Was it very awful? The birth I mean. One does dread it.'

'It was alright. As painful as you would expect, I suppose. It's worth it in the end.'

'Yes, of course it is. You must be so happy…and Arnold too.'

Carrie nodded. Yes…yes we are.'

There was a lull then Dorothy's eyes lit up. 'I've had a marvellous idea. Why don't you join us for tea tomorrow? You can introduce little John to everyone.'

Carrie blanched. 'No…no thank you. I don't mean to be rude, but I don't think it's a good idea.'

'Why ever not? Don't worry about the others, I'll put them in their place. They don't frighten me.' She giggled.

Carrie left her seat and wrapped the blanket even tighter around John. 'Yes, Dorothy, but they're not very nice to me. I know you mean well, but…we're different. You know we are. It's one thing your friends taunting me because of my situation in life, it's quite another when my new-born baby is in my arms. I know you understand.'

Dorothy got up and stood in front of her. 'Yes, yes, I do, Carrie. I think you're a very brave girl. It can't have been easy for you, giving birth on board. I just wish things were different. I hope you don't count me as one of those who would be disrespectful to you. I hope we'll be friends. If there's anything you need, please let me know.'

Carrie relaxed her shoulders and smiled at her, relieved to be off the hook. 'Thank you, Dorothy. I'd like us to be friends, too.' She turned and walked across the deck, her head held high. She clutched John's tiny body tightly against her. 'It's you and me, John,' she said quietly to him. 'You and me against the world.'

'I hear you've been fraternising with Dorothy Tremaine,' Arnold said as he buttoned his jacket that evening. 'Think you're like her, do you? Think you're one of them?'

Carrie watched Arnold as he smoothed his hand across his head which disturbed the thin strands of greasy hair covering his scalp, now red and peeling with sunburn. She could see his reflection in the mirror and the smirk on his lips. Then he tutted in exasperation as he tried to comb his hair, and Carrie frowned. 'Fraternising? I'd answer you if I knew what it meant.'

'You been talking to her, I heard. Making friends.' He sneered as he said it and her deep dislike of him ran hot through her veins.

'As a matter of fact she spoke to me, congratulating me on the baby. I do not think we're alike, I know we are not, and for your information I told her as much.'

Arnold swivelled on his heel, glaring down on her as she sat on the bed rocking John in her arms. 'What? What did you say to her? You better not have been rude to her, Carrie Dobbs. Her husband's a captain, a commissioned officer. You'll start a right royal row if you were insolent. You need to know your place, girl.'

Carrie got up and gently placed John back in the draw, now bedecked with cut-down cotton sheets and blankets that Nancy had found for her and turned to face him, determined not to show she was in any way riled by his rudeness.

'Well, isn't that what I just said? I politely thanked her for her kind words…and her invitation to take tea with her and her friends, but reminded her we are of a different class. She said she understood and that if I needed anything to let her know.'

Arnold narrowed his eyes and turned back to the mirror as he struggled to do up the top button of his jacket. 'Right. Well, we don't need anything so there's no need for you to go cap in hand to Mrs. Tremaine. She's a fine lady, she is. She won't want to have anything to do with you.' He turned to look at her again. 'And neither will the other fine ladies.'

Carrie folded her arms in front of her, wishing he would go and do whatever it was he had to do. 'I already know that, Arnold. They've made it quite clear.'

'I'm sure they have. I expect they know all about you.'

Carrie felt her breath catch in her throat. 'What d'you mean by that? What do they know about me?'

'For Christ's sake,' he yelled as he fumbled with his top button. ''Ere, get over 'ere, you're going to have to help me with this.' Carrie stared at him in horror. 'Well, come on, you stupid girl. I haven't got all bloody day. I'm going to be late. It's your bloody fault, keeping me talking.'

She crossed the cabin and stood in front of him, reaching up to the button under his chin. As she tried to get the button in the buttonhole her hand brushed the mottled skin on his neck and she recoiled, swallowing hard to keep her composure. His foul breath laced with alcohol and nicotine reached her as he breathed out, sighing with impatience.

'Have you done it,' he said.

She stepped away from him covering her mouth with her hand. 'Yes.'

He nodded. 'Right. Well. I've got to go.' He made for the door, but she stopped him.

'What did you mean when you said they knew all about me?'

He shrugged. 'They guessed our situation. The lads. They know what you are and they know he's not mine.' He nodded towards the baby.

Tears threatened as she realised any chance of her making friends with any of the other women when she got to India was gone. No one would want to know her for fear of their reputation being tarnished. It was something all classes had in common.

'You told them, didn't you? Why would you do that?'

'Like I said, they guessed. I didn't have to say much. You look what you are, Carrie Dobbs. They know a trollop when they see one. They wouldn't have had to be geniuses to work it out, and they're all a lot cleverer than you.' He turned to go then something occurred to him and he stopped and looked at her. 'You alright in that department now?'

Her eyes widened. 'Which department?'

He rolled his eyes and gave a low laugh. 'I thought you would have known what I meant, all the experience you've had on your back. I'm your husband. I've got rights.'

Carrie trembled, the threatened tears now running down her cheeks. 'No, I'm not alright in *that* department,' she said, her voice shaking. 'I've just had a baby, or p'raps you hadn't noticed for all the attention you've paid him.'

'Why should I give him any attention? He's not my kid, is he? I know whose he is, though. Your mother told me. Thought I had a right to know. She wasn't impressed, and neither am I. You need to learn to stick with your own kind, so any thoughts of elevating yourself by having friends like Dorothy Tremaine you can get right out of your head, Miss. And as for Johan Stern's bastard, if his own father can't be bothered with him I don't see why I should be. I'll be happier when you've had one of mine. And I won't be leaving it too long. We'll get a better house with more kids in tow, and a bit more pay, so you'd better think about that.'

Arnold slammed the door behind him and Carrie sank onto the bed. She closed her eyes as nausea overwhelmed her, breathing deeply like

Nancy had shown her when she was in labour, waiting for the sickness to subside. Feeling stronger she left the bed and knelt on the floor by the draw where John was sleeping peacefully. She gently placed her hand on the soft mound of his little body then bent and kissed his velvety cheek, breathing in his wonderful baby smell. She closed her eyes, and when she opened them again she looked determined.

'I have to do something, don't I,' she whispered to him. 'I have to change all this, John, because if I don't Arnold Bateman will ruin our lives forever and I will die of guilt and shame. Don't be frightened, my darling boy. I'll take care of us, I promise.'

Chapter 10

'Carrie. Carrie!' Dorothy ran towards Carrie from the officer's canteen. 'Carrie,' Dorothy panted. 'I haven't seen you for days. Where have you been hiding? I'd like you to meet Marcus.' She looked up at her husband proudly. 'Marcus, this is Carrie Bateman. I told you about her.'

Her husband, Captain Marcus Tremaine trailed behind her. He paused for a moment to light a cigarette, cupping the tip to protect it from the wind sweeping across the deck. He followed Dorothy looking curious, blew out a puff of smoke and nodded to Carrie. 'I hear you've already had an eventful journey, Mrs. Bateman. I hope everything went well.'

Carrie smiled although she was eager to get back to the cabin where she'd left John sleeping. She felt uncomfortable talking to this couple as if she were their equal. 'Yes, sir. It went well. He's a lovely baby. Not really given me any trouble yet. I came up on deck to get some air but it's stifling up here as well. There's nowhere to go to get away from it.'

'Yes, even the constant breeze doesn't take the edge off of the humidity. But I assure you ladies it's going to get a lot worse. India is always hot and humid, even when it rains.'

'Have you been to India before, sir?'

'Yes, when I was a boy. I doubt it's changed much. Very hot, very sticky. The custard apples are quite nice though.'

Carrie's eyes widened. 'Custard apples?'

'Oh, yes. You'll be able to pick them off the trees.'

Dorothy giggled. 'I think Carrie will have far more to think about than picking apples, darling.'

Marcus laughed. 'Yes, you ladies will be having mint juleps every afternoon and playing whist tournaments I don't doubt. Far too busy to be thinking about anything else.'

Carrie smiled and lowered her head. She was sure she wouldn't be drinking mint juleps with the other girls. She hadn't a clue what a mint julep was and she knew they wouldn't want her there. She couldn't think of anything worse. When she looked up Marcus Tremaine was looking at his wife as though she were the only other person on the ship. Carrie could see how much he loved Dorothy, and in truth it was the only thing she envied Dorothy for. She cleared her throat to get their attention. 'I'd best be getting back to John. I don't like to leave him for too long on his own. How long do you think it will be now, sir, before we reach Bombay? I'm keen to have John checked by a doctor, just to make sure he's alright before we begin the rest of our journey.'

'We'll probably load up again in Port Said before we go down the Suez Canal, and be required to wait for an escort, so that could take a day or more. Then the ship will go across the Red Sea to Aden, then on to Bombay. I'm afraid it'll be at least a week, Mrs Bateman. Actually I think we've made very good time. The wind must have been in the right direction. I'm sure we'll all be glad to get off this ship and on to dry land.'

'Yes, sir, I'm looking forward to it.'

'There's no need to call Marcus, sir when we're talking, Carrie,' Dorothy said, touching Carrie's arm. 'We're all friends together and we will all be living closely together even though he's your husband's commanding officer when they're on duty. Please call us Marcus and Dorothy.' Carrie smiled and nodded, then left the couple on the deck and made her way to the cabin. She inhaled a deep breath then released it slowly, steadying herself. She found meeting the other people on the ship such a trial, particularly when someone as kind as Dorothy tried to put her at her ease. She was so used to serving people she didn't know whether she should bob a curtsey to them. If Dorothy and Captain Tremaine had been visitors to Nightingale Lane it would have been something she would have been expected to do if she'd run into them for any reason. In fact the Sterns made it quite clear that downstairs staff weren't permitted upstairs when they had guests. Not even Mrs. Coyle. She knew Dorothy was being kind, but her familiarity and friendliness made Carrie anxious. Arnold had already warned her to stay clear of her and to know her place, and this was what she had been attempting to do. It seemed that Dorothy had other ideas. I'll have to keep below deck from now on, she thought. If it's going to be a week before we get to Bombay I'll need to be careful. It's just too risky to go up on deck when everyone else is there and I don't want to get on the wrong side of Arnold. I need to stay as far out of his way as possible or there's no telling what he'll do.

Chapter 11

It was the smell she noticed first. It wasn't that it was unpleasant, it was just very different from anything she'd ever known, the kind of odour that hit the back of the throat and could be tasted. She was shocked that it was so pungent even though they hadn't docked, and she wondered if the whole of India smelt the same. She thought about her mum, dad, and Elsie, and Alfie and Tommy, and the complaints of the stink of tripe and cabbage that always seemed to permeate the house because it was their constant diet. It was disagreeable she had to admit, but when your belly thinks your throat's been cut you'll eat anything. The whole of Whitechapel seemed to reek of it, it was just something they had got used to. Here was vastly different and Carrie wondered what the smell meant. Was it from what they ate, she wondered…or something else?

As the ship pulled into Bombay harbour, a gently curving seawall, Carrie stood by the ship's rail, a sleeping John in her arms. She looked down at his face, so tranquil and untroubled, and wondered what their new life would hold for them. Soldiers and their wives, missionaries, women who had come to India alone just for the adventure or to look for a husband stood around her. She heard their exclamations of wonder and delight…and trepidation from some. The constant breeze from the Indian Ocean ruffled her hair, lifting it from her shoulders and swirling it around her face. She inhaled as a wave of panic took hold of her making her breath quiver in her chest. The enormity of what was in front of her suddenly dawned on her and she felt small and insignificant. She had arrived in a strange country, thousands of miles away from home and everyone and everything she knew. She wondered what Johan would have made of it, this adventure she was on. Her heart sank when she realised he probably hadn't given her another thought. Had he realised she was no longer at 99 Nightingale Lane, she thought? She doubted it. The way he looked a Lizabet on their wedding day was the way he used to look at her when they were together. Was he so shallow that he could look at any girl like that as long as he was getting what he wanted? Did his parents know what they'd done and forced him to marry Lizabet? Is that why the marriage was arranged so quickly? Johan had told Carrie he loved her. Did he love Lizabet? Had Carrie meant nothing to him at all? She shook her head trying to rid herself of his image which pushed into her mind's eye. Johan was so handsome, a young man with a bright future, the sparkling, educated, cossetted only son of a very rich man. Why did she ever think he would want someone like her?

A tear rolled down her cheek and dropped onto John's blanket. She wiped her face on her sleeve and sniffed as Arnold pushed his way through the crowd and appeared next to her. He leant on the railing, a cigarette hanging from his lips. He puffed on it then took it from his mouth, twisting his body so he faced her. An arrogant smirk crossed his face.

'What's that for?'

She turned her face towards him. 'What?'

'You. Crying.'

'I'm not crying.'

'No,' he said. 'You'd better not be. Any other girl would give her right arm to be given a chance to travel and see the world. You don't seem to realise what an opportunity I've given you. Dunno why you're bloody-well crying.'

'Yeah, well, I'd give my right arm to be any other girl right now.'

His eyes narrowed, and he bent his body slightly towards her looking round to make sure no one else was listening. 'Get used to it, miss,' he hissed at her. 'You'd better start being the wife I want or I'll make your life hell.' He straightened up and she stared at him. 'You need to model yourself on your friend, Dorothy Tremaine. She knows how to behave even if you don't.'

'You don't want me anywhere near her. Make your mind up.'

He glared at her. 'Don't get smart with me, Carrie Dobbs. You know damn well what I mean. Just copy her. I need a woman like Dorothy Tremaine to make sure I get on further in my career, not some dowdy housewife who opens her legs for anyone. Try and act like a lady at least.' He dropped the butt of his cigarette on the deck and ground it in. 'Christ, if I'd know what you were like…'

She glared back at him. 'The feeling's mutual, Arnold,' she hissed back. His face darkened and she watched him swallow down his temper. He couldn't do anything to her on the deck because they weren't alone, surrounded by the other passengers. She was safe from him there. He would never risk making a scene in front of the other soldiers and their wives. His mates would never let him forget it. 'I'll never forgive my mother for landing me with you. You're meant to be my husband, but you're no husband to me. When you start treating me and John right I'll be the way you want. I'll cook and I'll clean and I'll smile at your superiors and your friends. But that's it. And for your information, your ladylove Dorothy Tremaine doesn't think much of you.'

His eyes widened and his face coloured up. 'Wha...what d'yer mean?'

'Look at me, Arnold. You say you want me to be like the others. Do I look like the others? Well, don't bother to answer, I'll answer for you. No, I do not, because you won't put your tight-fisted hand in your pocket to make sure I do. How am I supposed to compete with them when I look like a housemaid?'

'You were a housemaid,' he said grudgingly.

'Yes, I was, and I'm not ashamed of it. I worked my arse off at Nightingale Lane.'

He turned his head right and left to make sure no one heard her. 'D'you have to? Keep your voice down,' he whispered. 'Real ladies don't swear.'

'Why? I know what I am, and thanks to you so do they because you've made sure of it. Make you feel big did it, letting them know my baby wasn't yours?'

'I told you, I didn't tell them.'

'No, but you didn't stop them thinking it, did you? Or saying it. You and your so-called friends must have had a right laugh about it. So that's something else I've got to deal with when we get to wherever we're going. Not very bright, Arnold. They're already looking down their noses at me and that's down to you. Some of them won't even look at me, and they've completely ignored John. Do you have any idea how that feels?' He turned sulkily away and observed the colourful mayhem on the harbour. 'That's it, you ignore us too. You'd better hope I don't get my hands on any money when we're in Secunderabad because I'll be hightailing it back home to the people who love me.'

He spat out a laugh. 'Love you? They don't love you. They sold you, my girl, to the highest bidder. That's how much they love you.'

She swallowed hard and looked at him with such contempt it shook him to his core. After a few moments she spoke. 'You have no idea how much I hate you, Arnold Bateman. And I'm not your girl, and I never will be.'

She walked away from him, her head held high, and found a spot at the railings where she could see what was happening on the harbour side. She wanted to cry, but she knew if she let Arnold reduce her to tears there was no hope for her. She had to be strong, stronger than she'd ever been in her life. Standing around her were the people who would become part of her existence for the foreseeable future, including Arnold, and she dreaded it. Arnold was right about one thing; she was nothing like them. Being on board ship with the people who would be in her life had given her a clue as to the kind of society she would be part of. It was like an exclusive club, one to which she had yet to be given entry. Their lives were alien to her, with their constant partying and merry making, but she would have to find a way to be a part of the life she had been thrown in to if only for John's sake. For him she would do anything.

The ship moved in closer to the dock and the people at the harbour wall were bewildering to the astonished onlookers from the ship's decks. There were men, brown-skinned, some swarthy, dressed in loose linen tunics and baggy trousers tapered at the ankles, unloading boxes and crates from the hold. Some of them had lengths of brightly coloured fabric wound around their heads, and all were shouting in loud voices in strange languages with up and down singsong tones that carried on the breeze towards the ship. There were animals left to their own devices, milling about between the groups of men who didn't seem to notice their presence. Behind them, among the melee of people going about their business, were carts drawn by bullocks and horses drawing carriages of Europeans who had already made their home in the bustling city. A pier stretched out from the harbour into the shallows. Strolling along the pier or clustered in gossiping groups were women, young and old, dressed in saris in acidic colours of pink, green, orange, and yellow. Many of the saris were highly decorated with silver and gold thread that sparkled in the afternoon sun. The women were promenading, showing off their beautiful saris to their peers, the younger girls carefree and giggling in groups, unaware they were part of a mystifying tableau so very unfamiliar to the observers on the ship. Carrie was entranced, mesmerised by the dance that played out in front of her. She looked down at her plain dark-green cotton dress buttoned to the neck in a high ruffle and envied these women their freedom to wear such flowing garments in the jewelled colours of the rainbow. This is one of the first things I'll change, she thought. If I'm to become part of the society I've been thrown into against my choice I need to look like the women who inhabit it. Arnold Bateman will have to spend a bit more money on his investment and at the very least be a supportive stepfather of John too, even if he can't find it within himself to love him. She didn't feel guilty about it. He was aware of my situation, she assured herself. So, he needs to accept it and allow me to be the person I know I can be.

'What do you think?' Dorothy stood beside her, the feather in her straw-hat flickering in the breeze. She looked down at Carrie, a head shorter than Dorothy.

'It's overwhelming,' Carrie replied. 'I wasn't expecting anything like this.'

'Wait until you get into Bombay. It couldn't be more different from what we have become accustomed to in England.'

Carrie glanced up at her. You have no idea of what I'm accustomed to, she thought. The life you live is likely as different to me as the one I'll encounter in India. 'Do you know Bombay?' she asked Dorothy.

'Oh, yes,' Dorothy nodded. 'Very well. My parents came here twenty years ago, in 1895. I was such a little thing then, but when I reached seven I was sent back to England to go to school. My mother joined me a few years later.'

Carrie was wide-eyed. 'Where did you live? In England, I mean?'

Dorothy laughed. 'At my school, of course.'

'You lived at your school?'

'Oh, yes.'

'Without your parents?'

Dorothy momentarily closed her eyes and bent her head, then looked kindly at Carrie. 'It's how things are for us, Carrie. I expect you lived with your parents until recently, am I correct?' Carrie nodded. 'We have a different way of going on. I missed my parents dreadfully and I wasn't very happy at my boarding school, but I had to accept that my father's work took him to different continents and that I could not be with them. I know my mother missed me, and my sister, Leonora, but we just had to accept. It's what we women do, isn't it? Accept our fate.'

The sound of various Indian languages and strains of music reached the newcomer's ears as they disembarked from The City of London. Flocks of unfamiliar birds flew overhead, many diving into the swelling sea around the ship looking for food. Carrie, with John safely in her arms, and Arnold, made their way through the crowd of disembarking passengers to a bullock cart waiting to take them to a hotel.

'We'll spend the night in Bombay then get the train to Secunderabad tomorrow morning.'

'Where will we stay?' Carrie asked.

'In a hotel. And don't expect the Ritz. This is coming out of my army pay.'

She raised her eyebrows. 'Why would I expect the Ritz?' He glanced down at her without lowering his head, his mouth a straight line, and placing his hand firmly against her back pushed her in the direction of a cart. Before she stepped up to get in she attempted to give John to Arnold to hold, but he stepped back. She shook her head in frustration. 'Well, how am I supposed to climb in, Arnold? I've only got one pair of hands.' He looked around cautiously before reluctantly stepping forward and taking the baby from her arms. Carrie climbed into the cart and seated herself on the wooden bench, then glanced back at Arnold who was trying to hold John as far away from his body as he could. She sighed and reached out for John, who Arnold thrust towards her with relief then climbed in behind her.

As they drove through the streets of Bombay Carrie was fascinated and appalled in equal measure. There were crowds of people at every corner and down every alleyway. Market stalls littered the paths and spilled out onto the roads, peddlers selling everything from strange fruits and vegetables to lengths of sari fabric hanging from the fronts of the shops, swaying in the breeze sweeping in from the ocean. Oxen roamed the streets, untethered and it seemed without owners, until someone rounded them up with the switch of a stick and moved them down the street. Women stood in groups, gossiping and arguing with each other with no thought to the myriad people around them or who might be listening to their conversations. The noise was deafening.

The streets the bullock cart took them down were narrow and they were continually brought to a halt as they waited for people to get out of the way. The houses were like nothing Carrie had ever seen before; tall and narrow and painted in all colours. Down the alleyways the buildings were thrown together shacks, some painted as brightly as the saris the women wore, yet the cheerful colours couldn't hide the primitiveness of the buildings or how inefficient they were as family homes. Men, women and children sat outside the structures, preparing food, eating and meeting their neighbours. Countless people milled about as if they all had somewhere very important to go yet didn't actually get anywhere. Beside almost every building sat beggars; mostly men who lay against the walls, half-dressed, many wore only loincloths, some women, and even children who ran beside the bullock cart with their palms raised up to the travellers, grinning and looking for coins.

'Ignore them,' said Arnold. 'If you give to one they'll all come running, even those pretending they can't walk. We're not a soft touch, not for anyone.'

'How much further?' Carrie asked. The heat and noise was wearying her and her clothes were sticking uncomfortably to her body. She looked down at John in her arms who seemed to suffer no ill effects and had been rocked into a deep slumber by the swaying of the cart.

The bullock cart pulled up in front of a large shabby building painted ochre yellow and fronted by large double wrought-iron gates, the entryway to a large courtyard punctuated by straggly unkempt bushes.

'We're here,' said Arnold climbing out of the cart and running to the front to retrieve their luggage. Carrie waited for him to offer to hold John while she clambered off the cart but he didn't and she knew he'd not done so on purpose. She scowled at his back and struggled out of the cart, landing awkwardly on the dusty street. She smoothed down her skirt and raised her face to view the building.

It was set back from the street, the forecourt untidy with weeds growing up in between broken flagstones. Three stories high, each floor had a veranda edged with an intricately carved railing. The windows were shuttered against a veil of dust hanging in the air from the carts and horses going by on the dusty road outside. The front entrance was two doors, one of which was open and lead into a porch with a closed screen. The ambiance was of genteel shabbiness, a building which had seen better days and was once, in its heyday, very beautiful but had been left unmaintained, ravaged by dust, countless monsoons and the decay of years of neglect. Carrie considered it beautiful. Arnold observed it with a critical eye.

'Not much but it'll have to do. It's only for tonight. Tomorrow night we'll sleep on the train.'

'How many nights, exactly?' she asked him.

'Four. It'll take us four and a half days to get to Secunderabad. We've got a sleeper berth so think yourself lucky. Some of the women will have to sleep in the carriages.' He took their luggage across the courtyard and slid it into the porch, then knocked on the dividing screen. Carrie stood behind him waiting with apprehension. A man dressed in a brown brocade frock coat and white turban opened the screen and bowed to them. Arnold picked up the bags and went through into a large hall decorated in red and gold. The man smiled at them and welcomed them into the cool hall. Carrie was relieved to get out of the piercing sunlight and away from the constant noise from the streets. All that could be heard was the breeze rustling through the banyan trees lining the courtyard and the squawking of parrots flying overhead. When the door was closed again it was as if the street outside didn't exist.

'I'm Sergeant-Major Bateman,' said Arnold. 'I arranged a room for myself and my wife.'

'Yes, sir. We have been expecting you. I am Basu, manager of the Sundar Ghar Hotel. Please, let me show you to your room.' He took them up a flight of wooden stairs to the first floor and opened the door to a large room with long windows dressed in muslin drapes. Outside Carrie could see a veranda on which there was a bamboo table and two chairs. The walls of the room were washed in a watery yellow, and on the washed-out floorboards were rush mats. Above the bed was a muslin canopy that draped at the head of the bed. Basu swept his hand towards it. 'To protect you from mosquito, sir.' Arnold nodded as Carrie looked around the room.

'Excuse me,' she said. 'There's no cot. I need a cot for my baby.'

Basu looked dejected. 'I'm so sorry, madam. I did not know. There was no mention of a baby. I will get one of the boys to bring a cot. I'm so sorry, madam.'

Carrie smiled at him. 'Don't worry,' she said. 'He wasn't supposed to be here yet. You weren't to know.'

'You will need some refreshment, sir and madam. Please come to the dining room when you have become rested. There will be refreshment for you there.'

Carrie smiled at him again. 'Thank you,' she said. 'That will be lovely.'

When Basu left, Carrie lay John on the bed and pulled the blankets from around him. She removed his clothing and let him lay in his nappy. His skin was hot and clammy to the touch. She poured some water from a floral jug on the dresser into a small bowl and bathed him until he was cool.

'There you are, my little lad,' she cooed to him. 'That's better, isn't it? You were so hot.'

Arnold opened the door to a knock and two Indian boys stood on the veranda, one holding the cases, the other the makings of a cot. The first boy set the cases down by the window and then proceeded to assist the second to set up a cradle which they put by the side of the bed. When they had finished they waited for Arnold to slip them a coin but he didn't and they left.

'Shouldn't we have given them a little something? They probably don't get much,' she said to him.

He frowned as he slipped off his jacket and poured water from the jug into another bowl and began to wash. 'Why should I? They get paid, don't they?' He opened the smaller case and took his shaving equipment from a side-pocket and lined it up on the dresser. 'And while we're on the subject don't go getting close with the natives. The others in the regiment won't like it, and you'd better remember it when we get to Secunderabad as well. We'll have Indians working for us. They'll be servants not friends so make sure you don't get too friendly.'

She nodded and sighed. 'Is there anyone I can be friendly with, Arnold? I'm not allowed to talk to Dorothy Tremaine, and now I can't talk to Indians whose country we'll be living in. Is there anyone else you'd like me to stay away from?'

He snorted a laugh. 'Yeah. Me.'

Chapter 12

Basu had left them a pot of tea and some honey cakes in the dining room. By this time the hotel had begun to fill with soldiers and their wives, and Europeans from other ships. Two of the missionaries, a man and a woman who had travelled with Carrie and Arnold from England, were seated at one of the tables. They had to be contented with their own company as no one else seemed to notice them. When Carrie saw them she nodded and smiled and they returned it. Arnold glared at her but she turned away. He suddenly left their table and went to speak to some of the soldiers from his regiment. They all seemed to be young single men; there were no wives with them, and they were deferring to him. She realised that they were of a lower rank, something she was sure Arnold would relish because of the power it gave him, and when he came back to their table he was flushed with his own importance and belief in his superior status.

'I wonder if Dorothy and Captain Tremaine are staying here.'

Arnold spluttered into his tea. 'You do say the most ridiculous things. Of course, they're not staying here. This hotel is for the riffraff, not people of class like Dorothy Tremaine. They're likely staying at the Taj Mahal Palace.'

Carrie's lips twisted into a small smile. 'Are we riff-raff, then?'

'Not for too much longer, I hope. When we get to Secunderabad I want to make sure I get to the top of the tree. But we won't be doing that if you go around smiling at Indians and missionaries.'

'They're just people, Arnold. Like you and me.'

'They are not like me. They're nothing like me. When I return to England I want to go back as a non-commissioned officer, a captain, with everything that goes with it, including the social standing. It's why I've come to India, to change my life. And this is the best place for me to do it.'

'And what about me? And John. Where do we come in your plans?'

'You'll do as you're told.'

Later, after an afternoon nap which seemed a necessity to get away from the intense heat, Arnold announced he would be meeting his friends after dinner.

'You'll want to stay here with him, won't you?' he said pointing his thumb at John. 'And you don't have a baby carriage so you won't be going very far.'

Carrie frowned. 'I wanted to take John to be examined at a hospital. And then, I thought it might be nice to have a look around, you know at the town. I haven't come all this way to be stuck in a room.'

Arnold shrugged. 'I've already told the lads I'll be meeting them later.' He glanced at the baby. 'He's alright, isn't he? Didn't that nurse get someone to look at him for you?'

'Yes, but he wasn't a baby doctor. He was a soldier. He came to India to take care of soldiers, not babies.'

'Still a doctor. And I was there when he examined him. He said he was okay and that's good enough for me.'

Carrie knew there was no arguing with him. 'The soldiers you're going into Bombay with. They're the ones you were talking to earlier? The ones without wives. You have a wife. Should you not put us first? Why aren't you socialising with the soldiers who have brought their families with them.'

Arnold stood in front of the mirror fastening a tie at the neck of his military shirt. 'Oh, don't you worry about that. I will when it counts. When we get to Secunderabad I'll make everyone think I'm the most considerate husband at the station with a wife who will always be grateful for what I'm doing for her. Here…here I shall do as I please.' He turned from his grinning reflection and stared at her. 'I'm not stopping you if you want to go out and explore the town. I'd be careful though. There are all sorts in the streets of Bombay, and they'll want whatever you've got and probably won't ask before they take it. It's up to you, though.'

After dinner Arnold left Carrie standing in the hall and left the hotel with the other soldiers in his regiment. She watched him as he left by the front entrance, allowing the porch screen to swing back with a clang that felt like a slap in the face for her. A wave of anger made her skin prickle, quickly replaced by an overwhelming sadness. She remembered the conversations she and Pearl had had in their little attic room, the ones that went long into the night when they talked about the kind of man they hoped to marry. Never in her wildest dreams did Carrie ever imagine she would end up in a foreign country where she knew no one, with a man who treated her with such utter contempt. The man who called himself her husband. The one she could never love.

She climbed the stairs to the first-floor veranda and let herself into their room, looking around the four walls and wondering what she could do to fill the time that stretched out in front of her. She was not sorry to see Arnold go, but she itched to see what was on the other side of the gates shielding the hotel from the outside world. She thought about writing home to her parents and to Pearl, but wondered if her letters would ever get to them. Thinking about home made her desolate. It had been a hard life, but it was the one she knew well and there had been a kind of safety in it. Here, she felt as though she was abandoned, a woman with no one in the world to care for her. She had no one in her corner and there was no one else who felt like she did. Tears rolled down her cheeks as she stood by the door. She didn't want to cry because crying meant Arnold had won; had hurt her so much she couldn't recover, so she wiped her eyes on her sleeve and went across to the cot.

John was such a good baby. She could almost tell the time by him; he woke for his feeds like clockwork and the love she had for him was overwhelming. He had not whined at the heat and as long as he was near her he was contented. She adored him already, and in her heart she knew he would be her little friend. He was the one who would make everything she was going through worthwhile.

A gentle rapping on the door startled her. She remembered what Arnold had said about Bombay being a dangerous place and wondered if she should answer it.

'Madam. Madam. It's Basu, the manager.' Basu's voice came from the other side of the door and she ran to open it.

'Basu?'

He bowed, his hands pressed together as if in prayer. 'Madam, I saw you have no carriage for the child. I have one here for you. You can go out into Bombay like the other wives. They have all gone to see the sights. You should go too.'

He stepped to the side and pulled an old pram into the room. It had a rattan body and leather hood. The handle was worn with use and the gilding, a kind of gold paint, was flaking off where other hands had wrapped around it and pushed the carriage to who knew where. Inside the body of the carriage were beautifully embroidered pristine coverlets and an embroidered linen pillow. Basu grinned from ear to ear, so pleased that he could help the young madam from England.

'Oh, Basu, that's so kind. Thank you so much. And the linen is so pretty.'

Basu nodded and looked proud. 'My wife, Mrs Basu sewed them.'

'Please thank Mrs Basu for me. She's very clever. It's beautiful.' She smiled gently, feeling slightly embarrassed in front of Basu because Arnold had clearly abandoned her. 'My husband has gone into Bombay town. I could not go with him because of the baby.'

'Yes, Madam. I saw him leave with his friends. I thought you would like to go and see Bombay for yourself.'

She nodded and bit her lip. 'My husband says it's dangerous for a woman on her own, Basu. Should I not go?'

'If you stay on the main street you will be safe. Do not go down the narrow streets to the shacks where the peddlers are. They will no doubt approach you, even an English woman. On the main street there will be many people, men, women, and children. Do not pay the beggars. If you pay one you will pay all and they will not leave you alone.' She nodded. 'Be brave, Madam. There is so much to see.'

She grinned and nodded. 'I will. And thank you for your help. This is lovely.' She indicated the pram. When he'd left she raised her eyebrows and inspected the pram. 'Oh, John, this is an old one, but, it's better than nothing. I think we should go out. Everyone else seems be exploring.'

She changed her dress for a light floral cotton one that had belonged to Elsie. Carrie had altered it to fit her for after the baby was born. She hadn't known she would wear it so soon. It was a little tight in the bodice, but the limited diet on board the City of London meant she had lost most of the weight she had gained, so she was satisfied with how it looked. She brushed her long brown hair into a chignon and pinned it to the top of her head, then pinched her cheeks to get some colour into them. I'm a wife and mother now, she thought to herself. I need to look the part.

She lifted John from his cot and laid him in the pram. She'd fed him before dinner, so she knew she had a couple of hours before his next feed. Wheeling him out of the room her spirits lifted, and she found herself looking forward to going outside. She walked along the veranda, then realised she would have to get the pram down the wooden staircase. Basu and one of his boys were waiting at the bottom of the stairs.

'We are here, Madam, to help you.' They ran up the stairs and lifted the baby carriage, taking it down into the hall. Carrie nodded and thanked them. 'I'm so sorry. I have nothing to give you, but I promise I will get something for you for tomorrow.'

Basu shook his head. 'No, no, Madam, please, do not worry. We are pleased to help.'

The early evening sun was still intense, and she pulled up the baby carriage hood and folded the coverlet away from John to keep him cool. The hood provided plenty of shade for the baby and he looked comfortable and contented. This was the first time she had wheeled him in a pram and she enjoyed the feeling of having him in front of her. It meant she could see him all the time, and she found herself smiling and enjoying the walk through the streets. As she walked past the hotels and the tall houses the noise from the main street got louder and louder, and the smells of spices and garlic and street-food cooking on dozens of braziers lining the street was even stronger. Even though she had eaten the aroma made her mouth water and she was surprised that the smell of food so foreign to her would have this effect. For dinner the hotel had given them their idea of English food; pale meat, watery carrots, and hard potatoes. The food on the outdoor cooking stoves was bright and colourful, and Indians and Europeans stood in a group around each one, waiting for their share. Music came from many of the stores, strange lilting sounds that made no sense at all to Carrie, and certainly no tune she recognised. The marketplace sold everything, beautiful bright exotic flowers, pots and pans, fruit and vegetables in mounds on the street where shoppers inspected them before buying, and stalls where men made leather bags and belts or jewellery from precious metals and stone.

Behind all of this excitement and socialising were the native quarters, ramshackle dwellings crowded into tightly inhabited streets and occupied by families living in squalor. The shacks were painted in gaudy colours like their fashionable European looking counterparts in the centre, but that was where any comparison ended. Carrie thought about the house where she and her family lived in Hanbury Street, and how much they complained about having to use an outside privy they shared with the neighbours either side of them. Nothing would ever prepare the residents of Whitechapel for the scenes of mayhem down the alleys of Bombay.

Carrie wandered on, finding it more and more difficult to dodge the people who seemed quite happy to bump into anyone they encountered rather than finding a way around them. The baby carriage was knocked a few times and she decided to turn around and go back the way she came. It would soon be time for John's feed and she wanted to be safely back at the Sundar Ghar Hotel in good time. She negotiated the heaving crowd and was about to turn the pram to face the opposite direction when someone grabbed her arm.

'What're you doing here?'

She turned quickly in the direction of the voice to see Arnold standing next to her, a cigarette balanced precariously on his bottom lip. She frowned, worried it would fall into John's pram.

'What does it look like?' she said, pulling her arm away from his fingers digging into her flesh.

'I told you to stay in the hotel,' he said in a low voice.

'No, you didn't. You said I wouldn't be able to go out because I didn't have a pram. Well, someone got one for me. And no, I didn't ask them to. Basu brought it to the room because he knew I didn't have one. At least someone cares about me and John. Anyway, what difference does it make? I wasn't bothering you, and I'm going back now to give John his feed.' She looked past him and saw a young soldier standing by one of the street-food vendors. He kept glancing in their direction then looking away again. 'You with him?'

'We were about to go to one of the bars.'

'So, go then. I'm not stopping you.' She pushed past him and walked back down the street, dodging the bicycles, the oxen, the stray dogs and the myriad people, all squeezed into the narrow street. Then she thought of something and turned back. 'I need some money.'

Arnold frowned. 'For what?'

'I need a hat. All the other wives have one because of the heat.'

He fished about in his pocket and took out a note. 'Here's two and a half Rupees. That should be enough.'

'Doesn't seem much.'

'It'll be enough,' he said, and went to join his companion, who looked slightly embarrassed, then laughed loudly at something Arnold said to him. Carrie frowned, wondering why Arnold had made such a seemingly close friend of someone who was a lower rank in his regiment, but she shrugged thinking she didn't really know how everything worked. No doubt I'll learn soon enough, she thought as she began the return journey to the hotel. John had begun to stir, so she quickly made her way to a peddler selling hats and brought a round straw with a small posy of flowers on the brim, leaving her two Rupees. 'I'll give a Rupee to Basu,' she said to a now squirming John looking for his feed, 'and keep one for us just in case. We might need it.'

Chapter 13

The Victoria Terminus in Bombay was built along land on the Eastern shore known as the Bori Bandar. The vastness of the building with its octagonal dome topped by a huge figure of a woman took Carrie's breath away, and even Arnold seemed suitably impressed.

'I wasn't expecting this,' he said, a whistle of surprise leaving his lips. 'What the hell is this about?'

'It's beautiful,' whispered Carrie.

'It's Victorian Gothic,' a voice said behind them. 'Classical Indian with Italian influences.' Carrie turned quickly and found herself staring into the eyes of a soldier. Arnold stood swiftly to attention and saluted. 'Captain Lawrence, sir,' he said.

Captain Lawrence lit a cigarette, cupping his hand around the sizzling match. The flare highlighted the smooth contours of his face, and as he shook the match out he smiled at Arnold. 'Stand easy, Arnold. Time for all that when we get to the cantonment at Secunderabad.' He glanced over to Carrie. 'I take it this is your new wife. I'd heard you'd done the deed during your leave. Thought I'd never see the day. Please, introduce us.'

'Er, yes, sir. This is Caroline Violet Dobbs, my…my wife, er, known as Carrie. Carrie this is Captain Lawrence.' He cleared his throat. 'My boss.'

Lawrence frowned. 'Dobbs? Bateman, surely.'

Arnold looked flustered and Carrie couldn't help smiling to herself at Arnold's obvious awkwardness at having to admit she was his wife, and his mistake. 'Yes…yes, of course, sir. Carrie Bateman.' Lawrence held his hand out to Carrie. She gawped at it. No one had ever wanted to shake her hand before. She glanced up to find his dark brown eyes observing her and she felt her face burn. She took his hand, relieved she was wearing gloves, and bobbed a curtsey.

He grinned. 'And there's no need for that either, Mrs. Bateman. Your husband is a Sergeant-Major. You certainly don't need to curtsey to anyone.' He turned to Arnold. 'I'll see you when we get to the station, Sergeant Major Bateman. I hear there's a discipline problem amongst the men at the cantonment. Think they've had it a bit too easy. You'll deal with it, I'm sure.'

Arnold nodded and saluted again. 'Yes, sir, I'd heard the same. Don't worry, sir, I'll sort it out.'

Lawrence nodded. 'I know I can rely on you.' He turned his attention to Carrie. 'It was very good to meet you at last, Mrs. Bateman. I hope we can rely on you to be part of the society in Secunderabad. We're a territorial little lot and we'll need some pleasant entertainment. I'm sure Bateman here has explained it all to you.' He smiled at her and she nodded, not really understanding what he meant. He nodded and tipped his cap, then walked towards the station. Arnold grabbed her arm. 'We need to get moving. The train will be here soon, and if we miss it there'll be hell to pay.'

She nodded saying nothing, and pushed the pram towards the vast gothic entrance of the station crowned by figures of a lion and tiger. The hall was a complete contrast to the dusty outside; cool, with vast high ceilings, and echoing with a hundred voices.

'We need to find the booking office,' said Arnold, his need to get moving making his voice gruff and his patience thin. 'There it is, the Star Chamber. Come on, we need to get our tickets before everyone else has the same idea. I hate queuing.'

Carrie looked around at the stone arches carved with grotesque faces and foliage. The ceiling was a deep blue with gold stars. She sighed with wonder, entranced by everything around her.

'I've never seen anything like this before,' she said. 'It's like being in another world. Is Secunderabad like this?'

Arnold shook his head. 'No, nothing like this. It's all very utilitarian, but much better than where we've come from. And you heard what Captain Lawrence said. There will be expectations and you'll need to make sure you meet them.' She put her head down and didn't answer him. He frowned, looking cross. 'Now what's the matter with you?' He puffed out an exasperated sigh. 'It's not too much to ask, is it? It's what I paid for after all. I think you're getting a bloody good deal.'

'I don't want a deal, Arnold. You make it sound like a business transaction.'

He raised his eyebrows. 'Well, that's what it is. I've paid and you have to deliver. Christ, all you've got to do is be nice to people, serve drinks and smile. Even you can do that.' She closed her eyes and waited for him to pay for the tickets. She opened her eyes and watched him remonstrating with the ticket clerk about the price and her heart sank.

She wondered about how it would be in Secunderabad, the place that would become her home for the foreseeable future. Pearl had said it was an adventure, but Carrie knew she'd only said it to keep her spirits up when she was frightened of what she had in front of her. If only

Pearl had been there with her she'd know what to do. She was so much more streetwise than Carrie, and Pearl gave her a confidence she didn't feel when she was on her own. I've never missed you as much as I do now, Pearl, she thought. I thought I couldn't feel worse than I did when I was on the ship, but I'm thousands of miles away from you and I need you so much. She looked at John asleep in the pram.

'It won't be forever, sweetheart,' she whispered. 'I'll get away from Arnold Bateman as soon as I can, and we'll go home to where we belong to the streets of Whitechapel, a place I love. Just you and me, my darling. Just you and me.'

Chapter 14

The four-day journey by rail to Secunderabad Station was arduous, sweaty and arid, and Carrie felt every one of the four hundred and forty miles from Bombay to Secunderabad jangle and jolt through her bones. The carriages rattled across the Indian terrain with, it seemed, no concern for passenger comfort, and Carrie wondered if they would ever get to their destination. The juddering and shaking from side to side didn't bother John, in fact the rolling movement of the train sent him to sleep, which Carrie was grateful for. After a while Carrie felt a malady in her stomach, something akin to seasickness. The food offered to the travellers on board did nothing to quieten her insides; there was an abundance of curried meat, mutton chops, kidneys and chicken, the bones of old fowls made into a questionable soup, and not much else apart from rice which accompanied every meal. Sometimes when the train came to a halt, men dressed in calf-length cotton trousers and turbans would run up to the windows of the carriage, offering fruit and water which Carrie had been advised not to buy, as tempting as it was. She'd been told by a steward the food offered could be days old and kept in unsanitary conditions. She decided with regret to follow his advice.

The compartment in which she and the other wives were seated was allocated only to Europeans; Indian natives travelled on another part of the train, so Carrie was thrown together with those she had come into contact with on board ship, the girls she had done her best to avoid. This is worse than ever, she thought, they in their little groups of chattering girls, probably gossiping about some poor unsuspecting person, and me trying to stay away from them. Is this how it will be in Secunderabad? She was grateful that Arnold had secured them a small private berth which meant she could disappear with John if the need arose, pretending he needed to be fed or changed. It was the kindest thing Arnold had done for them, although she was quite certain he hadn't done it for her and her son's benefit, rather that he like to think of himself as officer material and didn't want to sit with the ordinary soldiers. She felt guilty using her son as an excuse to get away from the stares of derision or the silences that fell on the company when she appeared in the carriage and sat on one of the banquets, but it was the only solution to the problem she had had to face on the ship where it was so vast she could get away and be on her own, and certainly it wasn't a situation that Arnold helped to alleviate. She knew to complain to him about the way the women were treating her would be to risk his contempt for her even further and no benefit would be gained from it.

She wondered at the feelings of Indians towards those Europeans who had come from thousands of miles away to rule their country. She knew why the British military was sent to India. Arnold had given her chapter and verse one night when he'd drunk a bottle of brandy and was so drunk he could hardly stand. He had rambled about the mutiny in 1857 that had started in Meerut, resulting in the murder of so many innocents, women and children included which had sounded so frightening and abhorrent to Carrie and she hoped with all her heart it could never happen again, but it seemed that at the station in Bombay Europeans had simply appeared from nowhere, had spilled off the ships and the connecting trains and taken the most comfortably furnished carriages, pushing past Indians who had been waiting for the train, seemingly for hours. Many of them had camped on the platforms, rolled out bedding, cooked food for their many children on tiny stoves, and washed and dressed in front of each other, something utterly alien to her as someone who had only ever undressed in front of Pearl in their tiny room in Nightingale Lane. It felt very wrong that Europeans imagined they were better than the people who were born in India, their own country. Why are they not here too, she thought as she looked around the carriage with the ruby red velvet banquets and shutters on the windows? This is their country after all, where they were born and raised.

Many of the women Carrie sought to escape talked openly about their relief at not being introduced to 'the natives' at this early stage, and realised that most of them considered Indians to be inferior in the social standing, looked upon only as "good enough" for servants and care givers. She would turn away and gaze out of the window. Having come from what she knew they would consider to be a lowly background she had plenty to say on the subject, but knew neither they, nor Arnold, would appreciate her opinion.

Secunderabad lies in the southern part of India towards the Eastern terrain where the summers are incredibly hot and the monsoons come from late June, providing the landscape with a lush, rich setting Carrie had not expected. She was astonished at the countryside; green palm trees and parcels of arable land used for growing vegetables and rice stretched as far as the eye could see. Some of the fields were on the hillsides or situated on terraces, and on the flatlands there were oxen and water buffalo; animals working alongside the men and women in the fields. And it was very hot, hotter than anything she had ever experienced. Sometimes in the kitchen at Nightingale Lane she wondered how cook coped with the overwhelming heat from two ovens and simmering pans on a hob which was always alight during daylight hours. Even with the windows open in the carriages and the air blowing through on both sides it provided no respite from the intense heat. The incoming air was so warm it simply made the passengers even hotter.

Carrie sat quietly in a carriage that was relatively empty. Many of the other women had kept to their berths because of the unbearable heat, and she took the opportunity to leave the suffocating four walls of their tiny compartment and enjoy some time on her own. John was fast asleep in his cot and she knew he would be safe in the locked compartment.

She listened to the noise the carriages made as they went over the bumpy track. There was a kind of rhythm to the chug, chug, noise and it was quite comforting to her, even though it was accompanied by lots of lurching and shaking. She took the opportunity to look around the carriage. Some of the other travellers had remained inside the carriage, happy to take on the heat and the company of others. She recognised the missionaries who had been on The City of London. They were sitting closely together without speaking, both staring out of the window. The woman must have felt Carrie's eyes on her because she looked up and gave her a watery smile. Carrie nodded and returned it. She knows how I feel, she thought. Missionaries are second-class citizens as far as the other women are concerned, but at least she has her husband on her side. Others were keeping themselves to themselves, their noses deep in a book so they didn't have to converse with anyone else, or doing complicated embroidery, their heads down as if to say, "Please don't speak to me".

A loud peel of high-pitched laughter rang out from the back of the carriage. Carrie leant across the long banquet seat and peered down the aisle where a group of young women were playing cards. This was the "fishing fleet" she'd heard so much about when she'd wandered up to the top deck of The City of London, the educated young women who had been sent to India by their parents who had paid handsomely for their passage so they could find a husband amongst the officers stationed at the cantonments. Madness, she thought. I hope they don't end up with someone like Arnold. She sighed and looked out of the window. He had given her no reason to think he would suddenly become the husband to her he should have been, apart from when it was required of him. For show, she thought, when one of his unit was close, or one of his seniors, and only to make them think he was a man with a family, a "family man" who was taking care of her and John. If only they knew, she thought. If only they knew.

A rustle on the seat next to her brought her out of her daydream and she turned to find Dorothy staring at her.

'Penny for you thoughts, Carrie,' she said, smiling. 'You were miles away.'

Carrie shrugged. 'Was I?'

'Was it a nice place, wherever you were?'

'No, not really.'

Dorothy inhaled deeply. 'I'm guessing your thoughts were in the familiar streets of London where you live and not in the unknown alleys of Secunderabad.'

'Something like that.' She looked out the window again, wishing Dorothy would go back to her friends. She glanced nervously at the glass in the door separating their carriage from the dining car. She knew Arnold had been in there with his friends and she prayed he wouldn't choose this moment to suddenly return. If he saw her speaking to Dorothy he would be less than happy. She began to rise from her seat. 'Well, I think I'll...'

Dorothy put a gloved hand on her arm. 'Just a moment, Carrie, before you run away again.' Carrie lowered her eyes and sat down, wondering what Dorothy had to say to her, wishing she would understand and leave her alone. She raised her face and looked Dorothy directly in the eyes; beautiful, grey and staring at her with benevolence. Her features were soft, almost regretful. 'Is he kind to you?'

Carrie froze. Dorothy had caught her off guard and she hoped her expression wouldn't give her away. 'Kind to me?' She frowned, pretending not to know who Dorothy meant. 'I'm sorry, who do you mean, Dorothy?'

'Bateman? Is he kind to you?'

'Well, he...he, he does what he can.'

'That's not much of an answer.' She moved her hand away from Carrie's arm. 'And yet it tells me everything.'

'My life is very different from yours, Dorothy. I wish you would understand that.'

'You keep saying it, but we're both women and I think most women want the same thing.'

'I say it because it's true. You must know it.' She inhaled to steady herself. 'You married your husband for love, didn't you? And he married you for the same reason.'

Dorothy frowned at her. 'Of course. Why else?'

Carrie sighed and argued with herself about her next words to Dorothy, but her need to let her feelings out got the better of her. 'But that's the point. I hadn't planned to say this to anyone and if Arnold finds out I will be in a good deal of trouble, but you've asked me the question. I like you, Dorothy. We may be completely different and our backgrounds are like chalk and cheese, but you're the only person who has shown me and my baby any kindness since I left London, apart from the Indian manager at the hotel who I'm sure knew my situation without me telling him. His concern for me was written all over his face. I want to be honest with you. I don't love Arnold, and I can assure you he doesn't love me.'

She looked shocked. 'But you married him.'

'Yes, I did, because I had no choice. I was forced into the marriage by my parents, mostly my mother.'

'Why? Why would they make you marry a man you don't love?'

'Because they were ashamed of me. I brought shame on the family and it was something they couldn't forgive.'

Dorothy's steady gaze observed Carrie for a moment until realisation crossed her face. 'The baby. John isn't Arnold's.'

Carrie shook her head. 'No, he isn't.'

Dorothy looked flustered and Carrie thought it was probably the first time she'd been caught off-guard. 'I'm...I'm sorry, I didn't mean to... ' Dorothy breathed in then smiled awkwardly. 'I've embarrassed you. Please forgive me, it wasn't my intention.'

'There's nothing to forgive, Dorothy. I'm not embarrassed. I was silly...naïve my mother said. I believed a man when he told me he loved me. I loved him. Very much. I thought he would stand by me, but I was forbidden to tell him about John.'

'But why? Surely he should know he has a son.'

Carrie nodded. 'Yes, I thought so too, but my parents had other ideas. They said because he came from a different class and a different religion he would not stand by me, that John's could be anyone's and he would probably deny it. And Dorothy, they were proved right. He broke my heart because he married someone else without telling me it was going to happen. The wedding must have been planned all the time we were seeing each other.'

'How did you find out?'

Carrie hesitated. She felt that to tell this woman who came from such a privileged background that she was a maid in Johan's home might be a step too far, but she had already gone much further than she had intended. What was the point of keeping it a secret? It was secretiveness that had ruined her life. 'I worked for his parents. In their house. I was a maid.'

Dorothy gasped. 'Did he…take you?'

Carrie laughed. 'No, Dorothy. He didn't take me. I gave myself to him willingly. It wasn't like you think. I honestly loved him. He said he wanted us to be together, that we would make a life together, build a home. I believed him because it's what I wanted to believe. I shamed myself and I shamed my family. They might be poor but they know what pride is. It's all they've got.'

Dorothy shook her head. 'You poor girl.'

Carrie stood and gathered her things together, a book, a little flask of water, and she hoped her dignity. 'So now you know why we cannot be friends. I would imagine you will not want to speak with me again. You will not want to be seen with me. You will not want to share in my disgrace. All I ask is that you do not share what I've told you with your friends. They already despise me. If they find out what happened to me in London my life in Secunderabad won't be worth living. And it won't only be the women. Arnold would never forgive me, and I have to try and make some sort of a life in India. My home seems such a long way away and I'm beginning to think I'll never see it again which breaks my heart.'

'I can assure you Carrie, I will not share what you've told me, not with anyone.'

Carrie nodded her thanks, went back to her and Arnold's tiny compartment, and cried and cried.

Dorothy watched Carrie as she left the carriage and stepped into the corridor. She frowned at the girl's back, wondering what she could do to help her, thinking that she had an almost impossible job on her hands. Carrie was right when she said she wasn't like the other girls on the train who would make their lives in Secunderabad. She was not shallow or constantly looking for someone to belittle, only out for grabbing a man and expecting him protect the empire while she did nothing, and Dorothy still harboured a hope that she and Carrie would be friends. The officer's wives were a giggly bunch, constantly looking for someone to gossip about. It seemed to be the only thing they were good at. When one of the girls left the group they would talk about her in the most unflattering terms, ripping to pieces her appearance and the way she spoke, and if any of her relatives were tradespeople it seemed to be a matter for hilarity. When she returned to her seat around the table and someone else left they would gossip about her, the returnee joining in the personal demolition, not thinking for a moment that it was possible that the other girls had been discussing her while she was away. Dorothy had grown tired of it and had made it her business to avoid them as much as was deemed polite. When she had met them on deck they had made a point of trying to include her in their conversations, but she knew it was only because Marcus was a commissioned officer and they wanted their husbands on his shirt tails. There were rules in the society in which they'd been thrown. She knew how it all worked. Unfortunately, poor Carrie did not. She'll have to learn, she thought. She must learn if she is to survive. She's part of the Raj now, no matter what her beginnings were. The British society in India could be savage. She knew this because of her mother's experiences years before, and Dorothy doubted that things had changed much. The privileges of being part of such a group were great, but they came with a good deal of responsibility. A military wife in the Raj had certain expectations thrust upon her, and she had to rise to them or risk being trampled underfoot. India was a huge shock to everyone when they first arrived, but it was the British Carrie would have to win over. And she needs the tools to know how to do that, thought Dorothy, relaxing back in her seat, smiling to herself. And I'm the woman who has them.

Chapter 15

At the end of the fourth day of their journey, when Carrie believed she really couldn't take another day of dust and mutton chops, the train gradually ground to halt, billowing steam and dust onto the platform at Secunderabad Station like a great metal monster arriving in a cloud of vapour. Arnold was getting into a flap encouraging Carrie to move faster in gathering their things together in the tiny compartment, whilst doing nothing himself apart from barking orders.

'Get a move on, Carrie, for goodness sake. We have to find a cart to take us to the station and if we're the last out we'll never get one.'

She glanced up at him and shook her head with frustration. 'Maybe you could give me a hand, Arnold, instead of flapping around like a chicken with its head lopped off. I'm not one of yer soldiers in the unit, so you can stop ordering me about and help me get our things together. It may have escaped your notice but I have a baby to look after. I've to make John comfortable before we leave and I can't do that and pack our things.'

He ran his hand through his thin hair, making the oily partings even wider. The heat didn't suit Arnold. Not only did he look greasier than he had before, it made him tetchy too. 'It's your job. This is your job. It's what you're here for. It's what the wives do, organise everything so their husbands don't have to. Don't you know anything?'

'And as I said, the other wives down have a baby to look after. John needs me at the minute. He needs changing, Arnold. I doubt I'll get a chance later. The carts will just have to wait.' She lowered her voice and mumbled under her breath. 'And so will you for that matter.'

He looked out of the window and sighed. 'Look, look, they're all leaving. We have to get off this bloody train.' He began gathering up the bags, shoving one under his arm and lugging two more by hand. 'I'll meet you outside,' he said. 'Just don't take too long about it or I'll leave you here. I'm off to find some transport. I'm expected to see the unit into Secunderabad, you heard Captain Lawrence when we were at Bombay station, and if I don't do it I'll be for the high jump. Don't keep me waiting.'

She watched his retreating back as he squeezed out of the narrow door and walked down the narrow corridor, bumping into the door frames with their bags. Carrie wiped John's sticky body with a damp cloth and dressed him in a cotton smock. 'Poor baby,' she cooed. 'It's so hot, darling.' She wrapped him in a cool muslin, lifted him from the bed and placed him gently in the pram that the hotel had kindly donated to her, smoothing her hand across his downy head. 'It'll be alright,' she said softly, more to herself than to the baby. 'Everything will be alright.'

She was startled by a sharp rapping on the window and looked up to see Arnold's sweaty face pressed up against it. His hot breath fogged the glass and she could see his mouth moving.

'Come on, Carrie, for God's sake. We'll get left behind.'

Carrie took a deep breath and held it for a few seconds before she released it. She looked down at John in the pram, his tiny legs kicking, and she blinked back tears of remorse. 'I'm so sorry, John. I'll look after you, my darling, don't worry. I have you and you're all I care about.' Her glance settled on the window again where the vapour of Arnold's breath had left a smear. She gathered the bags together Arnold had left for her to carry and left the berth and put them over her arm as she pushed the pram down the corridors which were empty. Carrie could see they were indeed almost the last to leave the train apart from a few stragglers who were not with their party. After stepping awkwardly off the train, and with a helping hand from the Indian ticket inspector to lift the pram, she pushed John along the platform, past the families camping there, their bedding rolled up for another day of waiting, the cooking stoves, the children playing in the dirt, and made her way under an arch that led her to a ticket hall where there were queues in every direction, looking for an exit that would take her outside. Around the perimeter of the ticket hall were stalls selling hot, spicy snacks, sweets and sherbets, fruit stalls with colourful oranges and bananas, figs and dates. Hawkers approached her holding green coconuts, mangoes and glasses of soda, lemonade and raspberryade, bright red and as tempting as a punnet of juicy ripe raspberries. There were jugs of cold water on the ground and urns of milky tea next to them. Carrie would have loved some tea, but she dare not keep Arnold waiting any longer. As she made her way across the hall she could see a huge set of double doors leading to daylight, and waiting outside was a bullock cart with Arnold leaning against it, a cigarette hanging out of his mouth, his legs crossed at the ankle. As he bent his head to drop the butt onto the ground, a strand of thin hair fell in front of his face and he bad-temperedly pushed it back then slapped his hand against the cart. Carrie took a deep breath and straightened her back. Behind her a train had just arrived on the platform opposite the one where their train now silently waited to be reloaded, and it occurred to her that she was moments away from getting on that train, regardless of where it was going. Anywhere to take her away from the uncertain life waiting for her and John in the Secunderabad cantonment. 'But I don't have any money,' she said to herself. 'Arnold's made sure of it, and here in Secunderabad as in London, you can't get anywhere without money.'

'Well, thanks for that,' Arnold said, exasperated and sweaty as she joined him by the bullock cart.

'Thanks for what?' Carried answered frowning. 'What have I done now?'

He leaned into her, his breath hot on her cheek, his teeth locked together. 'Don't question me, Carrie Dobbs. I told you to hurry, didn't I? I have to be at the barracks before the men in my unit and now they'll have to wait for me thanks to you. You're a pain in the neck.'

Carrie ignored him and placed her bags into the waiting bullock cart then put her foot on the footrest and stepped inside, settling herself on one of the rough wooden seats around the edge. She smoothed down her skirts and waited for Arnold to lift the pram into the cart. She looked at Arnold who was staring at her. 'I thought we were in a hurry.'

He glared at her and narrowed his eyes, then hauled the pram and himself into the cart and went to the front behind the driver, making sure not to sit next her. He turned and tapped the driver hard on the shoulder. 'What are you waiting for, and hurry up about it. We're late.' He turned back and glared at Carrie again. She raised her eyebrows and shook her head, allowing her eyes to wander away from him and settle in the middle distance.

Outside Secunderabad Station there were crowds of people, Indian and European, either rushing towards the station or leaving it. As the driver pulled away from the station Carrie turned her head and looked back at the solid brick building with its archways and porticos that resembled a fort and wondered when the next time would be that she would see the station again. Arnold had assured her the army cantonment in Secunderabad wasn't far from the station, and Carrie believed this information as a sign because she knew to return here meant she would be escaping. It would be the first step of many in her journey home, a place that seemed so very far away from the alien place she now lived, one she would hold in her heart until she saw it again. And she would see it again, of this she was determined.

The cart bumped across lumpy roads strewn with debris and swerved to miss chickens running in front of them or other bullock carts coming in the opposite direction. There were no rules regarding road etiquette, no lines of embarkation. Carrie realised it was every man for himself. Horses rode swiftly past them, and the odd motor vehicle left them in the dust, but the atmosphere was quieter less busy and more rural. Bombay had been bursting at the seams, yet even with the occasional burst of activity on the roads Secunderabad appeared more sedate, the pace slower. Carrie was glad. As much as she'd enjoyed exploring the streets of Bombay and marvelled at the diversity of people there she had worried about John growing up in such a community. The streets had felt airless, layered with constant chatter in languages so alien to her, the strong aromas of street food offered to passers-by wherever she looked by vendors trying to scrape a living, mouth-watering if hungry, but its constant presence stomach curling in its overwhelming quantity. There was also a strong evidence of military personnel in the town; many of the bullock carts contained soldiers and their wives and families, a life Carrie knew she would have to get used to and be part of if she were to find her place within its confines.

Arnold lit another cigarette and turned his gaze on her through narrowed eyes as he drew on it. 'I hope you're gonna behave when you get to the cantonment.'

'Behave? How do you want me to behave?'

He turned away. 'Like a lady…if you can manage it.'

She laughed. 'Like you'd know how a lady behaves, Arnold. And will you treat me like one because I've seen no evidence of it so far.'

'When you behave like one you'll be treated like one. Just keep your mouth shut and when you do speak be careful what you say and don't speak out of turn. Let's face it, you know nothing about nothing so no one's going to be interested in anything you have to say. In other words just do as you're told and you'll get along fine.' He blew out a smoke ring. 'And don't go getting all pally with those above you, like Dorothy Tremaine and her friends. You've got nothing in common with them and it's best you stay away from them.'

'Right. So who can I talk to? And what if they talk to me? Am I supposed to ignore them?'

'You just busy yourself. You'll have plenty to do. You won't have time for gossiping, and there's no need to for you to talk to anyone because you haven't got anything to say that they'll want to hear. Am I making myself clear?'

She frowned and looked hard at him. 'What are you scared of, Arnold?'

His eyes flashed and she shrank back against the rough wooden seat. 'I ain't scared of nothing. Don't forget I'm a soldier and I'm the important one here. I'm here to do a job, an important job of protecting our empire, and it's your job to make sure I'm comfortable while I'm doing it. So you keep house and make sure that when we have visitors you don't heap shame on us. Do you understand?'

'I speak English, the same as you, so yes, I understand.'

'Good. Just be sure you do what's expected.'

'And what's that?'

Arnold sniffed and looked away. 'You'll find out when we get there.'

Chapter 16

Carrie stood silently in the doorway of the bungalow as the late afternoon sunlight dappled the scorched grass under the banyan and custard apple trees on the small lawn in front of the house. She held her straw hat by the rim, absentmindedly turning it round and round in her fingers, feeling the rough straw against her skin as she watched the *punkah*, the member of Arnold's staff who operated the huge fan swathed across the ceiling, pulling on the rope threaded out of one of the windows. Behind her, in the large vaulted room filled with light and shadows, the walls roughly whitewashed, John lay in his pram kicking his legs, mewling and making sucking noises, his belly ready for another feed. Carrie stared out into the cantonment at the other bungalows where her fellow military wives were busily making their homes, organising their husbands and fussing about how the furniture left behind by another family should be arranged. She squinted her eyes against the whiteness of the bungalow facades and breathed in the pungent smell of orangey-red hibiscus which grew in every garden.

'Carrie.' Arnold's voice interrupted her daydream and she turned as he entered the room from a narrow corridor that separated the living room from the bedrooms. He loosened the top button of his shirt and took off his jacket, flinging it on one of four rattan chairs placed around an oblong coffee table in the centre of the room, then stuck his hands in his pockets. 'Why don't you go and unpack. The bags are in the master bedroom.' He frowned as she stepped further into the room and went across to John, rubbing her hand across his downy head.

'That'll take me all of two minutes, Arnold. Making John comfortable is more important. He's ready for a feed now. I'll take him into the bedroom and feed him before I do anything else.'

'You won't need to worry about looking after him for too much longer. Every child at the cantonment has an *ayah* and he'll be no different.'

She straightened her back and stared at him. 'A what?'

'An *ayah*.'

She shook her head, frowning. 'What's that?'

'You mean, who's that. It's an Indian nanny. She'll take care of the child so you can take care of me. You'll need time to make the right connections here, organise social events so that I'm seen in a good light by the officers. I thought we could have a get-together here tomorrow night to welcome the unit to their new home. I want to be the first one to send out invitations. The others will be jockeying for position but they'll have to follow me if we get in quick which is what I want. You'll need to sort out the food, drink, that kind of thing…find out what people drink here, something cool and alcoholic I should imagine. Oh, and champagne. The kind of people who'll attend will want champagne and lots of it.'

'But…' Carrie frowned, shaking her head, feeling that everything was drifting out of her control. 'No, Arnold. No one is looking after John but me. He's my baby, my son. I'm his mother. And…and I don't know this person. Who says he's to have a nanny, anyway? No one asked me.'

'I didn't have to ask you. I did what I thought was right, what I know is right. No European woman looks after their own child here. And neither will you. All the children here have an *ayah*, from when they're babies up until the age of seven. Then he'll be sent back to England to go to school, a live-in school where he'll get a decent education and you can be free to do your duty and your job. And he'll have a wet-nurse too, so you can forget all that business,' he said, flicking his hand towards her breasts. 'It's disgusting anyway. We're sophisticated English military, not primitive savages. Why you couldn't use bottles like everyone else is beyond me. And don't look at me like that. You won't be searching for things to do while you're here, my girl. You'll have plenty to occupy your time believe me.'

'I know it didn't mean much to you, Arnold, but I gave birth on board a ship. There were no bottles. What would you have me do, let him starve? And believe you? Why the hell would I believe you?'

Arnold moved swiftly across the floor and snatched the front of Carrie's dress, pulling her towards him, his teeth clenched together in anger. 'Keep your sodding voice down,' he hissed. Carrie leant back, away from his anger and his alcohol laden breath, but then glanced behind him when a woman entered the room to see what the commotion was, her face contorted by concern.

She was as tall as Carrie, skeletally thin, her skin the colour of the spices with which she cooked and her complexion deeply lined. Her hair was pulled off her face and wound into a tight, greying chignon. Her dark brown, almond-shaped eyes quietly observed them with surprise.

'Sahib?' she said softly. Arnold stepped back and put a hand up to reassure her.

'No matter, Gita. Everything is alright.'

She nervously wiped her hands on her apron covering her sari, a rather plain piece of yellow cloth wrapped around her body, nothing like the beautiful jewel coloured saris Carrie had seen on her arrival in Bombay.

'Yes, sahib,' she whispered, her voice barely audible. She left the room as silently as she'd entered it and Arnold's eyes, full of contempt, roamed Carrie's face. 'Have some dignity, my girl,' he said, keeping his voice low. 'Don't you care what people think of you?'

'Why should I care?' she answered. 'I want to be allowed to take care of my son, Arnold. It's all I want. He's all I have here, and now you're telling me you're taking him away from me too.'

Arnold shook his head and grabbed his jacket from the chair without even a glance at John who, sensing his mother's distress, was now crying.

'Don't be so dramatic. I knew you'd be trouble but I didn't think you'd be a whiner. Feed him for goodness sake, then do what you want for the rest of the day. It might help if you went to meet the staff. Gita's the cook. We have a *dhobi wallah* to do the laundry and another *wallah* to do the cleaning. All you have to do is to make sure my household runs smoothly. Even you can do that with your scullery maid experience. I would have thought it would have come very easily to you.' He turned to leave. 'Oh, and don't forget,' he said, turning back with a smirk on his face. 'There's only one person you'll be opening your legs for, and that's me. Still, you'll be used to laying down for the boss, won't you, so it'll come easily for you?' The smirk left his face and his eyes hardened as he turned and left her with a now very distressed John.

Carrie picked him up and tried to sooth him while she unbuttoned the front of her dress. He latched on easily and she held him close to her, relishing the bond between her and her child, thinking it might be the last time she would be allowed to feed her own son.

John had drifted off into a contented sleep. Carrie derived so much pleasure from the knowledge that his tummy was full and he was secure and warm, and she was the one who had provided his comfort. She wondered at Arnold and how he could dismiss John's presence so easily, particularly as he'd said he wanted them to have their own child. His treatment of John didn't bode well that he would be an interested and loving father, in fact, the opposite seemed true. She also wondered about his lack of interest in her. Not once had he attempted to kiss her or to touch her. She rubbed her hand across John's downy head and frowned. Most men would at least have tried, but Arnold seemed to do everything he could to stay away from her. She hoped it would continue. Dolores had said that Arnold would expect her to be wifely in every way, including in the bedroom, but so far she had been mistaken. Carrie shivered. She couldn't bear to think about Arnold making advances to her, of lying down with him, of him knowing her like Johan had. And her knowing him in the same way. It made her sick to her stomach.

She left John sleeping and decided to explore. She'd seen Arnold leave the bungalow through the kitchen door and walk across the grass to one of the other bungalows, a visit perhaps to another family. He hadn't asked her to accompany him and her heart sank. A wave of disempowerment, of complete abandonment washed over her and she chastised herself. Why would I want to spend time with him, she thought? She knew Arnold was deliberately separating her from the very people she needed to get to know if she was to have any kind of life in Secunderabad. She inhaled sharply as tears pooled in her eyes; as angry with herself as she was with him. He was getting to her just as he'd wanted to, and she was allowing it.

'Memsahib.' Carrie started at the voice interrupting her thoughts. Gita put her hands together and bowed her head in the praying motion Carrie had seen many times since she had arrived India. It made her feel uncomfortable that another person felt compelled to do it, but she understood it. She, herself, had also been in a similar position in London, a position of subservience and powerlessness.

'My name is Carrie, Gita. I don't know the word you use.'

Gita raised her head and observed Carrie with questioning eyes. 'Madam?'

Carrie stared at her. 'My name is Carrie.'

'Madam.' Gita lowered her hands. 'I cannot call you that. The sahib…he will not like such…behaviour from me. I am here to serve you. Please, may I get you something, a drink perhaps? You must be very hot, not used to the heat in India yet. Perhaps some soda or maybe some chai? I can make it cool for you. It is very tasty…with cardamom and some sugar. It will give you strength.'

Carrie nodded. 'Whatever you think is best.' She watched as Gita made the chai tea, then cool the glass in a bowl of cold water. She passed the glass to Carrie with a napkin. 'Thank you, Gita. Is this tea?'

'Yes, memsahib. Chai. Black tea with spices and sugar. It is drunk very much here.'

Carrie sipped the drink, then smiled. 'It's delicious, Gita. Thank you.' Gita looked pleased. Carrie suddenly felt replenished and she realised she'd hardly had anything to eat or drink while they had been on the train. 'I need to look around the bungalow, Gita, to get to know my new home. Sergeant-Major Bateman has requested I do so. Perhaps you could show me the rooms.'

Gita nodded. 'Yes, Madam, of course.' She wiped her hands on a cloth then swept her arm out in front of her to indicate her workspace. 'This is where I do my work, Madam. For the sahibs and memsahibs. The kitchen, or *baawarchi khana*. I will prepare your meals and the sahibs meals here every day. And the milk for the baby when the wet-nurse is not here.' Carrie drew in a deep breath but decided not to say anything. She knew this was Arnold's idea and not Gita's. The kitchen was well-appointed with a small cooking range and plenty of cupboards in white wood, but little in the way of decoration. Everything in the bungalow was painted white and very plain. All Carrie could think about was the kitchen in Nightingale Lane, where everything seemed so much bigger and darker, and where Mrs. Coyle's voice filled the space with hustle and bustle and urgency. Then Pearl's face filled her mind's eye and she was overcome with sadness. Her grief at missing her friend got stuck in her throat and she fought to stop herself crying.

'Everything's white,' she said, her voice wobbling.

'For coolness, Madam.'

Carrie nodded. 'How long have you worked here?'

'I work…all my life, Madam, from when I was a girl. First I fetch water, the *pani wallah*, then wash sahibs and memsahibs clothes. Then make tea, the *chai wallah*, and clean house. Now I cook. I have worked upwards. To be a cook is a very good thing. My mother was cook before me.'

'Your English is very good, Gita. It's better than some of the people at home.'

'English is a language of Secunderabad and Hyderabad because of the many sahibs and memsahibs from England and Europe. We learn English.'

'What about your own language?'

'Urdu, Madam. Or Telugu.'

Carrie rolled the words around on her tongue and tried to say it the way Gita had. 'Urdu. Telugu.'

'Yes, Madam.'

'Will I have to learn Urdu?'

Gita shook her head. 'I think no, Madam. The other memsahibs did not learn. They always spoke English. It is why we had to learn.'

'What should I see now?'

'Perhaps the sleeping quarters, Madam, where you and the sahib shall sleep. And the room for your baby.'

Carrie glanced at her. 'John will sleep with me, in my…our room,' she said.

'Sergeant-Major Bateman said there shall be a room for the baby. His *ayah* will sleep on a cot next to him so if he wakes in the night you will not be disturbed. He requested this.'

'Will you show me?'

Gita led her down a corridor leading from the kitchen. At the far end was a small bedroom with a cradle and a low bed on which there was a mattress and a thin cover. Over the cot was a net arranged on a frame.

'What's that?' Carrie asked.

'It's to stop the mosquitos biting the child, Madam. If the baby is bitten it will make him very ill.'

Carrie ran her hand across her face, now moist with perspiration, wondering what kind of world she had stepped into.

'Memsahib? You've had *chota hazri?*'

Carrie frowned. 'I'm sorry, Gita. What's that?'

'Your break of the long fast from night until dawn. To eat. You must eat, Madam, after the journey on the train. Train can be very bad. The food. The cooks buy from villagers along the journey. Sometimes it is not fresh, not good for you. And you must keep strength. For the baby. You're feeding him, yes?'

Carrie's eyes filled with tears and Gita gasped as Carrie shook her head, inhaling a deep breath and looking away. 'My husband…doesn't want me to look after my baby. He says an *ayah* will look after him. Who will she be? Why is she better for him than me, his own mother?'

'Memsahib,' Gita whispered, pressing her hands down to gently quieten Carrie. 'She is not better for your baby than his own mother. She will help you. You are memsahib, wife of the sahib. She is…*ayah* to help memsahib. She is *ayah* for a long time, since a young girl. You will need help so you can do the things you must do for your husband. It's the way of things.'

There was quiet. Carrie looked into Gita's eyes and saw something there she had felt so deeply herself. It was subservience, the need to please, the fear of being abandoned if she didn't obey the master and his wife. This fear is what Carrie knew from an early age, the dependency on others to give her work so she could contribute to her family and pay her way. This was Gita's position now and Carrie wondered how much she knew about her and Arnold's sham marriage. Even though she was Arnold's wife with an opportunity to change her life, she also knew the societal values she lived amongst would prevent her from ever rising above the randomness of her birth. Arnold hated her and would never support her or help her transition into the society she had married in to.

She realised she had been staring. Gita's gaze was steady and unflinching. Her dark brown eyes observed Carrie for a long moment. She knows what I am, thought Carrie. She glanced out of the window to the other bungalows that shone bright white in morning sun. On the lawns and coming out of the bungalows were the young wives of some of the soldiers that were on the ship. They strolled between the banyan trees in twos and threes, like pastel coloured butterflies in creams, pinks and peppermint greens, and carrying lace parasols to protect them from the sun's already intense rays. The walked with their coiffured heads pressed close as they gossiped and giggled, their voices carrying on the still air.

Gita stood quietly, the palms of her hands pressed together. 'Memsahib, you wanted to see the rooms?'

Carrie averted her eyes from the scene outside and nodded morosely. 'Yes, I should see them.'

'And the *ayah*, Madam. You will see the *ayah*?'

A wave of anxiety flowed through Carrie. 'Perhaps later, Gita. I'll see her later. I just need to get used to all of this.'

'And your clothes? I should hang them up, yes? In your room.'

'No, no, Gita, I'll do it. Don't worry. I brought very little with me from England.'

Gita frowned. 'You will need something lighter, memsahib. Your dress…it is a very dark and heavy cloth. You will be very hot.'

Carrie nodded. 'Yes, yes, I know. I must ask Sergeant-Major Bateman. I should have the right things.'

As Gita led Carrie around the bungalow Carrie's mind was elsewhere. She finally realised just how unprepared she was for her new life in India. There were rules, she realised, controls and systems of the new society in India that she had yet to learn. And Carrie knew there was much to learn; the etiquette that woman like Dorothy already had instilled into them, and by which they would continue to live their lives even in a military station like Secunderabad, a world away from their British roots. Nothing would change for them because they were at the top of the hierarchy, it was in their interests for it to remain the same, and she, Carrie, would have to scrabble up the societal ladder as well as she was able, because she knew her husband would not be willing to give her his hand to help her scale it.

Chapter 17

Dear Pearl,

Sorry I haven't written before. I would have written sooner but I was so worried you would not get my letter. We arrived here in Secunderabad only two days ago. It seems like a lifetime since I last saw you.

I'm a mother now, Pearl, to a little boy. John. He was born on the ship on the way to India. I think you know why I've chosen that name. He's a lovely baby, very calm and easy to settle. It was a shock giving birth on a ship. There was only one nurse to help, and a ship's doctor to check John afterwards, nothing like I thought it would be. At least it's over. I'm afraid I can't say it's something I would recommend but it's worth it when you look into the eyes of your new-born. I'm so in love with him already. I can't imagine life without him.

When we got to Bombay we stayed in a hotel. I've never stayed in a hotel before. The people were very nice, and kind to me and John, kinder than Arnold, that's for sure. You were right about him, Pearl. He's a nasty miserable man who hasn't a good word for me and John. He's barely looked at him. There's no hope for us as a married couple, I'm afraid. I could never love him and he surely doesn't love me or the baby. Happily I've not had to do you know what yet. I hope it stays that way.

I miss you so much, Pearl. I never realised how much I loved London and how much it meant to me until I arrived in this strange country. Everywhere is dusty and dry and the heat is unbearable sometimes. Poor little John spends most of his time unclothed except for his nappy, and even that seems too much at times.

We're living in a bungalow. It's an Indian word meaning one storey house. If I can get some pictures I'll send them next time. We have servants here. Don't laugh. I know, it's funny isn't it, servants serving the scullery maid. I don't like it and I don't think I'll ever get used to it. My favourite is Gita. She's like the cook and the housekeeper but nothing like Mrs Coyle. Dear Mrs Coyle. I miss her too, and her funny ways, although they don't seem so funny now, not after what I've seen lately. We're having a 'soiree' tonight. That's what Arnold calls it. It means he's invited people to our bungalow for drinks and nibbles. Nibbles indeed. What a word. That's all we ever did wasn't it, nibble. There wasn't enough food around to do anything else. These nibbles are little bits of this and that, a bit like the Sterns had for their cocktail parties. Well anyway, it's what we've got for tonight. Gita helped me organise everything. Arnold even gave me some money to get a new dress. I had to go to a place called James Street where the shops are. Oh, Pearl, it's nothing like the West End. The shops are really fuddy-duddy and the clothes! Well, I managed to get a pretty primrose coloured cotton overlaid with chiffon. It's about all that can be coped with in this heat. It looks very nice and I feel much better in it. More like *the other girls here. I also bought some little buttoned shoes to match, and a tiny bag on a yellow cord. Arnold said he wants me to be the hostess but only the Good Lord knows how I'll manage that. I haven't got a clue.*

The other girls here aren't very friendly, I'm afraid. They were very unkind to me and John and put me right in my place when we were on the ship. They all know what happened to me, that I had a bun in the oven before Arnold and I was married. And that he's not John's father. Arnold made sure they all knew it, too. He's really made things difficult for me, but I have to get on with it. Where else can I go? There's just one who seems nice but Arnold has warned me off her saying she's too good for the likes of me. Charming, eh?

I hope you're all alright. Has William gone yet? You must be so worried. It doesn't seem to be ending, does it, this war? Not like they said it would. I wish you were here, Pearl. I know people always write that when they're away, but I really mean it.

I've written to my mum and dad, but if you see them tell them I love and miss them. I know what they did was wrong but they're still my mum and dad aren't they? And keep safe, Pearl. You and William. Look after yourselves because besides John I feel like you're all I've got. Please don't forget me.

Your best friend,
Carrie.

The bungalow was quiet. Carrie was with John, laying him in his cot while the *ayah*, Amrita, stood silently on the other side. Carrie glanced up at her and the *ayah* lowered her eyelids once and nodded slowly. Amrita had said nothing since they had been introduced by Gita the evening before; it was as though Amrita knew exactly what was expected of her, there was nothing for her to say, and why would Carrie object? Carrie had been swept along by Amrita's quiet countenance, her calm efficiency with John, and part of her felt calmed by her too. At their first meeting Amrita had simply held her arms out for John as if it were the most natural thing in the world. Carrie had looked quickly at Gita with concern and Gita's eyes had widened as if to say, he'll be safe. There's nothing to it. Trust her. So Carrie had. From that moment the *ayah* had not left their side, sitting quietly while Carrie fed John and not interfering until Carrie was ready to relinquish him. That night, the *ayah* had brought John to Carrie for his last feed before bedtime, then whisked him away to his bedroom. Carrie had stared after them and Gita had laid a gentle hand on her arm.

'Do not worry yourself, memsahib. I know Amrita very well. She will love your baby like her own. She will teach him, and play with him when you are busy. It is the way of things.'

Carrie had nodded and looked down at her hands in her lap. She swallowed hard to stop the tears that threatened to glaze her eyes. 'She seems very young.'

'Yes, she is still young, but very caring. He is your child, Madam. He is still your child. And you are to be busy. The sahib says there is much for us to do. Tomorrow night we will have many of your husband's guests here. And you will be the hostess. You are his wife and you will make the evening so pretty.' Carrie's eyes widened and a frown settled between her brows. Gita smiled gently and patted her hand. 'With my help, memsahib, of course. With my help.'

Carrie smiled at the woman who seemed to know what she was thinking. 'Thank you, Gita,' she whispered. 'Thank you so much.'

Carrie stood in the kitchen by the large pine table and watched Gita as she prepared the food for Arnold's guests. She wrung her hands together, the evening heat making her new dress stick to her back. In the shop on James Street the dress had given her confidence, but the sound of the guest's voices in the large sitting room had stripped any assurance she'd felt away. Now she was back to being Carrie Dobbs, scullery maid, not Carrie Bateman, wife of Sergeant-Major Bateman, and she knew why she wanted to stay in the kitchen. It was where she was comfortable, it was where she knew best, and in the kitchen she could remain invisible, a requirement of her past life where she was to be not seen and not heard.

She glanced out of the window into the increasing darkness wishing she could run away, through the lantern lit bungalows towards the lake in Secunderabad, the Hussain Sagar. She'd heard it was very beautiful, where people went for quietness and to think. There she knew she would find peace, a safe haven away from the vicious tongues of the women who were sitting in the most comfortable chairs in her home and expected to be offered hospitality. She hated Arnold for putting her through this. He knew the difficulties she'd had with some of the other women, yet here they were, the very ones who had made her feel so wretched, holding court in her home, their loud, flirtatious giggles ringing out at one of the soldier's crude jokes.

Gita efficiently placed canapes on a large platter and raised her eyes to meet Carrie's. She'd heard the disgusting joke and the women's over-loud laughter. She shook her head and as Carrie leant forward to take the platter from the table she stopped her.

'No, Madam. You are not servant. You are hostess. I and Aashi, my daughter will take the platters into your guests. You may fill glasses if a guest requires it, yes, but…you are not 'naukar', Madam. You must be hostess.'

'But, Gita…'

Gita gently laid a hand on her arm. 'Madam. I will be there,' she whispered.

Carrie nodded and inhaled a breath that wobbled in her chest then reluctantly turned and left the kitchen and made towards the sitting room. Gita and Aashi, Gita's teenage daughter, dressed in a sari of pale blue followed her, carried the huge decorated platters of exotic foods and sweetmeats. As Carrie stepped towards the other guests, another peel of laughter rang out which came to an abrupt halt when the owner saw Carrie. The other guests followed her gaze and immediately stopped their conversations. Carrie slowed but Gita pushed gently into the small of her back with the platter.

'Madam,' she said loudly to Carrie so the guests could hear. 'Your chosen food for the guests? Where would you like me to present it?'

Carrie looked around the room, then pointed to an ornate dresser standing against an unadorned wall. 'On there,' she said. 'I think it will be perfect.'

Gita nodded and went across to the dresser with Aashi following. 'And the drinks, Madam. May I help you pour?'

Carrie nodded. 'Thank you, Gita.' She swallowed hard then addressed the room. 'May I ask what everyone is drinking? Gita and I will refill your glasses. We don't want you to hold an empty glass.' Carrie smiled to herself. She remembered Mrs. Stern saying this once at one of her dinner parties.

First to step forward was Dorothy Tremaine.

'Carrie, darling,' she said in a louder than necessary voice. 'How lovely you look. The colour of that dress is divine, so spring-like, and the little shoes to match. Exquisite. You have excellent taste, my dear.' She thrust her glass forward and Carrie went across to the drinks cabinet, miraculously stocked with alcohol of every kind. She nodded her thanks to Gita who smiled and bobbed a slight curtsey. 'We have champagne, Dorothy. Would you like some?'

'Champagne! Did you hear that, everyone,' she said turning her head to the other guests and holding up her glass. 'We're being treated like royalty. And look at the label. Divine. Champagne for me please.'

Carrie poured champagne into Dorothy's glass until the bubbles almost spilled over the top and her eyes met Dorothy's pensive gaze. 'Just be yourself, darling,' she said under her breath. 'You're doing really well.' Carrie gave a small smile as some of the other guests came forward holding out their glasses. She didn't know whether the label on the bottle meant it was a good one, or whether it was one Gita had bought from the local merchant, but whichever it was it was popular and the six bottles she had placed in the drinks cabinet soon ran out.

'Arnold, old boy. You're letting us down. Out of champagne, apparently,' said one male voice who Carrie could see belonged to one of his superior officers.

Arnold looked cross and joined an awkward Carrie standing by the cabinet not knowing what to do. 'Why didn't you order enough?' he hissed. 'You must have known how much they'd need. You've worked in service all your life. You surely know how much people drink at these things.'

'I'm sorry, Arnold. I didn't order it. Gita did.'

'Oh, right, trying to blame the staff now are you?'

'No, that's not what I meant. If it wasn't for her we wouldn't have had any. You didn't say what you wanted. Can we not get more? There's a merchant on James Street. I think it's where Gita goes.'

He grimaced at her. 'Where do you think you are? You're not in someone's back room playing cards with the neighbours and can go off when you please to get more plonk. You're the hostess. You should know these things.'

Gita and Aashi came into the living room holding ice buckets complete with bottles of red and white wine. 'Sahib,' said Gita, breathless. 'We have the best wine here, sir. It comes from the cellar of the mayor. It is only the best.'

Arnold nodded. 'Very good. Serve it, Gita. Hopefully no one will notice. They've all had a lot to drink at the club already. And get that girl of yours to serve the food.' He threw Carrie a disgruntled look. 'We'll talk about this later. Maybe you can try and mingle with our guests. Just talk to them, damn it. That's if you're capable.' He wandered back to the little knot of male guests in the centre of the room and lit a cigarette shaking the match out and throwing it out of the window. Someone said something in a low voice and he bellowed with laughter, then turned and looked at Carrie. She lowered her head away from his gaze then turned away, sure they were discussing her.

'Memsahib?' Aashi was by Carrie's side, holding the canapes. 'Madam, you wish to eat? You must be hungry.'

Carrie shook her head. 'No thank you. I'm not hungry.'

'Madam,' Gita said. 'The baby. You must eat to feed him. Please, memsahib. You've eaten nothing all day. Please.'

Carrie stared at her. 'Did those bottles really come from the mayor's cellar?'

Aashi smiled at Gita and Gita nodded. 'Of course, Madam. Only the best for the sahib and his guests.'

Carrie laughed and took the platter from Aashi's hands, who gasped and turned quickly to her mother in horror. 'Let me do what I know best. It'll break the ice. I have to talk to these people. It's all I know. Follow me with tea plates and napkins, Aashi, and Gita, you follow with the wine. Are we ready?' The women nodded. 'Good. Let's go. Let's get these people fed and drunk,' she said, sotto voce, 'then maybe they'll go home.'

'You know we're pariahs, don't you?' said Captain Lawrence. 'Over in Blighty. That's how they see us.

'David, I don't think it's quite like that,' said Dorothy. I think you're exaggerating rather. In fact I think many of our circle back home envy us. They think we're having a wonderful adventure; that we're incredibly brave mixing with a race of which we really have very little knowledge, and wonder at us taking the risk that we could be slaughtered in our beds at any moment, day or night.' She turned to Carrie and winked. Carrie gave a small smile as she stood by Arnold, an untouched glass of white wine in her hand. 'And what about the girls who come out here looking for husbands. Most of them find someone to take them on. They wouldn't dare go back home to Mama and Papa without finding someone. It costs an absolute arm and leg to get out here.' She raised her glass in David's direction. 'I should imagine you're in their sights, David, the very kind of man they're all looking for.'

He laughed and returned her raised glass. 'They would need to be fast runners, Dorothy, to catch me, I mean. I like to do the choosing, not be the chosen.' Everyone laughed, Arnold loudest of all and Carrie wished he'd stop drinking.

She wondered at his need for alcohol no matter what the situation was. He would drink to celebrate and to commiserate; whatever the occasion, Arnold took to drink. Maybe he needs it, she thought, to feel part of this group of people we've found ourselves in. We're nothing like them, not even Arnold, although he feels his star is in the ascendant. During the evening his voice had become louder and louder, his laughter more and more animated, particularly when David Lawrence said anything, regardless of whether it was particularly amusing or not. Even when Carrie was serving the Sterns she had never felt the need to ingratiate herself in front of them. She had done the job she was paid for, and to the best of her abilities. Her thoughts went suddenly to Johan and she gasped. She hadn't thought of him for a while, whether by accident or design she didn't know which, but suddenly he appeared in her mind's eye smiling at her in the way that would make her stomach roll with love and desire. She took a quick swig from her wine glass and did her best to push the image away.

'You alright, darling?' Dorothy said, glancing quickly in her direction. Carrie nodded. 'Perhaps you need some air. It's rather stuffy in here.' Carrie nodded again and Dorothy took her arm and walked her out onto the veranda at the front of the bungalow. 'Sit, darling.' Dorothy pushed Carrie gently into a rattan peacock chair and sat opposite her on a lounger.

'You look beautiful, Dorothy,' Carrie said, smiling, her eyes on the stunning creation Dorothy was wearing. 'I love that dress. And is that the new length? Arnold would never let me wear something like that.'

'Oh, thank you, Carrie. I brought it over from London.' She looked down at the deep red velvet with red chiffon sleeves decorated with flashes of gold thread. 'This is a Paul Poiret. His new look is based very much on the Orient. I thought it was ideal for the kind of weather we have over here. The velvet is a new lightweight design.'

'And your husband doesn't mind you showing your ankles?'

She laughed. 'No, the opposite. Marcus loves it. He says he's proud of me and if a gentleman wants to look at my ankles he should have the pleasure.'

Carrie's eyes widened. 'What a lovely thing to say.'

Dorothy nodded. 'Yes, he's wonderful, although I did notice a few looks from some of the other girls. Not sure they approved but I don't care. They'll be wearing the same thing next week, mark my words. They haven't got an original thought between them.' Carrie looked down to her hands in her lap and twirled her wineglass in her fingers. 'And what about you, Carrie? You've done so well this evening. I can't tell you how brave I think you are. Bravo, darling.'

'I don't feel very brave. What I feel is out of my depth. I didn't order enough champagne, well, I didn't order any champagne. Gita did it. Then she saved my bacon by finding some wine from somewhere. Arnold wasn't happy. He more or less told me I was useless. I'm beginning to think he's right.'

Dorothy took Carrie's wineglass and placed it on a little bamboo table next to her, leant forward and took her hands in her own. 'Now you listen to me,' she whispered. 'You must stop thinking like that, Carrie. You are not useless. You've had a complete change of life. You've recently given birth...on board a damned ship for goodness sake, and you've put on this wonderful evening for us all. If Arnold is complaining, then I can assure you he is the only one. And even if Gita did help you, it's only what the rest of us would do. Do you think we'd go down to the merchants ourselves and haggle with them over bottles of champagne? Do you think I and the other girls would be standing at the kitchen table kneading bread to feed our husband's guests? Never. Ever. Carrie, I've never done anything like that. I can barely boil an egg. And as for Gita, she's a member of your husband's staff. It's what she's paid to do. If anyone should know that, it's you.'

'But he's so critical.'

Dorothy squeezed her hands then handed her the wineglass. 'Drink some more, darling. You need it.'

Carrie sipped at the wine and decided she had nothing to lose. 'He doesn't love me.'

Dorothy sat back in her lounger. 'I know he doesn't love you, and he probably never will. You told me on the train out here, didn't you, what it was all about, and now I can see it for myself.'

Carrie stared at her, her breath caught up in her throat. 'Is it so obvious?'

'It is to me. Marcus would never treat me the way Arnold treats you. I know what it is to be loved, Carrie, and you are not loved. I know exactly why you're here. It's almost like you're the opposite of the fishing fleet. They come out here to find a husband, usually someone with some status who, when they return to England, will give them the life their parents wanted for them. It's a terrible way to get a husband, but with the war and all the young men volunteering and being sent to the front, including those with any kind of standing in the community being recruited as commissioned officers, they probably feel they have no choice. You've come here to give Arnold married status. I worked it out when I discovered what had happened to you. And with a child as well he's viewed as a married man with a child; stable, committed and good for promotion. I hate to say it because that last thing I want is to upset you, but you've been used, Carrie. I can't imagine what your parents were thinking when they got you together with Arnold Bateman but I don't think they were thinking about you and the life you would have. There's nothing worse than being with a man who doesn't respect you.'

'Do you like him?' Dorothy raised her eyebrows but said nothing. Carrie's shoulders slumped forward. 'So what do I do? What would you do?'

'You must toughen up, darling, or you will not survive. I don't know if you've realised it, I rather think you may have, but it's brutal out here. This is not a holiday destination for bright young things. We're here to make our husbands' lives easier. I'm one of the lucky ones. Marcus would no sooner disrespect me than fly unaided. My father would roust him out and his reputation would disappear overnight, but in all honesty Marcus isn't that kind of man. You have a different situation with Arnold. What would your parents do if he abused you?'

Carrie's eyes glittered with tears. 'Nothing,' she said in a small voice. 'They wouldn't even know. My dad…he would care, but I'm not sure about my mother. He paid her you see.'

Dorothy looked horrified. 'What!'

'Arnold. He paid her to ensure I would accompany him. And she was happy because she'd already told me I had to leave our home because I was carrying John. It's not done in our community, to go with someone outside of it. Johan got married so I couldn't even tell him I was pregnant, in fact, my family told me not to tell him because it would ruin their reputation. I didn't know where to go, Dorothy. I had nowhere to go so I couldn't put up a fight because if I hadn't come out here me and John would have ended up on the streets, just two more people nobody wants. There are lots of them in London, mostly women. I don't think I have to explain what would have happened to us.'

'Oh, Carrie. I'm so sorry. We have no idea, do we, in my world. This is why the suffragette movement must win. Women must have a voice, otherwise this dreadful situation you're in will continue, and we can't let that happen.'

'The suffragette movement? Aren't they the ones who break windows and get put in prison? And you said men have volunteered for the army, Dorothy. I thought they were called up.'

'Oh, no. The young men going off to war have all volunteered. They want to do their bit for their country.'

'He lied to me,' she said, astonished.

Dorothy frowned. 'Who, darling?'

'Joe, from back home. He told me he'd been called up to fight, but he hadn't had he? He went because he wanted to. He left Molly and their little kids to fend for themselves to go off to war.' She shook her head. 'That's terrible.'

'Is it?'

'Don't you think so?'

'Not really. I think they're very brave men who want to do their bit for their country. Without them where would we be? Sometimes you have to stand up for what you believe in, even if it's not the safest or most convenient thing to do. Your friend obviously felt he should do something. He saw other young men leaving to fight and thought he should do the same.'

'But his family.'

'I know, Carrie but…bravery can't always be nice and clean and expedient. We all need to have something to fight for, particularly when what is happening is unjust. That's why I believe in the suffrage movement. I have stood with those women, I have listened to their stories. The woman who threw a brick through the window of Fortnum and Masons in London. She was arrested for causing havoc, for believing in her cause. And do you know that Fortnum and Masons sent their hampers to the women in prison, so they would have something decent to eat. They actually believed in what they were trying to achieve was admirable. These women have been accused of being unladylike, of being unseemly simply because they want to be equal to men. They are tough, Carrie. They grit their teeth and they will not allow anyone to sway them from what they know is right. Some who took part in the hunger strike have actually been fed by force with a tube down their throats, held down by men. It's a disgusting way to treat another human being just because they don't agree with men. Just think, if you had been equal to a man you could have stood your ground and refused to marry Arnold Bateman. You and your baby could have made a life together in London because you would have had as many opportunities as any man, and you wouldn't have been forced to live in a place that's wasn't your choice.'

'It wasn't a man who sent me here, Dorothy.'

'No, but it's a man who is treating you like a slave, an object, Carrie. It is a man who is making you feel small, who is trying to humiliate you in front of his friends. I know you think there isn't one person here you can call a friend. You must understand that I don't consider anyone here a friend, only my darling husband. And you, if you'll have me.'

'Arnold said I mustn't befriend you.'

Dorothy sat up quickly, looking astonished. 'Why ever not?'

'Because I'm not of your station. Because I was a scullery maid and you're a lady. We come from different worlds. In London I would probably be the one who cleaned and set the grate in the room you'd take tea in, the one who polished the silver spoon with which you stirred your tea, the one who would invisibly straighten up the room when you'd left. That was me, Dorothy. I was the one who did all that, and Arnold likes nothing better than to rub my nose in it. I've no doubt that after tonight I'll be in trouble, talking to you like this, away from the rest of the party.'

'I assure you, you will not. I think your husband has forgotten that we know where he comes from and who he is, that he comes from the same community as you do, and yet he is in your bungalow speaking quite freely with my husband, and his superior. David Lawrence will brook no ill treatment of you, Carrie. He would not be best pleased if he knew.'

Carrie shook her head. 'Please don't say anything, Dorothy. Arnold will make my life hell if he thinks I've been talking about him behind his back, especially to you. And if it affects his career my life won't be worth living. There's nothing I can do. I'm stuck here until I can find a way to leave and go back to London.'

'To what, Carrie, and to where?'

Carrie closed her eyes and swallowed hard. 'I don't know, Dorothy. I just don't know.

Chapter 18

'Memsahib, memsahib. May I speak with you?' Gita ran into the sitting room where Carrie was reading a letter from Pearl, at her side a Moses basket where John lay amusing himself and trying to roll from side to side. At two and half months old he had begun to smile and gurgle and play with his toes. Carrie was besotted with him and everything she did was for John, to keep him safe and secure and to benefit his happiness. She knew they would be in Secunderabad for some time yet. The previous two months had flown by and she had scarcely had time to think about anything other than running her household.

She had taken Dorothy's words to heart and they and Dorothy's support had given her strength. She had been shocked to discover that Dorothy supported the suffragette movement. Carrie had believed to be fortunate enough to be part of a certain society, the upper class as she saw it, would have been enough to satisfy any women, but she had quickly realised she was mistaken. She also realised that when Florrie had recruited Arnold Bateman as Carrie's husband, she had been utterly powerless. Her opinion had not been sought. There was no argument to be had. Florrie was her mother and Arnold was far older than Carrie. And Florrie had been paid. It had been a business arrangement that Florrie would never renege on because it would have meant giving back the payment Arnold had given her, the money which very likely kept Carrie's family in London from the breadline for many months. Carrie knew that Florrie felt that because she was her daughter it was Florrie's right to make the decision for the rest of her life. Arthur's opinion didn't come into it, because Carrie was sure if it had she would be at home in Whitechapel pushing John's pram down their street with Elsie and her own baby, a girl she'd named Rose.

She looked up when Gita came into the room. 'Yes, Gita. Is there something wrong?'

'Oh no, Madam. It is about the wedding.'

Carrie frowned. 'The wedding? Whose wedding?'

'It is the wedding of Aashi, my daughter and Devak Mistry. There will be…festivals, celebrations. I thought, Madam, you could be…part of it.'

Carrie leant back in her chair and looked at Gita for a long moment. 'Part of it? How?'

'You could join with Aashi and me, to help with wedding and decorate. I thought, Madam, it would help you.'

Carrie looked down at her letter and sighed. 'You're very thoughtful of me, Gita. I'm guessing you know I'm not really a memsahib, at least, not like the ones you're used to.'

Gita's expression tumbled into one of utter regret, her eyebrows knotting together. 'Madam. Please…'

Carrie drew in a deep breath. 'Well, you're right.' She looked up at Gita and smiled.' I think I'm more like you and your family than the women who came to India on the same ship. Their lives were very different from mine. I was in service before I came here. I did a job not unlike yours.' Gita nodded. 'Yes, memsahib, but it is not important.'

'It's not important to me, Gita, and I'm very thankful it's not important to you and your family. You've shown me every respect and kindness since I arrived in Secunderabad and I'm grateful for it, but I'm very much afraid it's important to my husband and his friends.'

'But Memsahib Tremaine, she is your friend, yes?'

Carrie nodded. 'She has tried to help me become part of her society, but to be part of it you must be like them. You must have their upbringing, their education, and their memories. I have none of that. I'm not ashamed to tell you, Gita. I'm not ashamed.'

'Why would you be ashamed, Madam? You know about life. You have worked to put food on the table. That is nothing to be ashamed of.'

'*We* know that. In our eyes it is something to be proud of. In our society we know we're important because without us our families will not survive. It's different in their society. It's all there for them from the moment they're born, the wealth, the society, it's like an exclusive club to which I'll never had admission. They will never understand.'

A protracted silence followed between the two women until Gita broke it. 'Madam. You must be strong. I have seen it…I have seen what they do.'

Carrie frowned. 'What do you mean, Gita?'

Gita's eyes widened when she realised she'd said too much. 'Oh, Madam, nothing. I…I see they are not the same as you. I have worked in this house for many years and I have seen many things. The sahibs and the memsahibs are not like us. They do not live the same way. They do not think before they act. They eat and drink so much,' she put her hand to her chin in thought, 'wasteful, I think is the word. They…do everything to…too much. And their lives do not have rules of faith, not like in India. Faith is…everything. They have so much. So very much, but they waste too much.'

Later that day, Arnold appeared in John's bedroom as she was putting him down for his nap.

'Where is the *ayah*? Should she not be doing that?'

Carrie straightened her back as she gently held John's fingers. 'Her husband is ill. She needed some time to take care of him. I told her to take all the time she needed.'

Arnold looked cross. 'You didn't think to ask me?'

Carrie leant against the cot and folded her arms. She felt herself bristle at Arnold's criticism of her. Yet again he'd found something to berate her for. 'Why would I ask you? You have your work, don't you? If I'd said anything to you, you would have said it was my place to run the house which is exactly what I'm doing. Make your mind up, Arnold.'

'That's not what I meant. The *ayah* is a member of staff. I hired her. It's up to me to decide whether she's required…or not.'

She walked past him into the corridor connecting the bedrooms and the living quarters. 'Well, it's too late. I've already decided.'

She went out to the veranda and sat in the rattan peacock chair. Arnold followed her, her answers to his questions unsatisfactory. She had overstepped the mark. She had made a decision that only he should make.

'Next time you must ask me. I'm not paying staff for doing nothing.'

'That's your decision, but I'm more than capable of looking after my own son. I think I've already told you that. It makes no difference to me whether she's here or not. The *ayah*, whoever she is will never have overall care for John. I'm his mother and I will be the one to oversee his care.'

Arnold clenched his fists and Carrie noticed his knuckles turn white with fury. 'I notice you and Dorothy Tremaine talk a lot.'

Carrie nodded. 'And?'

'I thought I told you not to get too friendly with her. She has…ideas she probably shouldn't have for a women of her standing.'

Carrie smiled to herself. So here it was. Here was the real reason Arnold didn't want her to associate with Dorothy. 'You mean her ideas about suffrage. Isn't that what it's called? I've never really taken much notice of it. Those women aren't like me. I thought you would have known that. I was too busy working my arse off to go on protests marches. Too many fires and grates to scrub and set, too many potatoes to peel, too much bowing and scraping to do. You know all about my life before, Arnold. I don't know why you're getting into such a tizzy about it.'

'A tizzy? I'm soldier, woman. I don't get into a tizzy. And maybe you could watch your language while we're talking, and in front of the servants. You don't seem to have any dignity.'

She stood and pressed her face as close to his as she could without inhaling his tobacco breath. 'Oh, I do, Arnold. I have dignity, but it's just not about pretending to be someone I'm not. I know why I'm here. The servants know why I'm here. They see no love between us, no signs of affection and certainly you have no feelings other than degrading ones about John, a poor baby who can't defend himself. Yet. I know who I am and where I've come from unlike you, and let's face it, if I didn't, thank goodness I've got you to remind me.' At that defining moment every ounce of hatred she felt for Arnold left her body and was projected towards him like a dart. It was as though everything around them had dissolved, the bungalow, the blazing hot sun in an azure sky, the banyan trees, the wagtails flying overhead and settling on the branches in flocks of twittering mayhem, everything stilled, everything stopped.

She came to on the veranda. All she could remember was a flash of something coming towards her face and connecting with her cheekbone in an explosion of pain. She lay there for a moment, trying to get her breath, struggling to come to terms with her awkward position on the dusty floorboards. She put her fingers up to her cheek, wincing at the tenderness slicing through the side of her face.

Raising herself up on her elbow she took a breath, then made a grab for the chair to help her get to her feet. Nausea rose from her stomach to her throat and she wretched. She put one foot in front of the other, her gait unsteady, holding onto the door frame around the bungalow's entrance. The sitting room was empty; quiet, cool, the same as it was before, as though nothing had happened, and she had simply imagined that Arnold Bateman had thrown a punch at her face and felled her and left her lying unconscious on the veranda. She wondered that he had attacked her in such a public place, but then she knew that most of the Indian Army Officers and their wives were at the Secunderabad Club, eating and drinking and playing cards. This is where Arnold spent most of his free time and where she knew he would be, carousing with his friends and not caring one jot about the violence he'd shown her.

Carrie staggered into the sitting room, sinking down onto one of the chairs and putting her head gingerly in her hands. A rustling sound in the corridor made her stomach roll with fear, terrified it was Arnold. She lifted her head slightly and breathed a sigh of blessed relief. Gita stood in the entrance nervously wringing her hands.

'Madam,' she gasped. 'What has happened? I must get doctor, yes?'

'No, Gita, please, I'll be alright.' Carrie knew the so-called doctor who attended the inhabitants of the cantonment was probably in the same place as Arnold; standing next to the bar in the Secunderabad Club playing drinking games. If you had reason to call a doctor in the Trimulgherry *mofussil*, which was what their station was called, you did not call for him.

'Oh, Madam. Your face. I…I don't know what to do.'

'Nothing. Nothing. Go about your work. Pretend you haven't seen me. No good can come of you getting involved.'

'Please, let me help you.' She called Aashi to assist her. 'Bring a bowl with warm water and a clean cloth. Hurry, girl.'

'Gita, if he finds you helping me it means you know what he has done and it will do you and your family no good. He will take it out on you, perhaps dismiss you. I couldn't bear it.'

Aashi joined them holding a bowl and some small scrupulously clean cloths over her wrist. In one of her hands she held a small bottle, brown glass with a cork stopper.

'What's that?' Carrie asked.

'It is pineapple juice mixed with turmeric and aloe. It will reduce the swelling on your face and help with the pain. It is something we use regularly so you need not be afraid of it. You must let me help you, memsahib.'

'Carrie. My name is Carrie.'

Gita sat back on her heels and observed Carrie. 'Madam,' she whispered. 'I cannot call you that.'

Carrie stared at her, her eyes glittering with tears, her understanding of the similarities between them greater than ever. 'Yes. Yes you can. It's my name. He is not here in the daytime and it's the time for me to be myself. When we are alone, when we're together in the house you can call me Carrie. I'm not a memsahib, I'm not better than you. My achievements are not greater than yours. I've done nothing or have nothing to deserve that word, that title, if that's what it is. It has no meaning for me, Gita. It isn't who I am. I am Carrie Dobbs and I always will be.'

Aashi placed the bowl next to Carrie's feet and Gita poured some of the liquid out of the bottle into the warm water then dipped the corner of a cloth into it and began to bathe the wound on Carrie's cheek. 'I have never seen this, Madam…Carrie. I have never seen a sahib beat his wife and cause her pain.' Her eyes met Carrie's. 'He is a cruel man.' Carrie nodded and closed her eyes. The warmth of the liquid and Gita's soft touch were soothing. Her head ached from where she'd fallen onto the veranda floor and when she felt the back of her head it was swollen. When Gita had finished she instructed Aashi to get rid of the evidence of their help then gently pulled Carrie to her feet. 'You must sleep, Carrie. Tonight is the Regimental Ball to greet the new soldiers. You are to go with Sahib Bateman. Had you forgotten?'

Carrie looked at her in horror. 'I can't go. Not like this. Look at my cheek. How can I face the others like this?'

'I'll help you,' Gita said. 'Aashi will make a poultice of pineapple and we will place it on your cheek while you sleep. You must rest. The pineapple will stop the swelling. We have cosmetics for Aashi's wedding. They will cover the marks.'

'I've never used cosmetics, I'm not sure I'm allowed to. The women here think they are used only by "certain" women and look down on them. I heard them say so when I was on the ship. They wouldn't speak to one of the women in the fishing fleet because she wore cosmetics to catch a husband. They said she looked like a woman of the night. I heard them when I was sitting on the deck by myself, laughing at her and saying bad things. They hate me already, Gita. Everything I do is wrong, and Arnold…he will criticise me.'

Gita shook her head and sighed. 'Don't worry, Carrie. Not colour, no colour will be used, but something on your face to help with dark marks. No one will know, I promise. No one will know. You must rest now. You will sleep this afternoon and Aashi and I will take care of your son while you sleep.' Carrie lay gratefully on the bed and drifted quickly into a deep sleep. Gita placed a light cover across her then stroked a hand across Carrie's forehead before closing the gauze curtains around her. Aashi entered the bedroom, her steps soft, her face etched with sadness.

'You must be careful, Talli. Sahib Bateman will not look kindly upon you for helping her.'

Gita nodded without looking at her daughter. 'She is the same age as you, Aashi. If this ever happens to you I hope someone will take pity on you and help you. She is in a foreign country and has no one. You have me and Auntie Shalini.' She shook her head and raised her eyes to her daughter's concerned ones. 'Men can be unfeeling. They do not understand a woman's heart.'

'And Devak Mistry. Why did you choose him for me? Does he understand a woman's heart?'

'He comes from a good family, daughter.'

'He makes trinkets.'

Gita frowned at Aashi. 'He is a craftsman, Aashi. He is making your wedding jewellery from the finest yellow gold and the most beautiful stones. You are very fortunate.'

'But I want to see the world. India is just one country. There are so many more to see, so many places to explore...like England and America. The streets are paved with gold there. People live in big houses and they have good jobs. Women are changing, Talli. I want to spread my wings. Memsahib Bateman has come to India from England. She has travelled on a ship across the sea. I have not even seen Bombay. I would love to go. The saris are brighter and more beautiful than ours and edged with golden thread. There are marketplaces selling everything you could want and houses painted all the colours of the rainbow. There are more people to meet and more things to do.'

Gita took her arm and led her into the corridor, shutting the bedroom door behind her. 'Yes, and Memsahib Bateman has married a man who strikes her and who doesn't love their child. She came to India from England on a ship with people she does not know to be beaten by her husband. Do you envy her?'

Aashi rolled her eyes then glanced at her mother. 'No, Talli. Of course not.'

'Then be grateful, Aashi. And be most, most careful what you wish for.'

'Will your wife be joining us, Bateman?'

'Yes, sir. She had some domestic requirements to attend to with servants but she will be here. Our *ayah* is unwell. She needed to be sure the child is cared for. She will be here soon.'

'I certainly hope so. I've yet to meet her. A little bird tells me she's rather friendly with Dorothy Tremaine.'

'Er, they seem to have found some common ground, certainly.'

'Mm, not sure it's a good thing, Bateman. Dorothy Tremaine is too clever by half. We don't need clever girls here. She should remember where she is. She knows how things are in this neck of the woods. We've come here to protect the Empire in the absence of the 9th Secunderabad Cavalry Brigade doing their bit in France. The 4th must uphold everything dear to the Emperor of India, King George V. It would seem we're not just defending the Empire from our enemies but from some unwanted musings from a few of our silly women. I hope your wife isn't one of them, Bateman. What do you think, my dear?' He turned to his wife, Lady Mabel Dimmock, commonly known as the *"burra"* memsahib, the Queen Bee of society and social leader of the Trimulgherry station, in Secunderabad and beyond. She was a woman of around fifty and had spent many years in India with her husband, Field Marshall Bruce Dimmock.

'A flash in the pan, my dear. Nothing for you to worry about. These girls want something they can't have. I'm so very glad we're here in India and not in London where they're causing an awful lot of trouble, and for what? It won't get them anywhere, I can assure you.' She crossed her arms under her not insubstantial bosom. 'These protestors will be squashed. Why on earth do they want to vote when men have been doing it with some success for years? Dorothy Tremaine's voice will fall on stony ground I can assure you.'

Her husband drew himself up and lifted his chin to look at the ceiling, deep in thought. 'Well, we must hope she never gets to meet Malcolm Darling. The man thinks equality is everything. We all know it will never work, particularly with the natives. It would give her new ideas. He is friend to that damned Bloomsbury woman, what's her name? The one with the strange ideas.' He looked to his wife for an answer but she didn't give it. 'Whatever it is, I must make a note to have a word with Colonel Tremaine about keeping his wife in order.'

Arnold's eyes went from one to the other as Field Marshall Dimmock and his wife spoke to each other as though he wasn't present and were sitting in their own drawing room instead of the Secunderabad Club where they were surrounded by people drinking, eating and playing cards. He knew he must also make a note to ensure Carrie didn't get too close to Dorothy Tremaine. He had a feeling his career trajectory would depend on it.

'Where have you been?' Arnold whispered to Carrie as she slid into the chair next to him at the long table. 'You're the last one to arrive. Are you doing your best to make an entrance, is that what it is? You've a long way to go before you do that.'

She turned and looked at him. 'What do you think I was doing, Arnold? Perhaps you haven't noticed.' Reluctantly, his eyes went to her cheek. 'Yes, that's right. I've been trying to hide the bruise and swelling on my face, the one you put there. I didn't think you'd be too pleased if I turned up at your Military Ball with a black and blue cheek. Would there not be questions asked? And what would I have said? Oh, don't worry, my husband punched me and sent me to the ground and left me unconscious. Is that what you wanted, Arnold?'

His face darkened and he turned away. 'Maybe you could keep your voice down and later engage in some polite conversation with people who matter this evening. It will do us some good.'

'No, Arnold. It will do *you* some good.'

The Secunderabad Club was a low building constructed over two floors punctuated by two small turrets either side. It was a beautiful structure fashioned out of white stone in the bungalow style, yet spread over many square feet. Inside was a restaurant, a bar, a games room for chess and other board games, and a ballroom where the Military Ball to welcome the newcomers to Secunderabad was being held. Outside, in the grounds was a tennis court, a croquet lawn and the beginnings of a swimming pool. Every whim was seemingly catered for.

The room was laid out with long tables running parallel with each of the four walls, in square formation and decked in pristine white tablecloths and sparkling silverware. Carrie eyed the three wine glasses at her place setting and wondered why anyone would need three glasses at one meal and the four sets of cutlery that seemed to all do the same job yet were of different sizes. In the centre of the tables were floral decorations in the red white and blue of the Union flag, and tall pillar candles on round mirrors to reflect the flames twinkling in the low light.

Her eyes wandered over the room and she was aware her primrose yellow dress, the one she'd worn to the drinks party at the bungalow was much too ordinary in comparison to the other woman of the company. They were dressed in their finest, dresses probably brought to India from the fashion houses of London, or even sent to Secunderabad by their servants back in England, and the men were handsome in their dress uniforms. Even Arnold's appearance seemed to improve in the wearing of such an impressive costume. She noticed it made the soldiers sit straighter with an upright air, and behave with more decorum than she'd witnessed on the ship from England where anything seemed to be acceptable.

She spotted Dorothy at the end of their table near the front, who saw her at the same time, and waved. Carrie returned her wave and smiled.

'Who are you waving at?' asked Arnold.

'Dorothy. She's over there with Colonel Tremaine, near the front, next to that fat woman in the old-fashioned dress and the red-faced man with the big white moustache.'

'Can you not speak like that? The woman Dorothy Tremaine is next to is Lady Mabel Dimmock, wife of Field Marshal Dimmock. She is the doyenne of our community and you would do well to offer her some respect. And you can forget Mrs. Tremaine. She's nothing compared to Lady Mabel and you would do well to remember it. They are the very people who will make a difference to us.'

'What would you have me do? Should I shuffle over on my knees and kiss her hand?'

Arnold closed his eyes with impatience, rubbing his forehead with a white gloved hand. 'No. I just want you to behave like a lady. I want you to speak with them on equal terms but with some deference. We are the new company here. They've been here for years, and Lady Mabel is at the top of the social pecking order.'

'Oh, is she. Well, she won't want to speak to me. In London I'd be clearing out her grates. She probably wouldn't even know I existed.'

'You're not in London. You're my wife and you will behave accordingly. It's why I married you, why I paid your mother a not insubstantial sum, and why I'm paying for you now. Everything you eat, wear, drink is paid for by me. I deserve some respect from you and I'm going to make sure I get it.' Carrie's eyes drifted back to Arnold as he spoke but then averted because she couldn't bear to watch his pallid face pulled into expressions of such disdain for her. She scanned the room while he spoke, his voice continuing to berate her in her left ear.

The first course was being served and she hoped it would be something she could stomach. Everything was so highly spiced, or made from things she had never come across in London and she had suffered for it. Gradually all the tables were served by Indian waiters dressed in white cotton suits and wearing huge colourful turbans. Their white gloved hands served soup with fingers of naan bread which

Carrie welcomed with delight. A plain vegetable soup without spicing was exactly what she needed and she ate with gusto, the first meal she had truly enjoyed since leaving London. Satisfied, she felt stronger and more able to get through an evening she had been dreading. Because of her hunger she had finished her meal quickly, so she took the time to observe the people around her. She recognised many of the soldiers from the ship and their wives. She noticed they sat in a group on the right-hand table, below where Dorothy and her husband were seated. It was clear they had imbibed freely of the wine on the table. The giggling and jokes had gone up a notch, and after a particularly loud guffaw by one of the men, Carrie glanced at Arnold. These were his men and she remembered Captain David Lawrence telling him that they needed to be taken down a peg or two when they met him at the station in Secunderabad.

'They're noisy.'

He glanced up from his soup. Carrie noticed some of the diced vegetable had settled on his moustache and her stomach rolled. 'They're letting their hair down. As long as they do the job they're paid to do when they should, they won't do any harm.'

'Will you join them later?'

'*We* will join them later, for drinks in the bar. I expect you to stand by me.'

After the company had finished dining everyone made their way through an elaborate archway into the bar while the waiters cleared the tables from the ballroom and made it ready for dancing. Carrie followed Arnold as he squeezed through the crowd of people standing around the bar. He spotted one of the soldiers in his unit and hailed him. Carrie smiled at the fellow and tried to look engaged, but the soldier completely ignored her and simply shook Arnold's hand, clapping him on the back like an old friend, turning away from her. Arnold didn't introduce them, and as Carrie knew no one standing near she remained quietly behind Arnold, not really knowing what was expected of her. Suddenly a hand on her arm pulled her to one side. It was Dorothy.

'Well, Carrie. What do you make of us all?' She looked around at the gathering jostling to get to the bar.

Carrie shrugged. 'I don't know, Dorothy. I don't know anyone.'

'Well, you know me, darling. Come and sit with Marcus and the others. Arnold's busy.' She threw a contemptuous look at Arnold's back which his friend saw but he didn't. The friend whispered something to Arnold who quickly turned, his expression and voice ingratiating. Carrie knew the toadying voice. It was the one he used when his superiors were close and wasn't a tone he ever used for her.

'Mrs Tremaine. You're looking extremely well tonight.' Arnold bowed towards her then straightened up, a smug smile playing on his lips.

'Am I? I'm surprised you noticed, Sergeant-Major Bateman. You seemed so…engrossed.' Arnold's smile slipped swiftly from his face and his cheeks coloured with embarrassment. 'I'm dragging your wife off for a while. I know you won't mind.'

Arnold shook his head. 'No, no, of course not. I want Carrie to enjoy herself.'

Dorothy raised an eyebrow then smiled at Carrie. 'Come on,' she said. 'I'm getting battered by the anti-suffrage brigade over here and I need some support.' She slipped her arm through Carrie's then thought of something and turned back to Arnold. 'By the way, Sergeant-Major Bateman.' Arnold's eyes widened and he nodded apprehensively, swiftly apprehending Dorothy was not about to be kind to him. 'Hasn't this dress had a previous outing?' She grabbed Carrie's hand and twirled her in a circle in front of him.

'Er, I…I…I'm not sure. Carrie sees to that sort of thing.' He swallowed hard and his eyes went from Dorothy to Carrie and back to Dorothy. 'I would have thought.'

Dorothy glared at him. 'Then may I suggest you think again. It just won't do, Sergeant-Major Bateman.'

Carrie was stunned. She knew Dorothy couldn't have known the danger she'd put her in because of how she'd spoken to Arnold, but she also knew he would take his humiliation out on her. Dorothy walked her across to a group of people sitting around a large rattan table in the bar. Field Marshal Dimmock and his wife were among them and Carrie sat nervously in a chair that had been pulled out for her next to Mabel Dimmock. She glanced over to where Arnold stood with his friends. He was staring at her with cold eyes and she shivered.

The discussion around the table had become heated. Lady Mabel was sitting on a seat made for two, a chaise where she could spread the skirts of her very old-fashioned, ornately decorated satin dress. The deep plum colour did not flatter the older woman's skin which had become dry and crêpey after spending too many hours in the Indian sun. The headdress she wore was also out-of-date; a tall cream feather attached to an ornate marcasite tiara fixed into her grey barrel curls. The feather fluttered dangerously each time Lady Mabel moved her head which she did regularly when she was trying to make a point to the rest of the company, which was most of the time.

'Of course,' she said in a very loud voice as Carrie took her seat. 'You young girls think life would be so much better for you if you were the same as your husbands. Do you not realise we do not need the vote nor would we ever use it if we were given permission. I hope if it was ever granted you girls would do the sensible thing and turn your backs on it. Why would you even consider it? We are fortunate to have husbands who have made their way in the world, and even more fortunate that they have chosen us to accompany them. Perhaps you should all think about what you would be doing with your lives or where you would be if it were not for their generosity.'

Carrie felt Dorothy bristle in the seat next to her. 'Lady Mabel, things are changing, and not just in Great Britain. Women are joining the suffrage movement all over the world. It has leapt great bounds in America in particular, and I can assure you they will not be distracted by a few arrests of their number. In London there are many woman of our class who are adamant we will receive the vote in this century, hopefully within the next decade. Why do you think it would be a bad thing? I'm afraid I don't understand.'

Lady Mabel's face darkened, and as she leaned forward to speak to Dorothy her satin skirt rustled. 'Because you are a woman, and women should know their place. I have always supported my husband. It is all I have thought about and concentrated on, and you should be doing the same, Mrs. Tremaine.'

'I'm sorry, Mabel, but your ideas are very out-dated. You are from a different generation whose only aim was to please a man. The women of our generation are very different. We want to have power over our own lives, to make our own decisions and to be part of the political landscape of our country. Many woman work at the same time as raising their families and they, indisputably, have a right to equality when they are not only raising the next generation but are also putting food on the table. Surely you can see that.'

An embarrassed hush settled over the company and Carrie looked from one to the other wishing she wasn't sitting between them. She glanced up to find Arnold frowning at her and she looked down at her hands in her lap. She turned her face to her right where Dorothy was sitting and saw Marcus slip his fingers around Dorothy's hand and squeeze it and she smiled to herself. Marcus Tremaine was a modern man who loved and respected his wife and listened to her views, possibly the only one who existed in Secunderabad, perhaps the whole of India. Her thoughts went to Arthur and Florrie and she giggled. Florrie didn't need suffrage to get what she wanted. The only one who suffered was Arthur.

'And what are you smirking at, Mrs. Bateman?'

Carrie looked up at Mabel Dimmock with wide eyes and met her intrusive gaze. 'Me?'

'Yes, you, dear. You were smirking at something. I suppose you agree with Dorothy.'

Carrie swallow and glanced at Dorothy who raised her eyebrows. 'I'm…not sure I know enough about it to comment, Lady Mabel. I've seen the marches in London but…well, I didn't think they were marching for my benefit.'

'Quite right too. Of course they weren't marching for your benefit. I can see you are a girl with, well, let's say basic sensibilities, not used to a certain society. I implore you to stay that way and not listen to Mrs. Tremaine's scurrilous ideas. They will only cause harm.' Carrie stared at her and said nothing, but it seemed Lady Mabel wasn't finished with her. 'And what do you intend to do with your time here, Mrs. Bateman?'

As Carrie was about to answer, Arnold appeared and stood behind her which made her nervous. Without his presence, Carrie felt that she could hold her own, but she knew he was waiting for her to say something acceptable. She wasn't sure how to answer Lady Mabel, but then remembered Gita's suggestion. Smiling, she said, 'I'm going to help my housekeeper organise her daughter's wedding.'

There was a collective gasp from the ten or so guests gathered around their table, then giggling from two of the soldier's wives. Carrie heard Arnold utter an expletive under his breath and Lady Mabel's complexion turned to stone. 'You're going to do what?'

Carrie inhaled a breath and felt Dorothy place a light hand on her forearm. 'I…thought…I might help.'

'A member of your husband's staff?' Carrie nodded. 'Why on earth would you do that?'

'Because she asked me.'

Lady Mabel sat back in her chair and glanced at her husband who shook his head. The other girls continued to giggle until Dorothy turned on them. 'Shut up, can't you?'

'I suppose this is your influence, Mrs. Tremaine,' said Mabel. 'The poor girl is unsound. Surely you know how wrong this would be?'

'Lady Mabel.' Carrie's small voice interrupted her and Lady Mabel turned her glare on her. 'Lady Mabel, it has nothing to do with Dorothy. Gita, our housekeeper asked if I would like to help. I agreed because I can't see why I shouldn't. She has helped me so why can I not return it.'

'Why should you not return it? I would have thought it was obvious. They are staff, my dear, and they are natives. The Indians serve us. We are the ruling class. Your housekeeper is your servant. She is paid…as a servant. It is not your place to help her. Goodness knows what would happen if this was permitted. It would unbalance everything we have come to know in India. The servants are in our homes to serve. You should dismiss your housekeeper. She should not be asking for your help.' She glanced up at Arnold. 'I'm surprised at you Sergeant Major Bateman, allowing your wife such freedoms with your staff.'

Carrie heard Arnold blustering behind her. 'I did not know, Lady Mabel, but of course, it will not happen.'

'I should think not. Just think what infectious diseases you may incur by mixing so closely with the natives.' She leant forward again, the feather in her headdress swaying dangerously as she warmed to her subject. 'They are not like us, my dear. They do not have the same habits, the same sensibilities. The men are…are rampant, and free with their susceptibilities. They do not have the intelligence or capabilities to govern themselves or to protect the empire which is precisely why you and your husband are here. You do not need to befriend your servants. There are plenty here within our own social class for you to befriend and I suggest you do just that, and *we'll* do our best to forget your faux pas.'

Carrie stared at her for moment than glanced around at the others sitting at the table. The girls were pressing their lips together; one had her gloved hand in front of her face to conceal her amusement. Dorothy squeezed Carrie's arm.

'Don't worry, darling,' she said quietly. 'It'll come to nothing.'

Carrie turned towards her, her eyes stinging with tears. 'What have I done? I don't understand.'

'I know, Carrie. I know.'

Arnold strode ahead of her down the long, tree-lined driveway leading away from the Secunderabad Club. He had waited until everyone had had enough to drink not to notice their absence, then had put his hand under her elbow and pulled her from her seat.

'We should go.'

Carrie glanced at the huge wooden clock above the staircase in the ballroom. 'But it's only ten thirty, Arnold. I would have thought you would have wanted to stay later.'

'I am staying later. You're leaving. I've organised a *dak-garry* to take you back to Trimulgherry where you can do no further damage.'

'A what?'

'A cart, damn it.'

'What if I don't want to go? Dorothy said she'll find me later. She'll wonder where I am.'

He shook his head. 'What you want is of no consequence. You've embarrassed me tonight, in front of my men and my commanding officers and their wives. I'll be a laughingstock. What were you thinking?'

'I still don't know what I've done that's so terrible.'

'Ask your friend Dorothy Tremaine. She'll tell you.'

At the end of the drive a cart waited. Carrie recognised the driver as Gita's husband, Radhav which gave her some relief.

Carrie ran to keep up with Arnold. 'You won't dismiss Gita will you? It's not her fault. She was just trying to help.'

Arnold stopped in his tracks and turned to look at her, pushing his hands into his pockets. 'Dismiss Gita?' He smirked and laughed with sarcasm. 'Why would I dismiss *her*? It's you I should get rid of. If I'd known what a liability you were…' He turned and pointed to the cart. 'There's your transport. Try not to get into any more trouble.'

'Can you take me to Hussain Sagar, Radhav?'

He frowned, then turned quickly to glance at Carrie. 'The lake, memsahib? The master said you must go to the mofussil, the Trimulgherry station. The lake…it is far.'

'I'll be alright. It's near James Street, isn't it? I can find some transport to take me back to the station. I'd like to walk near water, like I used to when I lived in London. St. Katherine Dock was just a walk away from where I lived. I went there to get away from things, like I want to now.'

'But, memsahib, the sahib will be very angry. He might beat us if you are not safe. Please memsahib, let me take you to the station. I will take you in the daytime. It is night and it is dangerous. Gita said I am to take care of you. She will be very angry too.'

Carrie sighed, realising her request of Radhav was too great. She was already concerned that Arnold would take her mistake at the Military Ball in front of Lady Mabel out on Gita, and if Radhav went against him too she wouldn't put it past Arnold to dismiss them both. She knew first-hand what that would do to them.

'No, no, of course. You must take me to Trimulgherry. I want to see my son. Take me back, Radhav.'

Radhav sighed with relief. 'Thank you, memsahib. Thank you.'

Gita was waiting on the steps to the bungalow.

'You are home early, memsahib. Carrie.'

Carrie dismounted from the cart and nodded. 'Yes, Gita. I'm back. How's John?'

'Sleeping soundly. He has not woken. Not once.'

Carrie smiled a humourless smile. 'No, well, he's a good boy.' She ran lightly up the three steps to the veranda, went into the sitting room and began to pace, her fingers linked tightly in front of her.

'Carrie?' Gita said in almost a whisper. 'Are you tired?'

Carrie shook her head. 'No, Gita, I'm not tired, but I need to tell you something.' She proceeded to tell Gita what had happened at the Secunderabad Club. Gita bowed her head as she spoke then turned away, a hand rubbing her forehead. When she turned back Carrie could see she looked exhausted.

'I'm so sorry, Madam,' she said. 'I am to blame.'

'You are not to blame. You were trying to help me, and clearly I didn't understand. I shouldn't have said anything, I just couldn't think of anything else to say. They all know each other. They all know what to talk about, but they talk about the same things all the time, the weather, the last badminton match, whatever that is. I suppose I could have spoken about John but Arnold wouldn't have been pleased.' She threw herself into a chair. 'Oh, I don't know. I keep getting things wrong.'

'Carrie, you must be yourself. Perhaps…perhaps you should do the things you want to do. Without the sahib's permission.'

Carrie glanced up at her and smiled. 'You think I should. You think I should go against his wishes?'

Gita knelt in front of Carrie and reached for her hand, leaning her head to one side. 'Not…go against his wishes, but, maybe to make up your own mind. Like Mrs. Tremaine.'

'You know Dorothy?'

Gita nodded. 'When she was a child. She came here with her parents to visit Lady Mabel Dimmock, but Dimmock was not her name then. She had not yet married the Field Marshall.'

Carrie frowned. 'So what was she doing here?'

'Like many of the young women who come to India, Carrie. To find a husband.'

Carrie's eyes widened. 'She was part of the fishing fleet.'

'Yes, that is what I've heard them called.'

Carrie began to laugh. She stood and began dancing around the sitting room still laughing. 'I'm so happy. It's really daft, but I'm so happy. That one little thing has changed everything. She's so…toffee-nosed, so…bloody snotty. She looks at me like I'm a piece of rotting fish under her big, ugly nose.' She grabbed Gita's hands, pulling her from the floor. 'Thank you, Gita. Thank you for being such a good friend.' She put her arm around the sparrow-like shoulders of the slender Indian woman. 'I'll never let anything happen to you, or your husband and daughter. Do you understand? While I am here you'll always have a job, I promise. I would fight Arnold for it if I had to. For some reason I don't feel scared anymore. And you're right, I need to make up my own mind and do the things I want to do. With or without Arnold's permission. This is the new beginning. Tomorrow is the day I take control of my own life.'

Chapter 19

Carrie woke with a headache. Her skin was clammy and even though it was the early hours it was even hotter than usual. She lay staring out into the darkness of the bedroom, the shapes of the sparse furniture making dark smudges against the walls. A rumble of thunder from far off echoed the mugginess of the bungalow. There was a storm approaching and she thought about what she'd heard of the monsoon season. It was late July and Gita and Aashi had talked about the great rains, the *"maanasoon"*. They said that Secunderabad and Hyderabad did not fare as badly as Bombay or Kerala where the rains washed away the mud streets and disrupted the markets and pulled down the roofs of some of the shanty buildings. Even the larger buildings in Bombay were not left unscathed. It changed the lives of people living in those places and yet the natives were used to it, some even looked forward to it because it broke up the parched air and dampened down the constant dust. As soon as the first large drops of rain fell, children ran out into the street, their arms aloft as if to greet the great rains, and splashed about in the water, having fun and crying out with joy as if it was a holiday.

She found the distant rumble almost comforting. It reminded her of when she was child playing in the streets of Whitechapel in the hot summer months when suddenly the skies would grow darker and darker and a heavy rain would fall accompanied by great rumbles of thunder and flashes of lightening. She would run into Florrie giggling with a delicious fear, and Florrie would yank the metal hair slides out of hair, worried that her daughter would be struck by lightning. Carrie often wondered that she had any hair left, she would pull so hard, but she was sure it was done out of love and misplaced superstition. Florrie seemed to live her whole life by superstition and tradition.

A flare from a fork of lightning lit up the room and she heard John stir in the other room. Carrie got out of bed and went into his room, pushing the net aside from the cot, and ran her hand across his dark hair which was damp with sweat.

'Oh, John,' she whispered. She took a muslin from a drawer and gently wiped his face, then his arms and legs, dabbing away the moisture that had settled in droplets on his skin. He stirred and opened his eyes, staring into the darkness without recognition. His eyelashes fluttered and closed again and she smiled her relief, then opened the door to the bedroom and went out into the corridor. It was cooler out there and she took a deep breath, but her throat was parched with the dryness in the air so went into the kitchen for water. Gita had left a jug on the stone floor in the kitchen covered with a cloth. She poured some water from the jug into a cup and as she turned was startled when she saw Arnold sitting at the kitchen table, a bottle of whiskey and a glass by his hand. In the darkness she hadn't noticed he wasn't beside her in their bed.

'Arnold. You scared me.'

'Did I?'

'What are you doing out here?'

'I couldn't sleep.' He looked up at her. 'There's a storm coming. It'll probably wake the boy.'

She bristled. Could he still not bring himself to say her son's name? 'The boy? You mean John.' He nodded and she gritted her teeth. 'And you're drinking whiskey, at this time. It must be, what,' she glanced at the kitchen clock, 'three o'clock in the morning? Why are you drinking alcohol at this time of the morning?'

He slugged the remainder of the whiskey down his throat and refilled his glass. 'Why do you ask so many questions? It's none of your business what I do.'

She sighed and made to leave the kitchen but he stopped her. 'Wait, for God's sake. Wait. You've got to try harder. You've got to make more of an impression. Some of the other women have befriended Lady Mabel and they've been invited to a charity open day they're holding to raise money to send food parcels to the front in France. Unfortunately, because of your performance the other night at the Secunderabad Club we haven't been invited.' He slammed the glass down on the table spilling some of the contents onto his hand and across the table where it dribbled onto the floor. 'It just won't do, Carrie. You must make more of an effort. We're getting left behind.'

'I don't know what you're talking about. My performance? All I said was that Gita had invited me to help her with Aashi's wedding. It sounds like a wonderful thing to do, and I'm one of the best people to do it with my experience at Nightingale Lane, yet it seems I said the wrong thing and I don't understand why.'

'Exactly. You don't understand why. That's the problem with you, you're not learning anything. You're not accepting what we have to do here to get on.'

'But I don't want to get on. What I want is to go home where I know everyone and everyone is like me. These people aren't my people, Arnold, and they're not your people either, but you won't admit it. Even Dorothy said you're determined to haul yourself up in society by your bootstraps.' Arnold blanched and his mouth was a straight line. 'And she's right isn't she? Where we come from isn't good enough for you anymore. You're trying to be something you're not.'

He narrowed his eyes at her and bared his teeth. 'And how would you know what I am...what I'm capable of? And you can tell high and mighty Dorothy Tremaine to mind her own fucking business. It's got nothing to do with her either. It's alright for people like her, they were born into it, the money and the position. I have to work harder for it, and you...,' he flung his arm out and pointed at her, 'you won't stop me.'

Carrie stared at him for a moment, then realising Arnold was drunk and beyond reason went into John's bedroom and closed the door. She gathered some blankets from a chest in the corner and made a bed on the floor next to his cot. A huge clap of thunder shook her and took her breath away. It was so violent it sounded as though it was right overhead. The rain began to fall in rods, striking the roof of the bungalow like the beat of an out of time drum. A wind got up and rattled the shutters and John began to fidget in his sleep, the clamminess and the unfamiliar noise of the thunder and lightning gradually waking him. Carrie took him to her breast and fed him. The comfort this gave him sent him back into a restless sleep and she was glad she had continued to feed him herself without Arnold's knowledge. He had told her a wet-nurse had been appointed to feed him but unknown to Arnold, Carrie had sent her away telling her there had been a mistake and she wasn't needed. Gita had nodded her approval and smiled warmly at Carrie when the young woman retraced her steps off the veranda. Carrie had worried then, that when Arnold found out he would be angry, but he was so bound up in his military duties and his quest to infiltrate himself into the upper echelons of the society of the station he hadn't noticed, and Carrie had breathed a sigh of relief, choosing to feed John in isolation, her absence from Arnold a welcome respite for her.

The next morning the sun rose again and quickly dried up the puddles that had been left by the downpour.

'Just a shower,' said Gita. 'Everything will be dry again in minutes. The sun will be fierce. Wear your topi if you go out, Carrie, and make sure John is in the shade. The hot sun follows a storm. It is just the way it is.'

'I've had another letter from Pearl. I'm going to read it first, then perhaps walk down to the pond in Trimulgherry. Would you like to come, Gita?'

'I...I would like it very much, Madam. Carrie. Yes, thank you. Read your letter first. I will make up a basket to take with us. We can shelter under the trees and you can eat.'

'And you, Gita. You will need to eat too.' Gita nodded, then lowered her face and smiled.

'We're going.' Arnold came into the kitchen and slammed his cap down on the table in triumph, then went across to the cabinet and poured whiskey into a glass.

Carrie looked up from the letter she'd received from Pearl, her eyes glistening with tears. 'Going where?'

Arnold didn't notice her distress and walked around the room, expansive in his speech, deliriously happy. 'To the charity open day. We've been invited, well, *I've* been invited, but obviously you will accompany me.'

Carrie nodded. 'Right.'

'Well come on, woman. Show some enthusiasm.'

'William has been killed...in France.'

Arnold inhaled and nodded, then bowed his head. 'I'm sorry to hear that.'

'Pearl is devastated. I wish I could be with her. I should be with her.'

'There's nothing you can do. Many men have been killed. She will have to make another life.'

'They were going to be married. They were engaged and she was planning their wedding. She wanted me to be her bridesmaid. She was so excited, so looking forward to her wedding day and being with William for the rest of her life. She thought they would have a lovely life together, him being a milkman an' all, she knew he'd never be out of a job. They planned to have babies. She loved him, really loved him, and he loved her.' Tears rolled unchecked down Carrie's cheeks and Arnold glanced at her, looking uncomfortable. 'She was going to have peonies.'

'Crying won't help.'

'I know that, Arnold, but I miss her so much.' She stared up at him, her face wet with tears as she pleaded with him. 'Could I go home, just for a while, so I can be with her? She needs me, Arnold.'

He frowned. 'Go home? This is your home and your place is beside me. I'm not without sympathy for her, but you're my wife and you must stay and help me run our household.' His eyes took on a hard look. 'Here's some money.' He fished a wad of notes from his pocket and peeled some off the top. 'Take Gita into Secunderabad, to James Street, and buy a dress. I think they're called tea dresses, for sunny afternoons and high society teas. I want you to look the part. Gita will know even if you don't, and make sure it reaches your ankles, not like that monstrosity Dorothy Tremaine wore to our drinks party. Marcus Tremaine must have been quaking with embarrassment. I mean, you could actually see the beginning of her calves. And buy a hat with flowers on it to match the dress, and shoes in the same colour with buttons. There's enough money there, but make sure you bring me the change. You must look like everyone else if you're to fit in.' Carrie stared at the money in his hand. 'Well, take it.'

'When am I to go?'

'You can go this afternoon. It'll probably be busy it being a Saturday but the open day is tomorrow so you need to get something.'

'How should we get there?'

'I've organised a motor vehicle.' Carrie looked at him in surprise. 'Don't get used to it. This is important to me and we've got to put right their impression of us.'

'Which is?'

'I wouldn't ask that question if I were you.'

James Street was busy. Carrie was utterly devastated at Pearl's news about losing William but the sounds, smells and sights of the crowded street lifted her spirits and she was filled with a new determination to return to her birthplace. This was the life she was used to, the excited chatter as people walked by, carts and vehicles on the road, and children running in and out of the crowd. The paths were populated by soldiers, some with their wives on their arms, and young women dressed in beautiful pastel gauzy dresses that fluttered in the warm breeze making them look like skittish birds of paradise. The overall atmosphere was one of excitement and the shops were very busy.

Carrie was fascinated by the jewellery shops where the windows were full of gold and silver necklaces and rings adorned with *Basra* or rice pearls. There were bangles studded with coloured precious stones and bracelets made of stained glass, items that Carrie had never in her life seen before, and she felt as attracted to their sparkle and shine as the shoppers around her. The saree shops were full to bursting with girls purchasing lengths of exquisite fabric to be made into Western designs by a *durzi* or *Kuttedi*, a tailor or seamstress. There were shops selling handicrafts and paintings, silverware and pieces of unusual furniture. There was even a large open fronted store selling automobiles. Every need was catered for, and Carrie was surprised at how different it was from Bombay, but as she looked around her she noticed it wasn't the natives of India lavishly spending money. It was the Europeans keeping the shops open, the military men and their wives, the men and women of the Indian Civil Service, and the fishing fleet who were forever adorning themselves in order to catch a husband. James Street was for the Raj.

Trimulgherry was a world away from Whitechapel, and Carrie acknowledged she had struggled to become part of it. As she and Gita walked along the street she felt her face pull into a smile, something she hadn't done for what seemed like forever.

'Do you come here, Gita,' she asked the woman who moved silently beside her.

'No. This place is not for me. I buy from the locals in Trimulgherry. The *box-wallahs*. I think you know them, Madam. You have seen them. They bring things to the house. All kinds of things. I know them and they know me. We can talk of price. I can get the best price. This place is for people with money.' She looked up at Carrie and smiled. 'Like you today, Madam.'

'You know, Gita, I feel as though I'm being bought by Arnold. He thinks money solves every problem.'

'Do you believe that, Carrie?'

'No. No, I don't. I know from bitter experience money doesn't come into it. Life is about people, about what they do rather than what they say. I'm afraid I learnt that the hard way.'

'Yes, Madam. I agree. We have had so little money in our family, yet Radhav and I have raised four boys and two girls. We have always had just enough, just enough to eat, just enough money to see us through, just enough work.'

'And will you keep working, Gita? When will you stop? You can't work for ever. The work you do, I know how hard it is. I used to work in a big house before I came here. I was a maid. It can be exhausting, and I don't mean to rude to you, Gita,' she smiled, 'I'm a lot younger than you.'

Gita stared at her and shook her head in astonishment. 'No, memsahib. You could not have been a maid. You could not have been like me.'

Carrie turned to her and raised her eyebrows. 'Gita, I feel more at home with you and Aashi because I know hardship, I know difficulty. I'm not like Dorothy Tremaine who for some reason has taken me under her wing. Of course, I'm very glad of it. Without her by my side at the social events I would be completely lost.'

'And your friend?'

Carrie lowered her chin and swallowed. 'You mean Pearl?' Gita nodded. 'Oh, Gita, I can't tell you how sad I am, but what can I do. When we arrived at the railway station in Secunderabad I promised myself and John that one day I would get back on that train and go back to England. It's all I want, to go back to everything and everyone I know. This…this is all wrong. This is not how my life was meant to be. I shouldn't be here. I should be in London, in Whitechapel with Pearl, comforting her, holding her tight and promising her I won't leave her side. I know I can't bring William back but…I could have cared for her.' Gita nodded. 'All I can do is write to her. The letter will take weeks to get to her and be of no use whatsoever. Arnold has refused to let me go to her.'

'I'm sorry, Madam. So sorry, Carrie.'

They stopped outside a shop selling fine fabric and dresses and looked through the window into the darkness inside.

'What do you think, Gita?'

'We should go into the shop.'

Carrie looked through the dresses hanging on rails and frowned. 'They're a bit old-fashioned,' she whispered. 'These dresses are the sort my mum would wear. I don't think they're right for me.' She glanced up and saw the shop owner watching her, and she smiled. 'Do you have anything for the younger woman?'

He came towards her, a small man with an abundance of black hair and piercing eyes, rubbing his hands together. 'This range is for the beautiful young English woman, Madam, like you. They have been sent from London.'

Carrie looked at Gita and pulled a face. 'Yeah, when?' she said under her breath. 'In the last century?'

Gita put her hand over her mouth and giggled. 'Carrie. He will hear you.'

'Good. These are awful. What am I going to do?'

They left the dress shop with the proprietor following closely behind, wringing his hands and almost begging them to stay in the shop. They walked quickly to get away from him, running through the crowd, doing their best to dodge the other shoppers. Carrie was in front and as she turned to see where Gita was, she bumped into someone. She turned to see a man sprawled on the ground, his face a mixture of recognition and surprise.

David Lawrence, Arnold's Captain got to his feet and brushed himself off as Carrie apologised over and over again.

'Captain Lawrence. Oh, my goodness. I'm so sorry, sir. Are you alright? Are you hurt?'

He straightened up and grinned at her. 'You're stronger than you look, Mrs. Bateman.'

'I'm so sorry, sir. I…we were trying to escape from a shopkeeper who wanted me to buy one of his horrible dresses. I'm surprised he hasn't chased us down the street.'

'Yes, some of them can be very persuasive in trying to get us to part with our money. Out clothes shopping, are you?'

She nodded. 'Yes, for tomorrow. For the open day.'

'It's a good cause. Mabel Dimmock knows how to encourage people. She could give some of these shopkeepers a run for their money, that's for sure.'

He looked at her and smiled and Carrie felt her stomach turn over. He was very good-looking; dark-haired with hazel eyes that roamed her face. The fierce sun in India had turned his skin olive brown and she felt her breath falter, cursing the blush she knew was creeping up her neck and onto her face.

'Well, um, I hope you're alright.'

'Yes. Yes, I'm fine.' She nodded. 'That's good.' She glanced at Gita who lowered her eyes.

'If you're looking for dresses I've heard the best one on James Street is Zaina's. It's near the monument at the far end, you know, the clock tower? I think it's where the other ladies go.'

She laughed. 'Thank you, sir. I'll go now. It can't be any worse than what we've just seen.'

He frowned slightly and momentarily put his hand on her arm. She felt her skin tingle under his touch. 'David, please. Not sir. My name is David.'

'Thank you, David. And I'm Carrie.'

'Yes, I know. Caroline Violet Elizabeth, if I'm not mistaken.'

Her mouth dropped open. 'How did you…'

'Dorothy. She said it was a beautiful name…and I agree.'

Carrie felt herself go even redder. 'Oh, well, thank you…David. It was my grandmother's name.'

He bowed slightly. 'You wear it very well.'

'Will…will you be at the open day tomorrow?' she asked, trying to appear as though it didn't really matter that he'd just said her name was beautiful.

'I hope so. I've been asked to lead an expedition into the hills but I'm thinking it'll begin on Monday rather than on our Holy Day, even though most of those at Trimulgherry are in and out of church as soon as they possibly can be without raising eyebrows. I'm sure they only go because they're worried if they don't they'll be thought of as heathen. I pity Father Clarke. His congregation shrinks by the week. He must wonder why he's here.'

'Do you go? To church I mean.'

'Yes, although I'm not particularly religious, and after some of the sights I had to confront in France I do wonder about our all-seeing God, but, yes, I go, if only to set a good example.' Carrie nodded and smiled and he lifted his cap to her. 'I must be on my way, Carrie. Good luck with your shopping expedition. Do try Zaina's. I'm sure they'll be able to help you there. I'll see you at the open day hopefully.'

She smiled, wondering if he meant he would hopefully be there, or he would hopefully see her. 'Goodbye, David.' She watched him walk away. He was tall, with broad shoulders and a confident gait, and as he made his way towards his car, his hands casually pushed into his pockets, she saw some of the women glance at him appreciatively then at each other, and raise their eyebrows as he passed. That he was an attractive man there was no doubt and she thought about how she'd felt when he spoke to her. She remembered those feelings. They were the ones she'd had when she'd spent time with Johan and she shivered.

'Are you alright, Carrie?' Gita asked her.

Carrie smiled. 'Yes, yes, come on, Gita. Let's get this over and done with. We'll go to Zaina's as David suggested, then we'll have coffee in that little restaurant over there.'

Gita visibly blanched. 'No, Carrie. Not a restaurant. I would not be allowed.'

Carrie stared at her in astonishment. 'Of course you're allowed. We're together. Our money is as good as anyone else's.' Gita still looked doubtful and Carrie put her arm around her shoulders. 'If it makes you feel better we'll sit at one of the tables outside.'

'Yes, yes it would, Madam.'

'Then it's decided.'

Carrie stepped over the threshold of Zaina's and gasped. The dresses were a world away from what she'd previously seen and she felt excited. Gita's face had lit up too and they both wasted no time in looking through the dresses on the rails.

'What d'you think, Gita? Which colour should I go for?'

After a few minutes searching Gita pulled out a dress and held it up. It was pale blue, with tiny white daisies all over the fabric. The sleeves were puffed and decorated around the trim which ended at the elbow with a small bow. The waist was cinched in to give a lovely shape and the skirt billowed beautifully, the perfect tea dress. 'I love this one. It is very beautiful. The colour will look very well on you.'

Carrie touched the soft fabric of the dress and imagined herself wearing it. It was everything Arnold had said it should be, but it was also very stylish and rather feminine. In her mind's eye she saw herself wearing the dress with matching pale blue shoes and bag, walking into the charity open day on David Lawrence's arm. Her heart fluttered and she inhaled a steadying breath. There was something about him that attracted her. It wasn't just the way he looked, but rather he had an air about of him of tenderness, perhaps even kindness, and in a man who had been so brave in the face of battle, those gentle attributes were very appealing.

'Yes, Gita. I think that might be the one. Well done. You're very clever.' She took the dress from Gita and grinned. 'Shall I try it on?'

Gita nodded. 'Yes, Madam, and I will find some shoes and a bag. I know what to look for.'

Carrie put a hand on her arm. 'I know you do, Gita. What would I do without you?'

Gita look pleased, then hurried off to the racks and racks of shoes and shelves of bags. An attractive Indian woman came out of a small office. She was dressed in a bright orange sari edged with gold. Every finger on her hands sported a gold ring and her ears were pierced and decorated with long gold earrings. When she saw Gita looking at the shoes she frowned and looked cross.

'What are you doing?' she asked Gita who turned quickly looking guilty.

Carrie came out of the dressing room. 'Gita is with me,' she said. 'She's helping me choose an outfit.'

Her demeanour changed instantly. 'Oh, madam. I'm sorry. I didn't realise you were together.' She clapped her hands and a girl came out of the office holding a tray with a glass of iced tea and some tiny spiced crackers. 'Please accept this while you look. It's very hot today and this is perfect for cooling.'

Carrie nodded her thanks. 'I'm sure Gita would appreciate some too. It looks delicious.'

The woman stared at Carrie and the girl frowned. 'Miss Zaina?'

'Er, yes, of course,' Zaina said. She turned to the girl. 'Another glass please, Varsha.' Gita was frozen to the spot, aware that Zaina was uncomfortable with her being offered refreshment. She was, after all, a servant, but this fact didn't seem to bother Carrie. 'Have you found something you like, madam?'

'Gita found this beautiful dress for me to try on.' She indicated the pale blue dress hanging on the curtain rail. 'And she's looking for some shoes to match, oh, and a bag. She has a very good eye for colour.'

Zaina eyed Gita with disdain and ignored Carrie's praise. 'Would you like me to find some shoes for you, Madam.'

Carrie looked at her in surprise. 'I think Gita is doing very well. Are you Zaina?'

'Yes, madam. And this is my shop.'

Carrie smiled. 'I can see why it's so popular. Your clothes are beautiful.'

Zaina glowed. 'Thank you. I do my best. Unfortunately it won't be for very much longer.'

'Oh, that's a shame. Why's that?'

'I came here to set up business ten years ago because I knew it would be a good place. We have many Europeans here now, the military, the Indian Civil Service, and the judiciary. Their wives all buy from me and there always seems to be something going on, a ball, a dinner party, official meetings they must attend. I have seen it all, madam, but my parents in Bombay are old. My mother is particularly frail and I must go to them. My father is unable to look after her by himself. It is my duty to take care of them.'

'I see. What about the shop? Who will look after it?'

'The shop will close, madam. It will be the end of Zaina's.'

An hour later, Carrie and Gita left the shop carrying three bags in Zaina's signature colours of orange and gold. In the largest was the pale blue dress with daisies and the matching clutch bag, the smallest held the shoes, and in the middle-sized bag was a straw hat, trimmed with cornflowers and daisies, the perfect accompaniment to round off the outfit perfect for a summer's day.

'Are you happy, Carrie?' asked Gita.

'I think what we've chosen is perfect. Thank you for your help, Gita. It's so lovely to have a companion. I don't feel lonely anymore. I wish you could come with me tomorrow.'

Gita threw her head back and laughed. 'That would never be allowed.'

'No, and I'm sorry. It's so silly all this dividing people up into boxes. You have been more of a friend to me than anyone since I left London.'

Gita smiled sadly. 'But, Madam. The difference is you have been willing to accept the friendship offered by an Indian woman. No one else would.'

Carrie linked her arm through Gita's. 'Then it's their loss. They don't know what they're missing.'

Chapter 20

Carrie waved to Gita as she ran up the steps at the front of the bungalow, then stopped when she realised the shutters had been closed. 'I know I opened them,' she said under her breath as she tried the veranda door which was also closed. As she pushed the door rattled slightly which meant it had probably been locked from the outside.

Gita began to retrace her steps when she realised Carrie had been locked out of the bungalow, and she joined her on the veranda.

'Carrie,' she said, sotto voce, her brow knitted with doubt. 'Do you not always open your shutters, Madam?' she asked. 'It's the only way to allow the early morning air to refresh your rooms. It will be very stuffy in the house.'

'Yes, Gita, you know I do. I thought Arnold was working on his papers at home today.' She shook her head. 'Perhaps I got it wrong. Maybe it's tomorrow.'

'And Amrita? Where is she?' Gita asked Carrie as she fumbled in her pocket for the bungalow key.

'She has taken John to her mother's house in Bowenpally. Her mother has had another baby and she thought it would be nice for John to spend time there with the other children. She has three small ones, the new baby and two more under five.'

Gita nodded. 'Yes, it is good for him to mix with other children.' She put her hand on Carrie's arm. 'There will be more children in your society soon, Carrie. John will have many friends.'

'I'm not sure, Gita. There doesn't seem to be much sign of anyone wanting to begin a family here. They're all having too much of a good time. Anyway, thank goodness you were here. I left my key inside. I didn't think I'd need it.'

Gita smiled. 'Today was very good, yes?'

Carrie returned her smile warmly. 'Today was very good.'

She let herself into the bungalow. The screen had also been locked, the first time it had ever been because it was not needed before, and inside the air was fuggy with cigarette smoke and the sourness of alcohol. There was hardly any light coming through the slats in the shutters, giving the room a gloomy feel. Carrie left her carrier bags from Zaina's on the sofa and narrowed her eyes to focus. On the desk were Arnold's papers, his pen thrown carelessly on the floor, the ink spilling from the nib and staining the rush matting. She bent to pick it up and used a wad of blotting paper to soak up the wayward ink. So he had been working here today, she thought. I was right after all.

She removed her topi and laid it next to the bags, shaking out her hair from the pins that had anchored it into a tight chignon, then decided to change her clothes. It was mid-afternoon, not quite time for Gita to return to prepare dinner and it seemed hotter than ever. She opened the shutters then went into the corridor which separated the living quarters from the bedrooms, glancing into John's bedroom and smiling indulgently at the brightly coloured soft toys in his cot that Gita had brought him from her house, the ones she had given her own children. She turned towards her bedroom, startled to see the door was also shut. They usually left all the doors open so that any cool air would freshen the rooms. She shook her head thinking she must have closed it before she left. Placing her fingers on the handle, she pushed down and opened the door.

Chapter 21

'The thing is, darling, they want to shut India out.' Dorothy sipped her iced tea then indicated to her maid to refill her glass. 'Another, Carrie?' Carrie shook her head and Dorothy continued her diatribe. 'They're afraid of losing face in front of each other. We…the woman of the raj are making it worse. Some of us have accepted this is not our country; that we are as much guests here as anything else, even though some people here would have us think differently, and have embraced a different way of life, a different culture. We were brought here to do a job. But others, like Mabel Dimmock, and those stupid girls who came to India on the ship with us feel they are in some way better than the natives of India. The men just get on with it because they have to, but it's the Mabel Dimmocks amongst us who perpetuate that we're somehow a higher race, a better breed, and should be treated with deference.'

'Even in their own country? It seems so wrong.'

'Yes, even in their own country. So don't be drawn into it. Find your comforts where you can, Carrie. If you have found friendship with Gita and her family then so be it.'

'I don't know how I would manage without her…and you of course, Dorothy. I want to help her with her daughter's wedding. It would be so wonderful to do something different, and would give me a purpose. It's not like I don't have any experience. I try to spend as much time with John as I can, but Amrita, the ayah is so good with him and he has really taken to her. She and her family are so kind. Her mother sends little treats back for John and Amrita is like his big sister. I trust her much more than I thought I would.'

'And Arnold?'

Carrie half closed her eyes and looked down. Nausea rushed into her throat and she swallowed hard not wanting to embarrass herself in front of Dorothy. Arnold had punched her in the face once, knocking her to the ground and rendering her unconscious, and had bullied her relentlessly since she had met him, but the burden she now carried was far worse than any of the pain she had suffered, or her constant fear of him.

'I have discovered things about him, Dorothy. Things I don't understand.'

Dorothy frowned and waved her maid away into the kitchen. 'What things?'

Carrie shook her head. 'I can't tell you,' she whispered. 'Anyway, I need to go back to my bungalow. It'll be time for dinner soon and he'll be wondering where I am. And I'm desperate to see John.'

Dorothy put a hand on her arm and her eyes widened. 'Why can't you tell me? What could be so terrible, Carrie?' She tried a smile but when Carrie didn't return it, it fell from her face. 'Is that why you came here this afternoon? To talk to me? Then you must, Carrie, if something is worrying you, you mustn't keep it to yourself. It must be bad if you feel you can't say it.'

'I just needed to get away for a while.'

She stared at Carrie and her face hardened. 'Is it something to do with when you lay together? Has he been rough with you? Has he hurt you? You don't have to put up with it you know.'

Carrie swallowed hard, her embarrassment talking about such things making her face redden. 'We…don't.'

'You don't what?'

'We don't…you know, in the bedroom.'

'So…it happens elsewhere? It's not so unusual. Marcus and I sometimes… How often?'

'Never.'

Dorothy stared at her, her mouth curved into a disbelieving smile. 'Never?' she cried. Carrie shook her head and Dorothy got up and began to pace the room, absent-mindedly straightening ornaments and plumping cushions on the many chaises in her sumptuous, highly adorned bungalow whilst still hanging on to her glass. 'So he must have a mistress, Carrie. I've not met a soldier yet who doesn't enjoy that kind of thing. I think it goes with the territory, letting off steam and all that, but…he's married. And you haven't been married long. One would have thought his looking for a mistress would be years away. Surely you want to add to your family before any of that goes on.'

'Does Marcus then?'

'Well, no. No, he doesn't. I can't imagine him ever doing something like that. We're so very close. And that side of things is, well, perfectly wonderful.' Carrie nodded, unsurprised that Dorothy's husband was faithful to her. 'This mistress. Do you know who she is?'

Carrie bit her lip and inhaled. She knew whatever she told Dorothy could not be taken back, but she trusted her, and the need to tell someone was far greater than the fear of speaking out.

'It's not a she,' she whispered, shaking her head. 'It's a he.'

Dorothy covered her face with her hands then sat and threw her arms around Carrie. 'Oh, darling, you poor sweet girl. I'm so sorry.' Dorothy released her then stood again and walked across to the window deep in thought. She turned and was filled with pity at Carrie's look of defeat and the tears running down her cheeks. She knelt in front of her, covering Carrie's hands that were in a tight knot in her lap, with her own. 'How did you find out?'

'Gita and I went to James Street. Arnold gave me some money to buy a dress for the charity open day. We weren't as long as I thought we'd be. John went to Amrita's family home to visit with her mother's children. I thought it would be good for him so I let him go and I was eager to find out how he'd got on. When we drove into the station I noticed the blinds were down in all the windows of the bungalow, and the shutters pulled together and I couldn't understand why. I definitely raised them this morning. I always do it. It's my routine. I open the blinds to throw back the shutters and let in the cooler morning air. I sent Gita home for an hour or two before she was due back to prepare dinner. Her husband has been under the weather and I knew she wanted to make sure he was alright.

'When I tried the front screen it was locked. Arnold said he'd be working at the bungalow that day, paperwork, you know the kind of thing. I just assumed he'd gone out for a while and had locked up. Gita gave me her key because I'd left mine in the house. I unlocked the door and went inside. I decided to change into something lighter so went into the bedroom.' She pursed her lips and puffed out a breath as tears rolled down her cheeks, then breathed in again, a breath that shook with distress.

Dorothy squeezed her hands. Take your time, darling. Take your time.'

'Arnold was in bed…with a young blond man, a boy really, not more than twenty. I recognised him as someone in his unit who'd met in the market in Bombay. Arnold had left the hotel saying he was meeting the men in his unit, thinking I wouldn't be able to follow him because I didn't have a pram, but the manager gave me one and I saw them both in the main street.'

'What did he do?' Dorothy said in a voice more like a whisper.

'He must have heard the door open because he sat up and just looked at me for what seemed forever. I…I suppose I stared at them because it felt like I was in a dream, a nightmare. Arnold had never approached me in the bedroom, and to be honest I was pleased because I didn't want to know him like that, and I didn't want him to know me either. I was so scared he'd want us to have a child together and I couldn't imagine how I would feel about it.' She shook her head. 'I don't love him, Dorothy. I never have. And it's not because of what's happened. He's just…unpleasant, bullying. He isn't a nice man. You know that don't you? How could any woman love a man like him?'

Dorothy got up and sat next to her on the rattan sofa. 'I must admit when I first met you I was surprised. You were far too young and pretty to waste yourself on a man like Arnold Bateman, and in all honesty I've never liked him. He's the kind of man we in the suffrage movement despair of most. He clearly dislikes women.' She glanced down at Carrie. 'You deserve so much better, you know. So much better.'

'He's my husband. I married him for better or for worse.'

Dorothy snorted. 'Oh, come on, that's taking things a bit far. When you made those vows you had no idea what kind of man he was. Don't get me wrong, Carrie, I'm not judging him, but he should never have married you, never have made you think you would have a normal marriage with him. What are you going to do about it? You can't want to stay married to him, surely.'

Carrie sighed. 'I'm not sure. I've moved out of the bedroom. Gita helped me take the single bed from the guest room into John's room. I could see Arnold wasn't happy about it because I'm sure he thinks if anyone finds out it'll look strange, but he didn't say anything.'

'No, I bet he didn't.' Dorothy clutched her hands wanting Carrie to make the right decision. 'You don't have to stay married to him, not now, not now you know who he really is. Perhaps I should speak to Marcus and ask him what you can do to put an end to this charade.'

Carrie looked aghast. 'Please don't. I'll deal with it, I promise. Please let's just keep it between you and me. Please, Dorothy. For now. Until I decide what must be done.'

Dorothy nodded, then leaned forward and kissed Carrie on the forehead. 'Yes, yes, okay. But Carrie you can't push this under the carpet. You're young and you deserve a better life than this. You don't have to accept it. You have to believe that.'

She stared at Carrie for a long moment with sad eyes, and Carrie leant forward resting her head on her knees, and wept.

The following day, the day of Mabel's charity affair, dawned overcast and humid. As Carrie lifted the blinds and opened the shutters she stared up into a heavy grey sky, her thoughts going to her new straw hat trimmed with daisies and cornflowers, and what would happen to it if it rained. She had been thinking about anything rather than the image of Arnold and the young man in their bed. It was beyond her understanding, far away from anything she had experienced before. She hadn't known such things happened between men, but now it was something she had been forced to face. Then her thoughts quickly went to David Lawrence and her heart leapt. Since meeting him the day before she couldn't get him out of her mind. There was something about him, the respectful way he spoke to her, his gentle demeanour that reminded her of Johan. She bent her head and could hear Pearl's voice admonishing her, saying, 'Yes, Carrie. And look how *he* treated you.' But Carrie felt instinctively that David Lawrence wasn't like Johan. David was older, more considered, and clearly made his own decisions without any family pressure. He was also Arnold Bateman's commanding officer.

Arnold came into the sitting room, fastening his cuffs, then reaching for his jacket laying on the chair.

'I'll have to meet you at the showground this afternoon. I've been asked to attend a conference with the boss about a trip he wants me and some of the unit to make into mountains. Apparently there are some insurgents causing trouble in one of the townships and we need to put a stop to it before it gets any worse.'

Carrie stared at him, waiting for him to say something, anything, about what had occurred the day before when she returned from her shopping trip with Gita. He seemed not to have any shame or explanation about her finding him in bed…their bed, with his lover, and yet she knew if she had been discovered in the same circumstances he would have turned his rage on her and beaten her, and made sure everyone knew about it. I must say something, she thought, or I'll never be able to face my reflection again.

'Why haven't you spoken to me about yesterday, Arnold? Do you think I'm just going to accept that you took someone else, a man, to our bed?'

'He raised his eyebrows and inhaled his impatience. 'It's none of your business.'

She pulled a face, then thought better of it when she saw his expression. 'Not my business. I'm your wife.'

'In name only. I've given you my name and I paid your mother handsomely for the privilege. And that's all it is, Carrie Dobbs, a lending of a name, an agreement for services rendered. You're hardly the catch of the century.'

'You lent me your name? We were married in church. You made vows, we both did, but they didn't include you getting into our bed with a man.' The slap knocked her sideways but she managed to remain standing. She put the palm of her hand to her face and held it against her cheek to relieve the pain. 'That's your answer for everything, isn't it, Arnold. A punch, a slap. You have no right to treat me like this. You mother wouldn't approve. She told me what sort of man your father was and how you've taken after him.'

'Oh, really? She stayed with him though, didn't she? And why was that?'

Carrie shrugged. 'How should I know?'

'Because she was in the same boat as you, pregnant with another man's child.' His lip curled with disgust. 'She got everything she deserved.'

'So he wasn't your father.'

'Oh, yes, he was. He made absolutely sure she didn't have the other one. He didn't want to raise another man's child. Why the hell should we? You women, you disgust me. You're all willing to open your legs to anyone who'll have you.' He made a step towards Carrie and she shrunk back aware he wouldn't resist striking her again if he had a mind to. He raised his hand and pointed at her. 'Make sure you're at the showground this afternoon, and you say nothing about anything. Do you understand?' She didn't reply. 'Am I making myself clear,' he shouted just as Gita arrived to prepare lunch and clean the bungalow. Carrie nodded and he glanced at Gita with a sneer before he left the bungalow, slamming the screen behind him.

'Carrie?' Gita said, frowning with concern.

'It's alright, Gita. Don't worry.'

'He hit you again?' Carrie turned her flaming cheek to her. 'Come with me. I will put something on it to take away the pain.'

Carrie followed Gita into the kitchen, her heart heavy and her head pounding from a headache where Arnold's blow had shaken her skull.

'Will you go today, Carrie? Gita asked her. 'Will you still go?'

'I must. I don't know what he'll do if I don't.'

'But your face.'

Carrie turned to her. 'Can you do what we did before, with the cosmetics, to cover it up? I don't have any choice, Gita. I don't know what he'll do to me if I don't attend. I must pretend to be the wife that I'm expected to be, while Arnold pulls the wool over everyone's eyes and playacts at being a husband...and a man.'

The skies had cleared, and a hot sun blazed onto the showground. Carrie stood at the gate, the skirt of her pale blue dress skittering delicately in the light breeze. Across the field were groups of people, men and women talking to their friends, drinking chilled wine and eating the Indian specialities offered to them by Indian servants clothed in white trousers, knee-length coats with mandarin collars, and brightly coloured turbans with swathes of fabric hanging down their backs. Carrie was filled with apprehension. She knew none of Mabel Dimmock's guests; there wasn't one group of revellers she could join with any comfort. Most of them, particularly the women with whom she'd sailed to India, had given her the cold shoulder. Even those who had softened slightly towards her, nodding when they saw her around the entrenchment, a small smile here and there when they were feeling magnanimous, now ignored her after her faux pas at the Military Ceremonial Ball which had become fodder for the gossipmongers. She knew she had made matters worse by befriending the natives, something no one else at the station would think of doing. Even Dorothy, who was striding towards her across the field.

'Carrie,' she called, waving as she walked. 'You came.' Carrie nodded and smiled, relieved to see her. 'You look stunning, darling. That dress, those shoes. They must be from Zaina's.'

'They are. But she won't have a shop for much longer. She's going back to Bombay to care for her parents.'

Dorothy looked horrified. 'Oh, good heavens. She has the best dress shop in Secunderabad. None of the others come close.'

'Don't I know it? I must have gone in all of them until I met David Lawrence and he told me the best place to go.'

'David?'

'He was on James Street. I bumped into him. Literally. Knocked him right over. I thought I'd killed him.'

Dorothy threw her head back and laughed. 'I don't think it's the only way you've knocked him over, darling, from what he tells me.'

Carrie felt herself go hot. 'What do you mean?'

'Oh, nothing. Don't take any notice of me.' She linked her arm through Carrie's and began to walk her towards a marquee where an auction was going to be held, and where everyone was standing outside mingling, waiting to be called inside.

'Now what about that other thing?'

'What other thing?' asked Carrie, knowing full well what Dorothy meant. Dorothy raised her eyebrows and pressed her lips together. Carrie shrugged and sighed. 'He didn't say anything, and when I brought the subject up, he did this.' She turned her right cheek towards Dorothy. 'So I've worked out the best thing to do is to say nothing.'

'But that can't continue, surely. So...he hit you because you questioned him about his lover. That's preposterous.'

'If I knew what that word meant I'd probably agree with you. He said it's none of my business, that he only leant his name to me to give me a name for my son and that I'm to do as I'm told and to say nothing about anything. That's my place, Dorothy, and I guess it's exactly where I am.' Dorothy shook her head and inhaled a long breath. 'All the time he's paying for me, like these clothes for instance, Arnold thinks he owns me. He paid my mother and now he's paying me. That's how he sees it, I know it. It's a business transaction. I'm just something to be bought and sold.'

'So do something about it, Carrie. Buy your own clothes.'

'With what? I have nothing, Dorothy. I don't think you understand. I came to India with nothing and I'll no doubt leave the same way, whenever that's going to be. It can't come fast enough as far as I'm concerned.'

The marquee was packed to the edges. Carrie stood with Dorothy at the back, clutching a glass of soda and wondering when Arnold would put in an appearance. It occurred to her he may have lied to her about where he was going. It was possible, she thought, that he was meeting the young man she found him with in their bed. Their bed. He'd insisted she sleep with him even though she hadn't wanted to, and she acknowledged what a hypocrite he was. Appearances. It was all he cared about. He was terrified that Gita and Amrita and Aashi, and the tea wallah and punka wallah would all know what was going on. Perhaps they knew anyway. Maybe they had known even before her. But it was far too late for him to be worrying about what anyone thought, and in any case he was arrogant and probably didn't care. He knew none of the servants would say anything because of the fear of losing their jobs. It was a fear he constantly held over their heads. She had heard him threatening the tea wallah with dismissal one evening because his tea was too milky, and complaining to Gita that her husband had let him down again even though Arnold knew he had been unwell. She closed her eyes when she thought of him and wondered how she would ever get herself out of his clutches.

The auction went without hitch. David Lawrence had offered to take someone out for afternoon tea to the highest bidder, and Dorothy had nudged Carrie, saying, 'Go on, darling. Make a bid. He'd love it if you won.' Carrie had smiled and shaken her head, but she'd been pleased that Dorothy thought David admired her. Mabel Dimmock made absolutely sure she won the opportunity to go out for afternoon tea with him, and Dorothy was in peals of laughter, wiping her eyes with a handkerchief when she saw the expression on David's face.

'Oh, brilliant. How wonderful. Look at David. He's positively appalled.'

'Shush, Dorothy. She'll hear you.'

'Good. I hope she does, silly old woman.'

'She's not that old.'

'Try telling that to David.' Dorothy squealed with laughter again.

Later, when they were outside the marquee and sitting in the sunshine, David Lawrence joined them. Dorothy looked up at him and burst out laughing again. She flung her arm over the back of her chair and grabbed one of his hands.

'That went well, darling. I don't think you were expecting that were you?'

He pulled a comical face. 'Well, she does have more money than anyone else. I suppose it's a sacrifice I'll have to make. It is for charity after all.'

'How much did she bid,' asked Carrie.

He smiled down at her and nodded. 'It was a lot. And if it helps someone it's a small price to pay. For me, I mean.'

Both Carrie and Dorothy erupted again and David offered to buy them a drink. 'Ooh, champagne for me please,' said Dorothy.

'Carrie?' he asked. 'Would you like champagne? How about a champagne cocktail. They're very refreshing in all this damned heat.'

'I've never had one,' said Carrie.

'Then let this be the first time,' he said with a smile. 'Dorothy?'

'Lovely, darling.'

When he returned he carried a tray on which there were three champagne cocktails, topped with raspberries and ice. He handed one each to Carrie and Dorothy, then sat in a chair next to Carrie.

'Go ahead,' he said to her. 'Try it.'

Carrie sipped her drink and gasped. 'Ooh, that's lovely.'

Dorothy smiled warmly and David laughed. 'How sweet,' said Dorothy.

David raised his eyebrows and smiled at Carrie's naiveté. 'So what's your normal tipple, Mrs. Bateman?'

Carrie shook her head. 'We never have drink in the house. My dad likes to go to the pub for a pint of ale, but the strongest drink we have at home is tea you can stand your spoon up in.'

David and Dorothy threw their heads back and laughed. 'Oh, Carrie,' said Dorothy. 'You really are very funny. It's so lovely to see that side of you. Long may it continue.' She put her hand on Carrie's and patted it. 'Well done, darling.'

Carrie shrugged. 'I'm not really sure what you mean, but, thank you anyway.' Dorothy and David swapped warm glances and both looked at Carrie. 'I wonder where Arnold's got to,' she said.

Dorothy released a breath of impatience. 'Yes, quite.' She took a sip of her cocktail. 'Not sure why you care, darling.'

David frowned. 'Dorothy! That's not worthy of you.'

Dorothy suddenly looked cross. 'Isn't it? I speak as I find. You know me well enough to know that, David.'

'Yes, but why? I don't understand.'

'No, David, you don't. You really don't.' Carrie looked from one to the other, feeling uncomfortable and worried. She stared at Dorothy and Dorothy shrugged.

'Speak of the devil,' said David. 'Bateman,' he called, waving to him. 'Over here.'

Arnold spotted them and faltered when he saw who Carrie was sitting with, then walked towards them, nodding to his superior then to Dorothy.

'Captain Lawrence. Mrs. Tremaine.'

Dorothy lit a cigarette and got up. 'Females first, Sergeant-Major. Bateman. You greet females first. It's how society works. Don't let Mabel Dimmock hear you get it wrong. She'll send you back to the front.' Arnold looked awkward and his face coloured as Dorothy bent and kissed Carrie on the cheek. 'You know where I am, Carrie. Any time, day or night. We girls must stick together you know.' She flashed a stony glance at Arnold and went back into the marquee where her husband was talking to a group of soldiers.

Carrie sat quietly with her head bowed, thinking she should have realised Dorothy wouldn't let things rest. Now she and Gita knew about Arnold, and Carrie was sure Gita would have told Aashi, her daughter, and perhaps even her husband that Arnold had struck her on more than one occasion. She knew from bitter experience that when you let knowledge out into air it had a funny way of multiplying and becoming uncontrollable. She said a silent prayer that Dorothy wouldn't say anything to David Lawrence. He was Arnold's superior after all and Arnold could lose his position if what had been going on was made public knowledge. She dreaded to think what Arnold would do to her if that happened.

'We should go and pay our respects to Lady Mabel, Carrie,' he said. 'And thank her for our invitation, particularly in the light of…' He looked down, turning his cap in his hands, then glanced in Carrie's direction.

David looked sideways, suddenly interested. 'In the light of…what exactly?'

'Well, sir. Carrie, that is, Mrs. Bateman didn't understand the ways of the mofussil… that we don't fraternise with the natives or the servants. She was asked to help with our housekeepers wedding…and she…well,' he looked embarrassed, 'sort of announced it in front of Lady Mabel as though it was something everyone does and that it would be deemed acceptable. I mean, we have to keep our distance from them, don't we, sir? Or how will we keep control?'

David Lawrence nodded as though carefully considering what Arnold had said. He stood and lit a cigarette, cupping the flame with his hand, a gesture Carrie remembered from the first time she'd met him at the railway station in Bombay. He turned and looked at her, his mouth a straight line. He's angry, she thought. He thinks less of me now. I've shown myself up for what I am. David dragged from his cigarette then released the vapour slowly into the air.

'I think if Mrs. Bateman is willing to give her time to helping with a wedding, which let's face it Bateman, isn't an everyday occurrence, I think it should be encouraged.' Arnolds face paled and he seemed to stop breathing. 'After all, it is a creative endeavour is it not, and one thing we do expect from our ladies is that they are socially creative, is that not so, Bateman?' David smiled and Arnold looked as though he might faint, while Carrie's heart thumped like a drum in her chest. He had taken her side. David Lawrence had taken her side against Arnold. 'I think on this occasion, Mrs. Bateman should be given the opportunity to be involved in an event so different from the ones we're used to, and hopefully your servants will work all the harder for it. I can see only positives.' He looked at Arnold, his face innocent and without expression.

'I…I suppose so, sir,' Arnold stammered. 'If you think it's acceptable. It's just that Lady Mabel…'

'Oh, don't worry about Mabel. She's coming to tea with me next week. I'll talk her round. I think she's quite fond of me.' Carrie lowered her chin to her chest and smiled to herself, hoping Arnold wouldn't see it. She heard him swallow and pictured his throat moving up and down.

'Yes, sir. Of course, sir.'

David nodded. 'As you were, Bateman,' then turned to Carrie smiling. 'Enjoy the rest of your afternoon, Mrs. Bateman. I believe there will be a bit of a party here tonight. I hope you'll attend.' Carrie looked up at Arnold waiting for him to say something.

'We'll be here, Captain Lawrence.'

'Good. I'll see you there.' Carrie watched David walk away, then waited for the bomb to fall.

Arnold put his hand on her arm and walked her across to where Lady Mabel and her husband were holding court. 'Looks like you'll be helping our housekeeper with her daughter's wedding.' Carrie looked up at him but he didn't make eye contact, as though he found it unbearable to look at her. 'Make sure you make a good fist of it, or I'll never hear the end of it.'

Carrie inhaled deep into her lungs, realising she had escaped a tongue-lashing from Arnold, then smiled to herself. Things were moving forward, and she had the party to look forward to that evening where David Lawrence would be present. She knew in her heart she should not have been craving another man's attentions while married to someone else, but knowing what she did about Arnold she realised that the 'marriage' she had signed up to wasn't a marriage at all, but a business deal, a convenience to Arnold and Florrie, and she was the one who had made it possible for them to get what they wanted. Now it was time for her to get what she wanted.

Chapter 22

For three weeks it rained, not as Carrie had imagined it would, like a never-ending waterfall as she had been told the monsoons brought with it, but just as she had become used to in London, an intermittent drizzle that seeped into everything it touched, and it was very welcome. It was still humid, the dank, clammy atmosphere that never seemed to dissipate no matter what time of the day it was, but there was also a freshness when the showers stopped. Carrie would take John outside, holding him in her arms as she strolled around the bungalow, breathing in the cleaner air that the rain had left behind until the atmosphere drew in again under dark, omnipresent clouds and the rain was released once again.

She had given Gita the good news that she could help with Aashi's wedding to Devak Mistry and Gita had been elated.

'Really, Madam. Oh, that is such wonderful news,' she said, clapping her hands. Then she'd frowned. 'But the sahib? He knows?'

Carrie nodded. 'Yes, Gita. He knows.'

The wedding day was set for the end of September when the rains had stopped and the weather was set fair. Gita's workload in the bungalow increased simply because of her nervous energy; if there was nothing to do she found something, she was everywhere, working very quickly, and the smile didn't leave her face such was her excitement.

The official betrothal, the *vagndana,* and the written declaration of their intent, *the lagna-patra,* signalled the visiting of the groom's parents to the bride's home. Gita told Carrie what would happen next.

'There will be a procession, Carrie, with drummers and musicians. It will be so wonderful but I am very nervous. Devak Mistry's parents will come to our home where we will give them refreshments. We must decorate our house to welcome them and show them they have certainly made the right choice of a wife and family. Everyone will be polite. We will bow and offer them the best seats and the best dishes, and we will be watching Devak and Aashi to make sure they follow tradition. This is the best thing we can do for her and it must be done properly because everyone will be watching us to make sure the customs are followed and Devak's parents will expect it.'

'It all sounds so wonderful, Gita. Aashi is very lucky. What will you give them to eat?'

Gita thought for a moment. 'Perhaps rice and lentil dumplings and gobhi porichathu.'

'What's that?'

'Fried cauliflower with curry leaves and paratha bread. It is delicious.'

'And then?'

'Red onion fritters with a jam made from chilies with *puli saddam*, tamarind rice. Very hot, very nice. And after, banana fritter with almond barfi and *boondi ladoo*, sweets Aashi and I will make for them to finish their meal.'

'And then?'

Gita was delighted at Carrie's enthusiasm. 'There will be prayers, *abhiseka*, to give thanks for bringing the young people together and to wish them a happy life in their future.'

'And the wedding will follow?'

'Not until the *Gruhapravesam* has been carried out. Devak and his father have built a small bungalow for him and Aashi to live in when they are married. This is a very modern thing. The *Gruhapravesam* is the blessing or warming of the house before they live there. It must be carried out before the wedding because they will go there after the ceremony and it can take a whole afternoon to perform. There is a blessing for the entrance called *Vastu Pooja*, and a priest conducts the *Vastu Shani* inside the home to create peace and harmony and stop any unsettling feelings. We then give the priest refreshment to thank him for his services. The house must not be left unattended for three days following the *Gruhapravesam*. Doors and windows must be unlocked, so we have paid someone to stay there for the following days. I expect this all seems strange to you, Carrie. But it is just our way.'

'No, please, it is so…different, and nothing like my own wedding. It sounds very exciting. You and your husband have taken so much trouble. I hope Aashi appreciates it.'

'Oh, yes, she does. She is trying to pretend she doesn't like Devak Mistry very well, but we know…' She tapped the side of her nose and smiled broadly. 'The meeting with the Mistrys will take place on Sunday. We have invited a *jyotishee* to deliver their *raashiphal*, their horoscopes, and I am sure the reading will show great happiness together.'

'What if it doesn't?'

'It always does. The *jyotishee* knows how to read the signs, and the signs are good. They have tender and loving aspects, with harmony and passion. We have chosen very well.'

The wedding took place the following week, at the end of September, as the days slid seamlessly into a spring-like October. Carrie became a helpmate to Gita, patting her down when she became anxious, helping to prepare the food which seemed to Carrie to be never-ending, although Gita assured her it would all be eaten, and taking part in the constant chatter about the wedding, the music, the costumes, the jewellery. Particularly the jewellery.

'Devak has made me something very special,' said Aashi. 'You know he is a very clever jeweller and I think it will be a piece like he has never made before.'

Carrie looked up from rolling chapatti dough and smiled. 'You sound very proud.'

'I am. I know I will be very well looked after.'

'Will you have children?'

'Mm, eventually, but not too soon. Everyone, including my mother, thinks we will have babies right away, but it's not what I want.'

'What do you want?'

'To get a job. A proper job, perhaps for the Indian Civil Service. I am capable of doing such a job, at least as good as any man. If I have children straight away I will forever be a mother and nothing else. I want much more, maybe to travel. I can have my babies later, when I'm more ready. I'm sure Devak will agree.'

Carrie nodded and smiled and wondered if she should put Aashi in touch with Dorothy whose views seemed to be similar to Aashi's, but she was quite sure Gita wouldn't thank her. She continued to roll out the chapattis in silence. She was fully aware of the best intentions held by the young, including herself. She was also aware of how family pressure could change those intentions, no matter how strong they were, and she was sure she would be hearing some very happy news not too far into the future.

'I hear the wedding went very well.'

'Yes, it was beautiful. Really something. The colours, the music, the food…and the ceremony was wonderful. I felt very honoured to be there.'

Dorothy smiled. 'You're a breath of fresh air, do you know that?'

Carrie tilted her head and looked at her. She thought Dorothy seemed a little sad, a little far away. They were at a leaving party at the Secunderabad Club for one of the civil servants who was going back to England. He had married in India, but his new wife was desperate to return to Cheshire where she was from, and he had capitulated.

'You look a bit down, Dorothy. Are you okay? There's nothing wrong is there?'

Dorothy breathed deeply and turned to Carrie with a less than cheerful smile. 'We're going home, darling. Marcus and I. Back to London.'

Carrie's mouth dropped open. 'What? No. You can't. I mean…oh, Dorothy, what am I going to do? No one else speaks to me, only you. Please don't go.'

Dorothy closed her eyes and lowered her head. Her face was pale and Carrie noticed her eyes were ringed with red as though she had been crying. This was not the Dorothy Carrie had come to know. 'It's my sister, Carrie. She's very ill, extremely so. She has children, so little, so close to their Mama, but I think…I think they will lose her.'

Carrie's expression changed and she put her hand to her face to cover her embarrassment. 'I'm so sorry, Dorothy. It's awful.' She looked away wishing she hadn't gone on so about Dorothy being the only one who spoke to her, almost begging her to stay. She looked back and put her hand on her friend's arm. 'I'm so selfish, aren't I? I'm sorry, Dorothy. You must be so worried.'

Dorothy put her arm around Carrie's shoulders and hugged her. 'I would love to stay. I feel I have found a real friend in you, so much more than those other silly wittering woman who have never had a day's difficulty in their lives. I was dreading coming to India, but you made it so much better. Just knowing you were here has helped me get through what I thought would be a nightmare.'

Carrie looked at her in surprise. 'How have I helped you?'

'Don't forget I've been here before, with my parents when I was a girl. Things haven't changed much. People like Mabel Dimmock are living in the dark ages and unfortunately she is the *burra* memsahib around here so she calls the shots. She hates me too, for being too…what did she say to Marcus? That I was too forward and had ideas that were incongruous to my upbringing and the ideals of my parents who must be terribly disappointed in how I've turned out.'

Carrie pressed her lips together to prevent herself from laughing. 'Well, I don't know what a lot of that means, Dorothy, but I think you've turned out fine.'

Dorothy giggled and kissed Carrie's cheek. 'Me too.' She released Carrie and stared at her.

'What?'

'We're leaving in two days. We must go now in case something happens to Leonora. There will be no one there to pick up the reins and it'll take at least three to four weeks before we get back to London. We can't rely on our parents to have the children. They're getting on a bit.'

'So soon?' said Carrie, her stomach flipping with anxiety.

Dorothy put a finger under Carrie's chin and tipped her face towards her. 'Now darling, I have to talk to you because there are couple of things I promised myself I would do before I go back to London. And they both concern you.'

Carrie's eyes widened. 'Me?'

'I want to make sure you're going to be alright. I know I must go back for my poor dear sister, but...I want to know you're safe. I must know you're safe or I'll worry all the time and never forgive myself if anything untoward happens to you.'

'What's going to happen to me?'

'Exactly. So...' She reached into her purse and pulled out a set of keys.

'What are they?'

'They're keys, darling.'

'I know, Dorothy. But what are they for?'

She pointed to the smaller one. 'This one is for my car.'

Carrie gasped. 'Your car?'

'Yes, I know. I've only had the damned thing for a couple of weeks. I was planning to take us all over when you'd got the wedding thing out of the way. Anyway, I want you to have it, to look after it for me until I come back.'

'I think you're forgetting something, Dorothy. I don't drive.'

'No, but you will. I've organised some lessons for you. You must drive, Carrie. You can't rely on other people to ferry you around when you're doing what you're going to do.'

'And what's that?'

She pointed to the bigger key. 'This is the key to Zaina's shop in James Street. I bought the tenancy. I was going to ask you to run it for me, and I was going to pop in here and there, but I'm going to be much too far away to pop in anywhere I'm afraid.'

'Dorothy, how can I run a shop? I don't have the first clue.'

'You see,' said Dorothy, vigorously shaking her head. 'I don't believe that. I've been hearing lots of things about Aashi's wedding, how you organised the decoration of the ceremony room, how you helped Gita with her outfit, and became Aashi's dresser. You even cooked much of the food. I also heard it was one of the best weddings this station has ever seen, and was in part, thanks to you and your ideas and your calm control. That is all you need. I think you love clothes, Carrie, and if Arnold was the kind of man who indulged you, you would have an extensive wardrobe.'

Carrie nodded and smiled. 'I have found an interest. I realised when I went shopping that many of the shops here don't sell the type of clothes women can buy in Bombay or Calcutta. I know they have to rely on catalogues to order the things they want and more often than not they don't arrive in time and the event has been and gone before they can wear them.'

'Zaina doesn't leave until the end of next week, so it will give you time to organise John's *ayah*. She will be able to bring him to you in the daytime and you'll probably see him even more than you do now. This is the spare key, and the owner of the building will give you the other key when you take over.' Dorothy gripped her hand. 'We can do this, Carrie. You can do it. I trust you implicitly and I know it will be a complete success.'

'I think we're forgetting something.'

'What's that?'

'Arnold.'

Dorothy's expression changed and she looked almost scheming. 'Don't worry about Sergeant Major Bateman. He won't give you any trouble.'

Carrie frowned. 'But…'

Dorothy looked closely at her. 'It's dealt with. You have no one to answer to. I promise.'

Carrie felt swept away by what Dorothy had done and was on the verge of tears. She had come through many changes, some she hadn't wished for and some she had relished, but she could see that what Dorothy had done would change her life. She swallowed hard, tears making her eyes glitter. 'You said there were a couple of things.'

Dorothy got up and held out her hand. 'My car's outside. We're going on a little trip.' Carrie looked across at Arnold who was standing at the bar, strands of thin hair hanging down the side of his face that he hadn't bothered to sweep across his forehead. His laughter was louder than anyone else's and as he brought a cigarette to his lips, the tips of his fingers were stained with the brown residue of nicotine. Dorothy raised her eyebrows. 'As I said, darling, you don't need to worry about Arnold anymore.'

Chapter 23

It was a beautiful evening. Dorothy had folded down the roof of her Swift motor vehicle, and she and Carrie wore long Indian scarves tied around their hair which trailed behind them in the breeze as Dorothy drove at speed.

'It's a beautiful car, Dorothy. Actually, it's only the second time I've travelled in a car. Arnold organised one for Gita and me when we went to James Street to buy my outfit for the Charity Open Day.'

'Yes, it's lovely, isn't it. Marcus ordered it for me to be delivered when we arrived in India but the waiting list for them is very long, so I had to wait a bit. I haven't really had the opportunity to make the most of it.' She glanced at Carrie. 'I want you to use it, Carrie. It will set you free, I promise. You can use it for getting to the shop on James Street, and also for taking John for days out. There are some wonderful places to see in India and I'm guessing you haven't seen any of them.'

'No, no, I haven't.'

'Well, there you are. It'll be perfect for you to make a life for yourself here.'

Carrie nodded but she couldn't help feeling apprehensive. 'I'm a bit nervous about driving. You seem to be very good at it.'

'You'll get used to it, darling. You'll be the envy of the *mofussil*, you wait and see. I've every faith you'll make some new friends because of it. People want us to be useful to them don't they? I'm not sure any of the other wives drive. They'll very likely hope you'll be their transport. Don't give in too easily, that's all I'd say. They've treated you abominably and your elevation to driver and business owner will give them a real shock. The other thing I want you to know is that people in trade are often shunned by the upper classes.'

'Oh? Why?'

'It's too obvious a show of having to work for a living, but don't forget to remind them if it wasn't for the fact their husbands were working, either in the Army or for the Indian Civil Service, they wouldn't be here sunning themselves on their verandas and sipping mint julep. Promise me, darling.'

'I promise.' Carrie smiled. 'I wish I was more like you, Dorothy. You're so confident and you have such modern ideas...and a husband who supports you in everything.'

'I know how fortunate I am. Marcus always puts me first.' She glanced at Carrie again. 'Don't let Arnold control you, Carrie. You are a very capable young woman. You just haven't had the opportunity to test yourself yet.'

'I have a feeling that's all going to change, thanks to you.' She looked about her and frowned. 'Where are we going, Dorothy?'

To the Hussain Sagar Lake.'

Carrie's eyes widened. 'Why? It's a long way from the station.'

'Not when you have a car, darling, which is the whole point.' Dorothy tightened her hands on the steering wheel. 'I've asked someone to take care of you while I'm away.' They turned off the main road onto the Necklace Road that follows the lakes perimeter and into Sanjeevaiah Park.

'Is it Gita?'

Dorothy threw her head back and laughed. 'No, it's not Gita.'

Dorothy drove them around the lake and Carrie marvelled at the beauty of it in the dusky light, a gentle breeze rippling across its surface.

'The lake,' she breathed, and glanced momentarily at Dorothy. 'It's huge.'

'Yes, and very beautiful at night. The lights will come on soon and you'll see how romantic this place is. The lake was built in the shape of a heart, for lovers I expect, but there's also a bird sanctuary and a fun maze. Families come here to relax. Perhaps you'll come here with John,' Dorothy said as she pulled the Sprite to a halt. 'We're here.'

'Where exactly?' Dorothy nodded towards a bench. Sitting on the bench was David Lawrence. Carrie felt her breath catch in her throat and she turned to Dorothy, her eyes wide with anticipation. 'Why is Captain Lawrence here?'

Dorothy shuffled round in her seat to face Carrie and took her hand. 'First of all, he asked you to call him David. He is only Captain Lawrence to the soldiers in his unit of which you are not one. And second...he is the person I've asked to keep an eye on you.'

Carrie was horrified. She felt herself go hot and cold in a matter of seconds, and with trembling hands she pushed her breeze swept hair out of her eyes. 'I don't know what to say,' she whispered. 'I never dreamt... Oh, my Lord, I'm so embarrassed. And when Arnold finds out my life won't be worth living. Dorothy what have you done?'

'Arnold won't find out. I know you like David. I know he's been kind to you because he is a kind and thoughtful man. I have known him for years. He was here with his parents when I was here with mine. He knows India like the back of his hand, and unlike some of the men here is madly in love with this amazing country. Please, Carrie. Happiness is waiting for you. Grab it, darling, with both hands.'

Carrie opened the vehicle door and closed it gently, then began to walk towards David. He held out his hand and as she got to him she clasped it. He smiled at her, his dark brown eyes not leaving her face for a moment, his expression one of joy and kindness.

'Carrie,' he said, gently. 'You came.'

Chapter 24

Dear Pearl,

I can't tell you how sorry I was to hear about William. I can't imagine how you must be feeling, and I wish with all my heart I could be with you to comfort you. At the very earliest, this letter will take a month or so to get to you. If only I could be with you. I'd give anything to come back home, but, you know who said it's not possible because I'm needed here to help him push his way up the ladder. If only I could turn back the clock.

Dearest Pearl I've had an idea. Things have changed somewhat for me here in Secunderabad. Dorothy has had to return home to nurse her ailing sister and care for the children. She rented a dress shop in Secunderabad that had become empty before she knew she must leave India so that she and I could work together, and in her absence she's given me the keys and asked me to run it, with Gita's help of course. Pearl, I'd love it if you would consider coming to India. I know it's a big thing, a big adventure, especially asking you to travel on your own, but you could help me with the shop and we would be together again like in the old days.

Take a deep breath, Pearl and really think about it. I'm not planning on it being forever. I'm determined to come back to Whitechapel one day. London is my real home and where my family is, but being here with me for a while would take you away from the bad memories and everything the war is doing to you all in London. I've heard some terrible things and it's made me so worried. You would earn more money than you're earning as a skivvy at Nightingale Lane, and you could put it by for when you return to England. Please consider it. We could look after each other.

I'll be holding my breath until I hear from you. Please come, Pearl. It would be so wonderful to have my dearest friend with me again.

Thinking of you always.

Lots of love

Carrie x

Chapter 25

Dearest Dorothy,

I'm so sorry to hear about your sister. One of Marcus's men told Arnold what had happened. Dear Dorothy, you must be desolate at losing your beloved sister and I am so sorry for your loss. I hope you and the children are bearing up. Poor little mites. How they must miss their mother.

For me, I must confess, I miss your company dreadfully. Life here was much more bearable when I knew you were just a short walk across the mofussil. You brought so much light into my life. Perhaps you'll come back one day, and bring the children with you. John would love the company of other children, I'm sure. There aren't many new children here yet, but I live in hope he will have some friends when he is a bit older.

The shop is doing very well. Gita and I are loving working together. She has changed so much, Dorothy, and not being in service has improved her confidence and belief in herself. She walks straighter now, and I've insisted she dress from the shop. She is a very beautiful woman with a lovely figure for her age and she's the perfect model. She and her daughter have both brought in new customers and we are often swept off our feet with how busy we are. Gita also has a very good eye for colour. Her choices are always spot on, and some of the dresses we have imported from England and France are stunning.

I hope you don't mind, but in the light of Pearl's dreadful loss and heartfelt grief I've invited her to Secunderabad if she can get a passage from England. I want to help her like you've helped me, Dorothy. She must be at rock bottom at the moment and I certainly know how that feels. I think it would help her take her mind off her troubles if she were to help out in the shop. We could do with another pair of hands. I thought she could stay in the apartment over the shop, at least for a while. I hope you agree it's a good idea and I'll eagerly await your reply.

Lots of love
Carrie x

Chapter 26

Dear Mum and Dad,

I know I've written before but I feel I should write again because I haven't heard from you. I hope you've received my letters, at least four now, because I've not received any news from you about home and I can only think you haven't received them. Could all my letters have gone astray? I'm desperate to know how all of you are, particularly little Rose and how she's thriving. I'm wondering why you haven't replied. I can't help but worry. If you don't want to write or haven't got time, please ask Tommy to send me a note. That's all I ask, to let me know you're all well.

Your little grandson, John is very bonny now. He's sitting up on his own and giggles and smiles all the time. He is a joy to me and I love him dearly, and I know the day you meet him you'll love him too. He needs to meet his grandparents and when he does I know you'll be important to him.

I miss everyone at home, Mum and Dad. No matter what happened in those dark days before I hope we can put the past behind us and be a family again. You all mean so much to me and I long for the day when we can all be together again, like we used to be.

Your loving daughter,

Carrie x

Chapter 27

The station in Secunderabad was busier than Carrie remembered it on her arrival six months earlier. Her thoughts went back to the day she first stepped off the train from Bombay and into her new life with Arnold Bateman, a man she called her husband, yet had never behaved like one to her.

October had brought with it sweltering weather, and she had raised the canopy over the Sprite so she and John, who was strapped into his carrycot on the back seat, wouldn't be burnt by the unforgiving sun that beat down on the earth like a furnace. She glanced into the backseat and smiled. John was in a deep slumber that had fallen on him as soon as she'd started the engine. She knew if ever he couldn't sleep, laying him in his carrycot and allowing the engine to idle was the way to sweet dreams for all of them, and she thanked Dorothy every day for the gift of freedom, and of sleep.

John had blossomed into a beautiful little boy. He was a happy, placid child, with a mop of curly brown hair and deep blue eyes. The conker-coloured hair, she knew, came from Johan, but the eyes were all hers and she was very proud of the way they sparkled, and reflected his sweet personality. She also knew that every time Arnold glanced at her boy, which was only when his gaze inadvertently fell upon him and he had no choice, he was reminded of who John's father was. This pleased Carrie more than she ever thought possible. She hadn't known she had those kinds of feelings in her, the ones where she felt as though she had exacted a much needed revenge for everything Arnold had put her through, for all the humiliation and pain he had inflicted on her, and she was no longer ashamed that he wasn't John's father. She was relieved, relieved and delighted that Arnold Bateman would never, ever, father a child, particularly a boy, because she could only assume that his dislike of women would be passed down, just as Arnold's father's unacceptable behaviour towards his mother had been passed down, like a trophy, to him.

Arnold hated women. He had proved it not just by the way he had treated his own mother, and in turn, Carrie, but also because he had taken another man as his lover. Carrie had been utterly shocked at her discovery of Arnold's predilection for young men, but as she had matured so had her willingness to accept those things outside of her understanding. It no longer mattered to her that he had no feelings for her other than those of disdain, because she didn't love Arnold, had never loved him and could never love him. She had also realised that it wasn't because of Arnold's choices in his personal life that she couldn't love him, but simply because he was the most unpleasant, hateful person she had ever met.

As Carrie sat in the car waiting, she heard the tumultuous sound of a train arriving at the platform, the unmistakable sound cutting though the chatter of the gathering masses. She opened the door and stepped out, then lifted John from his carrycot and settled him on her hip. She walked from the perimeter of the station into the huge grey baroque building with its turrets and flags, where the air was cooler and the aroma of the abundant food stalls was mouth-wateringly tempting.

Making her way to the main platform where she knew the train from Bombay had arrived in a cacophony of billowing steam and cranking of gears, and wheels grinding against the breaks with an ear-splitting squeal, she inhaled a deep breath, anticipation making her nervous. Was Pearl a passenger on the train, or had she been so hurt by her grief and fears that she couldn't bear the thought of leaving the surroundings she knew?

Her path to the platform through a stone arch was interrupted time and time again as she dodged the tidal wave of travellers moving towards her. There were many new Europeans stepping off the train. They looked as apprehensive as she had felt when she first arrived, and she had complete sympathy for them. They had likely travelled for weeks on unfamiliar transport from the other side of the world and had landed in a strange, dusty, colourful country where the inhabitants camped for days on station platforms with their cooking stoves and bedding. She could see it in their eyes, the uncertainty, the apprehension, and perhaps even dismay at their exotic and disorganised surroundings.

Carrie stood on tiptoe, peering over the heads of the travellers disgorged from the carriages. Where was Pearl? Had she decided the journey was too arduous, too dangerous for her to contemplate alone at a time of war? Had the money for her passage from England to India not arrived in time for her to travel? Or was it simply that her grief was so great she could not contemplate leaving the home she knew for an adventure that would test the hardiest traveller?

And then Carrie saw her...

Pearl had alighted from the train last of all the travellers. She was dressed in a faded pink tea dress patterned with birds, and dark brown buttoned shoes. She held a small suitcase and was looking around the platform and the myriad men women and children as though she had arrived on another planet. Strands of her thick red hair had escaped her straw hat and her eyes were huge in her pale face, now gaunter than Carrie had ever seen it.

'Pearl?'

Pearl's face broke into a relieved smile and they ran towards each other. Carrie flung her free arm around her friend's neck, and Pearl held Carrie so close she thought she would squeeze the breath out of her.

'Oh, Pearl, I'm so glad to see you. Are you alright? How was the journey? I've been so worried about you being on your own, yet here you are. You're so brave.' Carrie gently pushed Pearl away from her and looked into her eyes. 'Are you alright, sweetheart?'

Pearl's eyes flooded with tears and she nodded uncertainly, as if to convince herself. 'I miss him so much, Carrie. When he was away I'd counted the days to his return and it wasn't so bad. I had something to look forward to, but now…now there's nothing. It's broken my heart. And the thought of him going through pain…and the fear. I can hardly bear it.'

Carrie threaded here arm through Pearl's and walked her off the platform, through the bustling ticket office and out into the blazing sun towards the car. 'I know, Pearl. I'm so sorry. I know how much you loved him.'

Pearl nodded. 'He was my world, Carrie. I can't imagine life without him. We had such high hopes for our life together.'

Carrie squeezed Pearl's hand. 'I know. I know,' she said gently.

When they reached the Sprite, Pearl bent down and took John's face in her hands and rubbed his ruddy cheeks with her thumbs. 'God, he's gorgeous, Carrie, and oh, look at that hair. It's so like…' she stopped and pulled a face.

Carrie smiled. 'It's okay, Pearl, you can say it. It's like Johan's.'

Pearl shrugged. 'He's like his dad isn't he? What a shame he doesn't know about him. Anyone would be proud to have a little boy like John.'

Carrie kissed Pearl on the cheek. 'I am proud, Pearl. And he's got me…and you, and Gita, and Dorothy…and his *ayah*.'

Pearl's eyes widened. 'His what?

Carrie laughed again. 'There's so much for you to get used to. It took me a while I can tell you, but…yes, things are alright now. And you're here, and that makes everything perfect.'

She settled John in the carrycot in the back seat, indicating for Pearl to sit in the front passenger side then started the engine and pulled onto the track that led to Trimulgherry.

'You can drive, Carrie. That's very modern. I don't know anyone else who drives, not even Mrs Stern.'

'I've had lessons. Dorothy left the car for me to use. It's called a Sprite. Her husband, Marcus bought it for her, but as I mentioned in my letters she'd been called back home to nurse her sister and look after her sister's children. Unfortunately, her sister passed away and now it's up to Dorothy to raise them. I could never see Dorothy with children but she says she's enjoying being with them. She was very close to her sister. She must miss her.' She glanced at Pearl. 'You and Dorothy will get on really well, Pearl. I know you'll like her. She's very different, very opinionated and not what we're used to in the society we've been brought up in, but she has a heart of gold.'

'And Gita? She sounds wonderful.'

'Yes, she's a lovely person. Very homely and motherly. Exactly what I needed when I arrived here. She knew, you see, knew I wasn't like the others. Even though I was supposed to be her…well, boss, I suppose, her memsahib, I couldn't be like that. I didn't feel comfortable treating her as if she was less than me, which she plainly isn't.'

'Is it what other people do, then?'

Carrie nodded. 'I don't like the way the people in service are treated here. The thing is, you and I know what it feels like to be a servant, to not be seen and not be heard, to do the things them with all the money don't want to do. I can't treat human beings like that. Gita has been…like a mum, to be honest. She's really looked out for me, and she and her family have treated me like one of them. And, yeah, I got into trouble with the others for it.'

'Really? Why?'

'Because Europeans are not allow to have anything to do with the natives. It goes against the stupid rules of their society, yet she's shown me more respect and friendship than any of them, apart from Dorothy of course.' She inhaled a deep breath at the memory. 'Arnold was furious with me because I told everyone at the Military Ball I'd agreed to help Gita with her daughter's wedding. Honestly, Pearl, you would have thought I'd offered to murder someone instead of making chapattis. The other wives had barely spoken to me before that but they definitely didn't after. It was like I'd got some kind of disease.' Pearl looked worried and Carrie laughed. 'Don't worry. You won't come into contact with any of that.'

Pearl pulled a face. 'I'm glad to hear it.'

Carrie glanced at her again and smiled broadly. 'I'm so glad you're here. I can hardly believe it. I feel safe at last.'

'Do you?'

Carrie nodded. 'You were the person I didn't want to leave behind, Pearl. Only you. I miss Mum and Dad, and Tom and Alfie, but it's you I've missed the most.'

'What about Elsie? She's your sister. Little Rose is gorgeous. A beautiful little girl. I saw her walking towards Covent Garden pushing a pram and I went over to say hello and have a look. She didn't even mention you so thought I'd better not.'

Carrie's expression changed and a sadness overtook her. 'Me and Elsie…we were never that close. I feel very sad that I haven't seen Rose or been part of it all, but they sent me away, didn't they, Pearl. And they've never written to me. Even Elsie…or Tom. I've written to them loads but they've never replied. It's like I don't exist in their world anymore.' Pearl stared at her then looked away and bit her lip. 'Anyway,' she said, changing the subject, 'I'm taking you to the shop. I want to get you settled in the apartment. It's small but very nice. Dorothy had it all done up when she took on the lease. And then I thought we'd go for some lunch. There are some lovely restaurants on James Street.'

'A restaurant? Carrie, I've never eaten in a restaurant before.'

'Well, don't let that put you off. It's just like eating at home, except you haven't had to buy, prepare or cook the food. Or serve it to people who don't have the manners to say thank you.' She glanced at Pearl again. 'It's really quite nice.'

'The food on the train wasn't nice. And it wasn't much better on the ship.'

Carrie threw back her head and laughed. 'I did warn you.'

She pulled the Sprite up in front of the shop and switched off the engine.

'Well? What do you think?'

Pearl looked up at the sign on the shop. "Carrie's Closet". Oh, my goodness.'

Carrie grinned. 'It was Dorothy's idea. I wanted it to be named after her but she said the customers would want to be served by the name over the door. I suppose that's me at the moment.'

Pearl sat quietly looking around, her eyes flitting from one thing to another. The street was busy as it usually was at that time of day, the noise of carts, vehicles and people constantly in the background. 'I suppose it's a bit like London, only hotter.'

Carrie laughed. 'I think you'll find lots of things in Secunderabad are very different to London, Pearl, but…you'll have plenty of time to find out.'

They left the car and Pearl and Carrie, carrying John in her arms, went into the shop where Gita was rearranging shelves. She straightened up and smiled when she heard the bell on the door.

'You're back.'

'Yes,' said Carrie. 'And this is Pearl.'

Pearl and Gita said hello and embraced. 'It's so good to meet you, Gita. Carrie has written about you many times.'

Gita laughed. 'Oh, dear. Hopefully she is pleased with me.'

Carrie handed John to her. 'Always, Gita. Would you mind having John for ten minutes while I take Pearl upstairs to the apartment? You can close up for a few minutes if you like.'

Gita shook her head. 'Oh, no. The customers adore him. He sells as many dresses as I do. No need to close.'

Pearl followed Carrie up the winding staircase and through an archway to a door that led to the apartment. Carrie had cleaned everywhere herself and had put vases of flowers in the tiny living room that had a small kitchenette leading off it.

'Oh, Carrie. This is so pretty. Is it for me?'

'Yes, Pearl. This is your home for as long as you're here.' Pearl walked around the living room, nervously twisting her hat in her hands until her fingers reached out for the fine floral curtains at the windows and the tasselled cushions on the small settee. She bent to smell the flowers Carrie had placed on the table and when she straightened up there were tears in her eyes. 'Oh, Pearl. Don't cry. Please don't cry.'

Pearl shook her head. 'William would have loved this. I've never lived in a place such as this and I know he hadn't. It's proper luxury this is, proper posh, but I'm sorry, Carrie, I would rather have him any day.'

She burst into tears and Carrie enveloped her into her arms and held her close. 'Of course you would. Of course you would rather be with him. This is no substitute for the love you and William had, Pearl, but…I hope it will help you move forward when you're ready. If I could have come to you I would have, but now that I'm married Arnold has certain rights over what I do. There was nothing I could do but bring you here to me so I can look after you, and I will look after you. Me and Gita. We'll take care of you until you're strong enough to decide what you want for the future.'

Pearl lifted her head and nodded as she wiped her eyes and cheeks with a handkerchief. 'I know, and I'm grateful. I suppose I still can't believe I'll never see him again. It was so strange, Carrie. I'd just received a letter from him, from the front, and then his mum came round to our 'ouse to tell me she'd had a telegram from the war office saying he was missing presumed dead. Apparently there are lots of young men missing whose bodies they'll never find and William's one of them. It was like I could hear his voice in his letter, and then…nothing. If he was still alive he would have written before now to tell me how he is. His mum said the same. Neither of us have heard from him. He's gone.'

Carrie wiped her own tears threatening to fall from her chin and dried her cheeks on her sleeve. She swallowed before she spoke, her throat tight with sadness.

'This war has been so cruel. I wish they'd just stop it. All those men who've been killed, the future of the country just wiped out, and everyone at home left devastated. It makes me wonder what they're gaining out of it.'

Pearl nodded. 'The only comfort I have is that William said he was proud to do his duty. He was fighting for his country and I don't think he would have had it any other way. It's not like he was conscripted into the army. He volunteered like so many others. It was what he wanted and what he believed in, to defend his country for them what comes after us. It's how I comfort myself when I'm so sad I think my heart will shatter, to know he died doing what he believed in.'

Carrie smoothed Pearl's hair away from her damp face and squeezed her hand. 'You look done in. I'll make some tea. Why don't you change into something lighter? If you don't have anything go down to the shop and choose a few cotton dresses. Gita will help you. Have your tea first. I think you need to have a sleep as well. I'm going to take John home, then I'm coming back and I'll stay the night here at the apartment so you're not on your own. The ayah will take care of John while I'm away.'

Pearl looked astonished. 'But what about Arnold. Won't he want you at home?'

Carrie shrugged. 'I shouldn't think Arnold will notice. He has other things on his mind.' She patted Pearl's hand. 'I'll make that tea, and then you must sleep, and this evening we'll go out for something to eat. I want you to feel at home here, to get some of the old Pearl back.' She gave Pearl a sorrowful smile. 'We'll take care of you,' she said gently.

Pearl nodded, her eyes shaded with sadness. 'I know. I know you will.'

Chapter 28

Arnold was waiting for Carrie when she returned to the bungalow. He looked up briefly when she appeared at the door, then returned to his writing.

'Where have you been?' he asked without looking at her.

'At the shop of course.' She flung her hat onto the sofa and shifted John from her left hip to her right. The little boy clung onto the front of her dress pulling the fabric towards him so he could suck it.

'With John?'

'Why not with John? He's come with me before.'

Arnold nodded, then swivelled the chair so he was facing her. 'I think you've got something to tell me.'

Carrie glanced away on the pretext of rescuing her dress from John. 'Oh? Like what?'

'Like that guttersnipe, Pearl Watson has arrived in Secunderabad.'

'Pearl's no guttersnipe, and what if she is here? What difference does it make?'

'It won't make any difference to me. And you'd better make sure it doesn't make any difference to you. You're still my wife and you have duties to perform.' Carrie raised her eyebrows and Arnold's face turned to thunder. 'I suggest you take that look off your face, miss.'

'I know exactly what my duties are, Arnold. The question is, do you know what yours are?'

He got up quickly, sending the chair wheeling across the room. 'Don't overstep the mark. Your saviour, Dorothy Tremaine isn't here anymore. You're on your own, and it doesn't matter what she thinks, or how she's told you to behave. You'll do as I tell you, and I'm telling you, you won't be working in that fleapit much longer. There's more than enough for you to do here, and if there isn't I'll find plenty for you to do.'

Carrie knew this was the moment. She had thought it would take much longer to get to this point, but Dorothy had coached her before she'd left for England about how to handle Arnold when she was no longer in Secunderabad and Carrie was prepared. It was something she'd hoped she wouldn't need to do; threatening someone wasn't her idea of how to live her life, but Arnold was a different kettle of fish altogether, and it was necessary to handle him in the same way he handled everyone around him. This was fighting fire with fire and she knew it.

'Oh, really. Well, here's a news flash. You're not going to stop me working in the shop, and you're not going to stop me from seeing Pearl. Do you want to know why?' he observed her under half-closed lids. She saw his pronounced Adam's apple move up and down in his throat as he swallowed. She had him on the ropes. This was a Carrie he hadn't seen before and she wished with all her heart she'd shown him this side to her when they'd first met.

'The reason you're not going to stop me is because I'm not the only one who knows about your preferences. And if you push it with me, those people are going to make it common knowledge, and honestly, Arnold. I'm not sure it's going to do your career much good.'

She saw his jaw harden and she was prepared for him to lash out at her.

'You've discussed my private life. How dare you?'

'Actually, no, I haven't discussed you because I'm so ashamed of being married to you that I wouldn't want to discuss you or our life together with anyone. Do you think your servants don't know? This is the problem with people like you, you think that anyone who has to work in service must be stupid. Either that, or they walk around with their eyes shut. Now I'm the first one to admit that anything that goes on in a house stays in the four walls, it's what's expected when you work for someone and no one wants to lose their job, but it doesn't mean we don't see things, or hear things. They know, Arnold, and they're not the only ones.'

Arnold looked rattled, wrong-footed, perhaps scared. 'Meaning?'

'Meaning that there are some outside these four walls who know what's going on. Maybe one of your 'friends' has spoken out of turn. Have you ever considered that?' He said nothing, and Carrie picked up her hat from the sofa and made for the bedroom with a now sleepy John on her hip. 'Anyway, what all that means is, if you don't drop it I'm going to pack my things, and John and I will move out.'

Arnold's eyes widened. This was the last thing he would want, and Carrie knew it. 'You can't do that.'

'Yes, I can. And I will. And everyone will want to know why, won't they? And I won't need to tell them, because there are people out there who already know what's going on here. It's up to you really. We either keep it nice and friendly as in, we don't bother one another, or, I move out and you'll have some explaining to do. To be honest, I'm not bothered either way.'

Arnold threw her such a look of utter hatred it shook her to her buttoned shoes, but Carrie was determined to hold her ground.

'It looks like I don't have a choice.'

'You have a choice, Arnold. You've always had a choice. Your problem is you always make the wrong one.' She turned and went into the bedroom, closing the door behind her. She closed her eyes and inhaled a breath deep into her lungs, shaking with anxiety at what she'd just done. Leaning her back against the door she snuggled John to her until a smile played on her lips.

'We're winning, John,' she whispered into his soft hair. 'At last, we're winning.'

Chapter 29

'I want you to send her home. She has no place here.'

Carrie frowned and wiped her mouth on her napkin. The silence between her and Arnold had been heavily weighted and Arnold's glowering on the other side of the table was making her uncomfortable. She was relieved when he broke the ice by speaking, even if he was saying something she didn't want to hear.

'Why, Arnold. What difference does it make to you whether she's here or not, and she might be a woman and in your eyes something to be ignored, but she's also an adult and a human being. She's not a dog to be sent here, there and everywhere at your bidding.'

He forked a large piece of chicken into his mouth and answered her with his mouth full which made Carrie cringe. She came from a humble household that didn't believe in airs and graces and ideas that made you stand out, but she'd known from an early age speaking with a full mouth was bad manners. 'Why is she here? She's not part of this…not part of why we're here. We are here for a reason, Carrie, don't forget that, which is because of me. My rise in the ranks of my profession will affect you. You're my wife. We were married in the eyes of God, and no matter what our feelings are we must keep a united front to ensure our superiors have faith in us, in our…willingness to provide stability. We will need another child soon. You and I, a child of our own, to prove we're…as one.'

Carrie laid her knife and fork carefully across her plate and took a deep breath. This man, so full of hypocrisy and belligerence who spoke to her of God and marriage had sunk to the depths.

'And why am I here, Arnold?' He raised his eyes from his plate and stared at her. 'I'm a wife in name only, which, believe me, suits me just fine. There will be no child and you know it. You're kidding yourself as usual. You're using me to make you look respectable, I understand that, and I also understand you think it's your right because you paid my mother for my services. Well, here's what I think. I think you've had your money's worth out of me. I've kept my mouth shut. I've said nothing about our marriage to anyone who can do you harm. Yes, Dorothy knows but she is a friend and I have entrusted that secret in her care, not for you, Arnold, but for me and for John. Thanks to you I've had absolutely no respect from any of your so-called friends since I've been here. You didn't disagree with what they said about me, or stand by my side. You could have made it better, got them to think differently if you'd supported me, but your dislike of me prevented you from doing the right thing. That was your choice, and as I've said to you in the past, the decisions you've made have done you no good.'

'She has interrupted our life...'

'No! She has not. What you don't like is that I have a friend, one who knows all about you and where you come from, your roots and your humble beginnings that are exactly the same as ours. You would much rather your colleagues and superiors thought you came from higher ground, but the truth is, Arnold, that you came from the same breeding ground as Pearl and me, the dirty back-streets of Whitechapel.'

Arnold's jaw sagged when he realised that he had lost much of his power over Carrie.

'You seem to have been spending a lot of time at the shop in the evening. The shop doesn't open at night does it? You have a child here and...and responsibilities...here, at the bungalow. I know our arrangement is unusual but you still have duties to perform for us as a family.'

'And I fulfil those duties, although I'm surprised you're even mentioning John. You hardly look at him.' Arnold looked sullen. 'The reason I have been at the shop so much is because Pearl is unwell. Her grief for William has weakened her and she is suffering terribly with prickly heat and headaches. I'm very worried it'll turn into the flu. We have been warned against it. Dorothy has written from England to say it is very bad this time. I'm just doing what anyone would do, Arnold, caring for a dear friend and I'll carry on doing so with or without your permission. Of course I can't take John with me. If it's something that can be caught,' she shook her head, 'I don't think it is right now, but if it turns into something then I want John to be safe. Surely you can understand that. You didn't seem to mind him being cared for by an *ayah* when we first arrived.'

'That was different.'

'The only difference is that it suited you. Now it doesn't.'

Arnold clicked his fingers and Gita entered the room carrying the next course of sweet pudding. She looked pointedly at Carrie, placed the dishes on the table and went back to the kitchen. Carrie folded her napkin and placed it on the table.

'Gita and I are going back to the shop now. The ayah will be here in a few minutes to take care of John. Your time is your own, I thought you would have appreciated that. Go to the Secunderabad Club and see your friends. It's what you like doing, isn't it?'

Arnold shrugged. 'Do what you have to do, for now, but I still think she should go back to England. If she's struggling then maybe India doesn't suit her. Maybe she should go back to Whitechapel to her family and be looked after there. I don't see why you should take on the responsibility of her.'

Outside it was dusk, and lights were twinkling from the bungalow verandas. The night-birds had started up their calls. The loud alarm calls of the red lapwing and the hoots of barn owls had begun already. Carrie watched as one of the ghostly white birds flew slowly overhead, then nestled into a tree next to the bungalow with flapping wings that rustled the leaves, like the whisper of satin.

'What will you do, Carrie,' asked Gita, her eyes full of sadness. 'Will Miss Pearl have to go home?'

'Over my dead body,' said Carrie as she started up the Sprite. 'The cold season will be here soon won't it?' Gita nodded. 'How long?'

'Maybe a week…perhaps two, but it gets cold. So cold. I think you will be surprised.'

Carrie nodded. 'That's good. We know cold in England. We're used to it, and Pearl came in the warm season so she was bound to struggle a bit. She'll be alright. She's as tough as old boots really. Like me. Brought up with nothing, expects nothing.' She was interrupted by jackals calling into the increasingly dark night and she shuddered at their echoing cries. 'And it's not just being in India is it, her distress? Not just the heat?'

Gita shook her head and sighed. 'She is a broken girl, Carrie. Sometimes, when I am in the shop, I hear her crying above me. It will not matter where she is. Her heart is torn in two. Mending a broken heart so torn apart, is very hard.'

Carrie took a hand from the steering wheel as she drove towards James Street and placed it over Gita's clutched in her lap. 'But we'll try won't we, Gita? We have to try?'

Gita nodded again. 'Yes, Carrie. We will try.'

They found Pearl in the tiny living room, in her night clothes, her hair laying in unbrushed strands over her shoulders, sitting by the window and staring into space. She startled when they opened the door. Carrie's heart fell. This was so unlike Pearl, the girl who had been so optimistic and forthright when they'd worked together at Nightingale Lane. Carrie knelt down by her chair and smoothed Pearl's hair away from her face as Gita put water on the hob to make tea.

'Have you eaten, Pearl?' Pearl shook her head. 'You have to eat something, sweetheart. To keep your strength up.'

Pearl turned and faced Carrie. Her eyes were ringed red from crying. 'Why, Carrie? What's the point? Without him I've got nothing.'

'You've got you, Pearl. You're still here, and William wouldn't like to think of you like this. Please, eat and drink something.' She turned to Gita. 'Is there any food in the cupboard?' Gita opened each cupboard door in turn, then shook her head. 'Can you go down to James Street, to one of the street vendors? Something light, Gita, and nutritious.' Gita nodded and made for the door, then stopped and looked sadly at Pearl. 'What is it Gita?'

'A doctor perhaps, for Miss Pearl,' she said, sotto voce.

Carrie glanced at Pearl, her sallow skin, the perspiration collecting at her hairline, the look of abandonment in her eyes. 'Yes, Gita,' she whispered. 'I think you're right. I'll deal with it.'

By nine-thirty, Pearl was in bed and sleeping soundly. She had eaten a bowl of mulligatawny soup and a flatbread Gita had bought from one of the street vendors that regularly congregated in James Street as night fell. To Carrie's surprise she had eaten with relish, clearly starving, and it had filled her belly and lowered her gently into a comfortable sleep. Carrie sighed with relief. She feared for Pearl, knowing that if her mind was broken it would eventually break her body, and it was something she couldn't allow.

Smoothing back Pearl's hair from her face that glistened with a sheen of moisture from her fever, her thoughts went to David Lawrence. He was the only person who could help her find a doctor for Pearl, not a doctor of the body, because Carrie was certain this was something Pearl didn't need, but a doctor of the mind. She needed more than a friends' care to assist her in coming to terms with losing William, and as much as Carrie wanted to be the one to help her, she wasn't sure she could.

Gita finished in the kitchen and joined Carrie in the bedroom. She leant against the doorframe and watched as Carrie nursed Pearl.

'What will you do, Carrie? She cannot be left.'

'No, I'm thinking about it, Gita. I think I know someone who can help.'

'Captain Lawrence?'

Carrie stared at her. 'What? Do you know him?'

'I know he is a friend to you and Miss Dorothy, and a good man. My cousin Chaitali works in his house as housekeeper. She says he is very fair man, very good, very kind.'

Carrie nodded. 'I think he is the only one I can ask. There's no point in asking Arnold. He couldn't care less. He has said Pearl should go back to London, not because she has been unwell, he doesn't know how ill she is, but because she is here for me and he doesn't like it.'

'No, we know.'

'Do you?'

'Yes, Carrie. It is hard not to know things when you are working in someone's personal house. It is hard not to see things and hear things, even if we don't want to see them or hear them.'

Carrie rose from the bedside and straightened her skirts, then took Gita's arm and led her into the living room.

'And what have you seen and heard that you wished you hadn't?' She sat on the two-seater sofa with Gita next to her.

'I know he is not a husband to you. I know he has hurt you. I know I could lose my position in the house if he thought I had seen and heard things and I spoke of them to you…or anyone.'

'That won't happen, Gita. I wouldn't allow it.'

'But you cannot stay, Carrie. Why would you stay with such a man?'

'Isn't it what we do? Don't forget, this marriage was not my choice. This was an arranged marriage as much as any arranged marriage conducted in India. Your own daughter had a marriage ceremony this year. Did she choose her own husband?'

'No, but it is our way, it is what we know, and she accepted this. We chose…and we made sure we chose well. He will be good to her, he is good to her. His family is good. They come from a class who have a craft that has been in their family since old times. They make jewellery, the best, and the most beautiful. I am confident in their marriage.'

'But what if you discovered he'd been unkind to her, what would you do?'

'It would not be for me to do, it would be for her. If she left her husband and came home she would be in purdah, she would not leave the house, not for any reason. But…you know her, and she would not come home. She would go abroad, to another country so she could be a modern woman like the women in the West.'

'And is this what you think I should do?'

Gita looked up at Carrie, her eyes warm and steady. 'I think one day you will go back to your home, to where you came from, and when that day comes I will be very sad. You have become…like a daughter to me…I think of you like a daughter. You have shown me and my family more kindness than anyone has from the station. You are different, Carrie, yes, but you are also the same, because you are a woman, a beautiful woman who can love and be loved. It is not the right time for you to settle for what you have been forced to do. There is so much more for you to do and see, and one day you will find the one to join you.' Carrie looked down at her fingers entwined in her lap. Gita's words had settled on her heart and were gradually softening it, the lightness of her voice lulling her into calmness. 'I think there was a time when you thought you had found him.'

Carrie glanced up and smiled and found Gita smiling back at her. 'Yes, I thought I had found him. I thought what we were doing was his way of showing how much he loved me, but I was wrong. My mother said I was stupid, that I probably wasn't the first, and even though he married, I wouldn't be the last he would take advantage of.' She looked away, embarrassed. 'Yes, I thought he was the one.'

Gita reached for her hand. 'You have John.'

Carrie smiled again and thought of the little boy who brought her so much love and joy. 'Yes, I have John, and even after everything that's happened, I wouldn't change it. I love him so much.'

'You should go back to him now,' said Gita.

Carrie shook her head and stood, ready to go back into the bedroom to check on Pearl. 'No, Gita, I must stay. I don't think Pearl should be on her own tonight.'

'I will stay.'

'No, you cannot stay. Your family?'

'They will understand. You must go, and tomorrow you must see Captain Lawrence and ask him to find a doctor for Miss Pearl.'

Carrie put her arms around the sparrow-like shoulders of the woman in front of her and hugged her, the one for whom she held so much respect. 'Gita, how can I ever thank you? I'll find Captain Lawrence first thing and ask him to help us. You're right about him. He is a good man and I'm sure he will know what to do. I want my friend to be how she was, the happy, confident girl she used to be. We can't bring William back but hopefully we'll find the old Pearl.'

Chapter 30

The next morning, after Arnold had left for a two-day excursion to the Mahendra Hills, Carrie made her way across the station with John on her hip. Always aware of the social expectations of women, no matter how innocent her task, she felt taking John would make visiting a single man in his bungalow more appropriate. Her destination was Captain David Lawrence's bungalow, and although the prospect of seeing him again excited her, she was a married woman and could not be seen to be behaving out of that sphere.

She had thought about David a lot since Dorothy had left India. His kindness and respectful way with her had won her over, but she wondered if he was just a charming man whom everyone respected, or was his kind and caring demeanour with her exclusive? She wanted it to be, she knew that. He had stolen her heart; when she saw him, even if it was a glimpse across the station or at the Secunderabad Club when she was accompanied by Arnold, her stomach flipped. Yes, he was handsome, yes he was kind and softly spoken, his voice well measured and beautifully intonated, but was she being swept away by her feelings of abandonment in India, a country so unknown to her even now, her need for closeness with another man after finding out that Arnold's affections lay elsewhere and always would?

She could never love Arnold, could never have loved him, not because of his personal tastes; that was for him to decide, but because of his treatment of her, his wife and the mother of an eight month old baby, a woman who had travelled thousands of miles to a strange country and given birth on a ship with no facilities. He had never acknowledged how difficult and uncomfortable it had been for her. She accepted that John was not his, but she wondered even if he had been would there have been any show of affection for him, a proud fathers' affection and love for a beautiful little boy. She doubted it. There was absolutely no respect for her, or, she had come to learn, for the female species. He had treated his mother appallingly, had even championed his father's actions when he had caused her to lose the baby she had been carrying when she had first met him.

The closer she got to David's bungalow the more nervous she felt. He had not gone to the Mahendra Hills with his unit. Arnold had informed her with some pride that he, Arnold, was leading the party; that David Lawrence was needed to chair a meeting to prepare for a visit from a man from the west of India called Gandhi. She had heard the rumours that he was determined, by non-violent means, to obtain independent rule for India and was now the leader of The Indian National Congress, encouraging people like Gita and her family to rise up and verbally, and with a spirit of morality and independence, fight against those who were ruling them. She knew that the ruling class, according to Arnold, was very worried about Gandhi's growing popularity. Carrie had listened to Arnold and decided she had some sympathy with what Gandhi was trying to achieve, but she was certain Arnold would never agree with that view. She knew exactly how he felt about those he considered inferior to him. She wondered what David Lawrence thought of it, and she was almost certain his views would likely coincide with her own. He was a captain of men, certainly, but he was also fair and respectful.

As she got to the front screen of the bungalow Carrie bit her lip. If she could just stop thinking about him in those terms, look upon him as a man like any other, her stomach would not be somersaulting and a trail of perspiration would not be running down her back. The problem was he was not a man like any other, he had already professed an admiration and affection for her when Dorothy had taken her to the lake the night she had informed Carrie she was leaving India for England. He had taken her hand and told her to look upon him as a friend, that Dorothy had asked him to stand in her stead, and that he was honoured to do so until Dorothy returned to India and that she must turn to him if ever she needed help or assistance. This was one of those times, not for her it was true, but Carrie loved Pearl like a sister, so it would be helping Carrie too. She hoped their friendship would be enough for David Lawrence to want to assist them.

She gingerly held up a hand to knock on the front screen then lowered it and took a breath. She closed her eyes and when she opened them John gazed at her with his beautiful blue eyes, his chocolate brown hair ruffled by the breeze. She smiled at him and to her delight he smiled back.

'Alright, John,' she whispered. 'I know what I have to do.' She lifted her hand again and rapped on the screen. A few moments passed, then David Lawrence appeared through the screen. He was startled when he saw her. She saw his expression change and she wasn't sure if he was glad to see her, or embarrassed that she'd called on him at his home.

'Carrie.'

'David. I'm so sorry to disturb you at home, but you said I could call on you if I needed help. I should say it's not for me, but for a friend.'

'Of course, of course, come in, please.'

She stepped across the threshold feeling nervous, and went into David's large living room; typically masculine décor with brown furniture from home, yet softened with huge pieces of art he'd hung on the walls and brightly woven rugs underfoot. She breathed in as she got to the centre of the room, his smell, the unique cologne he wore, overlaid slightly with the pungent tobacco everyone smoked, so popular in India.

He followed her in, indicating for her to sit on a buttoned leather settee as he lit a cigarette and sat opposite her.

'How can I help? Oh, I'm sorry, Carrie, I should have offered some refreshment, particularly in this heat. I'm afraid I don't possess the hosting niceties you ladies have and I forget sometimes. What can I get for you, some mint tea perhaps or elderflower cordial?'

She nodded. 'Some cordial, please.'

'And John? Will he have a biscuit? I had some of my favourites sent over from England.'

She smiled and looked down at her son. 'John would love a biscuit.'

David nodded and, leaving his cigarette in an ashtray, went into the kitchen, returning with an elaborately decorated glass of cordial and a biscuit with white icing across the top. Carrie's eyes widened. 'He'll love that,' and laughed.

'Now,' said David, sitting in front of her. 'What can do to help you?'

'It's my friend, Pearl. She came over from England a few weeks ago. Her fiancé was killed at the front, and I so wanted to go home to comfort her, but Arnold said it wouldn't be possible. The passage cost so much and for me to go out there and return, well, he wasn't prepared to find the money, so I invited her here. Dorothy helped me with her fare. The trouble is, it's clear Pearl isn't well. She has stopped caring about anything, even herself, her appearance is awful, because she's pining for her William. Her grief is awful to see, and Gita and I have done everything we can, but we've come to a point where we can't go any further. I just don't know what to do. It's clear Pearl needs a doctor, a doctor of the mind, someone to counsel her and help her through it. Do you know anyone, David? I'm afraid this goes beyond anything or anyone I've come into contact with.'

David drew deeply on his cigarette, then stubbed the remainder out in the ashtray. He frowned, rubbing his chin, deep in thought. 'I'm not sure there's anyone like that in Secunderabad. Not much call for it I'd say, although sometimes I think some of the men need help with everything they've witnessed at the front.' He inhaled deeply. 'I think Bombay would be your best port of call.'

Carrie gasped. 'Bombay? But it's miles away. We'd have to pay for the doctor's train fare and even put him up in a hotel in Secunderabad because I'm sure one visit won't be enough.' There's absolutely no point my asking Arnold for help. He hates it that Pearl's here and has already suggested I send her home. If he knew how ill she was I wouldn't stand a chance of caring for her here.'

'I think it's the only place you'll find the kind of doctor you need. There's no one here like that, I'm pretty sure of it, and unfortunately there are some charlatans in Secunderabad who have set themselves up as doctors because they know they got a captive clientele, silly women who pay them for doing not very much. No, it has to be Bombay. Leave it with me, Carrie. I'll investigate…oh, and don't worry about the money side of things. I'm sure we can come to some arrangement with the doctor. The important thing is to find a good one, someone who understands what she's going through.'

'David, I don't know how to thank you.'

David held up a hand. 'We need to get your friend better. Her fiancé gave his life for his country. It's the least I can do. And you never know,' he said, smiling. 'I might need your help one day.'

David Lawrence was as good as his word, not that Carrie doubted him for a moment. Within two weeks, Doctor Angus Fraser was on his way to Secunderabad from Bombay.

'That's not a very Indian name, David,' she said when they met one evening at the Secunderabad Club.

'No, but he was recommended by a friend in England who knew him when he practiced in Scotland. Apparently he settled in Bombay after marrying into an Indian family, unusual for the times I know. Unfortunately his wife passed away after giving him a son and daughter, twins, only three years old.'

'Oh, that's very sad.'

'She caught the flu in her weakened state after giving birth and never recovered. If anyone knows how your friend is feeling, he does.'

Carrie shook her head sadly. 'She's not getting any better. Gita is sitting with her tonight. I don't know what I would have done without

Gita. She has been a rock for me. She is the only person I can rely on in Secunderabad…and you of course.'

David looked uncomfortable and Carrie's heart jumped. 'Have I said something out of place?'

'No, of course not, but there has been talk. The grapevine here is very active. I know you don't like to be involved, but many are. People are saying you're much too close to her. I'm just concerned Bateman will hear all the gossip. The people who are doing the most spreading are in his circle, in my own unit, and it can be very destructive. I know what has happened between you and Bateman, Carrie, Dorothy filled me in. She was aware she was putting me in a difficult position; Bateman is in my unit,' they both glanced across at Arnold who was holding court with some young soldiers, 'but she felt your safety was more important than the hierarchy of the unit. And of course she was correct.'

Carrie stared at him. Her stomach lurched and she had the sudden urge to kiss him, to place her lips against his and close her eyes. She imagined his strong arms around her, pressing her body to his and it made her gasp. David put his hand to her elbow to steady her, then swiftly lowered it again. There could be no impropriety between them, not even a light touch. 'Yes, yes, I'm fine. It's a bit warm in here that's all. I often struggle with the heat.'

'Do you need to go out for some air?'

'No. No thank you, I'd better go back to Arnold. He won't acknowledge my presence but if I'm not at least near him I'll hear about it later. David, thank you so much for all your help. I hope and pray Dr Fraser can help poor Pearl. I'm so worried for her.' She turned and walked towards Arnold, wishing with all her heart that the man she was walking towards was the one she knew she was in love with. Captain David Lawrence.

Within a week, Dr Angus Fraser was installed in a small, but neat and tidy hotel in central Secunderabad on a narrow alleyway leading off James Street. David Lawrence was unable to meet with him, his military duties had taken him to another station, but he had arranged for Dr Fraser to introduce himself by way of a visit to Carrie's Closet. Carrie was nervous about the meeting, and paced for an hour before his arrival. Gita put her hand on her arm and passed her a cup of tea to calm her nerves.

'You seem agitated, Carrie. Drink this and try to calm yourself. You'll be no help to anyone if you tire yourself.'

'But what if we don't like him, Gita? What if he's strict and harsh and doesn't understand why Pearl feels so ill? She won't thank me. When I said David and I had found a doctor to help her she was less than pleased, saying she didn't need a doctor and she would be alright if we left her alone. I won't pretend, I am very worried.' A moment later, the bell above the door chimed and a man who Carrie instantly knew was Dr Fraser bustled through the door. The first thing she saw was his beard, ginger in colour and parted by a huge smile. He was a large man, tall with broad shoulders, and his copious hair was as red as his beard. Carrie smiled to herself. This was a man in need of a haircut.

'Mrs Bateman, I presume,' he said, his Scottish brogue unspoilt by his years in Bombay.

'Yes, Dr Fraser?' She held out her hand which was engulfed as his fingers wrapped around hers. 'Welcome to Secunderabad. We're nothing like Bombay I'm afraid.'

He laughed and his blue eyes twinkled. 'Nowhere is like Bombay,' he answered, and Carrie liked him instantly. He smiled at Gita who had brought him some refreshment. 'Thank you. This is very welcome. And who is this lady?' he asked, nodding politely to Gita as he accepted the tea she offered him

'This is Gita,' said Carrie. 'My right-hand woman…and dear friend.'

'And the lady in question?'

'Upstairs above the shop…in the apartment. She is…not dressed today. And…unbathed, I'm afraid.'

'Aye, well, bathing is the last thing on someone's list of things to do when one is grieving.'

Carrie felt her breath catch in her throat. 'I…I'm sorry, Dr Fraser. I understand you are only too aware of how that feels. I'm so very sorry.'

'Yes, yes, unexpected, of course. Unfortunately, my wife wasn't very robust. The influenza took her. And now I have two bonny children to raise.'

'You have ayahs, nannies for the children?'

'Shilpa's mother, the children's grandmother. And a young woman who comes to the house a few hours a day to help out. And me, of course. I make as much time for them as I can. I have my patients. I must still attend to them.'

'Of course.'

'And with that in mind I should meet the patient. What's her name, her first name?'

'Pearl.'

'Ah, a good Scottish name. From which part of London are you?'

'Whitechapel.' He nodded knowingly. 'Are you ready to meet her, Doctor?'

'Yes, I think she and I should have a chat. She knows I'm here?'

'Yes.'

'And she's not very happy about it?'

Carrie wrung her hands and inhaled nervously. 'No.'

'No surprise there. It happens more frequently than you would imagine. Take me to her.'

Carrie and Gita took Dr Fraser up to the floor above the shop and waited in the tiny lobby that led into the living room. They were both holding their breath, waiting to discover what Pearl's reaction would be when he joined her in the place that had become her sanctuary, her safe place away from a cruel and unfeeling world that had taken her beloved William from her. It seemed to Carrie that Pearl now saw everything beyond her own space as dangerous, and everyone within it, the enemy. Her heart had been broken so decisively, with such force, there was nothing on earth that could encourage that heart to be mended, or at the very least, to begin the healing process. Carrie also worried that if Pearl decided not to see Dr Fraser, to send him away without allowing him to try and help her, not only would his journey from Bombay to Secunderabad been a waste of his time, but also a blow to her savings, money she had put aside for their futures. She didn't want to think of it as a waste, she would do anything to help her closest friend, but she knew there was always a chance that her idea of finding a doctor for Pearl could fall on stony ground, and therefore her friend would never be healed and the future Carrie planned for them would never be achieved.

Carrie and Gita listened silently to Dr Fraser as he spoke to Pearl, his voice low and gentle, neither cajoling nor admonishing, simply speaking to her with compassion and understanding. After a few minutes they heard Pearl sobbing, her voice broken and distraught as she explained to Dr Fraser how William's death had shattered her, not just in body but in her mind, how their plans to be married had been destroyed because he had been killed, that she could never find forgiveness for whoever it was who had taken his life, and because of this she had sunk into the very depths of despair. Carrie swallowed hard as tears rolled down her cheeks. Gita put a hand on her arm.

'He will help her, Carrie,' she whispered. 'He will help her.'

Carrie nodded and bit her lip. 'I hope so.'

Chapter 31

As the weeks went by, life began to take on a steady rhythm. Carrie did her utmost to stay away from Arnold whilst at the same time being the dutiful wife he demanded. Each morning she would rise early and prepare John for either accompanying her to the shop or to spend time with his ayah, who Carrie now looked upon as a friend. Amrita was a young woman with her whole life ahead of her. Carrie often wondered how she would ever meet a husband, knowing how important it was in her culture that she married, because her life consisted of caring for her mother's younger children at home in their village, and caring for John at the bungalow. Gita assured her Amrita would be taken care of.

'Already her family are considering young men for her, Carrie. She does not need to meet them. He will be chosen for her.' This had sent shivers down Carrie's spine, and she hoped Amrita's family would take more care of her than Florrie and Arthur had of her when choosing the man with whom she would spend her life. She often wondered if they had known what kind of man Arnold was, that he thought nothing of beating a woman and had only derision for his mother, they would have let her leave with Arnold so gladly, but then her thoughts went to Florrie. Florrie was a pragmatist. Arnold was a solution, and Florrie knew another one wouldn't come along so easily. Added to that, Arnold had paid her a not insubstantial amount of money, according to him. She hoped the money she'd received had been worth losing her daughter and grandson for. She wondered what had happened to it as she shook her head and tutted to herself. She could only hope it had made their life easier than the one she had left.

'Will I ever see you again?' she said aloud, with only John secured in the parcel seat at the back, and the parched trees on the track out of the station to hear her as she drove the Sprite to the shop on James Street. 'And do you want to see me? Will you ever want to see me and my son, or am I just a reminder of shame that you don't want and would rather forget?'

A deep sadness overtook her, and as she got to the road leading to the centre of Secunderabad she turned in her seat to look at John. 'How could she give up being your grandmother so easily?' John's face broke into a beautiful, heart-stopping smile and Carrie leant back and stroked his cheek. 'She has missed so much. No amount of money could ever be worth losing you. One day they'll know, they'll know they shouldn't have done what they did and they'll regret it. It will break their hearts because you are an angel. And we will have to mend those hearts again.'

The shop was already open when she arrived. Gita always rose early and was usually in the shop before Carrie. Carrie smiled as she opened the door and the little bell above it rang out her arrival.

'You love your job, don't you, Gita?'

Gita grinned and nodded. 'I thank the goddess Lakshmi every day for the opportunity she brought my way when you came into my life, Carrie. I am now thought of very highly in the village because I work for you. Villagers ask my opinion on everything, and everyone knows who I am. It has never been like this before. Before this, I was simply Radhav's wife. Now I am Gita, wise woman of the village, who has stepped outside of everything she thought she would be.'

Carrie had tears in her eyes as Gita spoke. 'Oh, Gita. I didn't know it meant so much to you. They need to know I couldn't have done it without you. You have changed my life too. I am honoured you're my friend.' She embraced the woman, noticing she seemed even thinner than usual. 'Gita. You've lost weight. Are you eating?'

Gita laughed and turned back to the racks of clothing where she was hanging new stock. 'Like a wolf with a catch, Carrie. I eat very well.' Carrie nodded, but a bud of anxiety grew in her chest. Gita took John from Carrie's arms and cuddled him.

'Dr Fraser is here.'

Carrie frowned. 'Already. He's very early today.'

Gita nodded and smiled. 'He is taking Pearl into James Street. It will be the first time she has left the shop in nearly two months. He wants her to spend Christmas Day with other people, although she has said she would rather be alone. She pushes it away when he suggests anything new.'

'Where is he taking her?'

'He said he is taking her shopping.'

'Shopping? Really?' Gita nodded. 'D'you think it'll be alright for me to go up to the apartment?'

Gita nodded again, and Carrie opened the door that led to the staircase to the first-floor rooms. When she got halfway up, she could hear Angus Fraser's gentle voice as he encouraged Pearl to step out of her safe place and venture out onto James Street.

'Now, Pearl, don't tell me you don't like shopping. I haven't met a woman yet who didn't love to trawl around every shop to find that very special thing, and then end up in the very first shop they went into.' Carrie stopped on the stair and smiled to herself. Here was a man who knew women. 'We don't have to go far. You will take the lead, and when you want to come back to the apartment for a nice cup of tea, we come back.'

Carrie stepped up the rest of the staircase and joined them in the living room. Pearl was pale, yet Carrie noticed there was a slight flush to her cheeks and her eyes were bright. Carrie went across to her friend to embrace her, and to her relief, Pearl returned it.

'You look better, Pearl. Much better. I hear you're planning to go out today.'

Pearl nodded. 'Yes, but Carrie I've got so little to wear. I feel so frumpy in the clothes I brought from London. They're all so dark and heavy. I've been watching everyone out of the window, the bright colours and beautiful soft floaty fabrics. I can't go out in what I've got.'

Carrie sat next to Pearl on the sofa and took her hand. 'Pearl, sweetheart, you're living over a dress shop. Finding something to wear should be the last thing for you to worry about.'

Pearl turned her face to Carrie's shoulder as if hiding what she was saying from Angus Fraser. 'I've no money, Carrie. I can't afford the dresses you sell. I came here to work and I've done nothing for weeks, so I've earned nothing. I feel such a burden.'

Carrie glanced up at Dr Fraser and was surprised to see the expression on his face which was one of gentle sadness. 'But you will earn, when you're properly better. You can help me and Gita in the shop. You can start with a couple of hours and then increase them when you're ready. And as for being a burden, I won't hear of it,' Carrie chided her softly. 'You could never be a burden to me. You're my best friend and you always will be.' Pearl looked into Carrie's face and tears filled her eyes. 'I'll go downstairs and get you some things to try on. Would that be alright?'

As she left the apartment she turned to see Angus Fraser sit in the chair opposite Pearl and take her hand in his own, then reach up to tenderly wipe away a tear from her cheek with his thumb. It seemed such an intimate thing to do, something a man would do for a woman he admired, not a doctor to a patient. She was curious as to Pearl's reaction, but she simply smiled at him and lowered her eyelashes, and Carrie couldn't help wondering if something had happened between them. She hoped Fraser hadn't taken advantage of Pearl in her darkest moments, but she couldn't deny that Pearl had become a different person since his arrival.

Her recovery had been a very gradual thing. At first she had put up barriers, telling Carrie that she didn't need a doctor and that time was a healer. Carrie had agreed with her, but told her that Angus Fraser had been recommended to David Lawrence and was a well-respected doctor in Bombay, and that if he could bring about Pearl's recovery faster then surely it was something worth considering.

'I don't want to forget William,' Pearl had said. 'I could never forget him, he'll always be part of my life even though he's not with me anymore.' She'd glanced up at Carrie, pleading with her eyes for her to understand.

'No one wants to take William's memory away from you, Pearl,' she'd said. 'He was your fiancé and you loved him. I know you still do, but you have a life in front of you, sweetheart, and I'm sure William would have wanted you to live it. I know how much he meant to you, but he would have wanted you to do what you could to get better. Live for him, Pearl. He was a brave boy who gave his life to his country so that you could continue without fear. It's time you did.'

Half an hour after Carrie had taken a selection of dresses to the apartment and Gita had helped her try them on, Pearl left the apartment for the first time in weeks. She had chosen a lemon-yellow dress that made her beautiful red hair flowing down her back glow like gold. A wide straw hat completed the outfit, and Gita had chosen some yellow buttoned pumps to match. Carrie had slipped Pearl some money in lieu of wages and she had smiled at Carrie gratefully.

'Treat yourself, Pearl,' Carrie said. 'Buy yourself a Christmas present. You deserve it.'

Pearl had clutched Carrie's hand and squeezed it. 'I'll never be able to thank you enough, Carrie, for what you and Gita, and Captain Lawrence have done for me. I'm ever so grateful.'

Carrie hugged her. 'I just want my Pearl back. That's all.'

That evening, when Pearl had returned from James Street and Dr Fraser had returned to his hotel, Carrie went up to the apartment before leaving for the bungalow. There was a feeling that had stayed with her all afternoon and she knew she had to speak with Pearl about it. The look she had given Dr Fraser had become imprinted behind her eyes and she needed to be sure Pearl was safe and in her right mind, that she wasn't being coerced into something she would later regret. She tapped gently on the living room door and Pearl answered.

'Come in.' Carrie peeped around the door and Pearl laughed. 'Come in, Carrie. I thought it was you. I know your knock.'

Carrie nodded and went into the apartment, then went across to the tiny kitchen and poured a pitcher of water into the kettle and placed it on the stove. Tea always accompanied those moments in life which stayed in our memories, and for a reason she couldn't fathom, she felt this was going to be one of them.

'How was your afternoon?' she asked Pearl.

Pearl sunk into the sofa and became quiet. She was breathing steadily, as if measuring every breath, the distance between each inhale and exhale equal. 'It's the first time I've left the apartment for weeks. I was very nervous, but Alistair, I mean…Dr Fraser gave me the encouragement and safety I needed.'

'What do you think of him?' Carrie carried two cups and saucers steaming with fresh tea across to the occasional table between the sofa and the chair and sat down, leaning towards her friend, hoping, perhaps even praying everything was as it should be.

'He's very kind, Carrie. He has been very kind to me.' She inhaled deeply. 'The thing is, he understands the loss I experienced when William was killed. He lost his beloved wife, he adored her you know, and it's how I felt about William. I think it's what I needed, someone who had been through it.' She leant forward and put her hand across Carrie's. 'Please don't think I'm ungrateful. You have been a true friend, the only one who actually tried to help me when I was in my darkest despair. Even at home in Whitechapel, I couldn't seem to make my family understand that I was wretched with grief. My mother said that I should grin and bear it because so many women had lost their husbands, and children their fathers; that I shouldn't behave as though I was the only one who had lost someone. What she didn't understand was that I was well aware of the devastation being felt by so many women and children in the country, but none of them knew William. Of course I understood, of course I knew that many hearts had been broken, but my heart had broken too, into so many pieces I thought it could never be mended.'

Carrie's eyes had filled with tears and she squeezed her friends hand to show her she understood. 'And is it healing, Pearl? Do you think it can be mended?'

'Something happened to my mind, Carrie. It wasn't just my heart that was broken. My mind became broken because of the unbearable pain I felt when I knew William had been taken from me and would never come back. It was like…it was like I'd been cast out into a storm so great I couldn't see where I was going or where I would end up. Even in the quiet of this apartment, the safety of these four walls, it seemed so far outside of what I was feeling inside, like I was in my own hell. I don't think I've ever been so frightened in all my life. And for a while I thought I wouldn't survive. I would either die in my sleep or by my own hand.'

Carrie gasped. 'No, Pearl. Never that. Please.'

Pearl patted her hand and leant back into the sofa. 'It has passed.' She smiled gently. 'I've found some strength…from somewhere. I know I'll never see William again, but the love we had was special, and I'll never forget it. And I'll never forget him and how brave he was to put himself forward for his country. Dr Fraser said this is how I should remember him, as a brave soldier who chose his path. And actually, Carrie he did, didn't he? William chose to go and fight. He knew what could happen, he knew he might die. We talked about it, but I was so naïve about what was happening over there, I just didn't think it would happen to him. Dr Fraser thinks I suffered a kind of shock to my system, something I couldn't cope with, which was why I became ill.'

'But you're getting better, aren't you? You're feeling better.'

'Yes. Yes, I'm better. The grief I feel now…I think it's normal grief for someone I've lost. Dr Fraser gave me some breathing exercises to do and some stretching exercises. Even going out today was part of my recovery. He says I did very well.'

'What will happen when he goes back to Bombay?'

Pearl shrugged. 'I'll have to be strong. I'll come and work in the shop to give me a purpose. He says it's what I need, a purpose in life. He says we all do.'

Carrie nodded. 'He's right. We do all need a purpose in life. As difficult as it was when I had John I don't know what I would have done without him. He gave me a reason to carry on, in fact, he was *the* reason. I had to be strong for him, even with everything I've gone through with Arnold. Knowing John needed me got me through it.'

'He said I could go to Bombay for a holiday, that I could stay in his house and meet his children.'

Carrie stared at her. 'Is there more to your relationship than a doctor, patient one, Pearl? I was a little concerned. You seem so close.'

Pearl shook her head. 'No. There has been no impropriety. He is just one of the kindest people I've ever met. I feel…safe, when I'm in his company. He has become a good friend. Our loss of the ones who meant the most to us has strengthened our respect for one another. He loved his wife so much, Carrie, but he had to remain strong for his children. That must have been very difficult, perhaps even more so for a man because children always look to their mothers, don't they?' Carrie nodded. 'But they became his purpose, along with his practice and his patients.'

'Will you go to Bombay?'

Pearl smiled benignly. 'Maybe one day. Not yet. I'm not strong enough for such a journey, or to be thrown into another person's life. It was very kind of him to offer me some respite, but I'm not ready for it. He's going to stay until the New Year. His family in Bombay don't celebrate Christmas as we do, and his children are well looked after so he will stay to see me through the festive season, then he will return to his family.'

Carrie left her chair and sat next to Pearl on the sofa. She clutched her friend's arm, then put her head on her shoulder. 'I've got you back, Pearl, my lovely wonderful friend. It's all I wanted.'

'And I'll never be able to thank you enough, or Captain Lawrence. How much must I owe him, Carrie? When will I ever be able to repay him?'

Carrie glanced up. 'Don't worry about that,' she whispered. 'It's not important. I'll see him tonight and I'll talk to him about it. Arnold and I are due to go to a dinner being held at the Secunderabad Club for one of the men in his unit, some sort of leaving do. For two pins I wouldn't go. I absolutely hate being dragged there and having to sit with Arnold pretending everything is as it should be. He likes to play the dutiful husband but I'm pretty sure most people know we don't have a real marriage. Anyway, I know there isn't anything to worry about as far as David's concerned. He was very willing to help us. David Lawrence is also a very kind man, a lovely man in fact.' She heard Pearl chuckle and she sat up. 'What?'

Pearl raised her eyebrows. 'And a very handsome man.'

Carrie grinned. 'Well, yeah, that as well.'

'Not that you'd noticed.' Carrie shrugged. 'Don't let him get away, Carrie. You've been through so much. I've learnt the hard way we have to take the opportunities that are sent our way. Life's too short to be holding back on anything. And I know you've got feelings for him. When you talk about him your voice changes.'

'Does it?' Pearl nodded, smiling and Carrie sighed. 'It doesn't make any difference how I feel. I'm married to Arnold Bateman and it seems as though it will have to stay that way. At least for now.'

Pearl shook her head. 'Why? You need to get out. You've got reasons. I don't know why you haven't done it.'

'It's not that easy. Where would I go? Arnold would make my life hell. And yes, I have the shop know, but it's not really mine. It really belongs to Dorothy, and if she returns things will change. I run the business as my own, and I'm saving like mad because one day, one day I will leave. I will go back to London, to Whitechapel, and I'll make sure me and John don't need to rely on anyone, but I don't have enough yet. I have a goal in mind, a ridiculous goal some might say, but it gets me out of bed in the morning. The more I work, the more I save, and the more I save the closer I am to achieving what I want. Whitechapel spat me and John out when we needed it most. I can't let it happen again.'

'So you will go back then?'

Carrie nodded. 'Yes, and if you're still here you can come with me. There will always be a home for you with me, Pearl. You know that don't you?'

'And what about Captain Lawrence?'

'I don't know,' Carrie answered, shaking her head. 'You're right about my feelings for him, but I just don't know.'

That evening Carrie accompanied Arnold to The Secunderabad Club for a leaving ceremony for one of the officers in his unit.

'We'll go in your car,' he said. 'Nice little thing that is. I don't mind arriving in it.'

Carrie felt her hackles rise. 'Dorothy didn't give it to me for your benefit, Arnold. It's meant for work. We should get another car or go by cart.'

'Cart? I'm not turning up to the club in a bloody cart. You can if you want to. I'll drive the car myself.'

'No. You won't. I'll drive.' The thought of Arnold sitting in the passenger seat beside her in the small car made her stomach turn, but she was determined he wouldn't take control of the only thing she could call hers, at least until Dorothy returned from England. 'Are you ready?'

He turned towards her, his white dress uniform would have been smart on anyone else, but on Arnold it just made him look even paler than usual. Carrie had long since realised there was very little that would make Arnold look smart, even though he was convinced he outshone every other soldier in the room, and he turned the glare of that light onto the young soldiers who had just joined the unit. 'How do I look?'

She glanced at him as she pulled on her gloves. 'Very smart, Arnold.' She waited for him to comment on her silver-grey sequinned column dress that skimmed her ankles and the white feather in front of her headdress, but he said nothing as usual. Carrie shook her head with frustration.

'Come on, let's go.'

On the journey he asked her about Pearl.

'When's she going 'ome? Out-stayed her welcome I reckon.'

'She's not going home. She's been ill and she needs time to recover. Then she's going to work in the shop for a while.'

'Yeah, well I should think so. She needs to earn her keep. We're not made of money.'

Carrie smiled to herself. No, we're not, she thought. But I am.

The shop had surpassed all their expectations. When Carrie had written to Dorothy to tell her how much it was earning every month, Dorothy had insisted Carrie begin a fund for herself.

I don't need it, darling, she had written, *but I do want you and John to have a nest-egg. And honestly, Carrie, you're the one doing all the work. It sounds like you're doing a grand job too. Just make sure Gita is looked after. I've heard she puts in a lot of hours. It seems to be in her blood, working herself to the bone, poor thing. It might be time for her to take a step back when Pearl feels well enough to take over. I'm so sorry she's been so unwell, but glad you've found a solution. I knew David would come through for you...*

Carrie had thought about nothing else since, that Gita was certainly not herself, yet she had stubbornly refused to rest even though Carrie had suggested it many times. She wondered if Dorothy was right, it was simply in her culture that she work until she dropped because she was apprehensive about what it would mean if she lost her job; that her family would suffer as a consequence. She needs time off, Carrie thought as she drove towards The Secunderabad Club, trying to block out Arnold's incessant self-important chatter. It will do her good to have some time to herself. I must make sure Arnold doesn't find out because he'll have her working back at the bungalow and she will not refuse because Gita doesn't know how to refuse anything.

Chapter 32

The mood in the club seemed rather sombre. Carrie had got past the point of worrying that the other wives barely acknowledged her; she knew she was seen as an aberration to the rest of the station. Even the Fishing Fleet ignored her. Strange though, she thought. When they come into the shop on their own without their friends they're as nice as pie.

She made her way to the edge of the room after taking a glass of sparkling wine from a tray. Arnold had instantly gone to the bar without a second thought for her, his usual behaviour when they mixed socially. It was almost like a game of chess; they both had their usual moves and accepted that the other would not be close. Carrie was glad of it. The last person she wanted to be close to was Arnold.

She glanced around the room at the other guests. Many of them were in little cliques, soldiers and their wives, some holding back while others were desperate to make their mark and become the Burra of the station, the Queen Bee of the mofussil. Carrie thought about when she was a scullery maid at Nightingale Lane, wishing she could be part of the beautiful set with their stunning clothes, clipped vowels and air of superiority. I've grown up, she thought. Now I know it means nothing. They're just like me. Cut them and they bleed, and make a lot more noise about it than my class would. Never again would she feel that someone was better than her simply because they had money. Carrie felt a warm feeling flow through her, a sense of knowing who she was and what she wanted. And she wasn't relying on a man to do it for her, to sit on his coat tails as he rose through the ranks in the military so she could boast about it to her friends. Everything she had now she could afford to buy herself. She had offered Dorothy a sum of money for the Sprite but Dorothy had refused, telling her that when she returned to Secunderabad they would go exploring together and Carrie could drive. Carrie accepted her generosity with good grace and took special care of the little car, somehow doubting Dorothy would return to the station.

She realised the way people at the station lived was unsustainable. No one could live like it forever. She had already been informed by Arnold that when John reached the age of seven he would be sent home to England to complete his education. It was true, she'd had to acknowledge. There were barely any children at the mofussil. There had been a couple of births recently, but certainly none older. Carrie was determined not to be separated from her son and this was at the foremost of her mind. Arnold had tried to take everything from her, her confidence in her abilities, her dignity, and her friends, and he had not succeeded. And he certainly would not succeed in parting her from her beloved little boy.

She realised she had taken herself in mind, if not in body, away from The Secunderabad Club and back to the streets of Whitechapel. She wondered about that place. Had it changed? How were her parents whom she had not once heard from since she had been in India; a year in April. Christmas in Secunderabad would be the first festive season she had ever spent away from home and she wondered how it would be. Most years, in London, they had so little, but with the cook, Mrs Coyle's generosity they had always managed to have enough to eat. Pigeon pie had been a regular on the Dobbs' Christmas table, accompanied by mashed potato and some greens. There would also be jars of strange things purloined from the Stern's cupboard at 99 Nightingale Lane, delicacies that Mrs. Coyle said had been there a while and Carrie might as well take home with her. It had become almost a Christmas parlour game, with everyone trying to guess what might be in the jars and only the bravest of them attempting to taste what was inside. Carrie smiled to herself at the memory and was then startled out of her reverie by a voice interrupting her daydream.

'You look very amused at something, Mrs Bateman.'

The voice brought her back to the present. Her heart jumped when she saw who had spoken the words and her breath left her body.

'Captain Lawrence. David. How lovely to see you. How are you?'

'I'm well, Carrie, but more importantly, how is your friend? Pearl isn't it?'

She nodded. 'Pearl is on the mend thanks to Dr Fraser. He has worked wonders with her. She's more like the girl I knew.'

'I'm very glad to hear it. Grief can be a terrible thing.'

'I'm glad I've seen you, David. I wanted to speak to you about Dr Fraser's fee. And of course his expenses. Will you let me know how much we owe you?'

He smiled gently and caught her eyes with his. Carrie had the urge cry, why she didn't know, but his kindness and gentleness shone from him and she wanted more than anything in the world at that moment to be taken into his arms and held, to be kissed, to feel his hands in her hair as he drew her body closer to his. 'You owe me nothing, Carrie.'

'But…'

He shook his head. 'Please. Don't worry. It was my pleasure to help you. I know Dr Fraser is very pleased with Pearl's recovery…in fact, he has nothing but high praise for how hard she has worked to regain her former health, and for you, of course.'

'You've spoken to him?'

'Yes, and we have come to an agreement over his expenses. He intends to stay until after the Christmas period. He will stay at the station in my bungalow.'

'Your bungalow?'

'Yes, Carrie. I'm leaving Secunderabad immediately after Christmas to return to the front. This…get-together is for me.'

Her eyes widen and she gasped. 'You're leaving? Why?'

'I'm to go to France to oversee another unit. Seems I've been too successful with my men here. I'm to go back where the men require more assistance. I just hope I can give it to them, poor devils.'

'David…please don't go.'

He laughed. 'Carrie, it's not something I have a choice in. Mahatma Gandhi's visit is in the week between Christmas and the New Year and then I must leave. If I could stay, I would.'

Suddenly the gong sounded for everyone to be seated. David wandered towards the front of the ballroom and Arnold joined Carrie.

'Why are you looking like that?' he said. 'You look like you've seen a ghost. Come on, we need to sit at our table. And please, try not to say anything stupid in front of my men. Best if you keep quiet I think.'

He put his hand roughly under her elbow and steered her towards the tables. Carrie felt like she was in a bubble, simply moving because she was being pushed. She sat with tears pricking under her eyelids. She hadn't known the leaving dinner was for David. If she'd known she wasn't sure she could have attended. Now she had to pretend everything was alright, that she was there simply as a guest, a bystander in the life of the mofussil, a bit-player in David's life, when really she wanted to be the most important part.

Arnold's impatience with her was palpable.

'What the hell is up with you? Are you ill? Please don't disgrace me again.'

Carrie took a deep breath. 'I feel a little under the weather. Maybe I need some air.'

'Can't it wait? They're about to make the speeches. You're probably hungry. Hope you can wait an hour. These things can go on a bit.'

She sat like stone, listening to the speeches about David and how much he would be missed in the unit. Occasionally she glanced at him. He had an elbow on the table, his face cast downward, and would only look up when someone made a joke about him that the ladies had to pretend they didn't understand. An hour or so later, dinner was served. Carrie picked at the food. As usual it was highly spiced until the cheese course when she felt she could eat something safely.

When dinner was over and a more relaxed mood had enveloped the gathering, Carrie whispered to Arnold that she needed some air and would go outside. He nodded impatiently, and she left the table with Arnold only vaguely acknowledging her leaving with a roll of his eyes. He didn't care, she knew. He was very busy discussing something with an extremely good looking, and rather effete young adjutant who had arrived in Secunderabad only the week before and seemed overwhelmed with the society he had been thrown into. She shook her head in disgust as she left the table, realising that the young man was probably Arnold's next target, but she also had to acknowledge that he seemed to be enjoying the undivided attention Arnold was giving him.

Outside, the air was still, with only the sound of the night birds as they roosted on the trees surrounding the club. Carrie looked back at the white building which looked almost ghostly in the increasing dusk, then wandered towards the small lake and sat on one of the benches. The scent of hibiscus and lilies hung in the air and she closed her eyes and breathed in the heady scent. It was a beautiful night, and Carrie sat silently, deep in thought, watching the water birds as they landed on the lake with a gentle whoosh and a brief flapping of wings. She was overwhelmed with sadness. Two of the people who had made her life bearable since she had arrived in Secunderabad were now lost to her. Dorothy had mentioned in her letters returning to India in the future, but Carrie was sure she would not. She was caring for her sister's children and she felt certain Dorothy only said it to placate her. She wondered if she would ever see her friend again.

And now David was leaving too. That she had fallen in love with him there was no doubt. He was everything she had ever wanted in a man, kind, gentle, strong, and utterly caring, and try as she might she could not push those feelings away. Every time she saw him she was aware of his nearness to her, his unique cologne, the lightness of his voice and the look in his eyes. He had an effect on her and she was undeniably attracted to him. She wondered if he had feelings for her, but it seemed an incongruous thought bearing in mind that after Christmas, he too would leave India. She sighed and swallowed the temptation to cry. If Arnold noticed he would not let her forget it and would certainly carp at her until he knew why, enjoying her distress.

Someone sat beside her and startled out of her thoughts. She turned slowly and stared at David, here heart beating wildly, hoping he couldn't read her mind.

'Life doesn't get any easier does it?' he said.

Carrie glanced back to the lake and shook her head. 'No. No it doesn't. And now you're going away to fight.' She turned to look at him. 'Are you afraid?'

He chuckled. 'You know, I'm not meant to say so. So many are giving their lives for their country. I've been at the front I know what to expect. I'm not sure if it makes it better or worse.'

'For better or for worse. Sounds like a marriage.'

'It is in a way. When you marry you tie yourself to another person, and promise to be by their side no matter what happens. Fighting for one's country is similar I suppose. Here, I've immersed myself into the culture of another country, while maintaining the rule of law of the one where I was born. I've stopped dissidents making trouble, arrested a few, but compared with what our men face at the front…it's incomparable.'

'And now you must go back.'

'Yes, there's no choice in the matter. If I could choose I'd stay here. With you.' His eyes met hers and she saw the deep sorrow he was feeling. 'I've never really been in love before. When the Fishing Fleets come over every season, my colleagues and their wives are intent on finding me a partner, but the girls who have been sent by their families seem only interested in bagging themselves a husband so they can climb the social ladder. You, Carrie. You don't care about that sort of thing do you?'

'Why would I? You must know where I come from. The class I've been brought up in is the one I've lived in all my life. I was born and raised in Whitechapel, David, not the leafy squares of London's upper echelon of society. Not Nightingale Lane, where I worked as a scullery maid before I came to India. I've known great hardship, experienced not having enough food to eat; been so hungry my stomach constantly growled and the only way I got away from it was when I went to sleep at night, that's if I could sleep. Most of the women here have no idea how that feels. I would imagine you don't know how it feels.'

'No, but I've known war, and I know the trenches. It gives a person a different perspective on life.'

She nodded. 'Yes. Yes, I expect it does.'

'And it makes you realise who is important in one's life, and you, Carrie, you have become very important to me. I…I wanted to tell you before I went away because I didn't know whether I would have the chance. I've…fallen for you. I've tried to push my feelings away because you're a married woman, albeit an unhappily married woman, but it makes no difference in our world. You're married to another man and that means you're unattainable.'

He reached for her hand. 'Carrie, I know this isn't right. You know it isn't right, but I can't deny the way I feel. Ever since I first saw you outside the train station in Bombay I had a feeling you and I were going to mean something to each other. You're a very special woman. I know how brave you've had to be, coming to a strange country, bearing a child on an old ship…living with a man who clearly doesn't love you. Do you love him?'

She shook her head. 'No,' she said in almost a whisper. 'I don't know how much Dorothy told you…?'

'She told me everything.'

'I don't want anything to happen to him. I have no respect for him, not because of the choices he's made, it's likely he can't do anything about that, but he could have treated John and me so differently. I know I made a mistake when I allowed Johan to lead me on, but I was so young, not just in years, but in experience. I didn't know anything about life, nothing at all really. Arnold has used it against me and made me feel like nothing, a no one, someone to look down on. The thing is, I adore John, and I wouldn't change a thing. I love him with all my heart. Arnold's never known that kind of love, never felt that depth of feeling for another human being. I don't think it's his fault.'

David shook his head slowly. 'I think you're being very kind to him.'

Carrie shrugged and released her hand from his. She turned towards the lake and watched the birds fly in a V formation across the silvery shimmer of the water, constantly moving, never still, the lights from the buildings twinkling in the dark. 'What's the point of feeling bitter, of wanting to get some sort of revenge?' She turned and looked at him. 'I have felt hatred for Arnold. I have known the depths of despair since I became his wife and travelled to Secunderabad. I could have found a place in my heart to like him if he had just treated me with kindness and a little respect. It wouldn't have taken much to turn it around, but

Arnold hates women and this fuels the way he treats us. I cannot allow that behaviour to change the person I am. I've never deliberately set out to hurt anyone but I've wanted to hurt Arnold, more than you'll ever know. I haven't acted on those feelings and I don't want to ruin his life. I just don't want to be in it and I don't want him in mine and John's.'

David leant towards her. He looked deep into her eyes and she felt lost in their depth, the richness of colour, velvety brown, the kindness and his attraction to her flowing from them. He put a hand under her chin and pulled her closer, then pressed his lips gently against hers. Carrie closed her eyes and was transported into gentleness and desire. He pulled her closer and she found herself wanting more, needing the closeness, the love and the longing, feelings denied her since she had become Arnold's wife.

Their kisses became more urgent, their need for each other paramount, until David reluctantly pulled away. 'You feel as I do.' She nodded and he smiled. 'I have hoped and wished and prayed that you would, not knowing whether I should make my feelings for you open, to show you that my love and desire for you is real.'

She inhaled deeply, then sighed. 'But you're going away and I'm still married, David. How am I to overcome that? Arnold will not let me go, and you, you must protect yourself from ridicule. You have a position of authority and now you are being sent to lead a new unit of men who will look up to you. I have made one mistake in my life where I allowed a man to lead me on then leave me when I needed him most. I've shouldered scorn and mockery from those who should have supported me and understood what I was going through. I cannot go through that again, and I can't allow you, a good man, to put himself in danger. You are free, free to do whatever you wish, with whomever you wish. I am not free, David, and if Arnold thought you and I had feelings for each other, believe me when I tell you he will not rest until he brings us both down.

He pulled her close again and kissed her. 'Hush,' he said. 'I know, I know all of that, but if I survive the war, Carrie, will you wait for me? Please say you will.'

'Yes, David, of course I'll wait for you. I can't imagine loving another man, or feeling for another man the way I have felt for you. I don't want anyone else. Just you, David. Just you.'

He kissed her again and smiled. 'This…weight I've been carrying around with me has pulled me down, made me morose because I wasn't sure if I'd got it wrong, if I was hoping for something I couldn't have, whether the love I have for you would be reciprocated. Can we meet? Somewhere private. A hotel? Before I leave. I want you, Carrie, more than you'll ever know.'

Carrie bit her lip. 'I want to, David. I want you, but…I'm married. If Arnold were to ever find out…I don't know what he would do. He has already tried to make my life unbearable, and it's only because of Gita and Dorothy's friendship that I've been able to be strong. I think we must wait, wait until I'm free of Arnold, and you're free of your duties to our country.' David looked crestfallen until Carrie took his hand and pressed it against her heart. 'I promise I will wait. Whatever happens from now, from this moment, I will wait for you, David.'

From a darkened room at the back of the Secunderabad Club, Arnold Bateman stood at a window looking out over the lake. He held a lit cigarette down by his thigh so that the burning tip would not be seen in the darkness by two people sitting on a bench below, thinking they were unobserved. He watched as Captain David Lawrence leant towards his wife, the woman he had paid for and given a home, and kissed her, seething with uncontrolled anger as she responded. As Carrie took David's hand and placed it against her breast, he hardened his jaw and ground his teeth in anger, then snuffed out the cigarette with his fingers, barely acknowledging the pain.

'Got you,' he murmured. 'Now you'll pay.'

Chapter 33

Gita was ill. Carrie had found her collapsed in the shop when she had arrived first thing, and she had insisted Dr Fraser take a look at her even though Gita protested she was alright and didn't need help. Carrie hadn't listened to her protests and had immediately locked the shop and driven Gita home. They passed vegetable markets, stalls selling lengths of fabric and accoutrements for home sewing, tables offering pieces of leather, some made into belts; the calls of the sellers fading as they left the commercial sector and got closer to the countryside. As they neared Gita's village the landscape became more rural, dry and dusty, with skeletal trees lining the dirt tracks leading to a collection of low housing consisting of shacks rendered with clay and roofed with bricks and reeds.

'Am I in the right place, Gita?'

Gita opened her eyes which were rheumy with exhaustion and half-covered with heavy lids that wanted to stay closed. 'Yes, Carrie. It is the house with the little garden in front. We are the only ones to do it. It is a Western thing I know, but a garden is so important to me.'

Carrie glanced across to her, her face etched with concern. I should have been tougher with her, she thought. I should have made her rest even when she resisted. Now look what's happened.

'You will rest, won't you, Gita? You will do as Dr Fraser said, stay off your feet, spend some time in bed and be good to yourself?' Gita nodded. 'I will check, you know. I will speak to your husband and daughter and tell them what the doctor said. I don't want to see you at the bungalow either.'

'But the sahib…'

'Never mind about him. I'll make sure he understands what's happened. If he tries to force you back to work at the bungalow tell your husband to come and see me.' Gita nodded again. She barely had the strength to move her head so Carrie was sure she couldn't do anything else no matter how much she wanted to do it. 'And don't worry about money.' Gita's eyes opened again and she stared at Carrie sadly. 'I know you need it and you will have it. Just don't tell the sahib, alright? And make sure you put enough away for medicine. If you don't have enough please tell me. You need the medicine Dr Fraser spoke about.'

'So I must lie,' she whispered.

Carrie swallowed hard, knowing this was something she shouldn't advise Gita to do, and that someone as honest and loyal as Gita would find almost impossible, but with Arnold who bore no excuses from anyone, there was no choice. 'On this occasion…I'm afraid we might have to. I'll try and keep him from you and your husband, I won't mention what's happened today, but unfortunately he seems to have a way of finding things out. How I don't know, he just does.'

Gita directed her to a small, square hut. It was modest and sparse in its construction, but even from the outside Carrie could see it was a home, one that was loved and cared for. At the front was a handkerchief sized patch of scrub where a narrow path had been fashioned out of bricks, leading to the front door.

'I am able to go in from here, Carrie,' Gita said.

Carrie raised her eyebrows. 'I'm sure you are, but I'm going to take you in. Wait there and I'll help you out of the car.' She went around to the passenger side and opened the door, placing a hand under Gita's elbow. The bone was sharp underneath her skin, and Carrie could see Gita's emaciated arm through the fabric of her jacket sleeve. Gently, she pulled Gita to her feet and walked her slowly into the little house.

Inside, it was dark and cool. There was a collection of mismatched furniture and a table pushed up against one of the walls. On the table were tiny ornaments, some photographs of Gita's daughter's wedding, and a shrine to Vishnu. At the far end was an opening covered with a piece of cloth. It reminded Carrie of the scullery in her parent's home and she smiled to herself.

'Where is your bedroom, Gita?' Gita pointed to the cloth and Carrie walked her across and pulled it aside. In the tiny room, no more than a few feet wide, was a bed covered in colourful fabric and some handmade cushions. Carrie settled Gita on the bed and lifted her feet, covering her with the fabrics. 'Please rest now, Gita. Try and sleep. I will get the medicine you need for now and have it sent to you. Would you like some water?' Gita nodded and Carrie went into the main room and looked for a kitchen area.

'We cook outside,' said Gita. Carrie went outside to the back of the house and found a cooking area where there was a pitcher of water and some metal cups. She poured some water into one of them and took it into Gita who drank it gratefully.

'Where is your husband?' Carrie asked her.

'He works for vegetable farmer today, delivering vegetables to the shops in Secunderabad.' Carrie nodded. 'And your daughter?'

'She is visiting her husband's relatives in Hyderabad. She will be back in the village tomorrow night.' Carrie nodded again and ran her hand across Gita's forehead, praying that it was just exhaustion that ailed her friend and nothing more. 'Please, Carrie, go back to the shop. I will wait for my husband to come home. He must cook tonight.' A little smile appeared across her face and Carrie smiled with her.

'Will it be the first time?' Gita nodded, still smiling, then sleepily closed her eyes and turned her face to the wall.

Chapter 34

Christmas advanced on them with great speed. Carrie spent more and more time in the shop, and thankfully Pearl was now well enough to help. The customers liked her down-to-earth manner, and her can-do attitude. Carrie was relieved to see the old Pearl.

'Are you enjoying yourself,' Carrie asked her on Christmas Eve.

'Y'know, Carrie, my whole working life since the age of fourteen I've worked as a maid, first as a tweeny, then worked my way up to room maid. I've slaved over ranges, cleaning them, blacking them, and polishing them to a shine which has taken hours. I've set fires for them upstairs so the poor things wouldn't feel the cold, and I've served at special occasions when it was as much for the guests to do just to say thank you, and often they didn't. I've never felt as much satisfaction from work as I do here. It's…it's a different world. And the way you've decorated the shop. It's so beautiful. I think you learnt something at Nightingale Lane. Maybe it did us both a service.'

Carrie nodded. 'You're not wrong, Pearl. I learnt about quality, and how less of a thing is often better than having too much of it. There's just enough glitter in here to make the shop sparkle from the outside to draw customers in. There's no colour because it would compete with those dresses we got from Paris. And it all looks lovely.'

Pearl fingered the sequined fabric on one of the mannequins. 'They are bright aren't they? I never would have thought women would wear anything like this. I bet they're not in London, what with the war 'an all.'

'Well, some of them are. I doubt the Sterns and their high-society friends are affected by the war.'

'I got a letter from me mum. No one's been called up yet, so Johan is probably still working for Mr Stern.'

'That won't last. They're dropping like flies on the front which means they'll begin the call-up shortly. It can't go on forever, can it? There won't be any young men left.'

'No, but there's still the older ones. Once all the young 'uns have been called up they'll start conscripting the married men. At least, they will if the war carries on.'

Carrie pulled a face. 'So much for the war being over before last Christmas. Got that wrong, didn't they?'

'Yeah, they did.'

Carrie dropped her gaze, then looked up at Pearl, wondering if she should say anything. 'How are you now, Pearl, y'know…about…'

Pearl looked wistful and shrugged slightly. 'Good and bad days. I lost the love of me life, but…well, you've been so good to me, and Gita was so kind. It helped me get over the very dark times. I didn't expect losing William to affect me like it did. It was like I was in a cloud, y'know, like the pea-soupers we get in London. The trouble with this one was it was only hanging over me, following me around even in the apartment. It wouldn't let me be until…'

'Dr Fraser?'

Pearl smiled and began rearranging the shoe closet at the back of the shop. 'Yes, Dr Fraser was the one who pulled me back over the line. He's a very wise man, and has been very kind to me. I'll never forget what you and him have done for me. Don't know what would have happened to me if I'd stayed in Whitechapel. Might have ended up in one of those asylum places, y'know like…what's it called, The Bethlehem Hospital? Sounds so nice, dunnit, but I'm pretty sure it isn't.'

They both shivered, then laughed. 'Hark at us. It's Christmas Eve and we're talking about asylums.'

'Well, if you stay with Arnold Bateman too long you'll probably end up in one as well. We'll be all girls together and cause 'em some havoc.' They both threw their heads back in laughter. 'And Florrie can come and visit. She'd love that.'

'Very funny. I can assure you she wouldn't. I'd never see her again.'

'You might not see her again anyway.'

'No,'

'How d'you feel about that? She did the dirty on you didn't she? Can't get away from that?'

'Yeah, well. She had her reasons. She was ashamed of what I'd done and couldn't bear the thought that our community might be talking about us behind our backs. And she saw it as another mouth to feed, and me with no job. There's no way I could have kept on working. All about money, see. I might have understood it a bit more if she'd picked someone who wasn't leaving the country, but she was determined to get rid of the problem. And she did.'

'My mum thought it was terrible, what she did. Less bothered that you were in the family way. She said it happened all the time and she didn't know what Florrie was thinking. She didn't even ask who the father was.'

Carrie nodded. 'Florrie's someone who cares too much about other people's opinions.'

'What about your dad? He couldn't have wanted you to go surely?'

'No, he wouldn't have wanted it. But what he wanted never got spoken about. It's me mum who makes all the decisions in that house, and I'm pretty sure Elsie was glad to see the back of me.'

'You're alright now aren't you, Carrie? Even with old grumpy knickers.'

'I'm alright because you're here, and because I have John.'

'And David Lawrence.'

Carrie's head snapped up. 'What?'

'Oh, come on, Carrie. It's obvious you're in love with him. And who wouldn't be? He's very handsome.' Pearl started dancing slowly around the room as though she was holding someone to her. 'And a captain, and rich, and...'

'Going to the front.'

Pearl stopped dancing and frowned. 'Oh no. When?'

'After Christmas. He's got to go back. No choice in the matter.'

Pearl went across to Carrie and put her arms around her. 'You're heartbroken. You must be. You and him, you could have had a life together when you got rid of that bastard. You can see what he feels for you. It's written all over his face.' She held Carrie at arms' length. 'Can't you go with him?'

'To the front?' Carrie cried.

'To London. Back home. To wait for him.'

'Like you did?'

Pearl sighed, her arms dropping to her sides. 'I know what you're saying, and I would never want you to go through what I went through when William was killed, but David's a Captain. He won't be in the same position as William was. He's got a better chance. William was unlucky.'

'Captains get killed, Pearl, just like anyone else. If he survives it'll be a miracle.' She sighed and gave Pearl a watery smile. 'I've promised to wait for him.'

Pearl grinned. 'I'm so glad,' she said. 'It'll give him something to survive for. You and John.'

Carrie took a deep breath. 'I'm still married, don't forget. And if we're to be together it's something I'll have to attend to, and if I know anything about Arnold Bateman it won't be an easy task.'

Christmas Day was a quiet affair in the Bateman household. Arnold was off-duty and spent most of the day getting steadily drunk. Carrie didn't mind. She had already planned to visit Gita in the morning and take some gifts for her and her family, then to Amrita's mother's house so John could spend some time with her children. She left early, knowing that the kind of Christmas children usually experienced back in England would not be forthcoming for John, and Carrie was relieved that at nearly ten months old, he didn't understand why Christmas is such an important festival.

For lunch, she and Pearl had planned to eat out at a small restaurant on James Street, then join the festivities at The Secunderabad Club in the late afternoon. Carrie had warned her it probably wouldn't be the usual Christmas fare.

'What's usual Christmas fare?' Pearl had asked, laughing. 'Eel pie and tripe with a bit of cabbage if we're lucky? Anything's got to be better than that.'

'Yeah, it was a bit like that, wasn't it, even with Mrs Coyle sending us home with stuff from the pantry.'

'Stuff no one wanted to eat, you mean. What the 'ell's a devilled egg for goodness sake.'

Carrie collapsed into giggles shaking her head. 'I don't know. We were lucky to get one from a hen, never mind one from a devil.' They had both laughed as they reminisced, but something inside each of them was left pining for the life they knew before, even with all its difficulties.

After lunch, when she got back to the bungalow with John, Arnold was dressing. He came out of his bedroom wearing his dress uniform. Carrie looked surprised.

'Are you not allowed to wear civvies even on Christmas Day?'

'Why would you want me to wear civvies? Like a soldier don't you?'

Carrie looked at him, a frisson of fear uncurling in her chest. 'I'm sorry, Arnold, I don't know what you mean. I just thought as it's Christmas Day, a public holiday, you would be able to enjoy the day without wearing your uniform.'

'Any man with a modicum of dignity will wear his uniform any day of the week, particularly when he's with his superiors. They'll all be wearing their dress uniforms, even Captain David Lawrence.'

Carrie's breath caught in her throat. He knows, she thought. Oh, my God, he knows. She swallowed down her fear and picked John up from where he was sitting on the rug. Her eyes went to Arnold. He was drunk, heavily so, and she knew better than most what he was capable of when he'd been drinking. She prayed she was right when she assumed he wouldn't touch her when she was holding her little boy. Arnold's lipped curled as he eyed from under half-closed eyelids.

'Think you've got one over on me, don't you?'

'I'm sorry, Arnold. Why would you think that?'

He leapt across the room and held a shaking finger up to her face, almost touching the tip of her nose. The whisky on his breath smelt sour and Carrie exhaled as he got near and tried not to face him. 'The reason I think that, lady, is because I saw you, I saw you, and 'im. Snogging 'is face off, weren't yer.'

Carrie's stomach rolled. She tried to look away, to get away, but he grabbed her arm. 'Don't walk away from me, Carrie Dobbs. You're no better than you should be. I saw you, and 'im with his hands all over you. You're a slut, always were and still are.'

Carrie's eyes narrowed and she pulled her arm away. 'And what about you, Arnold. What would you call yourself, eh?' He pulled his hand back and delivered a stinging slap against her cheek. Carrie managed to stay on her feet but John began to cry. 'What a man you are, if that's what you call yourself. That you would strike me while I'm carrying a child. You're no man, Arnold Bateman, at least not one I ever wanted to be married to. One day...one day I'll be free of you and it will be the happiest day of my life.'

Arnold stepped back, fastening the collar of his dress jacket as though nothing had happened and sniggered. 'Well, Mrs Bateman, I wish you lots of luck. More shame heaped on you. As if you don't have enough on your head already. By the way, I want you to drive me to the club. It'll look good for me to be seen in my wife's car being chauffeured by you.'

'No. No, Arnold. I'm taking Pearl with me. You can make your own way.'

'Are you going against me,' he yelled making John cry even harder.

Carrie nodded. 'That's right. I am. You'll stay away from me and my son. If you don't I'll tell everyone what you get up to on your nights off.'

Arnold shrugged and smirked. 'And you think they'd believe you? A tart like you.'

'There's no smoke without fire, Arnold. You remember that.' She turned away from him, trembling; her body rigid with anger and fear.

That he should hit her while she was holding John said everything about him.

In the bedroom she took one of John's muslins and soaked it in the pitcher of water, then held it against her face which smarted with pain. She knew by taking the blow and standing her ground meant she had received the full force of the blow, but she had been determined that he would not knock her down as he had before. And there was John. She looked at him in his cot, playing happily with the toys Gita had given him. Amrita would arrive at the bungalow soon and she wanted to be ready to leave. When she saw Carrie's cheek she would know what had happened and that would mean it would without doubt get back to Gita, the last thing Carrie wanted.

She had a strip-wash, then applied some makeup as Gita and her daughter had shown her, to conceal the angry mark on her cheek, the stamp of Arnold's hand. By the time Amrita arrived Carrie was ready.

'Will you stay the night, Amrita? Would that be alright? I might stay at the apartment this evening.'

Amrita smiled. 'Of course, madam. That is not a problem. I hope you enjoy yourself at your special festival.' Carrie smiled and nodded, then left the bungalow, thinking that since Arnold had been drinking all day and would certainly drink that evening, enjoyment was the last thing on her mind.

When Carrie and Pearl reached The Secunderabad Club the party was in full swing. Carrie pulled the Sprite up in the small forecourt and switched off the engine. As she made to get out of the car Pearl stopped her.

'Hold on, Carrie.' Carrie stared at her. 'What's wrong with your face?'
Carrie's hand flew like a reflex to her face. 'What?'

'That.' She pointed to Carrie's cheek. 'Where your hand's trying to hide it.' Pearl waited with raised eyebrows. 'He hit you didn't he?' Carrie pressed her lips together and lowered her face, then nodded. 'Why?'

'Because he saw me kissing David Lawrence.'

Pearl drew in a breath. 'Oh, Carrie. That was a bit careless. How did that happen?'

'It must have been the other night, here at the club, when I found out David was leaving. I came out for some air and he followed me. It was silly I know, but...I think David thought it would be our only chance to spend some time together. I didn't mean for it to happen.' She paused, wondering if she should tell Pearl what David had asked her. 'He asked me to go to a hotel with him.' Pearl's mouth dropped open. 'I said I didn't think it was right, but I wanted to, Pearl. I really wanted to.'

Pearl put her hand on Carrie's arm. 'Course you did, but you did the right thing. The way you feel about Arnold is understandable, but you're still married to him. A kiss is one thing, but…giving yourself like that to someone.' She looked hard at Carrie. 'It's different, isn't it? More important.' Carrie nodded. 'And if he loves you as much as he says he does, he'll wait for you. And Arnold's a bully and he doesn't mind using his fists. I dread to think what he'd do to you if he thought you'd slept with Captain Lawrence.'

'I know exactly what he'd do. It's not the only reason I didn't agree to meet David. I do know the trouble it would cause, of course, but I was thinking about him too. If his superiors found out it would ruin his career. I don't want to be responsible for that.'

Inside, the ballroom was decorated in the typically Victorian way, with huge Christmas trees in each corner, adorned with baubles and candles, and swathes of tinsel hung like bunting from wall to wall.

'This is beautiful,' breathed Pearl. 'Like fairyland.'

Carrie turned and smiled and grabbed Pearl's hand, pulling her across to a table. 'Let's sit here. We can watch people dancing.'

'Watch them,' cried Pearl. 'I want to be one of them, and so do you. Let's show these toffee-nosed sods how to have a good time.' Carrie threw her head back and laughed, so delighted to have Pearl with her.

When she was with Pearl she felt safe, a feeling she hadn't had in a long time. She remembered the day she'd married Arnold and watched Pearl walk out of the pub, making her way back to Nightingale Lane, thinking she would never see her beloved friend again.   I am fortunate, she thought. Things are hard, but I didn't know Pearl and I would be together again, yet here she is, my best friend in all the world. My sister, my soulmate; the best, most caring friend anyone could ever have. With her and John I know I can survive. I *will* survive. Everything. Arnold can do his worst, throw everything at me, but they'll still be with me, and right now, apart from David, they're all I need.

Carrie inhaled a deep breath, feeling relaxed after the events of the afternoon, until she felt eyes on her, her senses telling her she was being observed. She turned and there was Arnold, surround by the unattached men in his unit, his eyes boring into her back. His gaze turned to flint, narrowing as her eyes met his, and she turned away.

'You alright, Carrie? Pearl asked as she caught Carrie's expression. She lifted her chin and looked over Carrie's shoulder to where Arnold was holding court. 'Oh,' she said, her face hardening. 'Forget him. He doesn't deserve to have you and John. I can only hope that one day he gets what he does deserve.' Suddenly, she stuck her tongue out.

Carrie was astonished. She put her hand across her mouth to stifle her laughter. 'Did I just see you stick your tongue out at Arnold?'

'Yeah, childish, ain't I?'

'Oh, Pearl I love you. You're so funny.'

'Yeah, but I can get away with it. He wouldn't dare.' She pulled a face over Carrie's shoulder then patted her hand. 'Drinks, I think. Gin and It for me. How about you? The same?' Carrie nodded and watched as Pearl disappeared into the crowd at the bar.

Arnold appeared in front of her, looking in Pearl's direction. 'Your friend thinks she's clever, don't she?' Carrie said nothing, but continued staring ahead. 'You tell her if she does that again I'll wipe it off her face.'

Carrie lifted her head slowly. 'I'd like to see you try that.' She allowed a small smile to play around her lips and Arnold walked away, scowling.

'What did he want?' asked Pearl as she put the drinks on the table and sat down.

'Just trying to be clever.'

'He's got a long way to go before then, that's for sure.'

'Yeah, well.' Carrie took a sip of her drink and stared at Pearl. 'What?'

'How would you feel if me and John moved into the apartment over the shop with you?'

Pearl's mouth dropped open and her face shone with happiness. 'Oh, Carrie, I would love it.' Her expression suddenly changed. 'But what about Arnold? Leaving your husband. It's not done is it?'

'It's not done in London, but we're not in London, are we? Haven't you noticed, Pearl? Some of the rules are different here, at least that's how it feels. And the thing is, the reason we don't do things is because men have told us it's not right, and because we're worried about what people will think. That's why I'm here and not back in Whitechapel, after all, because Florrie was ashamed of me and what I'd done. She was terrified it would be found out by the people who live around us that I'd got a bun in the oven, knocked up by a member of the Jewish community no less, someone I worked for and someone I was supposed to look up to. If you met Dorothy you'd know things are changing for women, especially in Western countries, maybe not so much here. You've heard of the suffragettes haven't you?'

Pearl's eyes widened. 'God, she's not one of them, is she?' Carrie nodded. 'Oh, Carrie. They're always in trouble over something. What about that woman, Emily something. Ran out in front of a horse at the Derby and was killed. Why would she do that?'

'Emily Davison.'

'You know about her?'

'Dorothy knew her.'

'No!'

'Yep. Dorothy was a breath of fresh air here. When I first met her I thought she was like the others, but definitely she isn't. She even took on the Burra of the mofussil.'

'The Burra. What's that?'

'It's like the Queen Bee of the society at the military station. Ours here is Lady Mabel Dimmock.' She glanced across the room. 'Look, Pearl, that's her over there.'

'What the big one with the pasty face and the funny headdress?'

Carrie giggled. 'Ssh, yes, that's our Burra.'

'But why would anyone think she's head of anything? Look at what she's wearing. Looks like some curtains my mum had up at the windows years ago. Bet she's never been to the shop. Well, I know she hasn't. We'd never sell a rag like that.'

Carrie grinned. 'No we wouldn't.'

'You should challenge her.'

'Me? No thanks. I've got enough on me plate. I want to leave the bungalow without Arnold knowing, when he's on duty. I'll just pack our bags and go. I've got nothing else there, and it's not like Gita's working there now.'

'How is she?'

Carrie looked concerned. 'Better, I think, but not out of the woods. I hope it's only exhaustion she's suffering from and nothing worse. I couldn't bear it, and neither will her family.'

'She's a good 'un, isn't she?'

'She's been like a mother to me.'

Pearl glanced at Carrie, realising how much she must have missed her family. 'You'll see them again, Carrie.'

'Will I? What if they don't want to see me?'

'Why wouldn't they want to see you? You're a married woman, you've got a child and you run a business. Won't they be proud?'

'Not when I tell them I've walked out on my husband.'

'So, don't tell them.'

Carrie grinned. 'It's funny isn't it? It feels like we can do anything, just because we don't have the matriarchs of Whitechapel looking over us.'

'No.' said Pearl. 'We've got 'er.' She lifted her chin towards Mabel Dimmock and burst out laughing. 'Shall we have some fun?' She opened her bag and sprayed perfume from an atomiser on to her wrists, straightened her feathered headdress and got up.

'Pearl,' Carrie cried, trying to stop her.

Pearl giggled and walked across the ballroom to where Mabel was sitting. She curtseyed low in front of her and introduced herself. Carrie watched as Mabel flushed, then held out her hand as Pearl spoke to her, inclining her head in deference. Mabel, clearly delighted by the flattery smiled charmingly until Pearl turned and pointed in Carrie's direction. Mabel immediately drew her hand away and turned her head. Her husband flapped his hand towards Pearl as if to shoo her away. Carrie averted her eyes as a giggling Pearl returned to the table.

'Oh, my goodness, she doesn't like you does she? She was like putty in my hands until I mentioned your name.'

'Pearl, you're awful, but thank you. It's put everything into perspective. All they care about is status.'

'Let's enjoy ourselves, Carrie. We deserve it.'

They danced to every tune the band played, joined in with the Charleston, and Foxtrotted together around the ballroom. All eyes were on them, but they didn't care. When they'd exhausted themselves they fell into their seats, holding hands and laughing. A few moments later Arnold sat at the table opposite Carrie, his face etched with anger.

'You need to go home. You and 'er, you're making shows of yourselves.'

Carrie leant forward in her seat, her fear of him having lifted and drifted away like a black cloud. 'Go away, Arnold. It's none of your business what I do?'

'It's very much my business. I'm your husband.'

'You're her what?' said Pearl, taking a swig from her drink and looking over his shoulder.

Arnold blanched. He seemed wrong-footed for a moment, then rose from the chair and went quietly back to the bar, his shoulders slumped. 'That told 'im.'

'I'll have to leave now won't I?'

'Yeah, and it's the best thing you can do. Just don't leave it too long.'

Just before the Christmas Party came to a close, David arrived along with Angus Fraser.

'Oh,' said Carrie. 'I wasn't expecting to see them here tonight.'

'Dr Fraser said he had a meeting about a visit of someone important.'

'I expect he meant Mahatma Gandhi. David's spent a great deal of time organising his visit. I wonder what he wanted with Dr Fraser, though. Has he mentioned anything to you?'

Pearl shook her head. 'Well, he wouldn't, would he? I'm hardly important.'

David and Angus went to the bar, and Carrie noticed they seemed to make a point of not acknowledging her and Pearl's presence.

'It's probably for the best, Carrie,' said Pearl. 'After what happened to you tonight. You don't want to give Arnold an excuse for more of that.'

Carrie shrugged and nodded. She had to agree with Pearl, but her heart was telling her something different. 'Shall we go?'

'Yeah, good idea,' answered Pearl. 'We can talk about when you'll leave the bungalow and move into the apartment. I can't wait.'

Carrie was quiet on the way back to the apartment and Pearl kept glancing at her.

'You alright, Carrie?' she asked her, frowning.

Carrie nodded. 'Yes, I'm fine.' She glanced at Pearl and smiled. 'Tired I s'pose.'

'You will move out, won't you? Don't let him stop you.'

'I'm a bit worried about it. If he thinks I'm going to leave he'll do everything he can to stop me.'

'Then don't do anything to make him suspicious. Just carry on as normal. You could bring a few things over at a time, y'know, in the car every morning. A few drawers of clothes, some of John's bits and pieces. He'll never notice.'

'No, no, you're right. It's a good plan. I'll start on Monday, bring some of my clothes over and we'll organise the apartment so we find the best use of space.' She glanced at Pearl again. 'You do realise there'll be hardly any room.'

Pearl grinned. 'I don't care. Do you?'

Carrie returned her grin and laughed. 'No.'

Chapter 35

'Why is this visit so important? Pearl asked Carrie. 'Everyone seems to be on pins. I had a women in the shop this morning buying a new dress in case she sees him on his walk through Secunderabad which will take all of an hour. Barmy if you ask me.'

'Who was it?' Pearl looked up. 'Who bought the dress?'

'I think she's the wife of one of Arnold's friends. Brunette, quite pretty, but I thought she had a cruel look about her. She was quite rude to me.'

Carrie laughed to herself as she hung the new stock on hangers. 'Yeah, I know who you mean. She was the one who was so hateful to me when I first boarded the ship over here. She was horrible, even made snarky remarks about John. Needless to say I stayed in the cabin for most of the voyage.'

'If she comes in here again I'll stick a pin in her.'

'I'd love to be here when you do.'

'Will you go?'

'To the procession?' Pearl nodded. 'I thought I might take Gita. He's a hero to her, like a saviour of sorts.'

'Why?'

'He doesn't believe in segregation, and in South Africa where he used to live and work as a lawyer, he staged a non-violent protest about the tax levied on Indian immigrants. He was arrested and went to prison for it. But he ended the tax and since then he has become their hero. Now he lives in India in a spiritual monastery.'

'How do you know all this stuff?'

'David explained it to me when was organising the visit.'

'He doesn't wear very much, does he, Gandhi? I saw a photo of him in a newspaper.'

'He'll wear more than that on Friday. They call it a dhoti, like a big shawl wrapped all the way around him.'

'That's something I suppose. Do you think he'll come in here?'

'Into a dress shop.' Carrie laughed. 'I doubt it.'

'Talking of dresses, when's the day?'

Carrie took a deep breath. 'Sunday. Arnold's on duty. I'll move out on Sunday.'

'You haven't changed your mind, have you?'

'No. I'm looking forward to it, but I'll be glad when it's done.'

'Will you leave a note?'

Carrie stopped what she was doing and looked at Pearl. 'I hadn't thought. What would you do?'

'Bearing in mind the way he's treated you I would say no, but maybe something like, "I'm staying at the apartment for a while. I think it's for the best." What do you think? It's short and sweet and he'll get the message.'

Carrie nodded. 'Yeah, something short. He won't need an explanation. He'll know why.'

On the morning of the procession Carrie drove to Gita's house, and was heartened to see her sitting at a table with a cup of chai. She didn't appear to have lost any more weight, and Carrie had taken some gulab jamun, an Indian confection made with milk, flour and cream, deep fried and soaked in rose-water syrup. She knew they were Gita's favourite and she hoped they would encourage her to eat.

'Gita,' she cried as she went into the little house. 'You're looking better today.'

Gita smiled and held her hand up in welcome. 'Carrie. It's good to see you. I am feeling better today. I'm looking forward to the procession through James Street. What an honour it would be to see the Mahatma. It will be something I will always remember.'

'We've got time for a cup of tea,' said Carrie, 'and some of these.' She took the lid off the box and pushed them towards Gita, whose face lit up.

'Oh, yes, I like them very much.'

'I'll make myself a cuppa. Do you want another?' She pointed at Gita's cup and Gita passed it to her.

'Memsahib, I should be making refreshment for you in my house.'

'How many cups of tea do you think you've made me this year, Gita?'

Gita laughed and waggled her hands in the air. 'Many, many.'

'So I can make one for you occasionally, can't I? And we'll eat those lovely sweets, yes?'

Gita nodded. 'Yes, Carrie.'

When Carrie and Gita arrived at James Street it was busy to bursting point. Carrie had parked the Sprite some streets away, and she and Gita walked slowly towards the throng, Gita leaning on Carrie's arm.

'Are you going to be alright? Carrie asked her. 'I'm worried all of this might be too much for you.'

'I'm very good, Carrie. I'm so excited. To see the Mahatma is something I never expected in my lifetime.'

'Well, I hope we can see him. There's a big crowd.'

They continued towards James Street and met with a wall of people.

'I'm not sure about this,' said Carrie. 'How on earth will we get to see him if we can't see over people's heads.'

'He will know we're here even if he can't see us,' answered Gita. 'He is the Great Soul. He will know we are here.'

'He doesn't like us, does he? He thinks the British are trying to rule.'

Gita shrugged her sparrow-like shoulders. 'He dismisses no one. He opens his arms to everyone, but there must be fairness and respect in all things. Yes, he wants us to be allowed to be as we are, to follow our own culture and traditions without criticism, and he wants to get his message of hope and peace to everyone without using violence.'

Carrie's eyes widened. 'You…know so much, Gita. You have studied him?'

'I only know what I hear from the people who come through the village from the cities. There is much talk. They sit in the place where we gather and they talk, and the talk is of Gandhi. He makes us proud, proud to be who we are. And he is strong for us.'

Carrie nodded. Gita had surprised her with her passion, but then, she understood. When she discovered she was pregnant, a young girl without a husband and expecting a child, who knew she would lose her job and who thought her family would support her, her disappointment had crushed her. At that moment, when she was at her most vulnerable, she had wanted someone to take her hand and keep her safe and strong. But her vulnerability had allowed her to fall prey to people like Arnold Bateman who had poured scorn on her and her baby. Yes, she understood, so very well.

'Carrie!' A voice rang out that she recognised. It was David, standing by the podium, a lone soldier amongst the throng of Indian natives who jostled for the best positions.

'David!' She smiled and waved and he beckoned her forward. She shrugged and shook her head, holding her hands to her side as if to say, 'How?' He nodded and she watched in awe as he instructed the soldiers in his unit to carve a path through the crowd, standing firm to stop others getting though. He beckoned her and she walked Gita slowly forward towards the podium. 'What a position. Gita you'll be able to see everything.' The look on Gita's face was almost blissful, and she smiled widely, dipping her head to David to thank him. 'Thank you so much, David,' said Carrie. 'This is the best thing we could have done for Gita. She needs this.'

'I think many of our neighbours in Secunderabad need this visit. It will also show we are willing to work with everyone, that we're all here together, and that we understand their need to uphold their culture and traditions. I can honestly say I'm excited too. I've heard so much about the man.'

Suddenly there was a great shout from the opposite end of James Street. The crowd surged forward and Carrie and David stood firmly either side of Gita. Mahatma Gandhi walked slowly down the middle of the street. He was dressed in a pure white dhoti with simple leather sandals on his feet. He was a small man compared to those around him, yet had such charisma, such magnetism, that when he reached the middle of the crowd, silence fell. Many of those watching fell to their knees in worship. He placed his hand on the heads of many as he made his way to the podium.

'Will he speak? Gita asked.

David nodded. 'Yes, he will give a speech. He is a great orator I understand.'

Carrie watched in awe as Gandhi came towards them and finally stopped in front of them. Without warning, Gita stepped forward and knelt before him as tears rolled down Carrie's cheeks. She glanced at David. He too had tears in his eyes.

Gandhi placed his hands together as if in prayer, then leant and put a hand under her arm, raising her up.

'Do not kneel to me, sister. We stand together, side-by-side.'

Gita nodded and stepped back as Gandhi stepped up to the podium and began to speak. Gita's s face shone with admiration and Carrie could barely take her eyes from her. As Gandhi continued speaking Gita seemed to grow in stature. He spoke of their need to stand together, and to work with other cultures and traditions while upholding their own. The people around Carrie nodded and cheered, and she knew she had witnessed something memorable and very special.

Later, when Carrie had returned Gita to her home, they sat outside in the shade, drinking small handless cups of chai and finishing the sweets Carrie had brought with her.

'Well?' she asked Gita. 'What do you think of today?'

Gita smiled and half-closed her eyes, luxuriating in thoughts of the great man and how he singled her out. 'It was…the most wonderful day. I cannot wait to tell my husband and daughter and the rest of the village. He spoke to me, the Great Soul spoke to me. I will never forget it. Thank you, Carrie. Thank you for taking me. And please, thank Captain Lawrence again for me. I will remember it all my life.'

Chapter 36

Carrie placed the rest of John's things into a case and locked it. His toys had been taken in the Sprite the previous week, only his favourite felt rabbit remained, the one with which he could not sleep.

A small carpet bag held the remainder of Carrie's clothes. She put John in the cot with his rabbit and took the bags out to the car. She'd already written a short note to Arnold which she'd propped up against a jam-jar of wildflowers in the kitchen. She wondered at his reaction when he read it. If she knew Arnold at all, she knew he would quite likely explode with anger. There won't be any tears, she thought, no remorse or feelings of lost love. No, he'll think he's been done over, lost the game, not received value for money. It's too bad. I can't let what he thinks stop me from doing what I know is right for me and John.

She returned to the bungalow and lifted John from the cot, looking around the little bedroom she and John had occupied for nearly a year. There was sadness in her chest. This room where she and John had slept, the bungalow itself, had become their home, but it was never going to be forever. A forever home is the one you share with those you love. It couldn't be, could never be, because there was certainly no love between her and Arnold. What there was between them, a kind of simmering hatred, had poisoned the atmosphere, made her fearful and desperately unhappy and frightened for the future. He was her keeper, her jailer, and she his prisoner. A commodity, bought and paid for. It was a feeling that had shredded her confidence to tatters. Leaving Arnold, the bungalow and the mofussil was her escape. What shape her future would take once she had fled she didn't know, but she knew that every journey began with the first step and leaving the Secunderabad mofussil was the first step.

As she was about to leave she heard a noise in the living room. She hurried out of the bedroom with John in her arms to find Arnold sitting in one of the chairs, a whisky by his side, and a lit cigarette between his fingers.

'Going out?' he said patronisingly. 'Why the cases?'

Carrie froze. 'I'm giving some things to Pearl. She doesn't have anything for the season.'

He nodded and swigged from his glass. 'Got a child has she? That was quick. Might be better for you…and him, if you didn't lie to me.'

Carrie made for the door, but Arnold moved swiftly out of the chair and blocked her path. 'Let me go, Arnold. Us living together. It's purgatory and you know it.'

'I paid for you.'

'So you keep saying, but it's wearing thin and I reckon you've had your money's worth.' He lifted his hand but she stood her ground. 'Yes, you can hit me. Go on, if it makes you feel better, but it won't change anything. You don't want me, not in any way, and I don't want you. I won't allow John to be raised in such an atmosphere. This is your house, you've always made it quite plain where my place is, and now I'm giving you the chance to live the life you want. I'll never say anything to anyone about your choices, but I'm a human being and I deserve to live the life I want, just like you.'

He lowered his hand, and to Carrie's surprise, slumped in the chair looking defeated. 'You'll go to him, I suppose.'

'I don't think that's likely, do you? He left yesterday to join a unit in France. Men are being killed, Arnold. You know that, you've been there. I can't think about what might happen. It's more than likely I'll never see him again, but whatever I do from now on, I do for John, and only John.'

He glanced up at her, his eyes red-rimmed, resignation etched across his features. 'You'd better go then. I hope you're not expecting me to pay for you and the brat. I've done enough of that over the last year. Once you go there's no turning back. Once gone, gone forever. Do you understand?'

She nodded her head once, then left without looking back. Her heart thumped wildly in her chest and she could hardly breathe. She knew she had made a tumultuous decision, one that went against what everyone else wanted, including her own mother, yet Carrie left with her head held high. There was nothing about the mofussil she would miss. She had made no friends there apart from Dorothy and David and they were gone. And now so was she. And she was glad of it.

Chapter 37

A calmness settled over Carrie. If there was ever a moment when she felt she had grown up and become a fully-fledged adult, it was now. More importantly she was a mother, responsible for another human being apart from herself. It gave her a sense of place, a confidence in herself as a woman.

Having Pearl by her side had been the most fortunate stroke of luck, if it was luck that had brought them back together. Pearl was the person whom Carrie had cried over most often, the one she had desperately missed, the dear friend Carrie thought was lost to her for ever. They had shared a room at Nightingale Lane, a cold, unappealing attic with iron beds and sparse blankets that did little to keep them warm, where ice formed on the inside of the windows when it was winter, and where they'd shared their hopes and dreams in the middle of the night by candlelight, holding hands across the narrow space between their beds. Now they shared an apartment, compact, but one they had sweetened with colourful rugs, pretty tasselled cushions from the stores and street-side stalls on James Street, and vases of wildflowers picked from the hedgerows on their walks with John. They lived side-by-side in quiet harmony, respect, and a deep sense that their lives would always be entwined.

In the evenings they would close the shop and wander up the back stairs to the apartment, tired but satisfied they had achieved something. Pearl had become an expert in women's fashion, a revelation to her, but one she was delighted with. They would talk about the people they'd left behind, like the Sterns, Mrs Coyle, the cook at Nightingale Lane, the tweeny who never said boo, and their families, and wondered if their lives had changed as much as their own. They decided it couldn't be possible, because their lives were changed beyond recognition, and they had altered irrevocably. Both had suffered, Pearl in the loss of her fiancé, and the illness she had endured because of it, and Carrie because she had given birth, and been 'sold' to a man who hated women and who had abused her, wrecking her self-confidence and any belief she had in herself. They would toast each other with chai at the end of the day, saying they had come through it all, and were stronger and more determined to have a happy future because of it.

She thought often of Dorothy, a young woman whose life could not be more different from Carrie's, yet they had become firm friends.

Dorothy had told her that when she first met Carrie she had sensed she was a kindred spirit with an unshakeable strength that she admired. That Carrie had started life in one of the poorest streets in London and earnt her living cleaning grates and serving people like Dorothy, seemed not to matter to her.

Gita had become a friend from the very beginning. Carrie had wondered if she had seen something in the slight Indian woman that reminded her of Florrie, but Gita was a quiet, nurturing, selfless person, a personal description that Carrie could in no way attribute to her mother. She also knew that Gita would never treat her daughter the way Florrie had treated her. Gita's family were beyond poor, but Gita, as unwell as she currently was, was the backbone of her family, respected, perhaps even adored, and Carrie could readily understand why. Gita had helped to save her, had bathed her wounds and provided friendship and support, something Carrie would never forget.

And then there was David, the love she had found by chance, but something told her it was meant to be. She had already realised that if she had not married Arnold and made a life in Secunderabad it was likely their paths would never have crossed. He had shown her kindness and gentleness, his eyes held her with such warmth and understanding a shiver would unravel down her spine when he appeared in her mind's eye. Johan had given her John, and she could only thank him for it. She didn't want to think of him in a bad way. The time they had spent together had been delightful for her, full of promise and expectation. That those promises and expectations had not been fulfilled had led her to David, and she couldn't deny that fate had had a hand in drawing her towards the man she hoped and prayed would be her future, because it was in God's hands should David survive, and luck of course. Luck always played its part. And if he got through? Then, and only then, could she think of them building a life together, with or without Arnold's permission and agreement of a divorce, something unheard of within the society in which they had been raised. Carrie shook her head. It seemed he would always have a hold over her, at least until she could make their separation legal, binding, and without question.

The weeks flew by, and suddenly Secunderabad was plunged into the cooler weather of spring. Carrie had learnt that it wasn't just the designers of London and Paris who dictated what people wore at any time, but also the seasons. They had just received the new stock for the cooler months, beautifully cut jackets and skirts, silk scarves, buttoned Mary-Jane shoes in darker colours with bags to match, and Lyle cotton stockings in a multitude of colours.

'Will you wear this look?' Pearl asked Carrie. 'It seems very proper.'

Carrie smiled. 'It's definitely that. I'm not sure it's for me. Great for travelling though. I can imagine going back to London in an outfit like this. Can you picture their faces if you and I turned up, arm in arm, wearing one of these beautifully cut suits, a cartwheel hat with a feather, matching gloves and carrying one of those leather valises?'

'Of course I wouldn't return wearing anything less,' laughed Pearl.

'No of course not. Nor I.'

The girls laughed in unison, but both secretly wondered if they would ever return to the place they called home. Carrie was aware that David would probably never return to Secunderabad and she had wondered if it was time to say goodbye to the place she had fought so hard against and go back to London. If only I knew what was happening to him, she thought. If only I could see into the future I could make plans. And then there's John.

She glanced at the little boy who had just celebrated his first birthday, sitting on a rug in the middle of the room. He was playing with wooden blocks, building them up into a line of three and knocking them down, which he thought was very funny. Carrie smiled and bit her lip. I'll wait, she thought. We might hear something and then I can decide. She didn't have long to wait. Within two months she had heard on the grapevine that David was missing in action, presumed dead.

'Are you sure this is what you want, Carrie,' asked Pearl, her eyebrows pulled together in a frown. 'It's a big decision to leave everything you've come to know. What about the shop?'

'The shop has been a means to an end, Pearl, and I feel like I've come to the end of the road now that David's gone.'

Pearl frowned and shook her head. 'He might still be alive.'

Carrie lowered her gaze to her hands resting in her lap. 'He might.' She brushed a tear from her cheek. 'And he might not. I can't see how I'll ever know, we know so little about each other. It didn't seem necessary for me to know his address in London, and if he is ever found, surely that is where he'll be sent.' Her tears flowed thick and fast and she wiped them from her face with the heel of her hand.

Pearl was distraught. 'Where will you go?'

'Well, I can't go home. Florrie, Elsie and the others have never returned my letters, not in all the time I've been here.'

Pearl's mouth dropped open. 'What nothing?'

'No, not one letter.'

'Why?'

'Your guess is as good as mine, but it means they assumed they'd never see me again, that I'd be in India with Arnold forever, or at least for so long we wouldn't really be family anymore. When Florrie got rid of me she assumed it would be for good.'

'Can you forgive her?'

Carrie shrugged. 'She's my mum, but in truth we were never that close. She always preferred Elsie to me, and I think Dad and I always got on better. I would have appreciated it if he'd stood up for me more, especially when I got pregnant, but he was never strong enough for her. She always got the last word, no matter what the subject was.'

'Will you want me to come with you?'

Carrie stared at her, wondering when this question would come. 'You must do what's right for you, Pearl. I wrote to Dorothy last month and told her of my thoughts and plans. She said she, for one, was very happy I was thinking of returning to London because she's missed our friendship. I think she's the only one in London who has. It really must be your decision.'

'Everyone I love is either here or in London. If you leave I'll have no one. I can't imagine that. Doesn't seem right.'

'What about Angus Fraser?'

'What about him?'

Carrie pursed her lips. She hadn't wanted to broach the question of Dr Fraser but she felt it was the right time. 'He delayed his return to Bombay. There's only one reason he would do that, Pearl, and that's because of you. I know you said there's nothing between you, but I'm not sure he sees it like that.'

'I do like him, Carrie. He's a lovely man and he's asked me to go to Bombay to meet his children a couple of times.'

'Do you want to go?'

Pearl looked thoughtful. 'I think it's too soon.' Carrie nodded. 'But maybe later, when we've all decided what we want, perhaps I could return, when the time is right.'

'So you'll come back with me?' Carrie's heart lifted and she breathed a sigh of relief. She couldn't bear to be parted from Pearl again.

'Yes, Carrie. I'll go back to London with you. You supported me when William died. Now it's my turn to support you.'

Chapter 38

The return voyage was as arduous as the one outgoing, except that Carrie and Pearl knew what to expect, and John was now fourteen months old and more robust.

'I can hardly believe it was just over a year ago when we came here,' Carrie said as they sat in the dusty carriage, watching the changing landscape as they got nearer to Bombay. 'It's gone so quickly. I began the journey as a newly married woman and childless and look what's happened to me.'

'Did you tell Arnold we were going back to London?' asked Pearl.

'Yes. I felt I owed him that at least. He said it was the best news he'd had, because now he can lie about why we're not living together. He's going to tell everyone I have to go back because my mother's ill. It suits him, and I don't care what he says because there isn't one single person at the mofussil whose opinion I value or who cared about us. I honestly don't know what he's worried about. They probably haven't even noticed John and I aren't there. They can think what they like about me. They always have and they always will.'

'That was his fault. He could have made life much easier for you. It beggars belief why he didn't.'

'I never got to know him really, at least not the side of him that would have made me think it was acceptable to make a go of it. He never gave me a chance so…you're right, it was his fault.'

'And what about Gita? It must have been such a wrench to leave her.'

Carrie put her head down. 'Yes, worse than leaving my own mother. But I'm going to write. And send money to help her.' She glanced up at Pearl.

'Really, Carrie? I'm so glad you will. She deserves it.'

'Well, the shop is thriving, and now she's back to her old self she's determined to keep it going. I offered to close it down, Dorothy was willing, but Gita begged me to keep it open because she said it's the place where she's the happiest and it's a link between us. I made her promise to take someone else on so she's not entirely on her own and she can rest when she needs to, and she suggested asking her daughter to join her. It seems the hoped-for baby hasn't arrived yet, not even a twinkle in her eye. She's beautiful too and will look very well in all the fashions every season. And they'll both earn from the shop which will help them with better accommodation. I even suggested Gita could live above the shop in the apartment, but she said it might take some time to convince her husband of it. Yes, things have actually turned out alright.'

'Apart from one thing.'

Carrie looked at her with sad eyes and brushed away a threatened tear. 'Don't Pearl.'

'Aren't you tempted to think that he might still be alive? He's missing, isn't he? He might be found.'

'Presumed dead, Pearl. And no one's heard from him. Dorothy said he'd been writing to her husband, Marcus, but there's been nothing for weeks.'

'Presumed by who? They might be wrong. He might be in a hospital somewhere.'

'I don't think I'll ever feel for anyone else what I felt for him. Even Johan didn't come close. I've realised it was infatuation. I was young and inexperienced and fell for the first one who showed any interest. What I felt for David was real love. There was respect and need…and passion. And we hadn't even…you know.'

Pearl laughed softly. 'I don't think you're meant to…you know. At least *we're* not. Heaven knows who everyone thinks blokes, "you know" with, if we're not meant to do it.'

'Did you and William? Before he went away.'

Pearl nodded. 'Yes, just the once. I didn't want to let him go, Carrie. If I could have sewn him into my arms and kept him there forever I would have. And now I wished I had. He'd be with me still.'

'But that wasn't William, was it, Pearl? He knew what he wanted to do and he did it.'

'Yeah, he did, bless him. And he might not have ever forgiven me if I'd begged him not to go.'

A silence fell between them while they studied their own thoughts.

'We're going to Bombay, Pearl,' said Carrie. Pearl nodded. 'And we'll have to stay for a day or so before we get on the boat home. I wrote to Basu at the Sundar Ghar Hotel. He's keeping a room for us.' Pearl nodded again. 'And it's where Dr Fraser lives. You'll have time to visit him.'

Pearl quickly glanced out of the window. 'Oh, I don't know about that.'

'I do. Of course you must visit him. He's asked you to, so it's not like your visit will be unwelcome, and what would he think if he knew you'd been in Bombay and you hadn't bothered?'

'I…I don't know.' Pearl looked flustered. 'I hadn't thought…'

'Well, think, now, and when we get to the hotel I'll ask Basu to send one his sons with a note from you, saying you're in Bombay for a day or so, and would he like you to visit. If he says no, then that's that.' Pearl looked sheepish. 'Why are you looking like that? You like him don't you?' Pearl nodded. 'There you go then. One thing I've learnt this year is that if you want something you must try until you get it. And, Pearl, don't say it's too soon after William. Of course you'll never forget him, sweetheart, you loved him with all your heart. But…look what happened to him. He was so young, hadn't really lived his life, and it was taken away from him. Life's too short for regrets. There's no point in living your life by other people's rules. If you like Angus, even if it's only in friendship, why shouldn't you be friends?'

Pearl settled back against the banquette seat and pulled John onto her lap. She cuddled him to her, loving the warmth of his chubby body and the fresh clean smell on his skin. She rubbed her cheek across his soft curls as she realised Carrie had said everything that had gone through her mind since she realised that Angus Fraser might have a place in her life. Pearl had argued with herself, thinking that her attraction to Angus's kindness and gentleness meant that she was betraying William's memory, but she understood now that William had taught her how to love, without condition and with a full heart. She smiled to herself at the thought of seeing the ebullient, gentle giant who was Angus, whose stature and cheerful manner belied his tenderness and calm nature. Carrie's right, she thought. We're only friends, and if it were to lead to something more I can decide whether it's right for me. If it's not there's no harm done, but I'll have made a wonderful caring friend, and that can't be wrong.

Bombay was how Carrie remembered it, dusty and bustling, and full of noise. The women in their bright saris flocked together in groups in the main street, gossiping and giggling, and Carrie wondered what it was that made them so happy. The stalls selling everything but the kitchen sink were still there, and the air was filled with the calls of the vendors and the aroma of spices and flowers.

'I love it here,' said Pearl. 'I loved being in the shop in Secunderabad, but nothing beats the busyness of a marketplace. It's what I missed about London. I think it must be in our blood.'

'I agree. There's something very exciting here. It's probably as you say, the marketplace, the people, the feeling there's always something new about to happen. All we need now is a brazier and someone selling roasted chestnuts and it would feel even more like home.'

'And the people are so friendly. I stayed in a tiny hotel with just a couple of rooms, like a bed and breakfast I suppose, and the owner made me feel so welcome. She couldn't do enough for me.'

'We could learn something from it, too. I think it's why Gita, and you, were so popular in the shop. You know about customer service and how important it is. The customers came to love Gita and I have no qualms about leaving her in charge of the shop. She is a businesswoman in the making and I've no doubt she'll do well.'

'What will you do when you return to London, Carrie? I'll have to find work, I need to earn my living. I'll probably have to go back into service. What about you?'

Carrie nodded. 'Yeah, I'll have to find something. We'll see. I'll need to work, just like you?'

'Service?'

'Maybe.'

Basu was as good as his word and had a room waiting for them. It wasn't the same room she shared with Arnold; Basu seemed to sense it would make Carrie uncomfortable after her previous stay, and instead found them a beautiful suite with a tiny nursery alcove leading from the main bedroom. The twin-beds had elegant muslin canopies and pale lilac linens.

'Isn't he nice?' said Pearl. 'And this is beautiful. Funny isn't it, the hotel looks a bit shabby from the outside. You'd never think it was like this in here.'

'I think it's the dust,' answered Carrie. 'It gets everywhere, and I mean everywhere. In some ways it's worse here than in Secunderabad. It seems to batter the outside of the buildings with the constant toing and froing outside. It comes towards the buildings like a wave. It could definitely do with a lick of paint, but it's sort of charming, don't you think?'

'S'pose it is. I'm comparing it to 99 Nightingale Lane, where everything had to be pristine.'

'Mm, and uncomfortable and not very homely. I can't wait to see how they've fared since the war took hold. You know the government are bringing in conscription because of the heavy losses.'

'Johan?'

Carrie nodded. 'I expect so. Why not? He's of the right age. It will wipe that self-satisfied look off their faces, that's for sure. Mrs Stern will have an attack of the vapours when she discovers her beloved only son is being sent to war.'

'Is that revenge, Carrie?' asked Pearl, smiling.

'No, but when it comes down to it, war is a leveller. It doesn't matter what class we're in or where other people think we belong, or how much money you have, or where you live, whether in Nightingale Lane or in Whitechapel, we're all made of flesh and blood, and we can all be killed. The same weapon will kill anyone it hits, it doesn't pick and choose, or leave someone standing just because they think they're better than someone else. William died for what he believed in, a young lad from the East End. David is missing and very likely dead, an officer, someone who definitely was not from my class who was raised in the salons of Hampshire, although it didn't bother him. Johan will discover that the status he thinks he has in society will not protect him. That much he will learn if nothing else, and it's a very difficult lesson.

Pearl's note to Angus was swiftly answered with an entreaty for her to visit as soon as she could. As she made ready for the visit that afternoon, Carrie noticed her hands were shaking as she tried to button her shoes. Carrie knelt in front of her and pushed her hands away, laughing.

'Here, let me do it. You're a bundle of nerves, girl.'

'I know, isn't it silly? I am nervous, Carrie. What if the children hate me?'

Carrie sat up and frowned. 'Why would they hate you? No one could hate you.'

'Yeah, but they lost their mum didn't they?'

'And you're a friend, just visiting to give your condolences. That's all.' She pulled a funny face and they both laughed.

'Am I?'

Carrie got up from the floor and sat on the bed next to Pearl. 'I think that's up to you, love. Only you can decide.'

'What if he wants more?'

'Do you think he will?'

'It sort of felt like that, y'know, when we were in Secunderabad. Over Christmas. He didn't need to stay, but he did.'

'Well, there you are then. He likes you and you like him. You'll know when you see him. I'm a firm believer in gut-instinct. If your tummy does that rolling thing, I reckon…, I reckon you like him more than you want to admit.'

'Well?' asked Carrie when Pearl returned from her visit with Angus Fraser. She carefully removed the pin from her hat and laid the beautiful straw carefully on the bed. She was quiet, thoughtful, seemingly contented.

'They're angels, his children. They liked my hat. I'm not sure they'd seen one like it before.' Carrie smiled and raised her eyebrows. 'And did Angus like your hat?'

Pearl nodded. 'He did.'

'And you? What did you make of it all? What was the house like? And his mother-in-law? Did you meet her? Pearl nodded and Carrie's eyebrows knotted as she waved a hand at her friend. 'Well, what happened? Come on, Pearl. I thought you'd be full of it and wouldn't be able to wait to tell me all about it.'

'They're very nice, all of them, although I think his mother-in-law was a little suspicious, you know, watchful. I could feel her eyes on me all the time, like she wondered why I was there, but she wasn't unpleasant. Angus was attentive. We had tea, chai, with little Indian sweets covered in syrup, very sweet, and Earl Grey. I didn't like it. Too scented. I think I prefer the sludge at the bottom of me mum's teapot.'

Carrie giggled as she sat on the bed, pulling her knees up to her chest and wrapping her arms around them. 'And then what happened?' she asked, still laughing.

'The children climbed onto my lap. They are so sweet, like little dolls. The boy wore a funny little suit in bright colours with a stand-up collar and shiny trousers, and the little girl, the most beautiful dress in a bright pink taffeta with flowers embroidered around the hem. Underneath she wore tight taffeta under-things in a matching colour. Oh, and their hair, so dark and shiny, and their eyes so large and brown and full of excitement. Such sweet kids.'

Carrie inhaled comically. 'That's the children taken care of…oh, and the mother-in-law, but you haven't mentioned Angus. How was he?'

'Welcoming, of course. He asked me to visit, didn't he?'

Carrie leant her head to one side. 'I can feel a "but" in the air.'

Pearl sat on the bed and played absent-mindedly with her hat. 'I'm glad I went. I had to know, didn't I, whether thinking of changing my life was right for me. It was obvious he wanted me to consider becoming part of their lives, but it wasn't in the way we thought.'

Carrie frowned and put a hand on her friend's arm. She sensed disappointment in Pearl. 'What d'you mean?'

'He wants a nanny for the children, so his mother-in-law can take care of her parents.' Carrie's eyes widened in dismay. 'And I didn't feel… There wasn't that connection there, Carrie, between us, I mean. Don't get me wrong, he was as kind as ever, attentive, very…pleasant, but I didn't want to stay there. The house is still his wife's house, if you know what I mean. There are pictures of her everywhere, a huge portrait on the wall. She was beautiful, so beautiful, and I noticed his mother-in-law kept looking at it. She also said it was very fashionable in Indian high-society to have a British nanny.' Carrie's hands flew to her mouth. 'And I said I wasn't aware of that. She asked me what my plans were and I said I had a passage booked to England and I would be leaving tomorrow, to which she looked relieved.'

'And Angus?'

'His smile didn't falter. I think he might have been a little disappointed. We've all read stories about the widower falling for the nanny, but in truth I don't love him. I didn't get any of those feelings when I saw him again.' She looked up at Carrie and her eyes filled with tears. 'All I could think about was William, wishing he was here, that it was him I was talking to, sharing the time with. I wanted to tell him about my adventure of coming to India, of how I worked in the shop and sold clothes and met Gita and David. I wanted to tell him all those things, and I kept thinking, when I get back to London I can tell William, I can tell William, but I can't tell him, can I?'

Carrie wrapped her arms around Pearl's shoulders as tears ran down her cheeks.

'You and me,' she said. 'You and me are the same. We know what love is and we know what loss is. Dearest Pearl, I'm so, so sorry, sweetheart. I wish I could change things for you, more than anything, even more than I wish I could change things for myself. At least you know. You know you're not ready to find someone else yet. Maybe you never will be, and maybe I never will be, but if that's how it's meant to be, then it's how it's meant to be.' She turned Pearl to face her, rubbing the tears from her friend's cheeks. 'But we have each other, and we always will. You and me, we're a team. We'll take care of one another, and when John's grown up, he'll take care of us both.'

Chapter 39

Carrie and Pearl watched out of the porthole as the ship pulled into the docks at Southampton. The City of London had been their home for four weeks as they'd sailed from Bombay to England, and they'd anticipated this day like children waiting for Christmas.

'Oh, look,' said Pearl. 'It feels so strange, like I've been away for ten years instead of less than one. Do you think we'll settle alright after everything we've been through? I wrote to Mum to let her know I was coming home, but if I got a reply it's in Secunderabad waiting for me. Don't s'pose I'll ever get to read it.'

'I wrote to my lot too, but I shouldn't think it made a tuppence of difference. They won't be rolling out the red carpet for me, that's for sure.'

'They'll be pleased to see you though, won't they? Glad you're alright and you got home safely?'

'I shouldn't think Florrie could care less, and if she's thinking about anything it'll be whether Arnold will want a rebate on the money he gave her because I've come home. She'll be wondering why though, I've no doubt, and blaming me I expect.'

'And Arthur?'

'Dad'll be pleased, but he'll have to hide it. And Elsie will have a face on her like a bulldog, looking me up and down. And d'you know what, she will look me up and down. D'you know why?'

Pearl shook her head and they both turned away from the window. Carrie went to her trunk and pulled out two jackets, one in deep blue the other in forest green, with skirts to match. Two pairs of Mary-Jane shoes followed, with stockings in a paler version of the suits, and two little hats. Two leather valises followed.

Pearl's mouth dropped open. 'Carrie, oh, my goodness. You said when you returned home you wanted to wear one of those suits,' she cried.

Carrie laughed. 'Yeah, well now we can both wear one. Lovely aren't they?'

Pearl nodded, still stunned. 'Which one's mine?'

Carrie shrugged. 'You choose. They're the same size so I'm easy.'

'Can I have the blue one?' Carrie pushed the blue jacket and skirt across the bed, then the shoes, hat and stockings, and Pearl held them up in front of her. 'I can't wait to wear them.' She held the jacket against her, her eyes sparkling. 'Shall we get changed now?'

'Yeah, let's show the people of Whitechapel what they've been missing.'

They dressed quickly, both parading around in their brand-new suits and ending up in fits of giggles. Pearl put on a posh voice and began to walk around the cabin swinging her valise. 'I might go and visit the Sterns,' she said. 'Say I'm new in town and would they mind introducing me to society.' She stuck her nose in the air and walked towards Carrie stopping in front of her. 'Oh, 'ello,' she said in a plummy voice. 'Me name is Pearl Watson, and I've just come up from 'ampshire, don't yer know. I wondered if you wouldn't mind pointing me in the right direction for slumming it with the toffee-nosed nobs what live in this street.'

Carrie collapsed onto the bed in fits of laughter, then got up quickly for fear of creasing her skirt. 'Oh, Pearl, I dare you. Do you think they'd recognise us?'

Pearl put her hand on her hip. 'Why the 'ell would they recognise us? They never even looked at us. Me own Mum won't recognise me in this get-up.'

Carrie pulled a face. 'And mine definitely won't.'

They got the train from Southampton and arrived at Waterloo Station three hours later. John slept most of the way which Carrie was grateful for. He hadn't settled on the ship, had often been sick because of the ship's motion, and she was glad to get him onto dry land.

'I've arranged for our trunks to be sent on, Pearl, to your mum's house. I hope it's alright?'

'Yeah, course it is. Mum'll love it. She'll think herself very cosmopolitan because she's received trunks from India. No worries there.'

Carrie glanced at John and closed her eyes. She knew she should have been able to send them to her own house, but she was quite sure it would have gone down like a ton of bricks. She wondered how they would treat John, knowing one of Florrie's bugbears apart from everything else was the fact that he was Johan Stern's son.

'I'm dreading going home, Pearl, she said. 'Will you come with me? We can go to your mum's first if you like, but honestly, I don't want to turn up there on me own.'

Pearl glanced at Carrie with affection in her eyes. 'Course, Carrie. I get it, I really do. I always liked Florrie, but she's got a right reputation for being as 'ard as nails. We always used to say you lot in the family was always getting in the neck for something or other.'

They stood on the pavement. It was getting dark, and Carrie wondered what would happen when they saw her. Her stomach rolled with nerves and she glanced at Pearl and rolled her eyes.

'What if they didn't receive my letter?'

Pearl shrugged. 'By the sounds of it, it wouldn't make that much difference. Anyway, whatever happens, you'll stay at mine. Mum was over the moon to see us, wasn't she?'

Carrie nodded. 'Yeah, she was.' She looked down at herself in her forest green suit and Mary-Jane shoes, almost wishing she'd worn something more in-keeping with her surroundings. 'I just hope they don't think we're rubbing their noses in it, y'know, dressed like this.'

'Stop worrying, Carrie. Knock the bloody door, for cryin' out loud.'

Carrie raised her hand to knock. 'Here goes nothing.' She rapped on the door and waited. After a few seconds she heard a curtain being pulled away from the door. It was opened a few inches and Florrie's face peaked out.

'Oh. It's you.'

'Hello, Mum. How are you?'

'I'm alright.'

Carrie glanced at Pearl who managed a little smile. 'Can we come in?'

'Well, I don't know. The babe's just got off and we're making to get ready for bed.'

Pearl pushed the door open. 'For Chris' sakes, Florrie, let us in. Get that kettle on and let's have a cup of tea.' She stepped over the threshold pulling Carrie with her. 'Why the hell wouldn't you want us here? I don't get it.'

They went into the living room and Carrie gasped, her hands flying to her mouth. On the sofa lay Tom, his head and hands bandaged, and what she could see of his face was bright red with sores.

'Tom,' Carrie cried. 'What happened?' She turned to look at Florrie. 'What's happened to him?'

The curtain to the scullery was pulled back and Arthur appeared, wiping his hands on a tea-towel. 'Got burnt in an explosion at the tanning factory. The whole bloody place went up. He was lucky to get out, even with the injuries he's got. Some of 'em weren't so lucky.'

'Alfie?' Carrie said, fearful her younger brother had been one of them. 'Wasn't on shift, thank God.'

Carrie went across to the sofa and sank down next to it, her beautiful suit forgotten, her valise flung on the floor. 'Tom?' she said gently. 'Tom, can you hear me?'

'He hasn't spoken since it happened,' said Florrie. Carrie glanced at her. This wasn't the Florrie who had sent her away to India with a man she didn't know. She seemed diminished somehow, a pale version of the person she was.

'And when was that?'

'Six weeks ago.'

'And you didn't think to let me know? He's my brother after all, an' I still care about him.'

'What could you have done, being all the way over there? I didn't want to worry you, and at the time I didn't know you were coming home, did I?'

Carrie stood and faced her mother. 'So you didn't get any of the letters I sent?'

Florrie flushed. 'There's been a lot going on, our Carrie, more than you could know.'

Carrie put her hand on her hip and jutted her chin out. 'Like what? What was so pressing you didn't have time to write to your daughter, or was it because you thought you'd seen the back of me and that you'd never see me again?'

'It wasn't that.'

'It was exactly that,' Arthur said, speaking up at last. 'We weren't allowed to mention you, Carrie, and I know the reason why.'

Florrie stared at him. 'And why's that Arthur Dobbs?'

'Don't you Arthur Dobbs me, Florrie. It was guilt, guilt because she more or less sold you to some 'orrible bloke she didn't even know,' he said, looking at Carrie now. 'I never wanted it, Carrie, and I'm sorry I didn't speak up earlier. I let you down, girl, and I'm very sorry for not having the guts to go against her like I should have.'

'Where's Elsie?'

'Off with her new man.'

'Her new man? What happened to Len?'

'Got banged up, didn't he?' said Arthur. 'Took on one job too many and got done for it. You know what Elsie's like, wasn't prepared to wait. Anyway, I knew he wasn't any good, always knew it, told her I did, but she didn't listen. Too much like yer mother.' He glanced across to Florrie who put her head down.

'She wasn't sold off, then? What was it, couldn't you find anyone to take her? Carrie shook her head. 'Well, I'm here now, and we've got more important things to think about. Has Tom had a doctor? Shouldn't he be in the hospital?'

'He's been in hospital,' said Florrie, sulkily. 'They sent him 'ome yesterday for us to look after.'

'What about a nurse? He needs medical care.'

'They cost money.'

'Yeah, they do, which you have. The money from Arnold Bateman. You can use that.'

'All gone.'

'Gone? On what?'

'Living,' said Arthur. 'Now the war's taken hold the dock-masters are only hanging onto a handful of men. I got laid off. I know it was wrong to take money from Bateman, Carrie, but it's kept us afloat until now. If I'd known what would happen to our Tom…'

'We should go, Carrie,' said Pearl. 'It's getting late and mum likes to lock up before ten.'

Carried nodded. 'Alright.' She glanced at Tom, her heart breaking at the sight of him. 'I'll be back tomorrow afternoon,' she said. 'I've got something to do in the morning, I'll organise a nurse to come and see Tom and change his bandages. He needs proper medical care and those bandages need changing every day.'

Florrie stared at her with a hard look. 'And how will you afford that, lady?'

Carrie went up to her and put her face close to hers and Florrie stepped back, sensing this was a different Carrie to the one she'd sent away. 'None of your business, and if you'd had the decency to answer my letters and shown some interest, maybe you'd have found out.'

The following morning, Carrie left Pearl's and got the tram to Covent Garden. She wore an understated dress and coat, not wanting to stand out. It was clear the mood of the country was sombre. The streets were grey and the faces of the inhabitants were greyer. She was on a mission and the less attention she got, the better.

She wandered the streets, looking in the shop windows, passing the flower stalls that were almost empty, wondering how much further the country could sink before it landed on its knees. She sighed with sadness. Already conscription had made its mark. The younger men had been sent to fight and the streets seemed almost empty of them. The only people she saw were women with children and older people who walked aimlessly, as if they had no reason to be out, but needed to feel they weren't the only people left in the world. The poverty she had seen before she left London was nothing compared to what she witnessed now, and she realised that she had come back at just the right time, particularly where Tom was concerned.

When she thought of him lying there, looking as though he'd been to war himself, she realised his injuries were so great he would probably never be sent to the front to fight. She wondered whether he thought it was a blessing or a curse, then decided he was probably in so much pain even thinking would be too much for him. She'd hoped the war would be over before conscription began, but began it had, on the 2nd of March that year, and if the war continued for much longer, young Alfie would be sent, of that there was no doubt.

Pearl's mother, Doris had put Carrie in contact with a local nurse who had promised to visit Tom every day and change his bandages. She was a young woman with a family and had been overjoyed when Carrie had offered her the job of nursing Tom, because it meant she had a regular wage coming in. Her husband had been sent to fight and she had endured the struggles of those with nothing but each other. Not that there was much to buy. Carrie's heart had sunk when she'd seen the almost empty shop windows and the shopkeepers looking forlorn. The war had changed everything and she wondered where it would end.

Her thoughts accompanied her to Nightingale Lane, number ninety-nine, the house she'd come to see. She stood on the pavement in front of its greying facade and stared up at the windows, no longer sparkling with Christmas decorations, but dark and empty, like a body without a soul whose eyes were etched with sadness. The plush velvet curtains had disappeared, and the glass that she once polished until it shone like crystal was dusty and smeared with grime from the street.

The steps leading up to the front door had not been swept for months. A For Sale sign had been attached to the wrought iron railings with dirty string that trailed across the pavement. Carrie bent down and picked it up, laying it across the railings. The once pristine and palatial 99 Nightingale Lane was now empty. The rooms no longer resounded with laughter from the Sterns' daughters, maids were not running up and down the backstairs tying their aprons on as they arrived late for their shift. Mr and Mrs Stern were not in their drawing room, sipping tea from pretty china teacups and hosting dinner parties for the great and good, and Mrs Coyle no longer held court in the kitchen, bellowing at the tweeny to wash the pots so she could use them again, or fussing over intricate confections for the dining table. They were all gone, every single one of them. The life the house had seen was over, and as yet no one had taken up the baton to fill the house with the sounds of the living. The house looked abandoned and ghostly, and as tears welled in Carrie's eyes she wondered what could have gone so badly wrong for the Sterns that they should have lost their home.

She stepped toward the For-Sale sign and took note of the agent's name, Cripps and Prime, whose offices were in Covent Garden. She took a breath and raised her face to the second and third floors, then the attics at the top of the house where she and Pearl had become friends. The paintwork around the attic windows had begun to flake and a pang of regret went through her.

She had known happiness in this house. She had found her best friend and thought she had found love with Johan Stern. It was here she had conceived her son, late one night when Johan's parents had gone to the theatre with his sisters and they knew they were alone. He had pulled her into the drawing room and laid her down on the chaise longue and told her he loved her and he would do everything in his power to make sure they could stay together. He had convinced her his parents would accept her into the family, if she would only show him how she felt about him by allowing him to make love to her, and she had given herself to him willingly because she was sure she was in love with Johan Stern and that he was in love with her. If felt as though it happened decades before instead of just two years, and although she had been disappointed and deeply hurt when Johan had married, she couldn't deny that her feelings for him before then had brought her great happiness, even though his for her had been false.

She turned away from the house and retraced her steps down Nightingale Lane. Joe, the roasted chestnut man was no longer on the corner, stoking his brazier and filling it with plump chestnuts. He had gone to war before Christmas 1914, and she wondered if he had survived, if his wife and children had ever seen him again.

As she continued down the street, she pictured the children who were always to be seen, running in gangs, feral, out of control, having fun and shrieking with laughter, usually pushing a baby in a pram whose face was grimy and running with snot. What I'd give to have those days back again, she thought, a world with no war, young men walking the streets and not having to leave their loved ones. Poverty was one thing. War was quite another.

She reached the offices of Cripps and Prime and looked in through the window. A young studious-looking woman and an elderly gentleman with whiskers the colour of snow and a large reddish nose that gave away his love of whisky and cigars were sitting at two desks, their heads bent; their concentration fixed on the papers in front of them. Carrie wondered how much business they were doing in a time of war. Everything was in short supply, including money to buy property and she hoped fervently it would work in her favour.

They both looked up as the bell rang when she pushed open the door. She paused in the frame then shut the door behind her.

'Mr Cripps or Mr Prime?' she asked the gentleman.

He rose from his chair and made a slight bow towards her. 'Julius Prime, Ma'am. Mr Cripps is no longer with us I'm afraid. This,' he indicated the young woman sitting at the other desk, 'is his daughter, Matilda Cripps.'

Carrie nodded at them both in turn, then sat without being asked in the seat opposite Julius Prime's desk.

'99 Nightingale Lane.' She said. 'I understand it's for sale.'

'Indeed it is, Miss...'

'Mrs...Bateman.'

'Indeed it is, Mrs Bateman. Been on our books for about six months.'

'I understood a...a family lived there previously.'

'Yes, so they did, but the war, you know. It has cut many of us down, and not just those in the field of battle. Those in the financial world have suffered terribly. No investment you see, and no government contracts. Everything is going into the war effort.'

'And this is what happened to Mr and Mrs St..., I mean, those who lived there previously?'

'Exactly, Mrs Bateman. Are you interested in the property?'

'Well, there is a lot to consider, as you've said. We are in the middle of a conflict are we not?' Mr Prime nodded. 'So clearly the price would have to be...er, comparable to any property that has been left to decline because of the conflict.'

'Are you considering making it your home, Mrs Bateman?'

'I'm not sure, Mr Prime. That we shall have to see. I have business interests elsewhere in the world, and I certainly need a base to work from. I can only assume that because it has been standing empty for some while, the property requires some refurbishment. I'm correct in assuming this...I would imagine.' She turned her gaze onto Matilda Cripps, who stared at her through thick-lensed glasses without acknowledging her statement, then looked back at Julius Prime.

'It certainly needs a woman's touch, Mrs Bateman, that is true,' he answered. 'Perhaps you would like to visit the property. We have the keys. I can meet you there this afternoon at two of the clock if it would suit you.'

Carrie nodded. 'It would suit me perfectly, Mr Prime. I will meet you there at two o'clock this afternoon.'

Carrie shut the door behind her, the bell tinkling in her wake. She strolled down the High Street towards the tram stop, a surge of happiness flooding through her, and a satisfied smile playing on her lips.

 Chapter 40

'It's a bit empty in 'ere,' said Pearl, as she dragged a side-table into the drawing room. And what about curtains? We can't not have curtains.'

'Don't worry,' said Carrie as she dusted the skirting boards and the frames around the doors. Everything's being delivered this afternoon. It's going to take an age to get all the curtains up, but as you say, we can't not have curtains.'

'And will the boarding rooms be done first? What about beds?'

'The boarding rooms will be finished by tomorrow night. I've got Mrs Coyle and her daughter working up there now. They're making a grand job of the rooms, everything's in fine shape, it was just dirty.'

'Fancy you asking Mrs Coyle to work for you.'

'Why wouldn't I? She needed a job. She'd been out of work since the Sterns left and because of the war no one's been hiring. Her daughter was in the same position. She's got five kids to feed and she'd been laid off from the tanning factory because of the explosion.'

'All's well that ends well,' said Pearl, cheerfully.

Carrie straightened up and stretched her back. 'Do you really mean that? Really?'

'Yeah, I s'pose I do. The most wonderful thing would be if William walked through that door, but, I know he's not going to and I've accepted it.' She nodded, agreeing with herself. 'It's time to move on and working with you has made me happier than I thought I would ever be again.'

'We'll be alright, won't we?' said Carrie, smiling at Pearl with affection.

'Yeah, we'll be alright.'

There was a rap on the door and Dorothy appeared in the black and white tiled hall, her arms full of flowers and with two little girls holding onto her skirts.

'Hello,' she cried. 'Anyone home?'

'Dorothy,' Carrie cried. 'It's lovely to see you. Come in, yes, come in and see our handiwork.'

Dorothy swept into the drawing room and turned around as she surveyed the room. 'This is a lovely room,' she said. 'I've brought you some flowers. Thought they'd make it more like home for you.'

'Thank you so much,' said Carrie, relieving Dorothy of the huge bunch of flowers. 'By the way, this is Pearl, my best friend in all the world.'

Dorothy smiled and hugged Pearl, kissing her on both cheeks. 'At last we meet. I've heard so much about you.'

'And I, you,' said Pearl shyly, smiling at the elegant woman. She beckoned to Carrie. 'Give me those flowers, Carrie. I'll put them in some vases and put them in the reception rooms. They're so beautiful and they smell lovely.'

Carrie watched Pearl go then turned to Dorothy, her eyebrows raised. 'And who are these beautiful girls?'

Dorothy clutched the hands of both girls and pushed them forward. 'This is Seraphina. She's six, and Dottie, who's four.'

Carrie leant forward. 'Hello,' she said smiling. 'Thank you for coming to see me. Perhaps Aunt Dorothy will bring you back when we're all settled. Would you like to come for tea? We'll have some lovely cake and tiny sandwiches, just perfect for little hands. And my son, John would love to meet you.' The girls glanced up at Dorothy and she nodded.

'Yes, please,' said Seraphina. 'Dottie and I would like that very much.'

The girls ran off to sit on the window seat and Carrie's eyes followed them.

'Bless them,' she said quietly, then lifted her eyes to Dorothy's. 'How are you?' she asked her. 'Are you managing alright? It must be such a change in your life, Dorothy, almost a ready-made family.'

Dorothy nodded and swallowed hard. 'Yes, a bit of a shock to the system, but they're such little dears. I couldn't let anyone else take care of them, and Marcus adores them.'

'Are they living with you?'

'Some of the time, but when they want to go home to their father, they go. They choose what they want to do. They have a tutor whom they see every day for a few hours apart from Saturday and Sunday, so they have routine in their lives. I do think it's so important.'

'And what about you, Dorothy? You look a little tired.'

'Yes, morning sickness does that to you.'

Carrie's face broke into a smile. 'Dorothy,' she cried, hugging her. 'You're expecting.' Dorothy nodded. 'When? When are we going to have a new little arrival?'

Dorothy waved her hand at her, laughing. 'Oh not for ages yet. It's early days, but we're over the moon. And it'll be lovely for the girls to have a new cousin.'

'And a new friend for John.'

'Absolutely. Of course, it's a boy, so they can do boy things.'

Carrie threw her head back and laughed. 'How do you know that? Y'know, it might be a girl, Dorothy. There's always that chance.'

Dorothy nodded. 'I know, but we need more boys, don't we? I have a feeling this little one is a boy, and he'll be like my lovely Marcus. We need more men like him, especially now. We've lost so many of our young men.'

Carrie bent her head and Dorothy clutched her hands. 'Are you alright, my darling? The news about David was awful. I'm so sorry. You and he barely got started.'

'No, and if he hadn't been sent to France I'd probably still be in Secunderabad. Fate can be so cruel sometimes. We'd only just found each other, and I was devastated when I found out what had happened, but I have John and I had to grit my teeth and get on with it. I've found a strength I didn't even know I had. Losing David right at the moment when we'd promised to wait for each other was very painful. Why do all the good ones go, Dorothy?'

Dorothy shook her head. 'I don't know, darling. This war, it has ruined so many lives, and I've no doubt not just in this country. Families are being torn apart. There has to be a better way of settling differences without killing each other. Men, you see. They think war is the answer.'

'Are you still with the suffragettes?'

'Yes, but Marcus has begged me to concentrate on the girls and the new baby for now. He knows how passionate I get about things. I've agreed of course, but when things have moved on I'll be doubling my efforts to get our voices heard. I hope you'll join me, and Pearl. We all need to have our say.'

'Yes, Dorothy. I'd like to be involved. Of course I'll help.'

Dorothy sighed. 'I should be getting along. The girls' tutor is due in an hour.' She hugged Carrie to her. 'If you need anything, let me know, won't you, Carrie. I think what you're doing here is marvellous. Do you have any boarders yet?'

'Yes, my brother, Tom. He was injured in the explosion at the tanning factory. I have a nurse, a cook, and there's Pearl and me. We're as much as we need for now. When some of the young men are sent home with injuries we'll take them in and we'll nurse them and feed them up until they're back on their feet. The war office have agreed to send them our way. I wanted to do something to help. I saved everything I earnt from the shop and it was how I was able to buy this place which I got for a song. They wanted to get rid of it and I came along at just the right moment.'

'And with Gita running the shop in Secunderabad, it will help you keep it afloat.'

'Yes, and we can make sure your income continues, especially now there's a baby on the way, and Gita is so pleased she will be able to continue working there. She loves it and I have every faith in her that she'll run it at least as well as I did.'

Dorothy nodded. 'Wonderful. You've done a grand job.'

99 Nightingale Lane was lived in again, albeit in a very different way. Gradually, over the weeks and months the rooms were occupied by young men who had been wounded, whose injuries weren't profound enough to be sent to the over-subscribed hospitals, but who needed care and attention that couldn't be given at home, which Carrie and her team provided.

The house was never still. There was always someone new coming in to be looked after and once again 99 Nightingale Lane buzzed with activity. They all said Mrs Coyle's cooking was the best they'd ever tasted, and good food along with expert nursing and the right care and attention healed many of the young men enough to be sent home, at least for a while. Some of the men were sent straight back to the trenches to begin the fight again, but some were so badly injured they could not return.

Tom made excellent progress under Carrie's eye. His burns were attended to daily by the nurse and to Carrie's relief he began to speak again.

'I want to stay here, Carrie,' he said. 'I want to do my bit. I know I'll not be sent to the front, my hands have had it, but I can help here, can't I?'

She sat on the side of his bed and pushed his hair from his eyes. 'I'd hoped you'd say that. We need you here, and it'll be wonderful for the men coming here to have someone to talk to who has experienced injury and who has been nursed back to good health.'

'I'm sorry, Carrie.'

'What do you mean? What have you got to be sorry for?'

'I let you down. Well, we all did. I should have spoken up. Dad cried every night you know, after you left.'

Carrie closed her eyes, determined not to cry. 'Don't Tommy.'

'I can't imagine how hurt you were after what mum did.'

Carrie inhaled and smiled. 'Y'know, Tom, I learnt a lot while I was away. She might have done me a favour. Alright, I didn't think so at the time, but if I hadn't been sent to India I wouldn't have this place. I worked my socks off when I was in Secunderabad, built up custom, made sure people got good service. Let's face it, I know about service. And I saved everything I earnt. I couldn't have done that here. Look what happened to the Sterns.'

'What happened to them?'

'They lost everything. All their money. No one invested, no one saved. In less than two years all the money he had made over a lifetime had gone. We don't know about these things, do we? I don't know about markets and things like that, but the Sterns were in the wrong business, and they were arrogant. They thought nothing could touch them. They were very wrong about that. Julius Prime told me what happened.'

'What about Johan?'

'What about him?'

'Do you know what happened to him?'

Carrie shook her head. 'No, and I don't want to know. Me and John don't need him. We didn't need him then and we don't need him now.'

'Do you still love him?'

'No, Tom, I don't love him, and d'you know what, I don't think I ever did.'

Chapter 41

Carrie was woken by someone banging loudly on the front door. She got out of bed and dragged on her dressing gown and slipped her feet into her shoes, still half asleep. She opened her door to find Pearl on the landing.

'What the 'ells going on?' said Pearl. 'I don't like the sound of it.'

'No, neither do I. Will you come down with me?'

Pearl nodded. 'Yeah, come one, we'd better find out who thinks it's alright to wake God fearing people at this hour.'

They ran down the curved stairway into the hall. Carrie unlocked the door with Pearl peering over her shoulder. On the step stood two soldiers, both with a hand under the arms of a soldier they were supporting.

'Sorry, miss, to wake you at this hour, but this bloke needs some attention. We were given your address.'

Carrie nodded, fully awake now. 'Oh, right, yes, of course. Bring him in. What happened?'

'He was found wandering the streets. He'd been sent back from the front, been in one of the military hospitals but no one knew who he was.'

She opened the door wider and the soldiers brought the man in. He was filthy, and his face and hands were covered in dried blood. As they laid him on one of the sofas, Mrs Coyle came down the stairs, her robe tied tightly round her ample middle and her hair in curlers. Carrie looked up and beckoned to her.

'Mrs Coyle, can you make sure these soldiers get something to eat and a cup of tea.'

She nodded, asking no questions. 'Follow me,' she said to the soldiers. 'I've got some nice ham in the pantry and some bread I made this afternoon. You two look like you could do with something inside you.' The men obediently followed her into the kitchen and Carrie turned her attentions to the soldier they had brought in.

'Shall I get some soap and water?' asked Pearl. 'He needs cleaning up. Those wounds will never heal with all that filth on him.'

Carrie nodded. 'Yes, and some of that ointment from the nurses room.' She took the soldiers cap from his head. Pearl brought in a tin bowl and a soft cloth and Carrie began to clean the man's face. She wiped the cloth gently across his forehead, removing the blood that had flowed from a head wound, then after rinsing it out in the bowl, wiped his cheeks. She frowned then gasped. 'Pearl. Pearl,' she cried. She stood abruptly, her hands covering her mouth.

Pearl ran into the room holding a bottle of ointment. 'What's up, Carrie? What is it?'

'It's David. I think it's David.'

Pearl knelt down by the sofa and peered into the soldiers face. She turned to Carrie and put an arm around her shoulders, nodding. 'Yes, it's him. Oh, Carrie. He's alive.'

Gradually, they helped him shrug out of his great-coat and removed his blood-soaked jacket. He was utterly exhausted, barely having the strength to breathe as they worked to clean his bruised and bloodied body and bandage his wounds, but when Carrie held a cup of warm milk to his lips he opened his eyes and stared at her, tears streaming down his cheeks. His gaze was unswerving; he looked deep into her eyes and she smiled gently at him.

'Am I dreaming?' he whispered. 'Have I died and gone to heaven.'

She stroked his cheek. 'No, David, you're still with us. We're going to look after you.' She took his hand and put it to her lips. 'You're going to be alright, my love.'

He exhaled and relaxed his aching body against the sofa, a ghost of the man he once was, his cheeks hollowed out by lack of food, dark circles shadowing sunken eyes that had seen too much pain and anguish. 'I prayed for this when I was in the trenches. I prayed so hard, to see you again, to be with you, the only woman I have ever loved. An angel has answered my prayers.'

She put a soft finger against his lips. 'And we're together again. We're all together again. And we always will be. Nothing can part us now.'

Thank you for reading!

As an author, I love feedback. Candidly, you're the reason I continue writing about the characters you love. So, tell me what you liked, what you loved, and even what you didn't love. It would be great to hear from you, and you can write to me at info@andreahickswriter.com and visit me on the web _www.andreahicks-writer.com

If you're so inclined, I'd love a review of 99 Nightingale Lane. It's so wonderful for a writer when a reader loves a book enough to take the time to write about how it made them feel. Or equally, we can learn from you if you have a different view. Just a line, a phrase, or a few words, we appreciate you all.

Thank you for spending so much time with me.

In gratitude,

Andrea xxx

Historical Fiction at its best…the inspiring new novel by

Andrea Hicks

THE DANDELION CLOCK

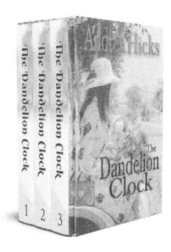

Made in the USA
Las Vegas, NV
08 September 2024

94980500R00156